A PLACE
CALLED
FEAR

OTHER TITLES BY KEITH HOUGHTON

No Coming Back
Before You Leap
Crash

Maggie Novak Thrillers

Don't Even Breathe

Gabe Quinn Thrillers

Killing Hope
Crossing Lines
Taking Liberty
Chasing Fame

A PLACE CALLED FEAR

KEITH HOUGHTON

A MAGGIE NOVAK THRILLER

THOMAS & MERCER

Text copyright © 2019 by Keith Houghton
All rights reserved.

Published by Thomas & Mercer, Seattle
www.apub.com

Amazon, the Amazon logo, and Thomas & Mercer are trademarks of Amazon.com, Inc., or its affiliates.

ISBN-13: 9781542014458
ISBN-10: 154201445X

Cover design by Ghost Design

Printed in the United States of America

For Lynn
My beautiful wife
For picking me up and never letting me down

Chapter One

FAT MAN IN A BOWLING SHIRT

In the shade of his straw hat, the manager's face looked like it had been drawn by a child. Everything exaggerated and bunched in the middle. "Welcome to Hector's Self-Storage," he announced as he rolled back the gate leading into the facility. "What can I do for you, amigo?"

The man kept his hands planted in the pockets of his hoodie as he stepped into the compound. "I'm looking for something private," he said. "As far from the street as possible. Something secure."

"In that case, you've come to the right place." A gold tooth lit up an otherwise dull smile. "Just so happens, security is our specialty. Come. I'll give you the grand tour."

The self-storage facility in Oak Ridge, Orlando, consisted of several back-to-back rows of rentable outside units running parallel with the street. Red roll-up doors set in beige walls. Everything tired and low key.

"I don't see any cameras," he said as he followed the manager.

There were none. He'd sneaked around the property in the dead of night, wearing soft-soled shoes and night-vision goggles. No security guards, either, and certainly no razor wire coiled on top of the walls.

The manager made a *What can I say?* expression. "Our customers are private people. What they choose to store here is none of our business. Protecting it—now *that* is." It seemed like a practiced answer, and came across that way.

The manager pointed at a window in the corner of the main building. It consisted of double-paned glass with a speak-through, like a teller window in a bank. "See the office?" he said. "It's manned twenty-four seven. Through the day, you'll find me there, watching over everything."

"And after dark?" Reconnaissance had shown him that no one stayed here after midnight. Lights at the entrance and in the office were left on, and a portable TV, its volume loud enough to hear at the gate, gave the impression that a security guard was on duty, when in fact the place was deserted.

"My eagle-eyed cousin works the night shift. Trust me, amigo. Nobody comes in or out without one of us seeing it."

It was a lie, and another rehearsed response.

"Best part?" the manager added as they walked across the cracked concrete. "If any unsavory characters come sniffing, we have deterrents." He lifted the flap of his two-tone bowling shirt to reveal a snub-nosed revolver stuffed in his waistband.

"Sounds like you have a good system in place."

"Only the best in town." The manager chuckled like it was a joke, which was exactly what it was; he just didn't know it. "That's why locals choose Hector's. We meet all your needs."

In one sense, he was right. Homework had shown that of the three public storage facilities located within a two-mile radius of Oak Ridge, this was the only one running on a shoestring. The lack of high-tech surveillance equipment was its best selling point.

The manager led him to the back of the lot.

The late-October sun was low, red clouds bleeding across the deepening sky. Long shadows, and the hum of rush-hour traffic.

The first whispers of *trick or treat* on the breeze. They came to a row of roll-up doors no larger than regular doors. The manager unhooked a bunch of keys from his belt and slotted a master key into a disc-shaped padlock.

"Once we get you the gate code," he said, "you can drive all the way back here. Come and go as you please. Night or day. No one will bother you, amigo. It's ideal for what you have in mind. Total privacy."

Although the manager had no idea what he had in mind, he was right about the location. Over the past days, and at all hours, he had stood on this same spot, unseen, evaluating. Back here, away from the street, there was no direct line of sight to the roadway, or the office, and tall trees overhung the units from behind. At either end of the row, high walls formed dead ends.

The manager hoisted up the door.

"How much?" he asked.

"A steal at seventy bucks a month."

A wave of warm air rolled out of the unit, bringing with it a faint smell of metal and dust, and something *biological.*

Pitch black inside.

"I need AC."

Florida heat could be punishing. Fragile things decayed fast in the tropical climate. Air-conditioning was a must if he wanted his *business* to remain undetected.

"You're in luck," the manager said. "AC comes standard. Just open up the vent at the back, and away you go." He reached inside and switched on the light.

On the corrugated metal ceiling, a fluorescent bulb crackled and came to life. Dead flies in the plastic cover.

The unit was about the size of a one-car garage. A simple rect-angular box with bare cinder-block walls and a poured cement floor. An electricity outlet in one corner, and a closed AC vent high up at the back.

Nothing fancy. But then, he didn't need it to be fancy.

Basic was best for what he had planned in here.

"I'll take it," he said.

The manager brightened. "Awesome. You won't regret it."

"Give me a minute?"

The manager nodded. "Sure. Take your time, amigo." He jabbed a stubby thumb over his shoulder. "I'll be in the office, getting the paperwork in order. Come see me when you're ready." He flashed his gold tooth again and walked away.

Once the manager was out of sight, he went inside, running his fingertips along the rough walls, inspecting every joint and seam. It was important to him that there were no holes, no cracks. The cast concrete was slightly warm, but otherwise sealed. He pressed his cheek to it, an ear, listening, hearing the faint hum of a distant fan system circulating air through the venting ducts.

In the middle of the floor, a large dark stain drew his eye.

It was probably paint, or oil. But it looked like old blood.

He went over and dropped to his haunches, touching his fingertips to the stain before bringing them to his nose and sniffing.

Definitely biological.

Someone had lost a ton of blood in here.

He wondered if it was a good omen.

Chapter Two

BREAKING THE BLOOD-BRAIN BARRIER

The clocks were about to strike midnight, and Maggie Novak had overindulged on finger food. Too much take and not enough give. The little black dress that had fit like a glove earlier in the evening now seemed a size too small. And to make matters worse, the only statement her ankle-strap stilettos were making was a guilty plea. Not quite torture, but close to challenging the Geneva convention.

Whose idea was this anyway?

Maggie sipped warm champagne, swaying to the music.

Up here, eleven floors above street level, on an outdoor terrace nestled between the Plaza towers in downtown Orlando, the New Year's party was in full swing. Glitter balls flashing and club music pounding. Everywhere she looked, glamorous guests in tuxedos and cocktail dresses, networking under the garlanded lights.

Above the DJ's stage, an arc of pearlescent balloons framed a banner that wished everybody:

HAPPY NEW YEAR FROM THE *CHRONICLE*!

Maggie drew a gassy breath, all at once feeling overheated and conspicuous, hurtling toward *drunk* at breakneck speed.

Where's Steve?

A passing waiter topped off her champagne flute before she could protest. "Compliments of the *Chronicle*," he said robotically.

Maggie saluted him with her glass and *drank*.

Every New Year's Eve, the paper threw one of these parties, the invitees consisting mainly of those who had made the headlines during the past year. Charity workers and fund-raisers. Lifesavers and philanthropists. Principally, real people going above and beyond to make a difference, and hardly anyone like her: a homicide detective invited here for just doing her job.

Maggie felt numb from the outside in.

Two whole months had passed since the resolution of the Halloween Homicide case—the case that had seen her deceased school friend seemingly rise from the dead and murder a mutual friend, then attempt to murder Maggie, too—and yet part of it still haunted her, the killings never quite far from her thoughts. Gruesome images of burning bodies populating her dreams, catapulting her awake in a cold sweat, convinced she'd heard bloodcurdling screams echoing through the empty house.

Of course, it was all in her head.

Steve, her psychiatrist boyfriend, had tried his best to get her to "open up," to talk about it, the therapist in him unable to accept that she just wanted to put it all behind her and *move on*. She had a handle on things. Her friend and her sidekick had both been caught and given long sentences. Neither of them was coming to get her. She knew that.

Even so, it didn't stop the dreams from coming nightly.

Captain Corrigan, her commander in the Major Case Section, had recommended she cash in her vacation days, take a few well-earned weeks away from work. Retreat to someplace she could

6

unwind her tightly coiled emotions. Essentially, unspool. But Maggie had respectfully declined, believing that the best way to deal with a cramp was always to run it off.

Champagne helped.

"Maggie! Maggie Novak! You look scrumptious!"

Maggie looked up from her drink to see Nick Stavanger elbowing his way through the crowd toward her, his bow tie and the top couple of buttons of his dress shirt undone. Stubble darkening his jaw, and his hair gelled back. In the right light, a skinny Ben Affleck.

"I could eat you alive," he said as he came up and kissed her on the cheek. He reeked of expensive cologne. "If only you were my gender of choice."

Maggie laughed. "You still wouldn't stand a chance."

Nick made a wounded face.

Nick Stavanger worked at the *Chronicle*, chiefly as a gossip columnist, but he preferred to think of himself as an investigative journalist—the same way he considered himself Maggie's best friend.

"What's this?" he said, clinking his glass against hers. "I thought you didn't like champagne?"

Maggie glanced at the drink in her hand. "Actually, it doesn't like *me*. This is my third glass, and I'm wasted."

Now it was his turn to laugh. "I hate these kinds of parties."

Maggie elbowed him playfully in the ribs. "Are you kidding me?" Despite Nick's comment, he was foot tapping to the thunderous beat and swaying at the hips. "We both know you're in your element here. Two hundred sweating strangers crammed in like sardines. Alcohol on tap and the paper picking up the tab. Give me a break, Nick. This has your name written all over it. The whole world knows you love your parties."

He laughed again, this time saluting her with his glass. "You're right, Maggie. I love *my* parties. Poolside and on my own terms.

7

Preferably, with swimsuits." He looked around at the sea of people. "All these strutting peacocks—it's my idea of hell."

Maggie watched him guzzle champagne, knowing that the real reason for his comment stemmed from his plus-one, Casey, being unable to attend tonight's bash. The two of them had recently come back together after a long breakup—Maggie playing matchmaker—and Nick fretted about anything that could interfere with what he called the *bonding process*. Besides which, outside his comfort zone, Nick was a terrible socializer.

"Like extracting teeth," he added as he scanned the crowd.

"No one would guess."

His gaze came back full circle. "The same could be said for you, Detective. Square peg, round hole, and all that."

Nick wasn't far wrong; she'd worn a brave face all evening. Smiling on cue and posing for press shots, softening the experience with champagne while she wished away the time.

A roar rose from the partygoers as the music died and the DJ announced the countdown to the New Year would soon begin.

"Don't look now," Nick said, "but I think your boyfriend is watching us."

Maggie spotted Steve standing on the DJ's stage, looking at her from across the waves of bobbing heads.

Like Nick, he had on a rented tux. But that's where the similarity ended. Steve's bow tie was still neatly knotted and positioned perfectly parallel to his chin. Not a single hair out of place in his *West Side Story* coif. Despite all the champagne she knew he'd drunk, as well as all his dancing—and he had busted quite a few moves this evening—Steve looked cool and composed.

The thought occurred: *What do I look like?*

She saw Steve lift his own champagne flute and point at it, mouthing the words, *Do you need another?*

Maggie shook her head, and then clung onto Nick's arm as the world spun.

In her ear, Nick said, "Aside from the dashing good looks, the athlete's body, and brains that make Einstein look like a simpleton, what exactly is it you see in Steve Kinsey?"

"Normalcy," she answered without hesitation. "When everything's up in the air, Steve's my grounding rod."

"If you want my opinion . . ."

"I don't."

"Steve's a bit vanilla."

"See, that's why I said I didn't want it." Maggie extracted her arm from his. "I knew you'd say something catty. I happen to like vanilla."

"Exactly. And that's the problem, Maggie. Right there. Everybody *likes* vanilla. But nobody actually *loves* vanilla. Vanilla is safe. Predictable. There are no surprises with vanilla. You know what you're getting every time."

Maggie narrowed her eyes at him. She went to speak, but changed her mind as she heard her phone ringing in her clutch.

"How convenient," Nick said. "Saved by the bell."

Maggie dug out her phone. "Don't worry. I'll get you back later." The number looked familiar, but she couldn't pin a name to it. "Hello?" she said as she answered.

"Hello, Maggie? Maggie, it's Sasha."

"Sasha?" It took a moment to register, for Maggie's intoxicated brain to assign the name to the voice and then to conjure up a face in her mind's eye. Sasha Young—the wife of Clayton Young, one of Maggie's fellow detectives in Homicide Squad—calling, by the looks of it, on her landline.

"Happy New Year, Sasha," Maggie said, then saw Nick shake his head. *Not yet.*

9

"I'm calling about Clay," Sasha said in her ear. "Maggie, I didn't know who else to call. I didn't want to trouble you. I was going to leave it until the morning. Let you enjoy your evening. I wasn't going to call at all. I told myself it was a mistake, and I shouldn't involve you in—"

"Sasha," Maggie said. "Slow down. What's wrong? Is Clay in trouble?"

"That's just it, Maggie. I don't know. He hasn't come home. I'm worried something has happened. I didn't know who else to call."

Maggie could hardly hear what Sasha was saying; the merry-makers had grown louder and rowdier as the countdown to midnight approached. She told Sasha to *hold on* and *don't go anywhere* while she found a quieter spot. She tapped on Nick's arm in farewell and handed him her glass. Then she left him looking slightly miffed as she weaved her way to a corner of the roof terrace.

"Sorry about that," Maggie said after she put the phone back to her ear. "I couldn't hear myself think back there."

"Maggie, is this a bad time?"

"No, not at all. I'm just at a party in the city. Sasha, it's fine. Did you say Clay is missing?"

"He's been gone almost two hours now. And I'm worried." Sasha sounded stressed, a reediness in her tone that instantly stirred concern within Maggie. "He should've been home ages ago."

Maggie glanced at her watch: two minutes to midnight, and a tangible sense of celebration rising in the air. "Do you know where he went?"

"To the store, he said. For milk. Can you believe it? Like we're in desperate need of any. We have a fridge full. And before you say it, yes, I tried calling him, about a hundred times. His phone just rings."

"Have you tried Andy?"

10

Andy Stucker was Clay's partner in Homicide Squad, and had been, on and off, for the better part of the past decade. Together, they were the longest-standing partnership in the murder team, and something of an institution. Stucker had joked on numerous occasions that the only way they were ever going to break up the partnership was when one of them died.

"I can't get hold of him either," Sasha said. "I was hoping you'd seen Clay."

"Not since this morning." Maggie tried to think back, but the alcohol was making everything hazy. She leaned against the cement balustrade that marked the edge of the terrace, each one of her senses feeling fuzzy and slightly askew. The dizzying drop to the street below didn't help, and she quickly turned her back to it. "There's probably an innocent explanation," she said. "Maybe he ran into someone he knows and got to talking. You know what a chatterbox Clay can be."

"Maggie, it's not like him not to let me know."

Maggie saw Steve working his way toward her, a champagne flute held aloft in each hand.

"Odds are he's gotten carried away and doesn't realize you're worried about him. I'm sure everything's okay."

"So why isn't he picking up?"

Maggie didn't have an answer. It was hurting her brain having to try to think coherently as it was, the alcohol objecting to any kind of clearheadedness.

"It's almost twelve," Sasha said. "Clay and I haven't missed a New Year's Eve countdown together in twenty-three years. It's not like him. I'm telling you, Maggie. Something's not right. I can *feel* it in my bones."

Steve came up and offered Maggie one of the glasses. She shook her head. He gave her a *Who's on the phone?* look, then sighed when Maggie mouthed, *Work.*

11

"What should I do?" Sasha was saying in her ear.

"Sit tight," Maggie said. "For now, at least, that's all you can do. You know what Clay's like. He'll be home soon, with flowers and an apology."

"And if he isn't?"

Maggie saw Steve tapping the base of one of the glasses against his watch.

"Give it some time," Maggie said. "Meanwhile, I'll notify Patrol and ask them to be on the lookout. He drives a red Nissan Sentra, right?"

"Yes. This year's model."

"Okay. Leave it to me. I'm sure it'll all work out fine."

"I hope so." She sounded disappointed with Maggie's response. "Call me either way?"

"Sure, Maggie. I'm sorry for troubling you. Have a good evening."

Maggie hung up and frowned at her phone.

"What's the emergency?" Steve asked.

"That was Clay Young's wife," she said. "She thinks he's missing."

"Missing?"

"She says he ran an errand a couple of hours ago and hasn't come home. Maybe I should go to her."

"Don't," he said, blocking her path.

Coming from Steve, it was odd behavior. Normally, he'd be the first to tell her to go, save the day.

"Steve . . ."

"She has sons, doesn't she?"

Maggie nodded. "Two. College age."

"Then she'll be okay. If it turns out not to be the case, I'm sure she'll phone back." He offered her the champagne glass again. "This time, Maggie, I insist."

12

Torn, Maggie took it.

Across the terrace, people started to chant in unison as the countdown to midnight got underway:

"Ten . . . nine . . . eight . . ."

"Maggie," Steve shouted, focusing her. "Look in your glass."

Maggie did. There was something resting in the bottom of the champagne. Something glinting. At first, she couldn't make out what it was. Then it dawned on her.

"It was my grandma's," he said. "Now it's yours."

" . . . three . . . two . . . one . . ."

Maggie didn't know what to say.

A deafening cheer erupted across the rooftop, and fireworks lit up the night sky, their explosions booming off the glass towers.

Steve dropped to one knee. "Maggie Novak," he shouted above the din, "will you do me the honor of marrying me?"

Maggie stared at the diamond ring sparkling in the champagne, her mind suddenly bouncing all over the place. She should have been overwhelmed with happy thoughts, ecstatic, but all she could think about was Clayton Young and why he hadn't come home.

Chapter Three

KEEPING PACE

M aggie woke with a start, her eyes taking a moment to focus on the alarm clock and the bright-red digits telling her it was just after seven in the morning. She let out a quiet groan and rolled onto her back, a fuzzy memory of *last night* skulking into her thoughts.

Her head ached like she'd been hit between the eyes with a hammer.

How much did I drink?

The party had fizzled out after one, she remembered, and she had a vague recollection of catching a taxi back home with Steve. Complaining loudly about the extortionate fare before falling through the front door and making drunken love on the stairs. Fumbling on the landing in the dark, laughing and kissing. Finally crashing into bed, sweating and exhausted.

Like landmarks emerging through a fog, snippets of the evening's partying came back to her: grainy images of eating too much, drinking too much, dancing too much, and Steve *proposing*.

The recollection came like a slap across her face, and Maggie sat up with a jolt.

Steve was snuggled up beside her in the bed, asleep, his hair tousled and the sheets pulled up to his chin.

Maggie stuck out her left hand, inspecting her fingers.

No sign of the engagement ring.

What did I do with it?

She tried to remember the course of events following Steve's proposal, but it only acted to intensify the pain in her head. She checked the nightstand. Still, no ring.

Where did I put it?

Steve moaned in his sleep, turning over and pulling the sheet off her.

Maggie swung her legs out of bed, then padded into the bathroom, switching on the night-light and grimacing at her ghostly reflection in the vanity mirror.

Death warmed over.

No other way to describe it. She looked like she'd been in a barroom brawl, her long dark hair mussed up, and her smoky makeup—which she'd forgotten to wash off—had expanded across her face, like ink on blotting paper, completely blackening her eyes.

From sultry to smudgy.

Maggie cleaned herself up, then downed a couple of Tylenol from the medicine cabinet.

Back in the bedroom, Steve was still fast asleep.

Quietly, Maggie dressed in her running gear, tying her unruly hair in a ponytail and feeding it through the gap above the adjuster in her official Orange County Sheriff's Office baseball cap. Then, mostly by touch, she searched for her phone, scouting out the bedroom and checking under discarded garments. She found Steve's phone stuffed in a shoe. But hers was nowhere in sight. She slipped out onto the landing, retracing her steps from the night before, finding her little black dress draped over the handrail and Steve's jacket slung over the post. She found her phone stuffed inside her clutch purse, left under the hall table.

She attached it to her Velcro armband, then turned toward the kitchen as she heard claws tapping on the tiles behind her.

Spartacus, Steve's eight-year-old Rhodesian ridgeback, was looking at her from the end of the hall.

"I'm sorry, Spart," she whispered. "Did I wake you?" She pouted at the dog. He yawned. "Can I make up for it by offering you a run?"

He plodded over, nuzzling his head into her hands. She ruffled his ears. Then she opened the front door, and they both slipped outside.

Cool air sucked the heat from her skin.

Spartacus watched her limber up in the driveway; then they headed out, taking it easy at first as they exited the cul-de-sac, applying a little more effort as they negotiated the steeper incline winding its way through the Hammocks.

The sun was an otherworldly glow in the east.

With the dog tight at her side, Maggie tucked in her elbows and upped her pace.

Maggie's regular running route wasn't a scenic one—no coastal cliffs or shell-strewn beaches—just the wraparound parking lot of the West Oaks Mall, with its crumbling asphalt and its tired trees. But she liked it—for as long as it lasted, that was. Recently, the mall had seen a decline in customer foot traffic, and Maggie suspected that at some point, redevelopers would come in, bulldoze the old mall out of existence, and build a new subdivision.

Then, where would she run?

She came to Clarke Road and crossed diagonally into the mall parking lot, the dark hulk of the mall building silhouetted against the gathering dawn. In the twilight, it looked like a scene from a postapocalyptic movie.

"Steve asked me to marry him," she told the dog.

He glanced up at her, keeping tight to her side.

"I know," she said. "It's freaked me out, too."

Why is that? she wondered.

Did she really think it was never going to happen?

She and Steve had been seeing each other now for over eight months, long enough to find out what made each other tick, and to consider their union serious. As far as she knew, their relationship was normal, healthy. They did regular stuff together, and their friends and family had grown accustomed to their being a twosome. And yet Maggie hadn't seen his proposal coming.

Why was that?

Usually, she was adept at predicting the things people were going to say and the way they were about to act. Not so with Steve.

His proposal had completely blindsided her.

Maggie ducked as she passed underneath low-hanging tree branches at the side of the road.

What answer did she give?

She realized with a start that she couldn't remember. Not her words, at any rate. But she could remember her physical reaction.

She'd laughed.

And Maggie was horrified at the thought.

She hadn't acted surprised. She hadn't shown any kind of excitement. She hadn't gone quiet with uncertainty. *Laughter* had been her first reaction to the idea of marrying Steve.

In all seriousness, he'd popped the question, and she had burst into a fit of giggles, blaming it on too much champagne and . . .

What?

Fear?

Her phone chimed on her arm. Maggie slowed to a walk and peeled it off the Velcro band.

"Stay," she told the dog.

It was a notification, alerting her to a voice message as well as to more than a dozen missed calls, all from the same landline number.

Heat bloomed in Maggie's chest.

Sasha Young!

The memory came like a punch in her gut, momentarily winding her.

In all the fanfare of the New Year's celebrations, she had completely forgotten about Sasha's midnight phone call. It would be easy to blame intoxication for her forgetfulness, but she knew it was the distraction of Steve's surprise proposal that had erased all memory of Sasha's plea for help.

Maggie had continued to get drunk, all thoughts of Sasha and her situation pushed aside.

What kind of friend did something like that?

Worse still, she realized, she had overlooked informing Dispatch to be on the lookout for Clay's car.

In Sasha's moment of need, Maggie had abandoned her.

Cursing herself, Maggie accessed the voice mail.

"Maggie, it's Sasha. It's after two in the morning. I know it's late. I've tried calling you several times already, but you're not picking up. Clay still isn't home, and he's not answering his phone. I'm scared something bad has happened. Please call me as soon as you get this."

Maggie saved the voice mail, then selected to return the call, hearing the number ring, unanswered.

"Don't look at me like that," she said, realizing the dog was looking up at her. "I know I messed up. Okay?"

She canceled the call, then selected Clay's cell number from her Contacts list. Almost immediately, his voice mail kicked in, and she left a short message, asking him to call her, ASAP.

"I just want to know you made it home okay," she said.

Then she resumed her run, wondering if the situation had resolved itself already while she had been sleeping off her night out.

She got her answer fifteen minutes later.

A call came through from Sergeant Lenny Smits, her immediate superior in Major Case.

"Happy New Year," she said as she took his call.

"Is it?" Smits's tone sounded more dour than usual. Even though one of his favorite sayings was *Humor me*, Smits wasn't known for his lightheartedness. "Sorry if I caught you at an inopportune moment," he said, clearly not meaning it. "What do you know about our missing detective?"

Maggie slowed to a walk, surprised that Smits thought she might know anything at all. "You heard about Clay?"

Smits made an uh-huh sound.

"To be honest, sir," she said, "I don't know much. Sasha called me just before midnight, saying Clay hadn't come home, and she was worried. I thought things might've resolved themselves overnight. Obviously not." It sounded like a weak excuse to justify her inaction. "Have you heard from her?"

"She's here," he said quietly, but in a way that told her it was both a concern and an inconvenience. "Mrs. Young is sitting on my couch as we speak. Consoling herself on my hundred-buck scotch. It's killing me."

"She's at your condo?" Maggie was surprised that Sasha had turned up at the Smits's home instead of at the Sheriff's Office.

"Trust me," Smits said, "her showing up like this came as an eye-opener to me, too. She said she'd called the office and was told it was my day off."

"And she couldn't speak with someone else?"

"Apparently not."

"How did she get your address?"

"I had the Youngs over for dinner once."

Maggie felt a pang of jealousy and pushed it away.

"Understandably," he continued, "she's worried over her missing husband. I heard you and he had an exchange of words yesterday and things got heated. You went one way while he went the other. Now he's missing. I want to know if your fight has any bearing on his disappearance."

Maggie slowed to a complete stop, the implications of Smits's words sapping her energy. Just the idea that she was complicit in some way was enough to knock her senses sideways. She began to speak, but Smits cut her off.

"Look, forget it," he said. "Mrs. Young is calling out my name. You can explain when you get here."

Chapter Four

WITHOUT A PADDLE

F our years ago, after her first partner in Homicide Squad had opted to take his retirement, Maggie had found herself partnered temporarily with Clayton Young. The union had existed only a few weeks, ending when Ed Loomis had relocated from the NYPD, but it had been a tough time for Maggie, and she'd almost quit the badge. It wasn't that Clay had been bad at his job. It was that Maggie had been too good at hers. And Clay hadn't appreciated what he saw as competition.

Now he was missing, and Maggie was outside Smits's condominium at Lake Eola Park in Orlando, her pulse still slightly elevated from her speedy drive over.

She took a breath, telling herself to *relax*. Then she rapped her knuckles against the condo's door.

"What's with the fancy running gear?" Smits said as he opened the door and looked Maggie up and down. "Did you run here on foot?"

Maggie made a face, wondering what other ways there were to run anywhere.

Smits had on gray sweatpants and a turquoise Tommy Bahama T-shirt with a hula girl print. His salt-and-pepper hair was tousled, and a thick coating of stubble darkened his jaw. He looked like he'd just rolled out of bed.

"You'll have to bear with me if I smell a little ripe right now," Maggie said. "I'm not the only one who didn't have time to change."

In fact, over the phone, Smits had given her a *get here or else* directive, and she'd sprinted home, leaving Spartacus in the kitchen before driving to Smits's city condo in record time.

Smits made an uh-huh sound and beckoned her inside, then closed the door behind her.

Maggie said, "Where's Sasha?"

Smits pointed down the hallway. "Living room."

Maggie looked. On the far side of the condo, the frail figure of Sasha Young was standing at the sliding doors leading out onto Smits's fifth-floor balcony, wringing her hands as she stared through the window. She looked skinnier than the last time Maggie had seen her, like her clothes were one size too big. Her short Afro hair, which normally glistened with product, looked dull, and there was a noticeable grayish cast to her skin.

Is that what twelve hours of husband worry does to a woman?

"She showed up an hour ago," Smits said, his voice low. "Distraught and in a mess. Said she was out of options and didn't know who else to turn to. The only way I managed to settle her down at all was plying her with alcohol."

"She called me just before midnight," Maggie said with a nod. "She told me Clay had been missing two hours at that point. I meant to issue a BOLO on his car, but I got distracted, and it slipped my mind."

"Not like you, Detective."

"Let's just say she caught me in a weird moment."

Smits nodded, but didn't push the matter. He offered to take Maggie's ball cap. Maggie took it off and handed it over. He hung it on a peg on the back of the door.

"Anyway," he said, "don't worry about the BOLO; it's done. I called Patrol right before calling you. Eyes across the county are now on the lookout for Clay and his car."

"Better late than never, I guess."

"Better eight hours ago," Smits said, and Maggie considered herself told. "Whatever's going on here," he said, "we're a long way behind it already. What exactly did she say to you last night?"

"Just that Clay hadn't come home, and she was wondering if I had seen him."

"And had you?"

"No. I was at the *Chronicle*'s New Year's party."

"So you didn't see Detective Young?"

"Not since earlier in the day, at the office."

"What did you tell her?"

"Exactly that. And that she shouldn't worry. That everything would be okay. I tried reassuring her."

Sasha was still staring out the window, as though hypnotized by the view across the lake, the slight rise and fall of her chest the only sign of life.

"Has she said anything to you?" Maggie asked.

Smits stuck out his lower lip. "She's convinced something bad has happened. And right now I believe her. But that's as far as I got. I thought you might have better luck."

"Because I'm a woman?"

Smits's gaze swung back to her. "No, Detective. Because I kept hitting a brick wall. The thing is, I can't have the spouses of my detectives showing up here whenever they have a fight. It's unprofessional. I was in bed, for Pete's sake."

"She didn't mention anything to me about them arguing."

"Me neither. It's just an assumption. It's New Year's. Why else would he stay away from his loving wife on New Year's?"

Maggie saw movement in the living room—Sasha wrapping her arms around her waist and holding herself tight.

"Okay," Maggie said, "let's speak with her."

Smits caught her arm before she could head inside. "Before we do, I need to know everything about your fight yesterday with Detective Young."

Maggie frowned. "For starters, it wasn't exactly a fight. Clay was angry about an article that Nick wrote in the *Chronicle*."

Now it was Smits's turn to frown. "Nick Stavanger, the columnist?"

Maggie nodded, her head hurting a little, and she realized she hadn't drunk enough fluids this morning.

Smits's eyes narrowed. "You and he are neighbors, right?"

"We're also good friends."

"His work is inciting."

"He prefers the word *awakening*."

"I don't care what he prefers, Detective. In my opinion, Stavanger writes provocative pieces. Seems he goes out of his way to get everybody's back up. Sooner or later someone's going to take exception to that barbed attitude of his and do something he'll regret."

Maggie felt a defensive response rising in her, but pressed it down. By design, Nick's articles were written to expose raw nerves and then to electrocute them. When a city commissioner accepted a bribe, or when a bad cop beat up on a good kid, Nick wanted people to sit up and take notice. For the most part, his pieces posed moral questions, his main intention being to call people out publicly on their private behavior. But his strong-arm tactics often rubbed people the wrong way, winning him the reputation of a rebel and someone who couldn't be trusted.

"Sometimes, Sarge," Maggie said, "the truth hurts."

"That depends on whose version of the truth it is." Smits gave her a *don't even come back on that one* look.

"Either way," Maggie said, "Nick's heart is in the right place." She wanted to say more, to defend Nick, but she knew that Smits's mind was already made up. Time and again, Nick had proven himself a loyal friend, and hearing anyone speak negatively about him didn't sit well with her. But people had a right to their opinions.

"Lucky for me," Smits said, still keeping his voice low, "I didn't read it. I had better things to do with my Saturday morning. Like playing golf with the mayor."

The mayor, Maggie knew, was sometimes the target in Nick's crosshairs, and she wondered if that contributed to Smits's standpoint.

"That said," he added, "I did hear Stavanger accused us of being heavy handed and negligent."

"We can't claim it doesn't happen."

"No system's perfect. Especially ones involving people. What part of it got Detective Young all worked up?"

"Nick used Lay-Z Creek's death in custody as an example of what he called 'OCSO's overzealous use of excessive force in certain arrests.'"

"Lay-Z Creek?" Smits rubbed at his sandpaper stubble. "The whiter-than-white rapper?"

"Actually, he was Latino."

"All the same, if I remember rightly, the kid was a prime suspect in an unsolved homicide."

"Only he was innocent, and he died in custody."

"He threatened Detectives Young and Stucker with a sword."

Maggie made a face, showing Smits that she disagreed with his defense. "The sword turned out to be a plastic movie prop from one of his music videos."

"But it *looked* real at the time," Smits said. "We've all seen the dashcam footage. As far as Detectives Young and Stucker were concerned, it *was* real. The kid left them no choice. For public safety, he had to be tased."

And the popular music icon had had a massive heart attack as a result, dying in the back of a sheriff's cruiser. The whole episode caught on a dozen smartphones and then spread to the internet. Cries of police brutality and calls for justice on social media. For most of last summer, the repercussions coming from the Creek incident had plagued the Sheriff's Office and those directly involved.

And Nick's article had brought it all back into the present.

In the living room, Sasha moved from the window, seating herself on a large couch facing the wall-mounted TV.

Quietly, Smits said, "Detective, let's you and I be honest here. Stavanger's the one who crossed the line. Anybody would think we got away with murder."

Maggie didn't take the bait. Wholeheartedly, she accepted that Nick's exposé may not have been the best approach to focus public interest on the arrest record of the Orange County Sheriff's Office, but his assertion about Creek's preventable death had been a valid one.

Creek's medical history had been public knowledge. He'd had cardiac issues, and half of his songs had been about his "broken heart." Although Maggie's professional loyalty lay with OCSO and her colleagues, a part of her stood behind Nick's rationale. Stucker and Young should not have used a Taser on the rap artist.

Smits seemed satisfied with her account, and he led her through to the living room.

Being here in Smits's private domain was a first for Maggie, and an eye-opener, too. Compared with his glass-walled office in the corner of Major Case, Smits's lakeside condo was surprisingly basic. Plain walls and no-frills furniture. Everything functional and tonally similar. Nice, but with about as much character as a wooden doll. The word *inoffensive* came to mind. Maggie liked simplicity, but she wasn't a fan of minimalism.

Sasha sat up straight as she saw them enter the room, bewilderment adding to the worry already etched on her face. "Maggie? I thought Andy was coming?" She looked at Smits. "I need Andy here. Where is he?"

"We don't know," Smits answered as he perched himself on the arm of the couch. "Detective Stucker is using up his vacation days and isn't answering his phone. I'll keep trying him."

"Knowing Andy," Maggie said, "he's probably sleeping off a heavy night." She followed it with a smile, but it failed to lessen the tension in Sasha's face.

"So," Smits said, "I called Detective Novak here instead, who probably wishes she was sleeping off her own heavy night, too. I hope you don't mind."

Sasha shook her head. "No, not at all." She patted the seat next to her on the couch. "Maggie, please."

Maggie went over, sitting down and taking Sasha's hands in hers. Sasha's touch was cool, shaky. "I'm sorry I missed your calls," Maggie said. "It's been a strange night."

Instantly, she regretted making the statement; without question, the night had been much stranger for Sasha Young than it had been for her, and her comment sounded more than a little lame.

Sasha's eyes flicked from Maggie to Smits and back to Maggie again. "You understand," she said, "I didn't have anywhere else to turn."

"It's okay," Maggie said. "You did the right thing contacting Sergeant Smits. We're worried as well. We want to know Clay is safe, too. He's one of us. We're here to help any way we can."

Sasha nodded, but she didn't look so sure.

"Can I ask you a few questions?" Maggie said.

Sasha nodded again, this time withdrawing her hands from Maggie's.

"When was the last time you saw Clay?"

"Yesterday evening, around ten."

"At home?"

"Yes."

"Were the two of you alone?"

"Yes. Just Clay and me."

"Where were your sons?"

Sasha made a face. "I'm sorry, Maggie. But how is their whereabouts going to help find my husband?"

Smits said, "Sasha. It's just the process we need to go through. All police work is the same. We need the basics first. The foundations, so to speak. It gives us something to build on."

Again, Sasha seemed uncertain. "They're staying with friends for the weekend. They're young men now, you know?" She seemed to add the last part as though to justify them not being home overnight.

"Sasha," Maggie said, refocusing her.

Her gaze came back. "Yes?"

"Correct me if I'm wrong, because my recollection of last evening's a bit fuzzy, but when we spoke on the phone, you mentioned Clay had gone for milk. Right?"

"Yes, that's right."

"I thought so. And I think you pointed out that it was odd behavior, because you felt you didn't need any milk."

"Right again," she said. "But it was my mistake. I panicked and wasn't thinking straight. We did have plenty of regular milk in the fridge. It was chocolate milk we were out of."

"Chocolate milk." Maggie glanced at Smits. He shrugged.

"It's one of Clay's vices," she said. "He insists on having a glass each night before bed. He's convinced it helps him sleep."

28

"Safer than scotch," Smits said.

"Has Clay gone for milk after ten before?"

Sasha nodded. "Oh, yes. Many times."

"Okay. And typically how long was he gone on those occasions?"

Sasha shrugged small shoulders. "I'm not sure. No more than fifteen minutes? The store's a minute down the road. Usually, he's back home before I realize he's been anywhere." Her gaze switched to Smits. "Can't you track his phone, or something?"

"Officially, Sasha, not without a judge signing off on a phone company data request." He said it as though he said it every day of the week. "The trouble is, it's a public holiday. Which means you're looking at midday tomorrow at the soonest. And that's being optimistic."

Maggie waited for Sasha to look back at her before saying, "Sasha, what were you both doing immediately prior to Clay leaving the house last night?" She was thinking about them arguing, but wanted to broach the subject softly.

Sasha seemed to give herself a few seconds to think about it before checking off the facts like a shopping list. "Let's see. Clay was in the den, watching the TV. I was in the bathroom, soaking in the tub. I could hear him laughing."

"So you'd say his mood was light?"

"I suppose I would, yes. He said he was looking forward to the fireworks. Clay loves that kind of thing."

"Were you still in the tub when Clay left?"

"Yes."

"Did he say anything to you?"

Again, Sasha seemed to allow herself a few seconds to think. "Only that he was going for milk and he wouldn't be long."

"Nothing else?"

29

"Let me see. He told me to enjoy my soak. Then, right before leaving, he kissed me on the forehead, and . . . he told me he loved me."

Sasha's last few words came out strained.

Maggie told her she was doing well, then asked about Clay's general mood of late.

"Upbeat," Sasha said, this time without a pause. "We have a vacation soon."

Smits nodded. "Havana, right?"

"Yes. At the end of the month. He's so excited. It's to celebrate his birthday. We've never been to Cuba. He's calling it our trip of a lifetime."

"I hear it's nice this time of year," Smits said. "You're going to have a ball."

Suddenly, Sasha's expression looked stricken, as though Smits had said the complete opposite.

Maggie asked, "It's Clay's sixtieth this time, right?"

Sasha nodded.

"How does he feel about turning sixty?"

"To be honest, other than talking about the vacation, he's hardly mentioned it. His attitude is, it's just another day and it's business as usual."

"So apart from Clay's mood being upbeat lately, how would you describe his state of mind over the last few months?"

"Normal, I guess. Why?"

"I'm just laying out the framework," Maggie said. "So you'd say he hasn't been worrying over something, maybe more than he would usually?"

Sasha turned out her bottom lip. "No. Nothing that comes to mind."

"He hasn't acted uncharacteristic in any way?"

Now Sasha frowned. "Can you be more specific?"

Maggie sat forward, knowing that what she was about to ask was not only difficult for her to say, but equally difficult for Sasha to hear. "Other than what you consider is Clay's normal behavior, has he been experiencing any mood swings or emotional outbursts lately?" Maggie thought about him verbally attacking her over Nick's article. She saw Sasha's frown deepen. "Has he expressed any feelings of disconnection and hopelessness? Has Clay withdrawn from family and friends? Has he—"

"Detective . . . ," Smits warned, cutting her off. "That's enough."

Sasha looked injured, like Maggie had slapped her across the face. "What are you saying, Maggie? You don't think he—"

"We don't," Smits said, preventing Sasha from finishing the sentence. "Absolutely and categorically not. No way on God's green earth would Clay do anything to hurt himself, or you." He stared at Maggie. "We don't think that. Do we, Detective Novak?"

Maggie sensed Sasha staring, too.

"No," she said at last. "You're right, Sasha. I'm sorry. I didn't mean to add to your worry. Clay's the last person I know who would—"

"Who would be that cruel to the woman he adores," Smits said.

But Maggie didn't share Smits's sentiment. If investigating homicides had taught her one lesson, it was that the only thing anyone could know with absolute certainty about anyone else was that nothing could ever be known about anyone else with absolute certainty.

Sasha pointed at an empty glass on the coffee table. "Please. I need another drink."

Smits got up, retrieved the glass, and went over to a cabinet in the corner of the room. He poured whiskey and handed it to her.

Sasha took a sip. "Thank you."

"Uh-huh." Smits looked at Maggie, tipping the bottle toward her. "Hair of the dog, Detective?"

She shook her head.

"Wise choice," he said, putting the bottle back in the cabinet.

Maggie looked back to Sasha. "Sasha, I need to ask another difficult question. Okay?"

Sasha seemed to consider the request, then nodded stiffly.

"How are things between you and Clay?"

"Fine."

It came out like a gunshot—a verbal bullet leaving her mouth a fraction of a second after Maggie's last word, the speed of her reaction ringing a warning bell in Maggie's head. She knew the lightning response could mean one of two things: either Sasha and Clay were madly in love, or this was the impression she wanted to give.

Sasha looked down at the gold band on her ring finger. "It's our anniversary this spring," she said. "We'll be married twenty-one years. We've chosen to stay together for better or worse. I think that says everything."

Maggie wondered how many of those years had been happy, then told herself to stop reacting negatively. Matrimony didn't mean imprisonment. There were just as many happy endings as there were horror stories.

An image of Steve's engagement ring flashed through her mind. A fuzzy glimpse of her extracting it from the champagne, sucking off the sticky liquid, and handing it back to Steve.

Did she say *no*?

Smits was looking at her with an expression that told her to stop making the situation worse and get on with it. *Clay was missing.*

"Last couple of questions," she said. "Does Clay have any medical condition we don't know about?"

Sasha looked up. "Such as?"

"Like something that may have struck him while he was out last night, incapacitating him and stopping him from coming home. His heart, maybe?"

Sasha shook her head. "You know my husband, Maggie. He's a fitness freak. He's fanatical about the gym. He eats all the right things. He keeps in shape. Our boys think he's a superhero in disguise." She smiled to herself, but it was fleeting. "On his last checkup, the doctor told him he has the heart of an ox. He has no health concerns."

Or, none that she knows about, Maggie thought.

Sasha turned to Smits. "By the way, I meant to ask. Do I need to file a missing persons report?"

Smits flapped a hand. "Don't go worrying about the paperwork, Sasha. We can look at doing that later, if we need to. And only when you feel up to it."

"I called the emergency rooms."

"And I'm guessing they had no record of him being admitted?"

Sasha nodded.

"That's good then. Positive."

Maggie waited until Sasha's gaze had circled back to hers. "What store did Clay go to?"

"Walmart."

"Where?"

"On the Trail."

Maggie knew the store in question. It was located on South Orange Blossom in Oak Ridge, within walking distance of the Young residence on Wakulla Way.

She turned to Smits. "We should get Patrol down there. See if anyone saw him in the store."

"I agree," he said and jumped to his feet.

Maggie waited until Smits had taken his phone down the hall with him before saying to Sasha, "I want you to think long and hard about this last question before giving me your answer. Okay?"

Sasha nodded, cupping the whiskey glass in both hands.

"Is there any reason, any reason at all, to think that Clay didn't intend on coming home last night?"

"I don't understand what you mean."

Maggie drew a breath, knowing how difficult her next words were going to be for Sasha to process. But she had to ask. "Could the need for him to go out for milk be a cover story, a way to get him out of the house?"

Now, bewilderment laid siege to Sasha's face.

Maggie leaned a little closer, keeping her voice to a minimum. "Sasha, did Clay have reason to be elsewhere last night? Maybe with a friend, or at a meet up of some kind?"

"Maggie, what are you trying to say?"

"Did Clay have any bad habits?"

Now, Sasha looked horrified at the thought. "You mean like drugs?"

"I know it's difficult to hear, but I need to know. You'd be surprised the things people get up to in their own time and in the privacy of their own homes. We all have secrets."

"I don't." Sasha's expression was taut, as though her skin was about to crack at any second.

"But does Clay?"

"No. Never. I'd know."

Maggie wondered at what point in a relationship a spouse would be able to spot if their partner were hiding something like a serious drug habit. A day, a week, six months, a year? If Steve started snorting cocaine tomorrow, in private, how soon would she be able to tell, if at all? Was he already doing it?

Maggie got to her feet as Smits came back into the room.

"Dispatch is sending a cruiser to the store right now," he said. "Let's see what Patrol comes back with."

"I think I'll head down there myself," she said. "Just to make sure they don't miss anything." She turned to Sasha. "I'll be in touch. In the meantime, stay strong."

Sasha nodded. "Thanks, Maggie. I'm sorry for your inconvenience, and for last night."

"It's no trouble, honestly. If things were reversed, Clay would do the same for me."

Smits followed Maggie down the hall.

As Maggie collected her baseball cap from the peg on the door, he asked her what she thought about the whole affair.

"I think, like you, I'm beginning to get a little worried," she admitted quietly. "We both know this behavior isn't normal for Clay. Plus, I've got a feeling there's more to this than Sasha's telling us. I don't know what it is right now. Maybe it's something or nothing. Maybe it's not even connected to Clay's disappearance. But something's off. I can sense it." She opened the door.

Smits put a hand on it. "You think she's lying?"

"I think she knows more than she's saying."

Maggie looked back along the hallway to Sasha Young still seated in the living area, sipping scotch.

"If she's faking that upset," Smits said, "she deserves an Oscar for the performance. Even fake tears are real tears. All the same, I'll get somebody from Victim Services down here to collect her. If this turns out to be the worst-case scenario, she'll need their support."

"And ours."

Smits looked back at Maggie and removed his hand from the door. "Keep me updated," he said.

Chapter Five

SURPRISE IN STORE

Maggie drove her newish Ford Mustang into the Walmart Supercenter parking lot on Orange Blossom Trail in Oak Ridge a little too fast, and the tires screeched on the blacktop. She hadn't had the vehicle more than a handful of months, and she was still enjoying putting it through its paces. The smell of new leather still got to her. She parked in the shade of a tree and kept her sunglasses on as she got out into morning sunshine.

Even at 9:00 a.m. on New Year's Day, the place looked busy. Probably, a few hundred people were already inside and crowding the pharmacy, in search of hangover remedies. For a second, Maggie considered joining them.

Peaky was the best word to describe how she felt right now. If anyone asked, that's what she was going with. *Peaky.*

She pulled down the bill of her cap as she crossed the lot, wishing she had applied sunscreen before dashing out of the house. Even through her shades, the sun seemed brighter than usual, its reflection dazzling in the car windshields.

She made a mental note to cut back on rooftop parties.

Outside the store's main entrance, a white sheriff's cruiser was parked on the crosswalk. No one inside. Maggie headed into the store, walking directly to the customer service counter located opposite the checkouts.

"I need to speak with the store manager," she told a female service representative.

"Is it something I can help with?" the assistant asked.

Maggie reached for her badge, then realized she'd left it at home, as well as her gun. Smits would kill her if he knew she was conducting sheriff's business without ID.

Extenuating circumstances.

Sure.

"I'm a detective with the Sheriff's Office," she told the assistant. "The deputies who came through here a few minutes ago—I'm with them. Can you point me in their direction? They're expecting me." On the ride over, Maggie had notified Dispatch of her imminent arrival at the store, asking them to update the deputies in attendance.

"Can I see your official ID?"

Maggie pointed at the Orange County Sheriff's Office emblem stitched on the front of her cap, as though it granted access to all areas. "You only get one of these when you work at the Sheriff's Office. Otherwise, I don't have any other form of identification on me."

"Oh."

"Look. It's my day off, and I wasn't planning on coming down here."

"What about a driver's license?"

Maggie shook her head. "That's just it. I left everything behind, even my purse." She leaned her arms on the counter. "If you can just have the manager come speak with me, that would be a big help. Tell him it's Detective Novak, and that he can check my credentials with the deputies."

The assistant didn't look so sure. All the same, she picked up the telephone and made the call. "The store manager will be with you in a minute," she said when she came off the call.

"Thank you."

Maggie retreated out of the way, her thoughts returning to Sasha Young and her using Smits's scotch as a painkiller. Maggie couldn't put her finger on it, but she sensed that Sasha wasn't being totally transparent.

Maggie's phone rang. She peeled it off her armband.

Steve.

"Hey there," he said after she answered. He sounded sleepy. "Where're you at? I'm guessing you're out running?"

"I was," she said. "Now, I'm at the Walmart on Orange Blossom."

She heard a rustling sound, as though Steve was sitting up in bed. "That's some run, even for you. What are you doing way out there?"

"On the hunt for Clay Young. It's a long story."

"Clay?" It sounded like Steve needed a moment to process. "You mean he still hasn't shown up?"

"Nope."

"Maggie, it's early. It's your day off. Now you're working Missing Persons as well as Homicide?"

Maggie knew Steve didn't mean it as a slight, but it sounded that way. "I go where I'm needed," she said.

"Well, they certainly like to stretch their girl power; that's for sure. You should ask for a pay raise."

"In the year of fiscal cutbacks? Who're you trying to kid?"

"You're worth every penny."

"Trust me. They won't even stretch to a *thank-you* card."

She heard him chuckle, then stifle a yawn. "Ouch," he said. "My head hurts. I need rehydrating. Do you have any soda?"

"Try the fridge."

"I will. How're you feeling this morning?"

"Peaky. I think I overdid it with the champagne."

"Oh, you *think*?" She heard him laugh again. "That's an understatement, Maggie. You drank the party dry. I don't think I've seen you quite so drunk. Do you know you lisp when you're tipsy?"

"I do, and it's something I don't talk about. Just one of my many embarrassing family traits."

Steve laughed. "You do me good, Maggie Novak. Listen, I'm going to grab a shower and then head back to my place. I need to pack."

Steve was attending a psychology conference in Atlanta tomorrow and for the rest of the week. He was flying out in the morning and wouldn't be back in Orlando until the weekend.

"I'll miss you," she said.

"No, you won't. Don't fib. You're married to your job."

Maggie's brain stuttered at the mention of the *M* word.

"Don't forget we have plans later," he said. "Your sister's, remember? The big New Year's get-together."

Maggie hadn't forgotten, but recent events had pushed it to the back of her mind. It was tradition: Nora inviting Maggie and their older brother, Bryan, and his family over for dinner on New Year's Day. It had happened without fail every year since their parents had divorced. The Novak family was big on such occasions. Maggie had no idea why, other than traditions were one of the few things that kept families together.

"This'll be my first," Steve said.

"Don't get too excited. It usually ends in chaos and tears. Remember, I survived a bunch of these dinners. I know what I'm talking about. Here's how it'll go down. At first Bryan will be nice.

But that's just to lull you into a false sense of security. Once he has you cornered, he'll try and foist his political views on you while Emma, his poor downtrodden wife, runs ragged after their three unruly children. Meanwhile, Nora, my lovely baby sister, with her inability to commit to any one argument for fear of offending someone, will agree with everyone's point of view while Kevin, her enslaved husband, backs her up. Trust me. My family is the definition of dysfunctional."

"And where will you be while all this is happening—stewing in silence and sitting on the fence?"

"Out on the lanai with a beer, and trying not to self-harm."

Steve laughed again. "Well, call me crazy, but I'm kind of looking forward to it."

"I'm happy for you, Steve. You live your life sunny side up. As for me, I just can't get excited about natural disasters."

She saw a young African American man in a blue shirt and chinos walking directly toward her through the checkout area, a Walmart name badge flapping on his chest pocket. He looked to be in his midthirties, with soft features and friendly eyes.

"Looks like my date's here," she said. "I have to run."

"Okay. I'll meet you at Nora's at four. That gives you most of the day to find your missing colleague. Let me know when you're on your way home?"

"Will do." Maggie hung up as the store manager came up and extended his hand in greeting.

"Detective Novak?" he said. "I'm Jeff Willoughby, the store manager."

She shook his hand. "Thanks for your time, Mr. Willoughby."

He smiled. "Please. It's Jeff."

Maggie smiled back. "Okay. *Jeff.* I appreciate your coming out here at such short notice and all."

"It's no problem."

"I explained to your colleague back there that I don't have my ID at hand . . ."

"It's okay," he said. "The deputies already vouched for you."

"They did?"

"Enthusiastically. The best detective in the squad, one of them said. Don't say it came from me, but I think he's a fanboy."

Maggie followed Willoughby across the shop floor. He had a slightly diverging stride, she noticed, having to correct his course every few yards. One of his shoulders hanging slightly lower than the other. They came to a staff entrance near the electronics department at the back of the store, and Willoughby tapped numbers on a keypad.

"Through here," he said, leading her down a short hallway.

Two deputy sheriffs in crisp spruce-green uniforms were standing in his office, talking between themselves: a young female, early twenties, with short black hair and big eyes; and an olive-skinned male, about thirty, whom Maggie immediately recognized.

"Deputy Ramos," she said as she entered the office. "It's been a while. How's your little boy?" Whenever Maggie ran into the deputy, she always asked. Last year, Ramos's five-year-old son had been diagnosed with a critical illness, and it had been touch-and-go, and Ramos had been out of his mind with worry. Fortunately, his son had gotten through the worst of it and was coping on medication.

"Felipe?" he said with a smile. "He's still on the mend, but things are moving in the right direction. I'll tell him you asked. You guys should meet."

"I'd like that." The words came out before Maggie could check herself. She wasn't in the habit of spending time with other people's children outside her close family, and the thought unnerved her a little.

Ramos prodded a thumb at his partner. "Oh, hey," he said. "Won't you know it; I'm being rude. Let me introduce you guys.

41

Detective Novak, this is my brand-new partner, Deputy Shaw. Two weeks on the force and already giving me a run for my money."

Maggie shook the deputy's hand. "Nice to meet you," she said. "I trust Deputy Ramos here is giving you the all-star treatment?"

"The best," Shaw answered, with no hint of a smile, her handshake equally serious.

Maggie sensed that, at least when in uniform, Shaw was all business and no play. Probably, trying a little too hard to make a good impression.

She couldn't be judgmental; this had been her, eighteen years ago. Braced to tackle the city's crimes single-handedly.

"Shaw is a quick study," Ramos said. "Makes me feel old."

"In all honesty," Shaw said, her face emotionless, "I have a great mentor. And that makes it easy. Deputy Ramos has been inspirational. I've learned more in the past two weeks than I did the entire time I was at the academy."

"Such is the way of the world." Maggie smiled at their mutual backslapping, wondering briefly if it stemmed from a place other than a simple teacher-student relationship. Then she dismissed the notion, knowing that Ramos was happily married and big on loyalty.

"So," Ramos said, "we gather one of the famous Deathtectives is missing."

Throughout the Sheriff's Office, the term *Deathtectives* had become the adopted collective noun to describe the eight detectives that made up Homicide Squad. The name had come about a few years ago, following an internal softball tournament in which *Deathtectives* had beaten *Drugbusters*, otherwise known as Narcotics Squad. Ironically, neither Maggie nor her colleagues in the unit referred to each other as Deathtectives. But it didn't stop the rest of OCSO from using the name.

"Detective Clayton Young," Ramos said, checking his notepad. "Reported missing around ten p.m. last night?"

Maggie nodded. "He told his wife he was coming down here for milk and didn't come home."

"They live close by?"

"Just around the corner."

Shaw said, "What are we hoping, ma'am?"

"That it's a false alarm and we can all go home."

Maggie saw Willoughby spin a computer monitor around on the office desk so that they could see the screen.

"All set," he said. "This is the security footage you asked to see."

Maggie glanced at Ramos.

"Pardon me, ma'am, but I took the liberty of requesting it. I thought you'd want to see it the second you arrived."

"You thought right." She pulled up a chair and sat down at the desk. "Okay, Jeff. Show us what you've got."

Willoughby dropped into his manager's chair and put his left hand on a computer mouse. "Okay. These are all our internal feeds from around ten last night."

The screen was split equally into a grid of sixteen rectangular images, each one showing a full-color video from various cameras located around the store. Lofty views along aisles and over sensitive areas such as the pharmacy and the electronics department. Time stamps in the upper right corner of each frame confirmed Willoughby's statement.

Maggie ripped her phone off her armband and logged into Major Case's secure cloud storage. She found a stock image of Clayton Young—a fifty-nine-year-old African American with the physique of a linebacker, posing for the press shot in a camel-colored sport coat and a white button-down shirt.

She passed it around. "Let's see if we can spot him." She asked Willoughby to set the playback speed to fast-forward, and they all focused on the array of images as marionette-like customers skipped up and down the aisles.

Maggie's gaze moved from one flickering frame to the next, looking for anyone resembling her colleague.

The store had been busy last night. Shoppers picking up last-minute foodstuffs and beverages. Lines at the checkouts and families with overflowing carts.

Twenty seconds in, Shaw leaned in and pointed to the image in the lower left corner of the screen.

"Is that him?" she said.

Willoughby paused the array. He selected the frame in question and expanded it to fill the screen.

"That's him," Maggie said.

Clayton Young was standing in what appeared to be the dairy section, a milk carton in his hand. He had on jeans, sneakers, and a white polo shirt open at the collar. He looked older than he did in the publicity photo on Maggie's phone, speckles of gray in his hair, but otherwise, it was clear he worked out.

One thing of note: Sasha had been telling the truth about Clay coming here. And another: Clay had been telling the truth about his reason for doing so.

The time stamp read 10:08:44 P.M., 31 DEC.

Maggie took a photo of the freeze-frame with her phone. Then she messaged a copy of it to Smits's cell number. "Okay," she said. "We've established he was here. That's good. Now, let's see where he went. Jeff, do you have external camera feeds as well?"

"We do." Willoughby reduced the image to thumbnail size and brought up the feeds coming from cameras overlooking the parking lot. This time, the screen split into quarters, showing four nighttime images. Deep shadows and tall lamp poles highlighting trees and car roofs. Customers strolling to and from their cars, some pushing carts. Kids running amok. The bright headlights and taillights of vehicles coming and going, and the majority of parked vehicles occupying the spaces closest to the store.

Willoughby fast-forwarded the feeds at maximum speed. In a blur, cars zipped around the lot, customers flickering across the screen. After a dozen or more silent seconds, Willoughby hit the brakes, dropping the playback to normal mode and pointing at the upper left frame. "There," he said.

The viewpoint appeared to be from above the main entranceway, from a camera positioned to look almost directly downward at the striped crosswalk between the store and the parking lot. From above and behind, Clayton Young could be seen walking away from the camera, a gray plastic Walmart bag swinging from his hand. As he reached the first of the parked cars, Willoughby directed their attention to the adjacent image. This was a longer shot across the lot from the same vantage point, and in it they could see Clay striding away from the store.

Near the top of the frame, Clay's red Nissan Sentra was just visible, parked on its own, almost as far away from the store as possible. The image quality depreciated with distance, which meant it was impossible to define detail. The farther Clay walked from the store, the grainier he became, until eventually he was nothing more than a moving smudge less than an inch tall.

"Can you zoom in?" Maggie asked Willoughby.

"Not in the raw format. But even if I could, the quality wouldn't improve any. All you'd see is a pixelated close-up."

On screen, Clay opened the driver's door and got inside the car. He'd visited the store all right. He'd bought his chocolate milk. Now, Maggie was curious to know where he went next, because she knew it wasn't home.

Unless Sasha's lying, she thought suddenly.

But it wouldn't be simply a case of tracking his car. Once Clay left the lot, it would be hard to monitor his movements. The traffic cameras dotted around the city's road network were few and far between, mostly located on the toll roads. And unless Clay had run a red light, his car wouldn't appear on any signal cameras.

Maggie's gaze snagged on the time stamp.

It read 10:36:15 P.M., 31 DEC.

"Wait a minute," she said. "Something's not right. According to the time, it took him almost half an hour to complete his purchase."

"That's easily explainable," said Willoughby. "It was New Year's Eve, and we had fewer checkout operators working. Waiting times were longer than usual."

In the recording, Clay's car hadn't moved. Not even an inch. Its headlights were still off, its windows still dark. The time stamp still incrementing.

Maggie leaned closer to the screen, her eyes trying to resolve definition out of the pixelated image. "Fast-forward for me, Jeff. Slowly, this time."

Willoughby upped the playback speed a little. Customers darted across the bottom of the image. Cars zipping in and out of the frame. All the while, Clay's car was unmoving.

Maggie kept an eye on the time stamp. "That's four minutes he's been sitting there." The time stamp continued to five . . . six . . . seven minutes. "Why isn't he starting the car and driving away?"

Then she got her answer.

But it was the last thing she expected.

Eight minutes after Clayton Young had closed the driver's door, the windows lit up, briefly turning fuzzy white, as though lightning had struck inside the car.

She shouted at Willoughby to stop the video.

Then, with fear burning through her chest, she leaped to her feet and ran out of the room.

Chapter Six

COMBUSTIBLE GASES

Maggie sprinted through the store, dodging customers, elbows tucked in, her running shoes cushioning the sound of her footfalls on the polished cement. Willoughby and the deputy sheriffs trailed a dozen paces behind; she could hear them clattering along behind her, calls of *Excuse us!* and *Coming through!* sounding in her wake. Even without her running gear, she would have outsprinted them. Her leg muscles were on fire, propelling her toward the exit.

A Walmart assistant, pushing a stack of plastic crates, stepped out into the aisle in front of her, and she tried to sidestep, but not soon enough. Her shoulder connected with the crates, sending them toppling and her into a spin. She shouted *Sorry!* corrected her balance, and plowed on.

Her mind raced.

She didn't want to believe her eyes, didn't want to believe what she'd just witnessed in the surveillance video, didn't want to be *right*. She wanted to be mistaken, to be absolutely wrong. She wanted there to be a different explanation to account for the flash of light inside Clay's car. Anything other than the thought burning through her brain.

But Maggie had witnessed similar things previously. One too many, in fact, to know there was no mistaking the cause of the windows lighting up the way they had.

She burst out into searing sunlight, increasing her gait as she cleared the busy crosswalk.

Directly ahead, at the far side of the parking lot, she could see Clay's red Sentra still parked in the shade of the tree. No other cars parked close by. And the sight of it stoked the fear in her heart. She ran, full speed, hardly breathing, covering the distance in seconds. Then putting on the brakes, her hand reaching out to open the driver's door. And then stopping dead, her fingertips an inch from the handle, her heart hammering as her eyes focused on the splash of blood on the inside of the glass.

Dry red rivulets, hardened in the heat of the sun.

Bile rose in her throat, and she clamped her mouth closed.

Clay was slumped in the driver's seat, his face slack and lifeless, a patch of bloody goo in the short frizzy hair on the crown of his head. More dried blood spattered on his shirt, the headrest, and up onto the headliner.

On his lap, a handgun in his loose fist.

Maggie's heart missed several beats.

Clay had shot himself with his police-issue .45-caliber Glock 21. By the looks of it, jammed the muzzle under his chin and squeezed the trigger. His brains, blown all over the insides of the car, misted blood spraying in all directions.

The bile surged again, burning at her throat.

Maggie couldn't believe her eyes, didn't *want* to believe them. The world spun crazily around her.

Clay had shot himself.

The realization shook her to the core.

This is going to kill Sasha.

Maggie heard a clatter of booted feet coming up behind, and she raised a warning hand. Ramos and Shaw slowed, both of them reacting with disbelief when they saw the blood on the window and Clay's corpse inside.

Ramos made the sign of the cross, muttering a silent prayer.

"How did you know?" Shaw said.

Maggie swallowed the acid in her throat and forced a breath, unable to drag her eyes away from Clay's lifeless face. "Muzzle flash."

Shaw stepped forward, reaching for the door handle.

"Don't," Ramos shouted. "Deputy Shaw. Stand down. This is a crime scene. Do not touch *anything*."

Looking scalded, Shaw backed away from the car.

Maggie told Ramos to fetch their patrol vehicle and set up a cordon. He nodded, jogging back toward the store. Shaw just looked at her with wounded eyes.

Hurt feelings were the least of Maggie's concerns.

Someone was going to have to tell Sasha that her husband was dead.

Maggie heard somebody throwing up, and turned to see Willoughby leaning against a tree a few yards away, doubled over and emptying his stomach contents onto the bark chips.

She stared at him, thinking it was a weird stunt for the human body to pull: to retch at the sight of death. It served no purpose she could think of. It didn't add to survival in any way, or act as a warning to others. If anything, puking at a death scene just got in the way of things.

Clay was dead.

The realization grabbed hold of her and shook her a second time.

What am I going to say to Sasha?

Her husband had told her he was going out for milk. He'd kissed her on the brow, said he loved her, offering no hint of what he had planned. Then he'd come down here, bought the milk, and then blown out his brains.

Who did something like that?

With her senses swirling, Maggie ripped the phone off her armband and called it in.

Chapter Seven

TIPPING POINT

The call of *Officer down!* acted like a siren, drawing just about every law enforcement officer on duty and within radio range. Not just deputy sheriffs on patrol but also police officers from Orlando PD, showing a united front and turning up even though this location was outside their jurisdiction. Dozens of cruisers converging on the supercenter, lining both roadways leading in and out of the property. Several ambulances pushing to the front, their sirens squawking.

From the center of all the activity, Maggie surveyed the scene, conscious of her dead colleague and the stink of Willoughby's vomit blossoming in the heat.

It was like something from a disaster movie. Flashing police lights as far as the eye could see. Cheerless officers gathering in knots, scratching their heads and asking for updates.

"You only see this kind of turnout for a brother in blue," Ramos commented as he came over to Maggie. "It's inspiring."

Inspiration was the last thing on her mind.

Under Maggie's direction, Ramos and Shaw had strung police tape between the parking lot trees, forming a circular cordon fifty feet clear of Clay's car. On the other side of the tape barrier, cruisers and police personnel packed the lot, Walmart customers corralled farther back, some standing on car hoods and filming with their phones. Organized mayhem. Inside the cordon it was a different matter. In the eye of the storm there was a complete lack of fuss and movement, as though the death scene had a dampening effect, deadening sound and muting color.

Chaos rotating around the calm.

Overhead, a police helicopter chopped across the blue, circling the scene, while another, belonging to WESH-2 News, hovered a little farther back above the supercenter.

"Smile for the camera," Shaw muttered, clearly not meaning it.

Already, a couple of big news vans had parked on the periphery of the parking lot, news crews setting up stalls. Maggie could see camera operators standing on A-frame ladders while reporters fed *live* tidbits back to the studio.

The circus had come to town, and everybody wanted a front-row seat.

Not just peaky—Maggie felt sick to the pit of her stomach.

All this commotion, all these eyes, all those lenses, all of it revolving around the red Sentra with Clay's dead body inside. The tape cordon provided a necessary breathing space, but even the cheapest smartphones could zoom in and relay the grim proceedings live to social media. Already, Clay's death had become a public spectacle. And this was just the start of it.

Ramos handed her an energy drink. "I picked it up in the store," he said. "No offense, but you look like you need it, ma'am."

She thanked him, then guzzled the drink.

From experience, Maggie knew it would take several hours for Forensics to fully process this kind of death scene, maybe another hour before the medical examiner would release it. Probably late afternoon at the soonest before the circus packed up and moved on. In the meantime, half a dozen hours of juggling and acrobatics, with Maggie acting as ringmaster.

Worst still, she knew that rigor would have set in overnight, effectively locking Clay in situ. Plus, he wasn't the smallest guy in the squad. It would take some planning and a lot of combined effort to extricate him from the car. Maybe even calling on firefighters to cut off the roof with their Jaws of Life and winch him out.

And their every move being broadcast live on local TV.

Maggie pulled the ball cap a little snugger on her head.

On the phone, Smits had instructed her to do nothing until he arrived, except secure the scene and sit tight.

He wanted to be here when they cracked open the car.

Then the real dance macabre would begin.

Happy New Year.

"They better get a move on," Ramos said to her, referring, she knew, to Forensics Squad. "He'll be ripe soon enough."

Maggie didn't want to think too much about it, but Ramos had a point. Even though it was early morning, the temperature was on the rise, and there were no clouds to lessen the intensity of the sun's rays striking the car. Enclosed in his metal-and-glass coffin, Clay's body would begin to break down, a chain reaction of disintegration that would grow exponentially as the heat increased, turning cells to slush and releasing odious gases.

For a second, the image of Lindy Munson, a seventeen-year-old girl broiled to death in a car trunk two months ago, flashed into Maggie's thoughts. That particular crime scene had been isolated, located on a quiet service road leading to Lake Apopka, with public access restricted and easily controlled. Not like here. When it came to open-air death scenes, this was probably the worst-case scenario.

Maggie glanced at her watch.

According to Dispatch, techies from Forensics had been notified and were en route. Minutes away. No word yet from the ME's

Office. It was a holiday, after all, and public services were running on fumes.

"Attention, everyone," Ramos said. "It's showtime."

Maggie picked out two familiar faces coming toward them through the officers crowding the cordon: the imposing figure of Lenny Smits, dark circles under his eyes; and the gray-haired, steely-eyed Wes Corrigan, the captain of Major Case. Smits had swapped his T-shirt and sweatpants for a somber suit, but by the looks of it, Corrigan had come directly from the golf links and was still in his golfing gear.

Maggie watched them sign in with a deputy manning the cordon, and then Smits hoisted up the police tape, letting Corrigan duck under before doing the same himself. Like her, both men wore blue plastic overshoes and blue vinyl gloves to minimize crime scene contamination. And like Maggie, both men looked understandably morose and uncomfortable, everyone hoping that this wasn't a taste of what the rest of the year had in store.

Corrigan acknowledged Ramos and Shaw with a nod and walked directly up to Maggie. "Detective."

"Captain."

"Caught you with your pants down too, I see."

She glanced down at her getup. "When I hear one of my people is missing, I come running."

A low rumble sounded in the back of Corrigan's throat.

Everybody at the Sheriff's Office knew that Corrigan was all about *his people*, as he liked to refer to those under his command. He considered everyone in the Orange County Sheriff's Office as family, quick to defend them and go above and beyond in the name of solidarity. But he was just as quick to throw them under the bus should any one of them break from the fold and betray the badge, even in the slightest way.

Maggie had stolen his punch line, and Corrigan had noticed. He didn't look appreciative.

"Give us the floor," he told the deputies.

Ramos and Shaw nodded and retreated to the cordon.

Corrigan waited until they were out of earshot before telling Maggie and Smits to come in close. Then he spoke, shielding his mouth with his hand. "Some of these news people are trained in lipreading," he explained, as though it was fact. "Let's keep this between the three of us." He looked at Maggie. "Okay. No padding. Is this as bad as we expect, or worse?"

Maggie wasn't sure how anything could be worse than Clay blowing out his brains all over the insides of his family car, but she kept any such comment to herself. She put her hand in front of her mouth. "From the arrangement of the body and the positioning of the gun, it looks like Clay turned his sidearm on himself."

Corrigan swore. "Do we know why?"

"Not yet. But I intend to find out."

"We spoke with the wife before coming down here," Smits said, covering his own mouth. "She dismissed the idea of Detective Young contemplating suicide. But Novak feels something's amiss with her statement."

Corrigan raised an eyebrow at Maggie.

"Just a feeling," she said from behind her hand. "My gut instinct has learned to recognize when someone is being conservative with the truth."

"You think she knew this was going to happen?" Corrigan said.

"Maybe not *this* exact setup. But she knows more than she's saying. I'm sure of it. It could be she knows the reason he did this."

"His trigger."

"Yes, sir."

Every suicide had one. That critical moment in which the balance between life and death was tipped irreversibly into the black.

"Okay," he said. "Run this whole mess by me, from the beginning."

His gaze stayed on hers while she brought him up to speed. She told him about Sasha's midnight phone call and Clay's trip to the store for milk, and how Maggie had watched security footage in the store manager's office, spotting the muzzle flash about seven minutes after Clay had returned to his car.

"And that's when you found him?"

"Yes, sir."

Corrigan swore into his hand. He glanced over his shoulder at the TV cameras pointing at the three of them from less than a couple of dozen yards away. His cool gaze revolved back to Maggie. "You work with Detective Young. Aside from his wife, you know him as well as anyone else. Did he or anyone close to him mention anything, or have any inkling he was in this state of mind?"

"Not that I know," Maggie said. She didn't need to date a psychotherapist to know that most suicides were surprise deaths, and that even those closest to the victim rarely noticed any behavioral clues hinting at their deadly intent. "I didn't hear any talk about Detective Young being depressed, or see any signs of it myself. But I don't claim to be an expert. I do know people who intend on committing suicide don't generally announce it beforehand. Not if they're serious about going through with it."

Smits said, "What about yesterday morning, Detective?"

Maggie saw Corrigan's brow wrinkle. "What happened yesterday morning?"

"Detective Young was in a bad mood," Maggie explained. "He was mentioned in an article that appeared in Saturday's edition of the *Chronicle*."

"You mean Stavanger's hit piece." Corrigan said the words through his teeth, like they were a curse.

"You read it, sir?"

"The miserable hack was attacking one of my people. Of course I read it. I'd consider suing if the chief editor wasn't such a good friend of mine."

"So there was a scene," Smits said. "Detective Young challenged Detective Novak because of her known affiliation with Stavanger. There was an exchange of words."

Corrigan's gaze narrowed on Maggie.

"It sounds worse than it was," she said. "And it definitely wasn't his trigger. Clay could give as good as he got. I doubt anything I said even made an impression."

Corrigan said, "Either way, I think we can all agree this is as bad as it gets. Hard questions will be asked. And the powers that be will want their answers. We need to get in front of this before the press start spinning their stories." He looked at Maggie from over the top of his hand. "Until this is wrapped up, I want you working this case night and day. Sergeant Smits here will assign your current workload to your fellow detectives. Speak with the wife again, as well as anyone else who might know something. There's a reason why Detective Young chose to end his life here last night. I want you to find it. The last thing we need is everyone speculating over why one of my people chose death over life. Understood?"

"Yes, sir." Maggie had already decided she would do exactly that, starting with the one person who knew Clay better than anyone else: his partner, Detective Andy Stucker.

"In the meantime," Smits said to Corrigan, "what *do* we tell the press?"

"Nothing. Other than to offer a *no comment*, we don't breathe a word. Instruct your people. We keep a lid on this, at least until Detective Novak has the right answers." He dropped his hand from his face. "Okay, let's do this."

As their huddle disbanded, Maggie heard the background chatter reduce in volume as everybody watching sensed the next step was about to be taken. She glanced around the cordon. Dozens of tense faces looking back. TV cameras trained on Clay's red Sentra.

Corrigan began to circle the car, cupping his gloved hands against each window and peering in through the glass.

"How's Sasha?" Maggie asked Smits. It was a dumb question, but she had to know; it had been eating away at her from the second she'd shared the bad news about Clay on the phone with Smits.

"Broken," he said and didn't go into detail. Not that he needed to. Sasha had just heard that her husband had been found dead, and in the blink of an eye, her world had ended. "I left her in the hands of the support worker," he added. "She's taking her to the Victim Service Center. I'll check in on her later." He nodded toward the Sentra. "How did this happen?"

Of course, it was a rhetorical question. They both knew how Clay's death had happened. By the looks of it, a .45-caliber bullet had tunneled through the flesh under his jaw, exploding across the cavity of his mouth, the slug piercing his soft palate before burrowing through his brain and bursting out the top of his skull.

There was no mystery in the manner of his death, just the motive behind it.

And Maggie didn't like not *knowing*.

"Okay," Corrigan said as he rounded the trunk. "Open her up."

Maggie hooked her gloved fingers under the driver's door handle and opened the door. Right away she heard a faint whirring sound coming from inside the car, like the air-conditioning had been left on and a leaf was caught in a fan.

But the engine was off, and the sound was out of place.

Instinctively, Maggie paused with the door open a fraction.

Then volcanic fear plumed in her chest, and she yelled, "Everybody back!"

She went to press the door shut again, in the same instant that the door pushed back, but with much more force. A hurricane wind lifting her off her feet and throwing her backward through the air. She saw the world tip sideways, and the ground came up, slamming into her shoulders. Maggie gasped. There was a moment of utter calm in which the thud of her heartbeat was all she could hear; then darkness washed over her and swept her away.

Chapter Eight

BACKGROUND RADIATION

When Maggie had just turned nine, Bryan, her brother, had gotten an electronics kit at Christmas. With it, he'd built several wacky devices, including a crystal radio set that Maggie had found fascinating—mainly because it had seemed like magic to her at the time.

How could a bunch of wires, coils, and capacitors pick up and play music when there wasn't even a battery to power it?

Far into the New Year, the crystal radio had taken pride of place in Bryan's bedroom. And when he wasn't home, Maggie had sneaked in, using their father's headphones to listen, not to the weak radio stations that the wire antenna picked up, but to the fuzzy reception in between.

The *mush*, as her father called it, was hypnotic. It reminded her of the sound she heard coming from the TV, late at night, after all the shows had ended. Waves of static, rolling in and out as she turned the dial.

Music for the soul.

Easy to lose herself in it.

When Bryan had found her perched on his bedroom window-sill one sunny Saturday afternoon, eyes shut and her senses lost in the white noise, he'd played a trick on her, claiming that angels were the source of the strange sound, and that it was their otherworldly voices she could hear, piping through the airways.

Of course, she hadn't totally believed him. But she hadn't totally disbelieved him either.

Something was making the sound.

Thirty years later, those same angels were chorusing in her ears again, almost drowning out the man's voice yelling at her to *get with the program* and *snap out of it*.

The voice was persistent, slightly annoying, and she felt obliged to say something.

She opened her eyes, blinking at the sudden brightness.

Everything was brilliant blue.

She blinked again as the silhouette of a man's head slid into view from the side.

"There you are," he said. "You had me going for a second there, Novak. I was *this close* to performing mouth to mouth. But Abby cooked a garlicky dish for dinner last night, and I don't think you'd appreciate my dragon breath."

Maggie coughed, spluttered. "Loomis?" Her head hurt, much worse than it had earlier in the morning, and her whole body *ached*. Her extremities seemed distant, reports of disturbances on the front line making their way slowly to her brain.

Slowly, her partner of the last four years swam into focus: Ed Loomis, with his dirty-blond hair combed back like James Dean, smiling calmly at her even though his eyes told a different story.

"How long have I . . . ?" She tried to move. Things hurt.

He told her to keep still while the paramedic checked her vitals; things could be broken. She sensed activity on the edge of her vision, somebody's gloved hands feeling the bones in her limbs, fingers feeling through her hair, following the contours of her skull, gently pressing the vertebrae in her neck. Maggie took the moment to assess, to allow her spiraling thoughts to catch up.

What happened?

She was on her back on the asphalt, staring up at an unblemished sky. Loomis kneeling beside her. He had on a brown suit and a white shirt open at the collar. A silver crucifix on a chain dangling as he leaned over her.

"You're going to be okay," he said. "Attention seeker."

She could hear people shouting, the wail of police sirens, the roar of a helicopter. A high-pitched ringing in her ears. She could smell rust and fireworks.

She coughed again. "What happened?"

"Bomb," Loomis answered without preamble.

"Bomb?" It sounded senseless, but it made sense.

"Bomb," he repeated.

"Don't mince your words, Loomis. Just say it like it is."

He laughed, but it was shaky, reactive. "Do yourself a favor, Novak, and leave the humor to the experts."

Like a blunt knife, full comprehension took a second to penetrate, to reach inside and prick her memory. But when it punctured through, panic gripped her, and she tried to sit up.

Loomis put a hand on her shoulder, pinning her down. "Not yet," he said. "Let the paramedic do her job."

A bomb? In Clay's car?

Maggie's thoughts were coming at her in a blur, too many to process all at once.

How had she survived a bomb blast and at such close quarters?

She'd seen video footage on TV of car bombings in the Middle East. Powerful explosions ripping through metal, lifting vehicles into the air and flipping them over. Obliterating everything within the blast radius. Red-hot fire and jet-black smoke. Shrapnel tearing the surrounding vicinity to pieces.

People died in car bombings.

Why wasn't she dead?

She saw Loomis glance over his shoulder. "Looks like it was in the front with Clay," he said. "You did the right thing closing the door when you did, Novak. It helped confine the blast." He looked back at her. "All the same, it's a miracle you're in one piece."

"Did you check no limbs are missing?"

"As a matter of fact, I did."

She remembered opening the car door and hearing a faint electronic whine. A noise that she now realized must have been the trigger mechanism activating.

"Pipe bomb?" she said.

"Maybe."

She remembered trying to shut the door again as the bomb detonated. A recollection of the door pushing back with brutish force, the wind knocked out of her as the shock wave bowled her off her feet. An image of her flying backward through the air, the earth tilting on its axis, her arms wheeling as the ground came up too fast, and then . . .

She tried to sit up again. "Smits and Corrigan?"

Loomis held her down. "Hold still. They're being seen to."

"How bad?"

"Injured, but alive. Getting medical attention."

A woman wearing paramedic gear leaned over her. A bright light flashed over Maggie's eyes. The paramedic asked Maggie to look left, then right, then left again. Smile, frown, show her teeth, stick out her chin. She told Maggie she'd taken a blow to the back of her head, and she would need to go to the hospital for a head scan, just to be safe.

Maggie blinked at the afterimages burned into her retinas.

"How do you feel?" Loomis asked.

"Like I was standing next to a bomb when it went off. Are you sure my fingers are intact? I can't feel them."

Loomis glanced at her hands. "All present and correct."

"Can I please get up now?"

"Not yet, Novak. Be patient, not the world's worst patient."

She flexed her fingers. The palms of her hands were stinging, like the skin had been stripped. "How long have I been out?"

"Less than a minute. I was just signing in at the tape when all hell broke loose. All I saw was you performing death-defying acrobatics. Scared the crap outta me." He squeezed her shoulder. She reached up and put her hand on his. "Do me a favor?" he said. "No more superwoman impressions. At least for today." He smiled again, but his voice cracked.

Maggie patted his hand.

The paramedic made a *thumbs-up* signal, and Loomis helped Maggie into a seated position. She coughed some more, and it took a second for her vision to stabilize.

All around her, sheer chaos in the Walmart parking lot.

Maggie got her first look at the aftermath.

The explosion had scattered the onlookers and many of the police personnel who had crowded behind the cordon. Those who had found safe distance were either staring back in shock, or on their phones. One or two in tears. A few with blood on their faces, wandering around and looking dazed. Paramedics running this way and that between parked vehicles. Police snapping out of it and starting evacuation procedures, corralling everyone back. Orders being shouted and hands pointing. Lights flashing. Sirens squawking. The only people staying put and focused were the newshounds.

Maggie spotted her ball cap on the ground, in the middle of a carpet of crumbled glass fragments. Beyond, she saw Smits sitting propped up against a tree, a paramedic attending to an angry cut on his forehead. When he saw her looking, he raised a shaky hand.

He had streaks of blood on his face and red patches on his white shirt. Maggie nodded an acknowledgment, and her brain protested with a clang.

As for Corrigan, he lay on his back farther out, a pair of paramedics working on him, their medical kits open and all kinds of paraphernalia scattered around on the ground. From this angle, she could see the soles of his shoes and one of his arms, flat against the asphalt. No movement in his feet or in his fingers. Bloodied fingers in one of his vinyl gloves.

Farther still, at the tape cordon itself, Ramos was kneeling on the ground next to Shaw. The young deputy was on her back, a fire department paramedic fixing what looked like a cannula to her arm.

Something stung Maggie's cheekbone, and she touched fingertips to the sudden pain.

"You got hit by glass," Loomis explained as her gaze came back to him. She saw him inspect her face. "A few cuts and lacerations, but no stitches necessary. Could've been worse." He showed her a pair of sunglasses—*her* sunglasses—a white scuff and a spidery crack in the center of one of the lenses.

"I liked those glasses," she said.

"You like your eyes more."

With Loomis lending a hand, Maggie got to her feet. The world swayed and landed on a tilt, then righted itself with a jerk.

Maggie got her first full view of Clay's car, postexplosion.

Apart from its missing windows, the Sentra didn't look like it had been the focal point of a traditional bomb blast. No raging fire blistering the bodywork. No black smoke gushing skyward. No twisted metal and melting tires. Just a ring of glass crumbs on the ground, and a scent of gunpowder in the air. Concussive force had blown the windshield onto the hood and thrown the driver's door wide open, leaving Clay's slumped body exposed and on show for all the world to see.

Maggie's senses swirled.

She heard Smits shout, "We need some tarps over here." And she saw one of the deputies rush over. "This whole scene needs screening," Smits told him. "Right now. I don't care how it's done; just cover the damn thing up." The deputy scurried away, rounding up his colleagues.

"Luckily for you," Loomis said to her, "it looks like it was a low-yield explosive. Otherwise, we'd be picking up pieces of Maggie Novak all afternoon." He hooked an arm around her waist. "Think you can walk?"

"Try stopping me." She put one hesitant foot in front of the other, realizing as she did that she had more strength of purpose than actual strength in her legs.

"Easy," Loomis said, catching her.

"I can't believe there was a bomb in his car. A *bomb*. It doesn't make any sense."

"Neither does Clay committing suicide, but these things happen." He walked her toward a shiny red fire department ambulance backed up to the tape, its rear doors gaping and paramedics waiting.

"Wait," she said, resisting. "I don't need to go to the hospital."

"Doctor's orders," Loomis said.

"I'm okay."

"Novak . . ."

"I just had the wind knocked out of me, is all. I'm needed here."

He made her look at him. "Listen to me, partner. You whacked your head pretty good back there. Hard enough to crack the concrete. I saw it bounce. You'll probably get a bill for the repairs."

For her benefit, Loomis was trying to make light of the situation, she knew, but her thoughts were heavy, holding her back.

"Loomis, seriously, I need to be *here*."

"No, you don't. You're done here for now. Bomb Squad are inbound. Just as soon as the paramedics can move the captain, we're all clearing out. There's nothing more any of us can do until they've swept the scene."

"The cordon needs to be pushed way back."

"I know."

"All the way to the street."

"I'll deal with it."

"There could be more devices."

"Novak, I've got this." He lifted the police tape and helped her under. "Besides, you'll just be in the way if you stay here."

A paramedic helped her into the ambulance.

"Which hospital?" Loomis asked him.

"Orlando Regional."

"Get checked out," Loomis told her. "Come back when you get the all clear." He slammed the doors shut, leaving her with a porthole view of the bomb's chaotic aftermath as the ambulance pulled away.

Chapter Nine

HYPOVOLEMIC SHOCK

The gurney was as hard as a mortuary slab, and Maggie couldn't keep still, every part of her itching to get back to the crime scene. Sitting around and doing nothing, when she could be somewhere else and doing *something*, always made her restless.

Why was there a bomb in Clay's car?

She must have asked herself the same question a hundred times, failing to come up with any answer that made any sense.

In the Walmart security video, she'd seen Clay open the driver's door and get into the car, minutes passing by before seeing the muzzle flash light up the windows. The bomb hadn't gone off when he'd opened the door, which told her that some of those minutes he'd spent setting a booby trap, one that would be triggered the second *somebody else* opened the door.

The bomb was meant for the first person to investigate his suicide.

The idea scared her.

To keep her thoughts from running away with her, she'd spent the last few minutes totting up the head count as one ambulance after another ferried casualties from the car bombing in Oak Ridge to the emergency department.

Like her, most of the walking wounded appeared to be victims of flying glass. But there were exceptions. Chiefly, people with more serious shrapnel injuries. The triage nurses were doing their best to assess patient priority, but with the casualty count still rising, the ER was being pushed to its limits.

Of course, despite the distractions, Maggie's thoughts were unrestrained.

The image of Clay, dead in his car, kept rushing into the forefront of her mind, like a subway train bulleting into a station. Glimpses of bright-red blood on the glass and lifeless eyes staring into infinity.

It wasn't enough to understand why Clay had chosen to take his own life; Maggie wanted to know why he had tried to take the lives of others, too.

Why had he turned his suicide into a death trap?

At a loss for an answer, she switched on her phone and almost dialed Steve's number automatically, without thinking about it.

She hesitated with her fingertip hovering over the telephone icon.

She'd almost dialed Steve's number a dozen times already while sitting here watching the comings and goings. But each time she'd almost called him, a voice in her head had urged her not to go through with it.

It was a dilemma. And Maggie wasn't the best when it came to personal dilemmas. Being pulled in two directions always made her feel split.

She stared at Steve's number, nibbling at her lower lip.

Why didn't she want to bring him in on what had happened?

On one hand, she felt he should be told about her near miss with death. As her boyfriend, he had every right to know where she was, that she had been hurt, but that she was all right, and that he didn't need to worry. He would understand. Being understanding was Steve's specialty.

But on the other hand, the fact that he hadn't called her yet meant that he hadn't seen the news. Right now he was probably unaware of her situation, too busy prepping for his trip to Atlanta. Chances were it would remain that way, too. Telling him now would only result in him dropping everything and rushing down here to comfort her, to be supportive, to be *gallant*. It was sweet, and it was endearing, but it could also be smothering, and right now she didn't need saving.

She lowered her phone as an intern came up to her. "Good news," he said with a quick smile. "Your scan results came back all clear. A spot of cranial bruising, and you might have a headache for a few hours, but apart from that you're good to go."

Maggie slid off the gurney.

"A word of advice," he said as she stuck her phone to her armband. "You should take it easy. At least for the rest of the day. It's possible you have a slight concussion. Take over-the-counter painkillers, and avoid operating heavy machinery."

Maggie thanked him and made her way out.

She spotted Smits near the exit, in conversation with a doctor wearing scrubs. The gash on Smits's forehead had been closed up with several butterfly stitches, and the blood had been washed from his face, but it still glowed on his white shirt.

She waited until he was alone before going over.

When he saw her, he put a finger to his lips, indicating she should refrain from speaking. He led her to a quiet corner before saying, "What the heck was that? This bomb came from nowhere. Caught us all napping."

Maggie released a breath. "It was certainly the last thing any of us expected; that's for sure."

"Theories?"

"Well, I think it's obvious Clay wanted to kill or maim the first responders."

"Over what? A grudge? Someone at the sharp end pissed him off and he decided to retaliate?"

"I don't know. Maybe. Though, I have to say, it sounds a little extreme, and not like Clay at all."

"I've got news for you, Detective. Committing suicide doesn't fit the bill either. But you saw it with your own eyes. Any thoughts on who he might've had issues with?"

"None. Realistically, there's no way Clay could predict who the first responders would be."

"All the same, let's narrow it down. Make a list of first responders on duty today. Cross-reference it with Detective Young's recent cases. See if anything lines up. For him to go to these lengths, someone must have really pissed him off. Plus, we need to look at anyone else likely to open that door first."

"Including us."

Smits's complexion seemed to pale at her words. "Including us," he repeated quietly.

The thought that Clay had deliberately tried to kill his coworkers from the Orange County Sheriff's Office was a frightening one.

"Anyway," she said. "It doesn't change the fact that a bomb is a pretty indiscriminate way to target a specific person. Maybe it was all about something else."

"Like what? To get our attention?"

"Doubtful. He already had it."

Smits rubbed a hand over the stubble on his chin; he wasn't the only one who had had no time this morning to prepare for a day on the battlefield.

"What then?" he said at last. "If Clay was nothing else, he was methodical. We know this much for a fact. So what are we missing? Talk to me, Detective. You're the bomb expert here."

She wasn't. Far from it. The closest Maggie had come to being any kind of authority on the subject was during her four-month stint as the acting commander of Bomb Squad two years ago while Jasper Carmichael—the current commander—had been on prolonged sick leave. In her short time overseeing the unit, she'd supervised the investigation, the safe removal, and the controlled explosion of a handful of suspicious objects, none of which had proven to be an actual bomb.

But she was familiar with crime motivation, and in that respect she knew that bombers were no different than any other garden-variety criminal who premeditated murder.

"There are two main types of bomber," she said, keeping her voice down as people passed by. "Those with a political agenda, whose goal is usually to sway public opinion and bring about regime change. And those with an attention deficit, whose aim is to make news headlines and create sensationalism."

Smits nodded. "Clay never struck me as an activist."

"He wasn't an attention seeker either."

"So which is he?"

"Neither. And that's what makes this whole thing harder to wrap your head around. Everything about it reeks of it being a personal statement. Only, Clay wasn't like that."

The surgeon that Smits had been speaking with a minute ago walked by and nodded at them.

"What's the word on Captain Corrigan?" Maggie asked.

"He made it out of surgery. They had to remove his eye."

"What?" Maggie was shocked.

"Shrapnel," Smits said. "It obliterated his eye on impact. Just like that." He clicked his fingers, making Maggie blink. "Apparently, he was lucky. If the shrapnel had penetrated any deeper, it would've been game over for the captain."

Maggie's shock stayed put, her mind scrabbling to process the news that Corrigan would never again see the world the same way, or look the same way.

"What about you?" Smits asked.

Maggie took a beat before answering. "Good, I guess, all things considered. A slight concussion. I'm all done here and about to head back. You coming with?"

"No." He rubbed at his unshaven jaw again. "You go ahead without me. I'll catch up. The captain's wife is due down here any minute. I need to be here when she arrives."

Maggie nodded. Although Corrigan was Smits's superior, they had been close friends since their patrol days. Naturally, Smits was deeply concerned for Corrigan's welfare, and wanted to show his support.

"We got lucky today," Smits called as Maggie walked away.

"How do you figure that?"

"I could've lost two of my best detectives."

Outside, the sun was almost directly overhead, shortening shadows and hurting her eyes. Maggie reached for her sunglasses, then remembered Loomis still had them. And her baseball cap was now part of a crime scene.

Staying in shadow, she used the Uber app on her phone to request a ride. Almost immediately, she received a notification saying her driver was two minutes out.

A deputy sheriff was pacing underneath the enormous silver-colored **EMERGENCY** sign at the corner of the street.

Deputy Ramos.

His shirt and pants were soaked with blood, turning the green fabric to black. He was on his phone, his shoulders rounded as he paced the sidewalk, his face fraught with worry.

Maggie's own phone rang in her hand.

It was her father's number.

"Hey, Dad," she said. "Is everything okay?"

"More importantly, Magpie, are you okay? I just this second switched on the TV, and you're all over the news."

Damage control, she thought straightaway.

"Dad, listen to me. Before you say anything else, I'm okay. I don't want you to worry unnecessarily. There's been an incident. And you probably saw me in a predicament. But I'm fine. Okay? I'm just on my way out of the hospital right now. I've been given the all clear. Honestly. You don't need to worry."

"You're sure?"

"Dad . . ."

"It's just that they're saying there was a bomb." He sounded panicky, pronouncing the last word as though it left a bad taste on his tongue. "You're on every channel. It's all they're showing. My little Magpie, flying through the air."

"Fame at last." She said it with a snicker, hoping to sound unfazed by her brush with death and give him the reassurance he needed, but she realized she didn't quite achieve it.

She saw Ramos stop pacing and stuff his phone in his pocket.

"Dad, listen to me," she said. "I have to go. Please, switch off the TV and quit worrying. I'm all right. I'll call you later. I promise."

"I can't help being worried," he said. "It's my job."

Maggie said her goodbyes and hung up. She went over to Ramos. "Deputy. Are you hurt?"

He glanced down at his bloodstained uniform. "Oh, this isn't my blood. It's Shaw's."

The memory of the young deputy flat on her back in the aftermath of the explosion came rushing back to Maggie, and a sudden concern for Shaw welled within her. "How badly is she injured?"

"Punctured femoral artery." His voice quivered as he said the words, intensifying Maggie's concern. "I managed to get a tourniquet on at the scene, stem the flow, but I'm telling you, ma'am, she lost a lot of blood. I don't know. Maybe too much. It was all over the place."

In Maggie's first week in Homicide Squad, she'd attended a crime scene in which a mentally unstable man had slit the throats of his wife and children while they slept. The blood had sprayed up the walls and soaked in the comforters, appearing black in the dark. Until that moment, Maggie had underestimated just how much blood the human body contained, and how much of it could escape when given the opportunity.

Ramos was looking at her with fear in his eyes. "She went into a coma on the way here," he said. "The paramedics said it's touch-and-go."

Maggie reached out, placing her hand on his arm. "She'll be okay."

But Ramos shook his head. "I should've seen something," he said, his eyes brimming with tears. "*Sensed* something."

"Deputy, you—"

"Ma'am. I'm trained for it." The tears began to roll. "Maybe if we'd been farther back, or if I'd acted sooner. Or, maybe if I'd—"

"Stop," Maggie said, squeezing his arm. "Don't do this. You're not responsible for what happened to Shaw. We can't plan for every unexpected turn of events. That bomb took everybody by surprise, no one more so than me. If you want to blame someone, blame me. I opened that car door. I triggered the bomb. You did your best. And I'm sure your partner knows that."

He nodded, sniffed, but he didn't look like he believed her.

In truth, Maggie only half believed her words herself; she'd seen one too many people bleed out to know that even if the victim survived, the sudden loss in blood volume often led to organ failure and long-term complications.

"Applying a tourniquet," she said, "was quick thinking on your part. You probably saved her life."

"It's not my first rodeo," Ramos said. "I've seen my fair share of IED injuries."

"Improvised explosive devices?"

He nodded. "I did two tours in Afghanistan. We had to make do. Be creative." He looked down at the dry blood on his hands and his uniform, a visible quake coursing through him. "But something like this, it just brings it all back. You know?"

"She'll be okay," Maggie said softly. "She's in good hands here."

He released a ragged breath. "I hope you're right, ma'am. She's a great kid. She doesn't deserve this."

Maggie felt bad for Ramos; she knew how she would feel if it were Loomis they were talking about.

A silver Prius came around the corner, its tires clipping the curb as it pulled up beside them.

"My ride," Maggie told Ramos. "I have to get back." She opened the passenger door. "Take care of yourself, Deputy. Keep me posted?"

He nodded, but his gaze was distant, someplace else.

◆　◆　◆

Traffic was jammed up tight on South Orange Blossom Trail as drivers slowed to grab a peek of the Walmart crime scene. Maggie told the driver to mount the curb and drive half on the sidewalk for the last quarter mile. He got about as far as the corner with Wakulla, and Maggie went the rest of the way on foot, the sight of the Wakulla street sign stirring up the dread in her belly.

Sasha and Clay Young's home was half a mile down that street at most. Maggie had only visited the house once, and she suspected its proximity to where Clay had taken his own life would likely prove to be a problem for Sasha continuing to live there. In fact, it was unlikely she'd ever shop at the store again.

The bottleneck in and out of the Walmart parking lot was crammed with law enforcement vehicles and police officers.

The cordon had been extended to encompass the entire property, and a few yards short of it, a team of CSIs from Forensics was waiting for the all clear to enter the crime scene, their white cotton coveralls stark against the black asphalt. Bags of equipment stacked up like luggage at the airport.

Maury Elkin, the county's chief medical examiner, was among them, talking with one of his assistants. Elkin's vitiligo—a skin condition that formed a jigsaw pattern of lighter patches on his otherwise dark skin—seemed luminous in the midday sun.

When he saw her, he hustled over. "Maggie," he said, giving her a hug. "I heard you were rushed to the hospital. Should you even be here?" He shaded his eyes as he scrutinized her face. "Are you all right?"

"I was given the all clear."

"But are you ready for *this*?" He motioned toward the car at the center of the crime scene.

Now that the cordon had been pulled back, except for customer vehicles caught in the chaos, the parking lot was mostly deserted. It was a strange sight in the middle of the day.

"No ordinary suicide," Elkin said as he looked back at her. "Clay is one of us. A brother. It raises the stress factor to a whole new level. So let me ask again. Are you *ready* for this?"

She rolled her shoulders. "I'm a bit stiff, and my head hurts. Aside from that, the doctors gave me the thumbs-up." She meant it as a positive, but it sounded like a poor excuse. Even so, she knew exactly what Elkin was getting at. Her fitness for duty wasn't in question here. It was her ability to completely detach her emotions, to erect an impenetrable wall between her role as lead investigator and as a grieving friend.

"Won't be easy," he said.

"I'd rather it be one of us than someone who didn't know him."

Elkin nodded. "Well said. He'd like that. The indomitable Maggie Novak exposing her soft spot, at last. On top of which"—Elkin dropped into whisper mode—"Clay tried to kill you."

Maggie was startled by his statement, and made no attempt to hide it.

Just as she had said to Smits, she was confident Clay had had no way to predict the identity of the person to open the car door. Yet the idea that she might have been his intended target was disturbing.

She realized Elkin was scrutinizing her face again.

"It's certainly a curiosity," he said. "Either we believe in chance, that everything happens purely at random. Or, we believe there's no such thing as coincidence, and everything happens for a reason. I wonder, Maggie, which camp your tent is pitched in."

Maggie blinked, momentarily at a loss for an answer.

Elkin's assistant called to him, and Elkin excused himself.

Dry mouthed, Maggie continued on to the cordon.

She signed in at the tape and asked the attending deputy for an update.

"We've evacuated the supercenter and the nearest businesses," he told her. "We've locked down all access points, and the cordon now follows the property line. As you can see, the press are digging their heels in."

Camped on the grass near the roadside, the news vans hadn't moved an inch. Several cameras on constant record.

"What about Willoughby, the store manager?"

"Holed up in his office. A warning, though, ma'am. He's not a happy camper."

Maggie couldn't blame Willoughby for being disgruntled. Right now, the cordon meant that his store was off limits to its customers. His business was hemorrhaging money by the second. Come the morning, lawyers would be talking.

"I'll need to speak with him again," she said. "Please have someone tell him to call me, as soon as possible." She jotted down her cell number on the log sheet.

"Will do." The deputy handed her a bulletproof vest. "Commander's orders," he said. "No one goes beyond this point without one."

Maggie thought it a bit late, but she put it on all the same.

A mix of uniforms and plainclothes officers were gathered next to a dark-green SWAT van parked where the original cordon had been earlier. Maggie recognized each member of High Risk Incident Command, as well as several of her fellow detectives from Major Case. The incident had also shaken a couple of top brass out of the tree, including Captain Wendy Velazquez, who oversaw Sector III's Patrol Division, and the big cheese himself, Major Daniel Oysterman, the division commander of Criminal Investigations. Whether in uniform or street clothes, everyone wore bulletproof vests and somber expressions.

Maggie spotted Loomis, standing head and shoulders above everybody else, and headed his way. When he saw her coming, he broke away from the pack and met her halfway to the makeshift command point.

"Not so fast," he said. "You've been given the green light?"

"Reporting fit for duty," she said.

"That was quick."

"I was first in line."

"How's the head?"

"Still attached."

"That's a bonus." He went to hug her, then seemed to notice the TV cameras pointing at them, and had a change of heart. "Any breaks or bleeds I need to worry about?"

"Nope. And it's cute that you do, Loomis, but you can stop worrying. At worst, I'm looking at a slight concussion for the rest of the day." She didn't mention that the palms of her hands were stinging like she'd placed them on a hot stove, and that her shoulders were beginning to stiffen and ache. "Any sign of Andy?"

"Not through lack of trying. He still isn't answering his phone. I've left multiple messages."

"Me too. He needs to be here. I know I'd want to be all over this if it were you in that car."

"Now who's being cute?"

"I mean it. Andy needs to know what's happened. We should send a unit around to his place."

"No point," Loomis said. "Stucker's in Titusville."

Maggie frowned. "What's Andy doing in Titusville?"

Loomis gave her a *Where have you been?* look. "Spending New Year's with his ninety-four-year-old mother."

"And you know this how?"

"Because it's tradition, Novak. Plus, he told everyone his plans before he went on vacation." He rolled his eyes. "Come on. You were physically there."

"But mentally I was probably somewhere else."

On the whole, Maggie didn't have a problem with Andy Stucker. He was a competent investigator. But he could be a little overbearing at times. One of those people who liked the sound of his own voice, especially during lengthier locker room talk, and Maggie had learned to preserve her sanity by tuning him out.

"We need to get somebody over there," she mused out loud. "Do we know his mother's address?"

"We don't. But I'm sure we can get it. Maybe ask Brevard County to drop by and tell Stucker to pick up his phone."

"Let's do that." Maggie looked at the SWAT van parked a few yards behind Loomis. The hatch was up, exposing flat-panel monitors and control consoles, and Jasper Carmichael looking back at her.

Jasper Carmichael was the commander of the Hazardous Device Team, colloquially known as Bomb Squad. He was thick cut and ex-military, his default expression one in which it looked like there was a permanent bad smell under his nose and the rest of his face was trying to crawl away from it. When he wasn't on call and commanding the unit, Carmichael worked full time in Major Case as a detective in Persons Squad. In Maggie's absence, he had assumed control of the crime scene.

He saw her looking as his cue to come over.

"Good news," he said to Maggie. "The bomb you set off—"

"Me?"

"Figure of speech, Novak. The bomb you *triggered*, it looks like it was the only device in the vehicle. My current assessment is it likely malfunctioned."

"It failed?"

The blast had seemed quite potent to her. Then again, she had been standing at ground zero.

"It explains how you came to escape with just a few cuts and bruises," he said. "Otherwise . . ."

Carmichael left it hanging, because they both knew things could have turned out much worse for Maggie had the bomb worked properly and to its full potential.

Beyond the SWAT van, Maggie could see Carmichael's team, wearing green Kevlar suits and blast-proof helmets, inspecting Clay's car like astronauts working on the lunar rover. Everything slow motion and precision perfect.

"Do you know what type of bomb it was?" Loomis asked.

"Pipe," he said. "Looks like it was wedged between the driver's seat and the door. Too soon to say any more. We're still piecing things together. It'll be tomorrow before we have the full breakdown."

Forensics would need to collect every bit of debris for reconstruction and analysis in the lab, Maggie knew. Every tiny shard of metal and fragment of wire. Put Humpty-Dumpty back together again, then use computer software to simulate the explosion.

"Just a thought," she said. "When you're done here, we need your people over at Clay's house."

"What's your thinking?"

"He built the bomb somewhere. We need to find the location and make sure it's safe."

Carmichael mulled it over in a second. "You think there could be more devices?"

"I think we can't take the risk. Who knows what Clay might've left lying around on a workbench somewhere. If there's even the slightest chance he didn't use up all the explosive materials . . ."

"Someone could be in for another nasty surprise. You're right, Novak. I'll get K-9 on it."

Maggie spotted Major Oysterman looking in their direction. Under normal circumstances, his lantern jaw stood proud, but today it seemed chiseled from granite. He summoned her with a backward nod of his head, and Maggie excused herself from Loomis and Carmichael.

She spent the next few minutes appeasing the top brass, primarily allaying their fears and reassuring them that, despite the chaos, the injuries, the media, the bedlam, that Major Case had everything under control.

"But do you?" Captain Velazquez asked, gaze piercing, when Maggie was done. "Corrigan's put you in charge. We have to be blunt here, Detective. No sugarcoating this. We have major concerns."

"I'm sorry to hear that. Let me help reassure you. What concerns do you have?"

"Conflict of interest, for starters."

"If you're referring to the argument yesterday morning, let me assure you both right now that—"

"We are not."

Maggie looked from Velazquez to Oysterman and back to Velazquez again.

"Your spat with Detective Young isn't our main concern here," Velazquez said. "It's your being the target of the bomb."

Maggie frowned. "Ma'am, with all due respect, have you been talking with Elkin? Because that's exactly what he said. Can I be straight with you?"

"Please."

"I know Clay. If he ever had issues with me, he made it known, and we always managed to thrash things out. It never festered. I don't believe for one second that I'm the intended victim. And I'll tell you why. There's no way Clay could've known I'd be the one to open that door. And here's the rub." She gestured at her high-tech running gear. "Look at me. I was running off a hangover when I was called out to this. It's my day off. I'm not even supposed to be on duty today. Clay knew that."

"All the same," Oysterman said, "it's a concern, for us. For now we're willing to go along with Corrigan's recommendation. But if it transpires you were indeed the intended target—"

"I'll recuse myself from the case," she said. "Absolutely no question. But I can assure you both it won't come to that."

Her words seemed to satisfy, or at least postpone any decision to replace her.

"What's the likelihood of there being more bombs?" Oysterman asked. "Ballpark figure."

"Right now, it's impossible to say."

Maggie knew as well as they that people who built bombs were in the business of causing widespread death and destruction, and that where one bomb existed, there could be others.

"But we need to assume they exist," Maggie said.

"What do you suggest?"

"We alert all first responders to be cautious, especially when approaching vehicles. Take extra precautions until we know there are no more threats of this nature."

Oysterman nodded. "There could be more targets out there."

Maggie couldn't accept that this was Clay's intention. Such thinking wasn't congruent with the man she knew—or, in keeping with the man she *thought* she knew.

How thoroughly did anyone really know anyone?

Already this morning, she'd given Clay's motivation a lot of mental airtime, mulling over the million and one variables, any of which could have come together in any combination to cause him to lash out the way he did. Without better information, the best answer she had at the moment was that Clay had suffered some kind of psychotic break, and Nick's newspaper article had been the straw that had broken the camel's back.

Pressure transmuting catcher into killer.

But then she'd reasoned that if this was indeed the case—that a sudden-onset psychosis had been his catalyst—would Clay have had the resourcefulness to construct a bomb?

Contrary to popular perception, homemade bombs couldn't be thrown together at the last minute with ingredients found under the kitchen sink. Clay had to have purchased the components in advance, every one of his actions premeditated, carefully putting all the pieces together before setting his trap. Plus, bomb making was a tricky process involving skill and a steady hand-eye coordination. A delicate undertaking in which one wrong move could have fatal consequences for the maker.

Could someone suffering from a mental breakdown have the capacity to pull off something like that?

Maggie wasn't sure, and she made a note to ask Steve.

She did know that the simplest way for Clay to hurt his coworkers would have been for him to walk into the Sheriff's Office on West Colonial and empty his Glock into every one of them. Not to place his faith in a bomb, hoping that it would do the job for him at random.

Maggie's phone rang, and she excused herself.

It was Smits.

"Detective," he said as she answered, "I'm afraid it's bad news."

A chill rose inside her. "Corrigan?"

"No. The captain's critical, but stable. It's the young deputy they brought in. The one you were with at the scene? I just heard. They pronounced her dead. She died on the operating table. Did you know her?"

Maggie felt queasy. "No, not really. We met just today."

Her gaze landed on a dried patch of blood a few yards away. It was a large red amoeba-shaped stain overlapping two parking spaces, turning the white separator line pink. Pints of Shaw's blood had spilled out, right there on the asphalt, then congealed, much of its water content evaporating in the midday heat.

"Congratulations, Detective," Smits said in her ear. "Your investigation just got upgraded from suicide to homicide. Ditch whatever plans you had. No one's going home early today."

Chapter Ten

SAFE INSTEAD OF SORRY

Maggie leaned against the hood of Loomis's minivan, massaging her neck and wishing she'd applied sunscreen. There had been no need for it when she'd ventured out for her run in the predawn light. But now the sun was high in the sky, and without even her ball cap to protect her face, it was bearing down on her like a blowtorch.

Her fingers located a knot in a muscle, and she winced as pain leaped up her neck.

Two hours had now passed since the blast had flung her through the air, and her back was stiff, dull pains lancing through her shoulders each time she tried to turn her head too far to either side. At some point, she'd need to apply ice or heat, or alternate the two, maybe reduce her sensitivity with anti-inflammatories.

The way things were going, she had no idea when that might be.

She took a swig of an energy drink and let her gaze wander.

As well as Loomis's minivan, a white Tahoe with Sheriff's Office decals was parked outside the Young residence on Wakulla Way. The vehicle had a metal cage barrier fitted in the back, and Maggie could see smudged paw prints on the glass. A hundred feet away on either side, patrol vehicles were positioned slantwise across the narrow lane, forming roadblocks. Deputies stopping and rerouting the occasional traffic.

The Tahoe belonged to K-9 Squad. Presently, two German shepherds and their handlers were inside the house, performing a thorough sniff and sweep for hidden bombs or explosives.

The notion that they might actually find something inside the home of her colleague made Maggie more than a little tense.

If someone had asked her yesterday, she would have stated with absolute confidence that Clay was the last person in the world she'd ever suspect of manufacturing a bomb. Then again, until this morning, he'd also been the last person in the world she'd imagine would take his own life, or murder someone.

Deputy Shaw's death played on her mind.

Maggie had listened with a lump in her throat as Smits had relayed the doctor's report, her heart aching for the young deputy's loss of life. Simply put, Shaw had lost too much blood, and she'd slipped into a coma on her way to the hospital. Surgeons had attempted to repair her ruptured femoral artery and to infuse blood, but her vitals had crashed, and all their resuscitation efforts had proven futile. Deputy Shaw had been pronounced dead, and Clayton Young had become a murderer.

A cool unease stirred in Maggie's belly.

She wondered how Ramos was holding up.

She'd asked him to keep her updated, but it was no surprise she hadn't heard from him. His thoughts would be on other things right now besides updating her—principally, his own self-recrimination.

Maggie could relate.

Two months after the fact, the Halloween Homicide was still taking its toll on her, dragging her mind through the tangled razor wire of self-censure. The endless *what-if* debates in which she played out various scenarios in her head, trying to determine if alternative courses of action could have changed the outcome.

Steve called it *counterfactual thinking*, and reminded her that even though it gave her a sense of control, the control was illusory, and that investing mental energy into the process was counterproductive to her long-term recovery.

In short, *talking* was the only way to go.

But Maggie had refused his offers of therapy, believing it best to keep her work and her love life separate.

It wasn't always possible.

Maggie was conscious of the fact that she cherry-picked the principle, choosing to uphold it when it suited her.

Why was that?

Luckily for her, Steve wasn't offended. Being selective was all part of her defense mechanism, he'd explained, and he didn't take her silence on the subject personally.

Maggie heard a dog bark, and she refocused on the Young residence across the street from where she was standing.

Clay and Sasha's home was a single-story ranch-style dwelling with peach-colored walls and a large oak tree dominating most of the front yard. In comparison to some of its neighbors, the property looked neat and tidy, a freshly painted white picket fence creating a formal entranceway around the front door.

Maggie could see movement through the windows.

The car bombing had set into motion what was called an *emergency exception*. On the grounds of public safety, the special circumstances allowed them warrantless entry into the Young residence. Over the phone, Smits had talked Sasha into giving up her house keys—saving her front door from being busted open—and a blue-lit patrol car had sped to and from the Victim Service Center in the city to fetch them.

There had then followed a heated debate on the best way to enter the house. Carmichael insisting that Clay had already set one booby trap, wiring the car door to trigger the bomb, and that extreme caution was called for. Maggie arguing that Sasha had left the house hours *after* Clay, and that she would have noticed if a bomb had been attached to the back of the front door.

Finally, with the debate deadlocked, Maggie had taken the initiative, and Sasha's keys, and unlocked the front door, allowing the dog handlers entry. For the last fifteen minutes, damp muzzles had snuffled through the Youngs' private lives.

Of course, Maggie was sensitive to the situation—she didn't like the idea of strangers riffling through her personal things—and she'd reminded the handlers to be as respectful as possible.

This is the home of our dead colleague.

Maggie's phone rang.

"Maggie, it's Jeff Willoughby," a voice said after she accepted the call. "I'm told you need to speak with me?"

"I do. Thanks for getting back to me, Jeff. Can you do me an enormous favor? I need copies of those security tapes. Everything you have from ten through eleven last night. If you can put them on a flash drive, that will be great."

"I'll see what I can do. In the meantime, Maggie, when do I get my store back?"

She glanced at her watch. "It's going to be a while yet. I promise, we'll be out of your hair as soon as we can."

"Will it even be today?" His deflation was edged with an understandable amount of frustration.

"Absolutely." She saw Loomis walking toward her. "Listen, Jeff, I have to go. Thanks for your ongoing patience. Let me know when the flash drive is ready?"

"Sure."

Maggie hung up. "Everything okay?" she asked Loomis as he joined her. His Wayfarers were perched on the end of his nose, his eyes prowling the street. He looked uncomfortable, like he had heat rash and couldn't settle.

"Incoming," he said under his breath. "Vultures at three o'clock." He drew her attention to a WESH-2 News van slowing to a stop on the other side of the roadblock, where it mounted the curb and parked on the grass outside a neighboring house. Doors sliding open and a news crew jumping out.

"That's all we need," she said.

"We're today's big story," Loomis said.

"And tomorrow's landfill." Maggie noticed one of the dog handlers appear in the front doorway of the Young residence, a German shepherd sitting obediently at his feet. He motioned at her to join him. "Looks like we're wanted," she said.

"What've you got?" Loomis asked the handler as they crossed the front lawn.

"It's both good and bad news," he said as they gathered in the small entrance hall.

"Give us the good first. I need some cheering up."

"The house is clean for explosives."

Maggie was surprised. "Not even trace?"

"Put it this way," he said, "nothing the dogs were able to detect. And that's the important thing to remember. It doesn't necessarily follow there's no bomb-making equipment squirreled away here, somewhere. It just means it's not contaminated with the compounds the dogs are trained to detect. Forensics may luck out."

"What about tools?"

"There's a box in the garage. It contains basic stuff. Hammers, screwdrivers, a handsaw. To be honest, the tools look hardly used."

"Clay wasn't a handyman," Loomis said. "*Home improvement* were two of the dirtiest words in his vocabulary."

"What about the spaces the dogs can't reach?" Maggie asked. "Like the attic."

The handler turned out his lip. "Even if a suspect hides contraband out of range, such as above head height, trace usually contaminates other stuff they touch around the house. Door handles, stair rails, that kind of thing. Even if they wash their hands, the trace ends up on the towel. The dogs are trained to detect such things. They didn't find anything."

"So, chances are, no bombs were made here?"

"Now *that* I can't say for sure. Like I say, Forensics will need to do their thing first. You need to keep in mind, even the strongest odors disperse over time. It's possible explosive materials were kept here at some point, but it's so long ago that no trace still exists."

"If that's the good news," Loomis said, "you better hit us with the bad."

The handler breathed in. "There's no sign of a workshop or even a workbench at this location."

"Which means," Maggie said, "the bomb factory is still out there."

"Correct."

"We need to widen the search," she told Loomis. "It's possible Clay rented some space somewhere."

Maggie thanked the handler. *Good job.* He collected his partner, and together they walked their dogs back to the Tahoe.

"What now?" Loomis said as they watched the dogs leap in the back of the vehicle.

"As uncomfortable as this is," she said, "we perform a manual search here first before searching anyplace else. Forensics are tied up at the death scene. It could be a while before they're done. If there's no bomb-making apparatus to find here, let's see if we can find anything else that helps us understand why Clay committed suicide." She wiggled her fingers. "Got gloves?"

He smiled. "Does the pope wear white?"

While Loomis fetched his crime scene kit from the minivan, Maggie studied the framed school photographs of Clay's boys in the hallway, knowing that it would be some time before these happy faces ever smiled this way again.

◆ ◆ ◆

Maggie's instincts were right. Searching the Young house proved as difficult as she had imagined it would be.

Like rummaging through a dead person's pockets.

Clay had been more than an acquaintance. He'd been her teammate—occasionally partnering with her, sometimes partying with her—and although Maggie and he hadn't always seen eye to eye, she had considered him a friend.

Sifting through his personal effects wasn't just weird; it was unsettling. And, more so than usual, her sense of intrusion was prominent, challenging her to cease and desist.

No such luck.

To compound the feeling, she'd elected for just Loomis and her to search the Young residence. Ordinarily, a team of investigators would be required to systematically search the premises, each person allocated to a different area to help minimize the chances of cross contamination of evidence. But Maggie was conscious that they were intruding on Sasha's private domain, and she wanted to avoid adding to her pain.

The fewer intruders, the better.

"You should see his boxing memorabilia," she heard Loomis call from the den. Loomis had been in Clay's man cave for a while now, periodically oohing at some new keepsake he came across. "Signed photographs of all the heavyweight champions, going back to the Rumble in the Jungle."

"Clay boxed in his youth," she called back. "He was a south-paw, like Marvin Hagler. He could've boxed professionally, but he tore a shoulder ligament and never fully recovered."

"And you know this how?"

"Because I show an interest, and I listen."

Maggie was in a small home office, inspecting an assortment of hardbacks and monthly magazines stacked haphazardly in a bookcase. She hadn't expected to find a manual on bomb making, not exactly, but she had found a biography on Ted Kaczynski, also known as the Unabomber, as well as other books on famous murderers.

As far as she knew, Clay had never professed to be a huge reader of anything other than the sports pages.

She slid the Unabomber biography out of the bookcase and perched herself on the corner of the office desk, leafing through the pages. She glimpsed black-and-white photos of various kill locations. Victims, before and after. Blast damage and debris. Color shots of Kaczynski himself, as well as the famous police composite sketch of him in a hoodie and aviator sunglasses.

Was this biography of a killer Clay's inspiration to kill? she wondered.

She kept turning pages.

She came to a complete copy of the Unabomber's manifesto, phrases highlighted in yellow and quotes marked out in Day-Glo orange. Notes written in the margins in red pen. Maggie was no expert in the field, but the handwriting looked like a woman's.

What is Sasha's interest in the Unabomber?

Maggie took photos with her phone, then returned the biography to the bookcase.

Did Sasha know more than she was saying?

A secure gun box was bolted to the top of a three-drawer verti-cal file cabinet. Maggie examined Sasha's bunch of keys, picking out a key that looked like it might fit. She tried it in the lock, and, sure enough, it worked. She lifted the lid and looked inside.

Empty.

No spare clips for Clay's standard-issue Glock. No box of 9 mm rounds. No cleaning cloth, or any other paraphernalia.

Maggie thought about her own gun safe at home, the little shelf stacked with boxed bullets, the empty magazines, her permit to carry a concealed weapon. She locked the box and turned her attention to the file cabinet itself.

Sasha, she knew, worked as an editor at a publishing house in the city. It was possible the cabinet contained confidential information on clients and contracts, or no such thing. Either way, Maggie had to tread carefully.

When it came to the limits of their search, this was where the line blurred. Perusing private documents on the grounds of an "emergency exception" lay in the gray area between bona fide investigating and unreasonable intrusion. It didn't give her license to examine sensitive material that lay outside the scope of the search. They were looking for bomb-making materials, not whether Clay was behind on his utility payments.

As an investigator, Maggie had to be aware of overreaching her authority. To do so could jeopardize the chain of custody and bring into question the validity of evidential finds. It was vital she recognized what areas fell inside the search parameters, and avoid those that didn't.

Even if she found papers providing proof of illegal activities, none could be used as evidence in a court of law. Not if the crime was unrelated to their search. Not unless she applied for a court order to conduct a second search, on the basis of prior knowledge, and even then it wouldn't be cut and dried.

But there was a loophole.

Motive, she told herself as she pulled open the top drawer.

Most suicides fell into one of three camps: emotional stress, societal stress, and financial stress. Clay had shot himself for a reason. She needed to know if that reason was documented in some way, such as in a record of mortgage defaults, accumulated debts, or even in a medical report describing a terminal disease.

Everything else she could overlook.

The drawer was filled with date-marked file folders going back at least ten years, all relating to Sasha's editorial role at the publisher.

Maggie moved on, finding more of the same file folders in the second drawer.

Third time lucky.

The bottom drawer was less full, this time containing what appeared to be personal documents.

Maggie reminded herself to be selective. She wasn't interested in love letters or car loan agreements.

Maggie tiptoed her gloved fingertips across folders until she spotted what she was looking for. A file marked INSURANCE.

Whenever somebody died in suspicious circumstances, it was standard practice to identify those who stood to benefit from the victim's death. Suicidal deaths being no exception.

Of course, in cases of murder, it didn't necessarily follow that the person in a position to gain the most was automatically a prime suspect. But in cases of suicide, sometimes the person who stood to lose the most was also the one to gain the most.

Not all gains were monetary. Recipients profited in all kinds of ways: upon death, contracts became null and void; commitments ceased; debts dissolved.

A timely death could wipe out a financial crisis.

Maggie spread the documents over the desk.

Both Clay and Sasha had separate life policies payable on death. In each case, $100,000 going to the surviving spouse.

The policies had been taken out eighteen years ago, when their boys had been babies, and were set to expire at age sixty. In both cases, the payout wasn't a bank-breaking amount, but it was enough to ease any fiscal burdens.

Clay's policy was scheduled to expire at the end of the month, the day before his sixtieth birthday. Four weeks away.

Did she believe in coincidence?

Maggie debated taking a photo with her phone, then put the documents back in the folder.

She knew where they were if it came to it.

She was about to close the filing cabinet when she noticed what looked like a notebook lying in the bottom of the drawer.

She took it out, letting the pages fall open in her hands.

It was an account book, with columns of handwritten numerical values going back years. Most of the entries written in black pen, but many in red. Maggie had seen ledgers similar to this before. Some people were old fashioned and liked to record their financial outgoings on paper, especially if they were on a tight budget. But this was slightly different. Here, she could see what looked like gains and losses, generated from the most volatile kind of capital venture: sports betting.

There were entries for horse racing at Gulfstream Park, greyhounds at Sanford, wagers placed on a variety of sporting fixtures scattered across the state.

Maggie had had no idea that Clay was a serious gambler. She knew he'd been *into* his sports and was especially passionate about his beloved boxing. But she had never witnessed any of his sports betting firsthand.

Many addicts were adept at hiding their addictions.

She wondered if he'd been a big gambler all his life, or if it was a more recent manifestation. A harmless hobby that had become an obsession without him realizing it, turning into a problem and taking over his personal life.

She knew that gambling addictions were as serious as any other kinds of addiction, and that addicts required counseling to help reset their brains. She knew that, if left unchecked, it wrecked marriages, ruined careers, spiraling out of control and becoming all-consuming. She knew that some addicts couldn't cope with escalating debt and the destruction it brought to their personal lives, choosing suicide as their only way out of the jam.

Is this what happened to Clay?

Maggie refocused on the ledger.

On each page, the right-hand column appeared to be a running total of all the preceding entries. A black matchbook was being used as a bookmark on the last page of entries. Maggie turned to it, letting the matchbook drop into her gloved hand.

In bold red pen, the cumulative total read:

-$59,896

Maggie took a moment to evaluate the amount. It was a minus figure. A loss. This time, she took a photo with her phone, knowing that the ledger didn't qualify as an official document and therefore came with fewer legal restrictions.

Minus sixty grand.

In anyone's book, the loss wasn't pocket change.

Maggie wondered if the Youngs' household purse strings had stretched to absorb the loss, or if this was a debt owed.

Her answer came a moment later as her gaze caught on the matchbook still in her hand.

In pink, three words were printed on the black cover:

And on the reverse:

THE SPACE COAST'S PREMIER ADULT HOT SPOT

Curious, Maggie opened the flap. Inside, someone had scribbled:

You owe me $39,840

Maggie couldn't swear to it, but it looked like the handwriting of Andy Stucker, Clay's partner. The spidery scrawl and the slight leftward lean of the letters was the same style she'd seen in countless of his reports. Stucker also had a habit of putting a slash through his zeros, like he was a computer programmer. The same was evident here.

Did Clay owe Andy all this money?

Maggie mulled it over. There had been times when she had helped Loomis out of a sticky financial spot, and vice versa. Unexpected expenses arriving before payday. That's what partners did for one another. In their line of work, having a partner's back wasn't restricted to firepower support in the middle of a shoot-out. It crossed into all aspects of their lives. If they could help each other out, it was a given. So it came as no big surprise to think that Clay had borrowed money off his partner. What was surprising was the amount.

Forty grand wasn't to be sniffed at. It was a small fortune. People didn't have that kind of money lying around in loose change. Most people worked hard all their lives just to save up that kind of money.

But Clay had blown that much and more on gambling.

And it looked like his partner might have picked up the tab.

Maggie took several photos of the matchbook, then tucked it back in the ledger, and the ledger back in the cabinet.

Why wasn't Andy answering his phone?

A half hour later, Maggie decided that their work here was done, that they needed to broaden their search for Clay's bomb factory, and she and Loomis made their way outside into bright sunshine. Aside from the clues that Maggie had found in Sasha's home office, and shared with Loomis, they had come up empty handed.

"We need to look elsewhere for answers," Maggie said as they crossed the lawn.

"Any ideas where to start?"

"My first stop would be with Andy. If I'm right about the note in the matchbook being from him, then it looks like Clay owed him a ton of money. We need to speak with Andy, face to face, as soon as possible. See if the debt is real and if it had any bearing on Clay's state of mind. Plus, Andy needs to know what's happened here today."

Loomis stowed his crime scene kit in the back of his minivan and slammed the hatch. "Okay. Let me call Forensics. See if we can get some techies down here."

Maggie noticed a neighbor staring at her as he put trash in a garbage can in his front yard. He was taking his time, probably using it as an excuse to snoop at the goings-on next door.

Maggie went over. "Sheriff's Office, sir. Anything I can help you with?"

He looked uncertain, as though his trash ploy had been exposed and she was calling him out on it. "Just wondering," he said. "I don't want to pry. But did something happen to Sasha?"

Maggie stopped at his wire fence. "What makes you ask?"

"You guys being here." He closed the lid on the cart.

Maggie glanced behind her at the police activity outside the Young residence. It made for quite a spectacle on such a quiet lane. "What makes you think it's Sasha?" she said, looking back at the neighbor.

"All the arguments they've been having lately. Things being thrown and whatnot. Of course, it's none of my business, but I saw Clay getting right in her face a couple times."

"Was he ever physical with Sasha that you saw?"

"Hard to say for sure. Just the sound of them arguing and stuff smashing. Sometimes deep into the night."

Maggie made a mental note to check the Youngs' garbage cans for broken possessions.

"How long have you been their neighbor?"

He looked up at the sky, as though for inspiration. "Going on fifteen years."

"And this arguing, it's a recent manifestation?"

"Well, I guess they argue regular, like all couples do."

"But more so lately, is that what you're saying?"

"Yes, ma'am."

"Arguing about what, do you know?"

She saw him shift his weight from one foot to the other, as though realizing he'd said too much already. "Last thing I want is to get anyone in trouble."

Maggie put her hands on the chain-link fence. "Sir, have you seen the local news today?"

He shook his head. "No. Should I?"

"Clay's dead." She watched his reaction.

"What?" His eyes grew wide, and his color paled. He took half a step back. "Did she . . . did she kill him?"

"We're still determining what happened." Maggie heard her name being called, and she looked around to see Loomis waving at her from the minivan. A female crime scene investigator in a blue CSI windbreaker was standing next to him. Maggie looked back at the neighbor. He had retreated several steps. "Excuse me," she said. "I may come back to you for a statement. Okay?"

"Sure," he said, not sounding it.

Maggie returned to Loomis.

"They found Clay's cell," he said.

The CSI handed Maggie a clear plastic evidence bag. The label had been filled out and the bag sealed with red tape.

Inside, Maggie could see a phone in a black rubber case.

"I was just telling Detective Loomis," said the CSI. "I found the phone in the foot space of the vehicle. Passenger side. Next to the carton of milk. I checked to see if it was still operating after the blast. It was."

"You need to see what came up," Loomis said.

Maggie took the bag into the shadow cast by Loomis's minivan. She pressed the power button through the plastic, and the screen brightened, showing the messaging app and a text conversation between Clay and Andy Stucker.

"That's how it was when it came on," the CSI said. "I didn't change anything."

The last lengthy exchange was dated a few days ago—some mindless banter between two grown men behaving like adolescents—but the final two messages, both sent from Clay and separate from the last conversation, were listed as Yesterday, 10:48 p.m.

The first read:

Walmart on Orange Blossom

Meet me in the parking lot ASAP

And the second simply said:

They know

Maggie looked up at Loomis. "I don't care if Andy's on a retreat in the Himalayas. We need to speak with him. Right now."

Chapter Eleven

SMOKE AND MIRRORS

Of course, Maggie knew that Andy Stucker wasn't on a retreat in the Himalayas. He was much closer, within driving distance, and her Mustang was pushing the speed limit as she drove with her foot down into Titusville on Florida's Space Coast.

Fifty minutes had passed since the text messages had propelled her and Loomis into action.

First off, after updating Smits, Maggie had dispatched a patrol unit to Stucker's Orlando apartment to confirm he hadn't come home earlier than expected. Then she'd called Human Resources, hoping that Stucker's next of kin details were on record. Luckily, a clerk was working the holiday. She'd checked into Maggie's request and come back with an address for Stucker's mother, but no land-line number.

Then, while Maggie had run back to Walmart to collect her car, Loomis had spoken with his contact in the Brevard County Sheriff's Office. Out of courtesy, BCSO had dispatched a patrol unit to the Titusville address. But word had come back to them that no one was home.

That was forty minutes ago, and Maggie and Loomis had spent most of the journey east speculating on what Clay had meant by the words *they know*.

Every way Maggie looked at it, it was an ominous statement, and other than hinting at a secret, its meaning was probably impossible to guess without more information.

Who were "they," and what did they "know"?

As for Clay's attempt to summon Stucker to the Walmart parking lot on New Year's Eve, Maggie was sure it could mean only one thing:

Stucker had been the target of Clay's homemade bomb.

It seemed obvious after the fact, but Maggie was keeping her options open until they spoke with Stucker in person.

Why would Clay want to kill his partner?

Making assumptions was easy. Hard facts were what they needed, and the fact that Stucker still wasn't answering his phone had left them with no choice but to drive to Titusville and hope that their paths crossed.

They know.

People didn't commit suicide for no reason.

Something or someone had pushed Clay off the bridge.

Is that person Andy Stucker? Maggie wondered.

Was the answer hidden in the text message?

If so, Stucker was probably their best bet to decode it. Plus, since they had no way of knowing whether the car bomb had been a one-off, or Clay had planted other devices, Stucker needed to be aware of the threat.

It all felt messy, and Maggie detested mess.

Her phone chimed on her arm.

"Got it," Loomis said and tore it off her armband. "It's a message from Carmichael," he said, reading the screen. "Forensics confirms no signs of bomb-making equipment in the house."

Maggie wasn't surprised. "I guess we suspected it from the start," she said. "Sasha isn't blind and certainly not stupid. She would've noticed if Clay were putting a pipe bomb together in the kitchen. The smell of explosive material alone is enough to give the game away."

Loomis pointed at the lane she needed to be in, and Maggie swung the Mustang into it. "Which means," he said, "Clay had access to other premises. An office maybe, or an RV."

Maggie glanced sidelong at him. "An RV."

"Recreational vehicle."

"Loomis, I know what an RV is. It's just a random pick, is all."

"Stranger things, Novak." He reached for the dash and turned the radio off.

Maggie glanced at him again. "What's wrong?"

"Feeling restless," he said with a sigh. "This has got to be the worst New Year's on record."

"Don't hold your breath," she said. "It's only just begun."

There were more dark days ahead, she knew, starting with a visit to the morgue, probably sometime tomorrow.

Even though Clay had died from a self-inflicted gunshot wound, procedure dictated that they would still need to hear the official version from Elkin before his autopsy report could be added to the case file. The visit wouldn't go easy on their nerves, she knew. Trips to the morgue never did. But this time the degree of discomfort would be multiplied. It would be their friend lying on the steel plinth.

"Why do you think he did it?" Loomis said as Maggie took the exit off Columbia Boulevard and onto US 1.

"Plant the bomb?"

"Commit suicide."

Now it was Maggie's turn to sigh. It would be a lie to say the same thought hadn't been bugging her, too. From the second her

105

brain had processed the sight of Clay sitting dead in his car with his gun in his lap, she'd asked herself the same question, over and over, seemingly every minute since.

Why did Clay kill himself?

"Right now," she said, "it's anyone's guess. Clay was a private person. Apart from Sasha, it's unlikely he talked to anyone about his feelings."

"There's no saying Stucker will know anything either."

"Maybe we'll never get to the truth. That said, we should check with Clay's family doctor. See if Clay sought professional advice."

Clay was the first of their team to die. And even just a few hours after his death, a black hole had appeared in their world, sucking up logic and crushing it out of existence.

Sometimes suicides never made any sense.

In Loomis's hand, Maggie's phone chimed again.

"Elkin," he said, reading the message. "He estimates at least another three hours before he releases the death scene."

"Tell him we're hoping to be back in town by then, and thanks."

Loomis sent the reply, then switched his gaze to the passing scenery. The overgrown Florida landscape, visible for most of their journey, had given way to man-made structures. Automotive shops and strip malls. Nail salons and fast-food restaurants. The staple diet of civilization.

"Titusville hasn't changed one bit," Loomis said.

"You've been here?" she asked.

Loomis nodded. "A lifetime ago. When I was a kid. We vacationed in Orlando a couple of times, doing all the expected touristy things, like theme parks and airboat rides. This place still looks like a butthole in the middle of nowhere."

Maggie followed his gaze to a passing strip mall, with its flamingo-pink stucco walls and its aging marquee signage. It looked like it had been built in the sixties and stuck in a time warp ever since.

It was a familiar sight for her, too.

In her childhood, Maggie had visited Titusville several times with her family on their day trips to Kennedy Space Center to watch shuttle launches. She remembered their dining here, but she had no recollection of where, or even if it had always been the same restaurant.

She did recall, however, the thunder vibrating through every bone in her body as the orbiter had risen from its launchpad on a plume of white incandescence, a matching giddiness bubbling up inside her. She remembered the wonderment in Bryan's eyes and Nora cowering from the deafening roar. She remembered the enchanted grin plastered on her father's face and her eternally cheerless mother muttering about the absurdities of space flight, and that everything was just a *show*.

"Next right," Loomis said.

Maggie turned off the highway onto Riverside Drive, the ubiquitous pink and beige buildings giving way to detached properties and glimpses of the steel-blue Indian River through the shoreline trees.

Unlike most of the buildings they'd passed along the way, the homes here were upmarket and in better shape. An altogether nicer neighborhood. Private boat docks and big colonial-style houses overlooking the water.

Loomis let out a low whistle. "Are we sure this is the right location?"

"According to HR."

After a half mile they came to a large redbrick house surrounded by stately trees, and Maggie pulled up on the curbside grass alongside the river.

Loomis whistled again. "Who would've guessed Stucker came from money. The dude's always crying poverty. Never pays for anything."

"How do you think the wealthy stay wealthy?"

A breeze caressed Maggie's skin as she got out of the car. She was conscious that she was in desperate need of a shower.

"If it turns out he's here," Loomis said as they crossed the street, "I'll let you do the honors. You've known Stucker longer than I have. It'll sound better coming from you."

Maggie wasn't sure how anyone could make their kind of news sound any less awful than it was. She hadn't forgotten the hopelessness and bone-shaking upset she'd felt twenty years ago when she'd learned that her high school friend had perished in a house fire. The information had come from a softly spoken TV news anchor, but it had been no less hard hitting.

"No sign of Andy's truck," Loomis said as they walked up the gravel driveway.

"Brevard County said no one was home."

"Except, his mom's supposed to be housebound."

Wide concrete steps led to a big front door, a Christmas wreath hanging from the brass knocker. Three tall Georgian-style windows on either side, with a further six on the second floor and three attic windows jutting out of the sloped roof.

Loomis put a finger on the bell push. A double chime sounded somewhere deep inside the house.

"How was the party?" he asked while they waited.

"Blurry," Maggie said.

"That good, huh?"

Maggie lifted a hand to knock on the door.

Loomis blocked her. "Novak. Give her a minute. She's an old lady."

Maggie heard the sound of a lock mechanism turning, and the door opened to reveal a young woman in a skimpy black kimono. Bright-red lipstick and black hair, her expression a hard mixture of stony and bored.

"If you sell religion," she said with a Slavic accent, "I have plenty of it."

She reminded Maggie of a young Chrissie Hynde, the singer in the Pretenders, right down to her razor-sharp bangs.

"Excuse us," Maggie said. "I think we may have the wrong address. We were expecting Mrs. Stucker."

The woman seemed to brighten. "Mrs. Stucker?" She pronounced it *Stoo-kah*. "Believe it, yes. I am she. Mrs. Stucker."

"You're Andy's *wife*." It took a second for it to register. Maggie glanced at Loomis. "We didn't know he was married."

"Yeah," Loomis said. "He kept that one quiet."

The revelation was unexpected, and it took a moment for it to sink in, especially since Stucker had always been someone who Maggie had thought too set in his ways to wed. Not only that, Maggie would never have paired him with the young woman standing in front of them now; Stucker was old enough to be her father.

"Congratulations," Loomis said.

The woman waved a hand. "It was small service. Just Elvis and two witnesses." She flourished her wedding band. "See. We are sick with love." She batted long lashes at Loomis.

Maggie saw him start to flounder and said, "Mrs. Stucker, we need to speak with Andy as a matter of urgency. Is he home?"

The woman folded her arms. "My husband is fishing."

"Fishing?"

"On his boat. In the lagoon."

Maggie was reluctant to believe her, intuition telling her that the woman had given her a rehearsed answer. To Maggie, it could mean only one thing: Stucker was someplace else entirely.

The woman was staring at her expectantly.

Maggie said, "We tried calling Andy. Left voice mails. Do you know if he has his phone with him?"

The woman shrugged.

"Is he with anyone else we could call?"

Another shrug.

Maggie sighed deliberately loudly. "Do you even know when he might be back?"

"Soon," she said. "My husband never misses lunch." She looked Maggie up and down. "In meantime, I am curious. You are tax inspectors?"

"We're Andy's colleagues," Maggie said. "Detectives Novak and Loomis."

Now the woman's hard expression softened slightly. "Hold the phone. You are Novak and Loomis? I hear many things about you."

Loomis said, "Not all bad, I hope."

She tilted her head at him. "Some, yes. For example, you speak only and always of twin babies. And you"—she swung her gaze back to Maggie—"you are lesbian. Yes?"

Maggie felt her jaw drop. "Excuse me?"

"It is okay. Also, I am free spirit." The woman stuck out a bony hand. "Please. I am Klementina. You are welcome to my home."

No expense spared. That was Maggie's first impression as they followed Klementina through the riverside house, Maggie's running shoes squeaking on the polished wood floor.

Everywhere she looked she saw antique furniture and fancy fixtures. Persian rugs and chandeliers. It was like something out of an Agatha Christie novel. Ordinarily, such lavish decor didn't impress

Maggie, but given she'd seen Stucker's basic bachelor apartment in South Orange, this was nothing short of a poke in the eye.

"Who is this guy?" Loomis whispered to Maggie as Klementina led them to a spacious room at the back of the house.

The living room was tastefully decorated in warm earth tones. A large black-and-white photo portrait of the loving couple hanging above the mantel, and tall windows overlooking a big swimming pool.

"Nice," Loomis said. He'd gravitated toward a large accent cabinet, his hands unable to resist the assortment of framed photographs covering its surface. "You guys get hitched in Vegas?" He picked up one of the photographs, holding it so that Maggie could see its subject matter. It showed Andy Stucker in a black tuxedo and Klementina in a white wedding dress, standing in front of the world-famous **WELCOME TO LAS VEGAS** sign. Big smiles on their faces and confetti in their hair.

Both corners of Klementina's lips curled upward. "Handsome man."

Loomis nodded. "For sure. Not bad for an old dude. Full-on lady-killer."

Maggie said, "Klementina, we were under the impression Andy's mom lives here. Where is she?"

"Moved out. Now she enjoys nursing home by sea."

"So," Loomis said, drawing a circle with his finger, "you guys live here together?"

"Presently, only weekends and holidays. We plan family. Then we live together on permanent basis." She picked up an ornate cigar box and opened the lid, shaking it at Loomis. "Authentic Cuban cigar?"

"We appreciate your hospitality," Maggie said. "But we don't smoke."

Loomis paused with his hand halfway to the box. "What she said," he said.

"We sent a patrol car around earlier," Maggie said. "You didn't answer the door."

Klementina brought her gaze back to Maggie. "I was busy shaving legs." She closed the humidor with a snap, then placed the box back on the table.

Loomis picked up another photograph, this one showing the loving couple at Disney World. "How did you guys meet?"

"Mutual friend. Pay attention. I tell story. Fill up time while you wait."

Maggie listened as Klementina explained in her pidgin English how she and Stucker had met and fallen madly in love, apparently at first sight, and how their whirlwind romance had led to them becoming married within weeks after their first meeting.

It was all news to her and felt a little disjointed. For his own reasons, Stucker had kept the information to himself, never mentioning any of it at the office. Maggie wondered if Clay had known all about Stucker's Russian romance, or even if he'd traveled to Vegas to be Stucker's best man. She knew they had been there together several times on gambling weekends.

Why had neither of them mentioned it?

As Klementina began to walk Loomis through the plethora of photographs on the cabinet, Maggie excused herself to use the bathroom. Klementina gave her directions to a first-floor powder room, and Maggie left them to it.

Already, it was two o'clock in the afternoon, and Stucker was nowhere to be seen. Realistically, they couldn't just hang around here all day hoping he'd show. They were needed elsewhere. The death scene beckoned.

Maggie locked herself inside the powder room and tried Stucker's number again. After a couple of rings, she heard the same uninspiring voice mail requestor kick in.

Why wasn't he picking up?

She left yet another voice mail, this time informing him that she and Loomis were at his riverside home and that he should meet them here ASAP. Then she placed both hands on the rim of the washbasin and, for several quiet seconds, stared at her reflection in the gilded mirror, frowning at her bloodshot eyes.

"You look like the living dead," she told herself. "No more burning the candle at both ends."

She half smiled at herself, but her reflection sneered.

She ran the tap and splashed cool water over her face, then cupped her hands and guzzled until her thirst abated.

A hundred miles an hour—that's how the events of the day had been up to now. No time to properly absorb the magnitude of what had happened, or simply to take a moment to *breathe*, never mind to *think*. The day had been a runaway train, rushing at her headlong, with Maggie racing from one set of points to the next, trying to realign the tracks before the wheels skipped and everything crashed.

She turned her back on the mirror and phoned Smits.

"The captain's doing okay," he told her after she asked. "His wife's at his bedside. Aside from losing the eye, his prognosis is good. I just this minute got back to the crime scene."

"Any news?"

She heard him sigh. "Where do I begin? The tarpaulin screens are up, and a flatbed carrier is here, standing by to transport the wreck to the lab. Otherwise, there's an eerie silence."

"What about Elkin?"

"Still working out the best way to extract the body. Even so, he's confident we should be all done here by five at the latest."

Maggie pictured her coworkers standing in a grim line along the police tape, showing solidarity for their fallen colleague, all eyes focused on the red Sentra, a hush over the proceedings as everybody watched the medical examiner do his thing. Elkin's fastidiousness was renowned. It's what made him top of his game. Elkin couldn't be rushed. He'd keep his cool, even with Major Oysterman breathing fire down his neck.

Maggie knew it could be dark before the circus pulled up stakes and left town.

"What's happening with the Deputy Shaw situation?" she asked.

The whole drive from Orlando, Maggie hadn't been able to shake the image of the young deputy far from her thoughts. Each time she'd pictured Shaw, staring at her with wounded eyes, it had been juxtaposed with the image of the bloody patch in the parking lot.

She heard Smits sigh again. "You haven't caught the news? Somehow, the press got wind of her death, and her face is all over the TV. Captain Velazquez has spoken with the family."

"How are they?"

"Goes without saying they're devastated. She was their only child. Just twenty-two."

"It's awful," Maggie said. "Young deaths are the worst kind." Not just awful, she knew, but frightening as well. The world could change in the blink of an eye. "Have you heard from Deputy Ramos?"

"Her partner?"

"I'm worried for him. We spoke briefly outside the hospital. But that was before Shaw died. Ramos administered first aid at the scene and was with her in the ambulance. He was pretty cut up as it was, blaming himself for failing to protect her."

"I expect you told him it wasn't his fault."

"I did. But I think it fell on deaf ears. You know what it's like, Sarge. It's human nature to blame ourselves." Maggie had done it, and still did to a certain extent. "Ramos was standing right next to her when the bomb went off. And he came out of the ordeal physically unscathed. An experience like that can bring home our own mortality. Make us think it's our turn next."

"Or, that we're invincible."

Although it wasn't like Smits to be perceptive, his point was valid. In Maggie's experience, a near miss with death could send survivors one of two ways: either retreating into their shells or acting oblivious to risk. A couple of years ago, she'd been involved in a high-speed pursuit on the interstate in which the fleeing vehicle had hit the median barrier, flipping over and rolling a dozen times. Bits of broken vehicle strewn all over the place. Miraculously, the driver had climbed out of the wreckage without a single mark on him. But instead of counting his blessings and surrendering to his pursuers, the injection of invincibility had caused him to disregard risk. He'd fled across the oncoming lanes, not getting more than a dozen yards before a passing truck flattened him.

"The thing is," she said, breathing out, "I'm worried he'll go to pieces over the news of her death. I feel we should reach out. Be supportive."

"I'll mention him to Victim Services."

"Speaking of which, do we have an update on Sasha?"

Sasha, too, hadn't been far from Maggie's thoughts all day. It was bad enough that her husband had taken his own life, but for her then to learn that there was a possibility he'd also tried to kill his colleague would surely magnify her suffering tenfold.

"Don't worry about Sasha," Smits said. "She's being looked after."

By a stranger, Maggie thought. *On the worst day of her life.*

"She needs to be at home," Maggie said. "Surrounded by four walls that are familiar. Once she's settled in, we need to speak with her again. We've established Clay didn't construct the bomb at home, which means, if this is his doing, he built it someplace else. We're thinking a rented space. Sasha could know that information."

"No," Smits said.

"No?"

"Absolutely no. She's too delicate right now. She needs a minute to recover. I'm worried if we're too pushy, it'll tip her over the edge."

"Sarge, I—"

"Detective. Listen to me. You're going to have to get your information from another source. For the moment, Mrs. Young is out of bounds."

Maggie bit down on her natural response to argue the point, deciding against it. She'd just have to go about things the long way.

"Did you speak with Detective Stucker yet?" Smits asked.

"No. We're at the house right now. Andy isn't here. We're waiting for him to come home."

"Does his mother know where he's at?"

"That's just it. Andy's mom is in a care facility." Briefly, Maggie explained about Klementina and the Vegas wedding. "It makes me wonder what else he's been keeping from us."

"In what way?"

"Take the text message, for example. Clay urged Andy to meet him ASAP. But Clay knew Andy was an hour's drive away in Titusville for New Year's."

"Unless he wasn't."

"My thought exactly. Before the holiday, Andy made it known he was spending New Year's with his mother. Now we know that was a lie. What else could he be lying about? His wife says he's gone fishing. But I don't believe her either. Something just doesn't feel right. I'm thinking, if Andy did pick up Clay's message last night, it might explain why he isn't here."

"Well, he isn't here either, Detective. That's for sure. And I guarantee he would be, if he knew what's happened to his partner. You need to establish a timeline. And while you're at it, press that brand-new wife of his for information. Detective Stucker has been incommunicado since last night. People don't just drop off the face of the earth. Find him."

On her way out of the powder room, Maggie checked her phone for missed calls. There were none. Steve's continued silence meant he hadn't heard the news yet. Right now, his ignorance was her bliss.

Back in the living room, Klementina was discussing what sounded like economics with Loomis. He'd stopped his hovering and had landed on a couch facing Klementina. They both looked up at Maggie as she came back into the room.

"Give me your handcuffs," she said to Loomis.

Her instruction brought a frown to his face, but he handed them over without question.

Maggie dangled them in front of Klementina's face. "No more obfuscation," she said. "Either you tell me where Andy is, right now, or I'm placing you under arrest for obstruction."

"What?" Klementina looked like she'd been slapped across the face. She glanced at Loomis, seemingly for his intervention. But Loomis just shrugged.

"Show me your hands," Maggie said, waggling her fingers.

Klementina scooted back in her seat. "Wait," she said. "No arrest. I spit it out. Okay?"

"We're listening."

"My husband . . . he is at gentleman's club. There, it is said. Now get pen. I give you address."

Chapter Twelve

SPACE FOR RENT

The gentleman's club was located a mile south of the Stucker residence, at the end of a sandy lane that ran at a right angle to the riverfront. The buildings in this part of town looked older, many dilapidated. Small businesses with boarded-up windows, and empty offices with FOR LEASE signs behind dusty glass.

Titusville had deteriorated in the past quarter century, Maggie realized, seemingly no one willing to reinvest and regenerate after the end of the space shuttle program. Everything paint flaked and in desperate need of updating.

She saw a broken marquee sign standing at the entrance to a derelict strip mall—Moonshot City—and a strange sadness settled over her. It reminded her of her father. Like this town, twenty-five years ago, he had been vibrant and energetic, full of life and promise. Booming. But just like Titusville, he was showing his age, and it was a worry.

"What's Stucker doing at a strip club?" Loomis said as they passed the mall.

"Do you need me to spell it out for you?"

"I mean, it's fine, on any other day, and if he were single. But this is New Year's. And Stucker has a cute wife waiting at home."

Maggie gave him a long sideways glance. "Cute?"

"You know what I mean. My heart belongs to Abby. But that doesn't mean I can't make professional observations about the opposite sex."

"In the line of duty."

"You bet."

Maggie chuckled. "Well, you better get your inspector's note-pad ready, Detective. We may be about to encounter more cuties."

She slowed the car to a stop outside a single-story, windowless building with white stucco walls. It sat in the middle of a sandy wraparound parking lot bordered by chain-link fencing, a dozen cars parked on the potholed concrete—including a black Ram pickup truck that looked like Stucker's. The entranceway consisted of glass double doors underneath a faded red canopy. Above it, neon tubing formed the name of the venue.

"The Orbit Club," Loomis said as he read the signage. "Isn't that the same thing you found on the matchbook in Sasha's home office?"

"It is," Maggie said, her curiosity growing.

They got out of the car and made their way toward the entrance, faint dance music coming from inside.

"Doesn't exactly look like the Space Coast's premier adult hot spot," Loomis muttered.

There was a bouncer at the door. A chunky guy with pinhole eyes and a spider tattoo on the front of his neck. One of his eyes was blackened, and the knuckles on both hands looked raw.

"Membership cards," he said as he stuck out a paw.

Loomis showed his badge. "Sheriff's Office. We need to speak with one of your clients."

"Not without a warrant."

"Excuse me?"

"This is private property. Access is reserved for members only." He seemed totally unfazed by their presence.

"Let's go at this another way," Maggie said. "Why don't you phone your boss and tell him that unless he invites us inside right now, we'll vet every single person who steps in and out of these doors. I don't think his clientele will appreciate the Sheriff's Office taking an interest in their personal details. Do you?"

The bouncer thought about it for a moment, then turned aside and spoke quietly into his cell.

Loomis held his badge up to a camera above the entrance.

"The boss wants to see you," the bouncer said as he faced them again. He jabbed behind him with a thumb. "Around back."

They made their way down the side of the building.

A metal door was located at the back corner. As they approached, it swung outward to reveal a bald-headed man in cargo shorts and a jazzy Hawaiian-style shirt. He was in his midfifties, with permanent ridges in his forehead and sunspots freckling his cheeks.

"In all the strip clubs in all the towns in all the world," he said without a hint of mirth, "you find your way to mine. What the hell are you guys doing here?"

Maggie said, "We could ask you the same, Andy."

Stucker's dimly lit office doubled as a storeroom. Boxes of booze stacked to the ceiling. Bottles rattling as dance music thundered through the floor. At one side, a large one-way window provided a private viewing into the club itself. Through the grubby glass,

Maggie could see a buxom girl in a gold lamé bikini, waitressing for a bunch of seated patrons, not all of them men. Gazes transfixed on two scantily clad dancers cavorting onstage. The club's decor had a *space* theme, Maggie noted, a revolving glitter ball projecting a steady stream of stars across the black walls and ceiling.

"Level with me, guys," Stucker was saying, his voice hoarsened by a lifetime of cigar smoking. "Did Clay put you up to this?" The second he had heard their news, he'd collapsed into the only chair in the room, effectively leaving both Maggie and Loomis standing. "Seriously," he said. "Is this some kind of sick New Year's prank? Because, take a long look at this face; I'm not laughing."

Maggie brought her gaze back inside the office, having seen enough of the club to know that it wasn't a place she ever wanted to buy a drink. "No joke," she said. "Clay's dead." She blew out a breath. "I know it sounds unbelievable, but I can't put it any simpler than that. The only reason we're here at all is because we couldn't get hold of you."

"All day," Loomis added.

"My phone's off," Stucker said.

"No kidding."

Stucker gave Loomis the finger. "Like I said, it's a holiday. I have this rule. My phone stays off for the duration of the holidays. Y'all should know that."

"This was an emergency."

"Like I'm supposed to know the difference." Stucker rubbed a hand over his heavy brow. "Jeez. So it's real. Clay's dead?" He pronounced the word like it was the first time he'd ever used it.

Maggie nodded.

Stucker clenched his fists and pounded them on his desk. "This is insane. How can he be dead? We just spoke, yesterday."

In seven years of knowing Andy Stucker, Maggie had never seen him looking quite this shaken. Even when he'd had a close shave with death a few years back, he'd laughed it off, as though he did it on a daily basis. Now, despite the whirring desk fan blowing air directly at him, sweat beaded his face, and dark patches were spreading under his arms. Universally, Stucker had a reputation of being something of a hard-ass. Yet here he was: shaking like a leaf—as though he'd just been diagnosed with a fatal illness and he had mere days to live.

"It's a lot to take in," Maggie said. "We're still processing. Aren't we, Loomis?"

"Fact," he said with a nod.

Stucker let out a moan and rubbed a hand over his forehead again. "I'm just having a hard time buying it, is all."

"So are we."

He stared at her with strained eyes. "Let me get this straight once more. You're saying Clay killed himself *and* set off a bomb."

"That's right."

He glanced at them both in turn. "Does any of that sound even remotely like Clay to you guys?"

It didn't. And it was a hard pill for them all to swallow.

But the facts couldn't be interpreted any other way. They were black and white. Everything pointed to Clay setting up the booby-trap bomb and then shooting himself in the head.

"We've seen the evidence for ourselves," Maggie said. She brought up a picture of the crime scene on her phone and turned the screen to face him. It showed the red Sentra with its shattered windows and Clay slumped inside, the top of his skull blown out. She saw Stucker gulp. "None of us want this to be true, Andy. Clay was one of us. But a lot of people were hurt in the blast. And a deputy died from the injuries she sustained."

Stucker rummaged in the desk drawer and brought out a brown paper bag, scrunching it to his mouth. "Hyperventilating," he said as he breathed into it.

Maggie glanced at Loomis.

Loomis mouthed the words *Attention seeker*.

"I can't believe he did this," Stucker said into the bag. "It's not like he was depressed or anything. In fact, he was on a high. Excited about our plans for the weekend."

"Plans?" Maggie said. "What kind?"

"The McIntosh-Gonzalez clash in Atlanta. Big, big deal."

"A boxing match?"

"Title fight," Loomis said. "It's touted as the heavyweight bout of the decade." He saw her questioning look and added, "I don't just read the funnies."

"We've had the tickets for months," Stucker said as he removed the bag from his lips. "Five hundred bucks a pop. We were making a weekend of it. Rooms at the Four Seasons. Dinner reservations at Kaiser's Chophouse. Clay couldn't wait. Neither could I. Now I guess that's all been given the kibosh." His strained eyes found Maggie again. "Jeez, I just remembered. Sasha. How's she holding up?"

"Like you can imagine. Smits says she's managing to keep it together. But it's not looking good. She could do with your support right now."

"Sure," he said, nodding. "Just as soon as I've got things covered here, I'll head back to Orlando."

The waitress in the gold bikini came up to the one-way glass, refreshing her lipstick in the mirror.

Loomis watched her from inches away. "Didn't know you were in the entertainment business, Stucker."

"Yeah, well, it's not how it looks, or what you think."

"I think it looks like you're running a seedy strip joint in your spare time." He looked back at Stucker. "Tell me when I'm close."

"Give me a break," he said. "My partner just died. I don't need you being judgmental, Loomis. You're no saint yourself. Besides, I'm doing nothing illegal here."

Maggie squinted at the county compliance certificates on the wall behind the desk. "So what is the real deal here, Andy?" she asked. "Are you the owner? The bouncer called you *boss*, and I can't help noticing your name is on those invoices, right there on your desk."

Stucker glanced at the mound of paperwork in front of him, as though registering its presence for the first time. "It's my family business," he said. "I manage it in my spare time. My mom's the legal owner."

"Your mom?" Loomis said. "The same mom you shipped off to a home the second you moved Klementina in."

Stucker gave him the finger again. "My mom inherited it from my old man when he died in '98. Originally, this was his baby. He started it back in the sixties, when the space program was really taking off. Made a small fortune."

"I guess it explains the big riverfront property," Loomis said.

Stucker snickered and leaned back in his chair. "Except for that house, there's not much of any fortune left. Turnover went into a steep decline after they canceled Apollo, and things never really recovered. These days a big chunk of the profit pays for my mom's astronomical nursing fees."

"Did Clay know about this place?" Maggie asked.

He looked up at her. "Do you keep secrets from your partner?"

Maggie chose not to give him the satisfaction of a reply. It was true: she didn't withhold everyday stuff from Loomis. Certainly, not pertinent case information. Sharing helped keep partnerships healthy. But some things, especially private things, she never shared, not with anyone, not even with Steve.

"How have things been between you and Clay recently?" she asked, changing tack.

"Same as always. Clay and me, we're like brothers. Tight."

"No fights?"

"Why would there be? Everything was good with us. Best friend a guy could have. Why? What are you getting at?"

"Last night," she said, "Clay sent you a text message, asking you to meet him in Orlando. It sounded urgent. Do you know why that was?"

Stucker's eyes narrowed. "Come again?"

"Right before Clay killed himself, he sent you two text messages."

"He did?" Stucker looked confused. His gaze flicked to Loomis and back to Maggie again.

"You haven't read them?" she said.

"No. I . . ." He fumbled his phone out of the desk drawer and powered it up. "I was busy with something else last night."

"Such as?"

"Such as it's none of your business."

Maggie saw him open the messaging app on his phone and bring up the text conversation with Clay.

"The final message is the big mystery," she said. "I'm interested to know what you think it means."

She saw his eyes widen as he read Clay's words. Then he tossed the phone on the desk and put the paper bag to his mouth. Instead of using it to subdue hyperventilation, he doubled forward in the chair and vomited into it.

"Nice," Loomis said. "Rough night, Stucker? Something disagree with you?"

Stucker shuddered and retched again, a dark stain spreading across the brown paper.

Maggie put her foot against the wastebasket next to the desk and pushed it underneath the bag. "Do you need a minute?"

"I'm good," Stucker said as he came up for air. "Delayed reaction."

Even so, Maggie gave him a few seconds.

Stucker spat a mouthful of goo into the bag and wiped his lips on the paper. Then he dropped it in the wastebasket.

Maggie said, "Andy. Right now we believe those texts were the last messages Clay wrote before taking his own life. That means they're significant. The first text urges you to drop everything and rush to his side. The second implies someone found out something he didn't want anyone to know about. Can you shed any light on either?"

"Doubt it. I have no idea why he sent those texts." He ran a hand over his face, mopping up sweat. "Truth is, we can speculate on what he meant all day long. You know as well as I do, Clay had being cryptic down to a fine art. Check the rest of his texts. You'll see what I mean. I can't even tell you who he means by *they*."

"Enemies?"

"Your guess is as good as mine. The three of us know making enemies is par for the course in this job. Every bad guy we bring in has a chip on his shoulder. Take your pick. But I can tell you where you should start looking." He pushed the wastebasket toward Maggie with his foot. "That lightweight reporter friend of yours."

"Nick Stavanger?" Maggie felt her insides harden.

"For sure. A blind man can see that cheap chop job of his crucified Clay."

"I read the article," Maggie said, holding back her instinctive response. "I know Nick doesn't have a filter, but he didn't report

126

anything that wasn't based in truth." She chose her last few words carefully, knowing that even though Nick had reported the incident accurately, certain emotive points had been embellished to stir up public unrest.

Stucker banged his fists on the desk again. "Don't defend that piece of crap. It was a character assassination, pure and simple. I haven't seen Clay that angry in a long time."

"Clay didn't kill himself because of that article."

"Yeah, and you have no way of knowing what effect it had on him."

Maggie's chest tightened. Stucker was right. With Clay dead, it was impossible to know exactly how deeply Nick's exposé had penetrated Clay's tough exterior, puncturing an irreparable hole in his heart.

Did Clay kill himself because he couldn't live with Nick's article?

The thought made her nauseous.

"What about Clay's creditors?" she said, redirecting.

Stucker leaned back in the chair. "Creditors?"

"Clay's moneylenders."

He scooped a blob of phlegm from the corner of his lips and wiped it on his cargo shorts.

"The people who funded his gambling addiction," Maggie explained. "Could *they know* be referring to them?"

"Creditors," he repeated.

Loomis rolled his eyes and breathed out an expletive.

Maggie said, "Don't act dumb, Andy. I found a ledger at Clay's home. It contained a betting record going back at least ten years. I know the two of you went weekending on casino cruises out of Port Canaveral. You know exactly what I'm talking about."

"So what? Clay was a meticulous guy. It's no surprise he kept good records. What was Sasha's take on it?"

"We haven't discussed it yet. Let's just say it made for interesting reading. Did you know Clay was up to his ears in debt?"

"Show me anyone who isn't. Sure, I knew he owed money. I didn't know how much, or to whom. I didn't pry. It was none of my business. Clay liked to gamble. So what? It was his one weakness, poor guy. We've all got demons, Novak."

"It was more than that," Maggie said. "From what I saw, Clay had a *problem*."

Stucker folded his arms. "Your point being?"

"I don't know. Work with me here. I'm just trying to figure out why Clay killed himself; that's all. Sift through a hundred variables. It kills me knowing he felt he couldn't come to us with his problems. Instead, he sat in his car last night, all alone in that parking lot, and blew his brains out. Don't you want to know why?"

Stucker rested his fists on the desk. "Goes without saying."

"So why are you being difficult?"

"I don't know. Maybe it has something to do with you guys coming down here and poking your noses in my private life." He saw Loomis about to pick up a bottle of Russian vodka and told him to keep his mitts off.

Loomis said, "Trust me. We don't want to be here any more than you want us here."

Maggie waited until Stucker's gaze had come back to hers before saying, "Did Clay ever ask you to lend him money?"

"Yeah. Sure. Sometimes. Cash flow was always an issue with him."

"Did he pay it back?"

"Whenever he could."

"How much does he still owe you, Andy?" Maggie was thinking about the handwritten note she'd found inside the flap of the matchbook in Clay's ledger.

"A few grand."

Maggie brought up the picture of the matchbook on her phone. "Would almost forty grand be more accurate?" she said, showing him the image on the screen. She saw the lights come on in his eyes. "Am I in the right ballpark?"

Stucker spread his hands on the desk. "Okay, you got me. Clay owed me a ton of money. So what? It's irrelevant. I was cool with it."

"So why the note?"

Stucker sighed. "You probably don't know this about Clay, because he hid it well. But he had a problem remembering numbers. I think it was a form of dyslexia or something. Anyway, when he was here a couple weekends back, he asked me to write down exactly how much he owed. That's it. No big deal."

"Were his other creditors equally cool?" she asked.

Now he shook his head. "Man, if you think Clay killed himself because he owed some loan shark money, you're barking up the wrong tree. Those backstreet bookmakers he dealt with, he wasn't intimidated by those guys. If anything, it was the exact opposite. He had them eating out of the palm of his hand. They knew they were onto a good thing with Clay. Whatever he owed them, it was a small price to pay for his . . ." Stucker's words trailed off, and he clamped his mouth shut.

"For his what, Andy? For his turning a blind eye?"

Maggie was repulsed at the idea, but she was aware that it happened: that an element of those employed in law enforcement accepted bribes to look the other way. Corruption was the way of the world. Cities were built on it, and politicians were funded by it. She knew Clay had skyrocketing debts. It wasn't a stretch to think that he'd given preferential treatment to those he owed.

Stucker pointed a warning finger at her. "You need to tell me what's really going on here, Novak. You guys didn't come all this way just to tell me Clay's dead. Level with me, or this little reunion is over."

The stink of vomit had begun to creep into Maggie's nostrils. With her foot, she pushed the wastebasket back toward the desk. "All right," she said. "Here's the rub. Clay texted you, asking you to meet him."

"Yeah. I already get that."

"As far as we know, it was the last rational thing he did, right before turning his gun on himself."

"Grisly details aside, I get that one, too."

"Before which, he placed a booby-trap bomb in his car, set to explode the second the driver's door opened."

Stucker feigned a yawn. "Come on, Novak. This is getting old. I wasn't born yesterday. I get all that."

"So why don't you get that right now everything points to you being Clay's target?"

Stucker blinked.

"In other words," Loomis said, "Clay wanted you dead, Stucker. That's why he sent you the text. He was counting on you opening that door before anybody else."

"Only," Maggie said, "you didn't come running, did you? You stayed away. You must see how this looks from our angle."

Stucker let loose a nervy laugh. "You guys have got to be joking, right?" He glanced at them both in turn. "Right?"

Neither Maggie nor Loomis said anything.

"You're way off base," Stucker said. "And I'll tell you why. If my best friend wanted me dead—which we all know is BS—he didn't need to go to all the trouble of building a bomb and hoping I'd take the bait. Who does that kind of thing anyway? Bombs are sloppy.

The easiest thing would've been to come out here and shoot me. He knew where I was. He could've waited outside the club after we closed last night and popped me one in the head." Not being diplomatic, he mimed the action of a gun, shooting himself in the temple.

"We didn't say it was perfect," Maggie admitted.

No homicide theory ever was. Until the lead detective declared case closed, every homicide investigation was considered a work in progress, with the theory adapting and adjusting to fit each new piece of evidence as it was presented.

Right now it was too soon to have all the answers, and although the evidence seemed to be leading one way, experience had taught Maggie to be open to taking alternative routes if new paths to the truth were exposed.

A homicide investigation was like climbing a mountain. It took planning and careful steps to reach the summit.

But Stucker seemed intent on grounding them at base camp.

"Clay luring me into a death trap," he said. "It isn't even close to being believable."

Maggie wanted to argue otherwise, but all at once she didn't have the strength for it. Not now. Not with Stucker. Not when their colleague was probably on his way to the morgue.

"And as for that text message," Stucker continued with a scoff. "I mean, come on, you guys. Be a little bit more creative here, will you? Who sends a cryptic message like that right before committing suicide? Think about it. If Clay wanted to make sure I came running, why didn't he just call me up on the club's landline and speak to me? The number was in his phone. Why didn't he tell me he was going to kill himself? He knew I was an hour's drive away, but I would've been back in Orlando like the devil was on my tail."

"Maybe because he had to be cryptic," Maggie said. "Maybe the two of you were involved in something with serious blowback. Something someone could exploit if they found it out. Use as blackmail."

"Oh, yeah? Like what?"

"Like running a strip club, for example. You know as well as I do, Andy, that it would be remiss of me if I didn't wonder if all this is a front for something else."

Maggie's last sentence seemed to hit a raw nerve, and Stucker jumped to his feet. "We're done here," he said. "Get out. Both of you. Get out before I do something you'll regret. This conversation is over."

Chapter Thirteen

BORDERLINE

Maggie didn't feel like talking much on the ride back to Orlando. The night before had caught up with her again, and her hangover was back with a vengeance. Needles behind her eyes and in the back of her throat. The day was winter bright, and her spare sunglasses from the glove compartment were doing little to ease the sun's intensity.

She stopped for gas on the outskirts of Titusville, and while Loomis used the restroom, she used the pit stop as an excuse to pick up peanut M&M'S as well as two vanilla coffees to go. She hadn't eaten a thing all day, and her system was crying out for a sugar fix.

She tore open the M&M'S, thinking about the moment Stucker had thrown them out of the club.

He'd acted insulted. But Maggie had detected an underlying unease. It was the same thing she'd sensed during her conversation with Sasha in Smits's apartment. The same lack of transparency that always piqued Maggie's curiosity.

Now she was thinking she'd approached the entire thing from the wrong angle.

The passenger door opened, and Loomis dropped into the seat. "Two of the best hangover remedies of all time," he said as he shoveled a fistful of M&M'S into his mouth. "So, what are we thinking?"

Maggie started the engine. "That your table manners leave a lot to be desired."

Loomis crunched candy. "I mean about Stucker. He definitely knows more than he's saying."

"I agree. But I don't think it has anything to do with the club." She swung the car out of the gas station and followed signs for the interstate. "I know Andy can be thickheaded at times. But he's not stupid. If the club has been operating since the sixties, you can bet your bottom dollar it's a legitimate company, with business accounts and IRS records."

"So why has he never mentioned it?"

"Probably for the same reason you've never shared with him your passion for childish video games."

He glanced at her. "Privacy?"

"Embarrassment."

Loomis almost choked on his mouthful. "Here's an update for you, Novak. Those games are pure adult entertainment."

"The same can be said for the Orbit Club."

Maggie took the I-95 on-ramp, headed south. Traffic was light. They hopped off the interstate after a couple of miles, taking the parkway to the Beachline. As the expressway opened up, Maggie's phone rang through the car speakers.

"Steve," Loomis said, reading from the screen on the dashboard.

For a second, Maggie debated the pros and cons of answering the call, temporarily torn between keeping Steve in the dark and turning the spotlight on her own evasiveness. Then she succumbed to *doing the right thing* and pressed the button on the steering wheel to accept his call.

"Are you taking advantage of my easygoing nature?" Steve said after she answered. His tone was calm, but his choice of words told her he *knew*.

Maggie's stomach dropped. "You've seen the news."

"I have. You can imagine what's been going through my mind."

Terror.

"Steve," she began, "first things first—we're on speakerphone, and Loomis is with me. Secondly, please know that I'm not seriously injured. Aside from some stiffness, I'm totally fine."

"It's okay," he said. "Since you didn't call, I figured that one out."

Steve didn't sound pissed, but then it wasn't always easy to tell when he was pissed. According to her girlfriends, Steve Kinsey was a rare breed. One of the few men who was able to check his emotions and rein them in before opening his mouth. It was a great trait to have on paper, but in practice it could throw unexpected curveballs.

"I know your silence is your way of protecting me," he added.

Now Maggie felt bad. "Steve, I should've called you. I'm sorry."

"Maggie, honestly. As long as you're okay, so am I."

But she sensed it wasn't the case, and she couldn't hold it against him.

Purposely, she'd decided not to call Steve from the hospital to let him know about the car bombing. She'd known then that it was a mistake, as well as unfair, and that he would feel abandoned and hurt once the news did break. But she'd done it all the same.

Why?

The answer, she guessed, was less about obligation and more about independence.

Did his marriage proposal scare her *that* much?

"It's been nonstop all day," she said with a sigh. "I didn't want to worry you unnecessarily, especially when we both had stuff to do."

It was a poor excuse, she knew, but she hoped he would be gracious enough not to give her a hard time over it.

"So what happened?" he said. "The last I heard, this was a missing persons case."

Maggie brought him up to speed. A lot had happened in a short space of time, and she heard Steve take several sharp breaths as she recapped her madcap day.

When she was done, he said, "If you're only just on your way back, I take it we have no hope of making Nora's on time?"

With a jolt, Maggie remembered their four o'clock invite to dinner. "What time is it?"

"After three," Loomis said.

"Oh." The time had completely run away with her. "In that case, Steve, no. Nora will blow a fuse. Listen, let me hang up and call her right away. Explain I'm running late."

"I'll do it," he said.

"You're sure?"

She heard him laugh. "Maggie, you and I both know you'll only end up inflaming the situation and making it a million times worse. Let me talk with Nora. Smooth things over. How late should I say?"

"Well, things are being wrapped up at the crime scene, so let's say six? It'll give me time to shower and change first."

"Six it is. See you then."

Maggie said her goodbyes and then drove the rest of the way to Orlando hardly speaking to Loomis. He didn't quiz her about her decision to keep Steve out of the loop. He knew her well enough to know when to leave her be. The reality of Clay's death was finally sinking in, and it was taking her down with it. She didn't resist.

She let it settle over her, going with the flow and encouraging her feelings to run their natural course. Tears in the corners of her eyes and a lump in her throat. Every now and then she checked the rearview mirror, wondering if she might spy Stucker's truck racing up and passing them at breakneck speed. But she didn't see it. And by the time they had arrived back at the Oak Ridge crime scene, both Clay and his car were gone.

Chapter Fourteen

NO HOPE FOR THE FUTURE

W eeks ago, as he'd listened to the sounds of children crying *trick or treat* on the street, he'd wondered if life had been this complicated when he was younger. Times had seemed simpler back then, summers longer, hotter. People older, poorer, but somehow happier. Stuff cheaper, but generally better, made in the USA. No such thing as social media, or stress. No one hooked on Facebook, or anxiety meds. And no one imagining a future quite this *dark*.

Past perfect. Future tense.

Was this everybody's impression of their childhood?

Better times.

Or did the warm glow of nostalgia taint memories, the way that time faded old photographs, making them seem only fonder?

The difference these days was that everything and everyone was disposable. They called it *progress*. Now, when stuff broke, instead of being repaired, it was replaced with shinier stuff. The same went for people. When relationships broke, instead of observing their vows, people substituted the dull for the shiny.

The whole wide world in a constant state of renewal.

But everybody living alone in the global village.

When he was younger, he'd wanted to make a difference. He'd believed that one man *could* make a difference. Give him the right tools, the know-how, the incentive, and he could change the world.

He'd been naive to think that way.

A grain of sand on the beach could never hold back the tide.

The world didn't work like that.

As a family man, he'd learned that change was painstakingly slow, creeping through society and civilization. Cities and fashions gradually reshaping themselves over time. As a career man, he'd learned that change could be sudden, brought about through violence and bloodshed. Life extinguished in the blink of an eye.

Sometimes it was too much to cope with.

He'd worn a brave face for a long while now, reining in his emotions and carrying his cross on the inside. For the sake of his family, he'd continued on as normal, screaming silently into his pillow at night and cursing the universe for abandoning him. And then recently, his burden had doubled, becoming too much for any man to bear.

Without question, he couldn't go on like this.

Things had to change.

In one hand he held a gun. In the other, a handful of bullets. Both, he knew, were useless without the other.

Weeks ago, he'd listened to the sounds of children crying *trick or treat* on the street, knowing that real monsters existed, and that he had the power to put them to death.

All it would take is a single bullet.

Chapter Fifteen

WHERE THE HEART LIES

A noise jolted Maggie from her sleep, and several seconds passed before her brain made sense of her dark surroundings.

She was in her backyard, slumped in a padded lawn chair a few feet from the smoldering firepit. A pashmina over her shoulders and ruby embers glowing through charcoal ash.

A little achy, she sat upright, surprised that she had fallen asleep. She took a moment to gaze around, wondering what had woken her. As far as she could see, there were no neighbors' lights visible through the trees. No breeze rustling the palm leaves. No artificial sounds breaking through the background cacophony of chirruping crickets.

The time on her watch read 3:13 a.m.

It had been almost midnight when she'd come out here, wired and convinced that sleep would be too much to hope for, especially after her mixed-bag evening at Nora's.

Things hadn't gone well from the start.

It had been after seven when she'd finally arrived at her sister's house, walking into awkward silence and to scowls from her siblings. Cries of "Aunt Maggie!" from her nieces, followed by cuddles from the kids and then a long supportive hug from Steve. A tall glass of cold Shiraz—doctor's orders, Steve had said—and a plated meal, incinerated in the oven, virtually inedible. The grown-ups seated around the dining table while the kids watched the latest Disney Blu-ray in the family room.

Without going into detail, Maggie had apologized for her lateness, explaining that "things" had been wrapped up at the crime scene a little later than expected, after which she'd raced home to shower and change and to apply a little makeup to compensate for the fact that she was looking subhuman. She hadn't stopped all day. Bryan repeatedly telling her it was "okay"—they *understood* her job came with certain expectations and *priorities*—while his body language betrayed the fact that he was tired of hearing her excuses.

Maggie had bitten her tongue, but once or twice she'd bitten back as well, and the evening had ended prematurely, on a downer. And even before Maggie had finished eating, Bryan had employed his infamous "I'm up early for work in the morning" card, and he and his wife, Emma, had gathered up their three children, bundling them in the minivan while Maggie stood in Nora's front doorway, saluting with her empty wineglass and shouting that she'd see them all again next year. Nora taking her to one side in the kitchen and pointing out that yet again Maggie had ruined a perfectly nice family get-together. *Did she do it on purpose?* And Maggie telling Nora that she'd lost a friend today, and that she could live without her endless disdain.

Nora's cheeks had brightened cherry red.

Out on the street, Steve had suggested Maggie follow him back to his place. After the day's events, he didn't think it was a good idea for her to be alone tonight. Better that she spend the night at his house, where she could blow off steam to her heart's content. Tell him all the horrible details about her day. He called it *relive and release*. But Maggie had declined, saying she was beat and that

141

tomorrow promised to be equally grueling. The sensible thing was an early night.

Alone, Maggie had returned to her house on Wineberry, the drive home and her runaway thoughts electrifying every cell in her body, pushing the prospect of sleep further from her grasp.

She'd resisted turning on the TV news for fear of hearing speculations and untruths, not knowing if she had the energy for it after running the emotional treadmill all day. But then she'd succumbed, curious, curling up on the couch in the den with a glass of red, watching and wincing as she saw herself being blown off her feet, the windows of Clay's car exploding, fragmented glass peppering the crowd, pandemonium breaking out. Her curiosity turning into dismay as the news anchors talked about what they were mistakenly calling the "Suicide Bombing in Oak Ridge."

The whole bloody mess repeated *on the nines*.

Sickened, Maggie had sloped off to bed around eleven, tossing and turning and eventually giving up and wandering out to the backyard. Lighting the firepit and staring up at the star-speckled sky, her mind ablaze with thoughts of Clay.

Clay, feeling isolated, his spirits crashing to earth.

Clay, without any way to turn, choosing death over life.

Clay, desperate, putting the muzzle of his Glock against his jaw and squeezing the trigger.

Then, unexpectedly, sleep had taken her, here on the patio.

She remembered now.

Clay had visited her while she slept—a dream in which he was alive and sitting in the passenger seat of her black Ford Mustang, parked on a desert valley floor surrounded by eroded mountains. A blazing sun pinned to a violet sky. And Clay smiling at her as the inside of the car filled with watery blood.

In the dream, Maggie had been rooted to the parched earth, every muscle paralyzed. She'd wanted to yank open the car door and let out all the blood before Clay drowned. But she was stuck, frozen beneath the searing sun, her sense of helplessness forming a cold spike at her core.

And as the watery blood had completely covered Clay's face, she'd watched, petrified, as he'd jammed the gun under his chin and mouthed the words *Your turn next.*

Then the entire roof of the car had burst open, a tremendous blood geyser rocketing skyward. And Maggie had woken with a jolt, here, slumped in the lawn chair.

She leaned out of the chair to stoke the embers in the firepit.

It was pointless, she knew, to rack her brain over Clay's reason for committing suicide. Without better information, his motivation was anyone's guess. And guessing only went so far. As an investigator, Maggie used guesswork the same way an artist used a rough sketch. Guesswork was a guide, something to build on and never the whole or the finished picture.

The embers crackled, tiny fiery shards rising on the heat.

She heard a thudding noise coming from inside the house—a muffled rat-a-tat-tat—and she turned in the chair to listen.

Is this the noise that had woken her? she wondered. It sounded like somebody banging a fist against the front door.

Curious, she went inside, moving by touch through the darkened house and into the hallway.

Someone was at the door. She could see the bulky shape of a man through the glass panel next to the front door, a green uniform illuminated in the yellowy porch light.

She put one eye to the peephole, then opened the door.

"Deputy Willits?" she said, recognizing the barrel-chested deputy sheriff standing on her porch. "It's late. Is there an emergency?"

She saw his eyes widen.

"Detective Novak?"

He seemed genuinely surprised to see her, as though he was expecting somebody else to answer the door.

"You know," he said, fingering his trim moustache. "I swore he was trying to pull a fast one."

"Excuse me?"

He jabbed a stubby thumb over his shoulder. "The old guy. He showed up at the Sheriff's Office. Said he was looking for his bird. If you ask me, he seemed confused. I offered him a ride home. He said he lives here."

Maggie looked beyond Willits to the white sheriff's cruiser parked across the foot of her driveway, its headlights casting long shadows across the cul-de-sac. She could just make out the shape of a man sitting in the back seat.

"He gave this address?"

Willits nodded. "Yes, ma'am. Of course, I didn't know you lived here until you opened the door." He glanced over his shoulder. "He's a nice old guy. No ID, though. I was hoping he was right about the address. You know what it's like once Social Services get involved."

"It's my dad," Maggie said in the same moment she realized it.

Willits looked back at her. "It is?"

"You said he was looking for his bird, right?"

"Yes, ma'am."

"Well, he calls me his magpie. So now you know. Come on."

With Willits in tow, Maggie made her way to the cruiser, worried for her father and his reason for being away from home at this time of night.

She opened the car door, and her father climbed out. He was dressed in what Maggie always thought of as his *professor getup*: brown corduroy pants and tweed blazer over a white shirt and knit tie. Snow-white hair combed in a side parting. Bright twinkly eyes.

He's looking old, she thought with a start.

144

"Dad," she said. "Are you okay?"

He gave her a hug. He felt thin, feeble. He smelled of tobacco. "I am now," he said as he let go. "I told this nice deputy that this was the right place. Didn't I, son?"

Willits nodded. "You did, sir."

Maggie closed the car door. "Dad, what's going on? Why did you go to the office?"

"I was worried," he said. "I know you told me not to be. And I know you told me you were all right. But I couldn't sleep. Every time I closed my eyes, I kept seeing you in that explosion. I needed to know you were still okay."

"Why didn't you just call me?"

"I couldn't find my phone. I looked, but it's vanished into thin air. Going down to the Sheriff's Office seemed the obvious thing to do."

"But, Dad, it's the middle of the night."

Maggie saw him think about her comment, and it occurred to her that he might have been drinking. But she couldn't smell alcohol on his breath. And apart from his poor timing, he seemed coherent enough. Besides, drinking wasn't something he did.

"I guess that explains why my neighbor seemed a bit uppity when I asked him to call me a taxi," he said with a sheepish laugh.

She held his hand. "As long as you're okay."

"Best of health." He smiled, as though to confirm it.

But it didn't stop Maggie from wondering if there was more to his turning up at this hour than a timing error. She made a mental note to have him checked at some point. Put her own mind at ease.

"You got this, ma'am?" Willits said.

She turned to him. "Yes. Thank you, Deputy."

"No problem." He nodded his acknowledgment. "Y'all have a good morning." Then he went around to the driver's door.

"Thanks for the ride," her father said.

145

"Anytime, sir."

The deputy got inside the cruiser and made a U-turn in the street. And as the car lights receded, Maggie noticed Nick standing in his bedroom window across the street. He waved, and she waved back.

"Come on," she said to her father. "It's late. Let's get you home." She looped his arm and walked him up the driveway to her Mustang. She opened the passenger door, but he hesitated with a hand on the rim, his gaze on the house.

"I'll always think of this place as home," he said, his eyes twinkling in the street lighting. "We had some good times here, Magpie. Didn't we?"

"When the whole family lived here, I guess."

Maggie was the first to admit that hers had been a happy childhood. Both parents in education, with all the school breaks to spend with their three children. Her only issue, if she was being picky, being her position as the middle child. Often overlooked. She couldn't speak for the years after she and her siblings had moved out, though. Those were the years in which the cracks in her parents' marriage had widened into fissures, then rifts, splitting them permanently apart.

Maggie went back inside the house for her keys and phone. As she joined her father in the car, he asked if they could drive with the top down, and Maggie lowered the roof before pulling out of the driveway.

"How's the dog?" he asked as they drove through the cul-de-sac. "Couldn't help noticing the blanket in the back, and the smell."

"Spartacus is fine," she said. "But are you, Dad?" She glanced sidelong at him as she turned out onto Hammocks Drive. "Is everything okay with you? It's just strange, your looking for me in the middle of the night like this. You've never done anything like it before."

"You've never been blown up before."

Maggie experienced a pang of guilt. "All the same, it's dark. You should've realized I'd be home."

He smiled, almost to himself. "At my age, time has little meaning, other than it's running away from me faster than I can keep up. I hadn't heard from you since the morning. You said you'd phone back. You didn't, and I got worried. I wasn't thinking about time or location. Just you."

Another pang of guilt lit up inside her. "Dad, I'm sorry for panicking you. Things got a little hectic today."

He flapped a hand. "And you forgot about your old man. It's okay, Magpie. I know your work comes first. And I respect that. You and I are cast from the same mold. Besides, my memory isn't what it used to be either. The only thing that matters is you're okay, which you are." He smiled at her and patted her knee. "Now do your old man a favor and put the pedal to the metal. I want to feel the wind in my hair while I still have some of it left."

Chapter Sixteen

THE BUGLE CALL

Maggie scanned the tense faces of those gathered in OCSO's main conference room, unable to recall ever seeing quite so many of her colleagues here all at the same time.

The place was packed to capacity and heating up. People seated around the long table and shoehorned into every available space. Detectives and high-ranking officers from Patrol Division standing shoulder to shoulder along the edges of the room. Everybody from the top brass down. Not just detectives from Homicide Squad—huddled with Maggie and Loomis at the back of the room—but all those able to attend from across the Violent Crimes Unit as a whole.

Two of their own had died, and although attendance wasn't compulsory, the meeting was impossible to miss.

Maggie's gaze focused on the big TV monitor suspended on the far wall, at the side of the doorway. On screen, two portrait photos were displayed side by side and had been all the while the room had filled up. One was the stock image of Clayton Young that Maggie had pulled up on her phone at Walmart yesterday, in which Clay was posing for the press shot in his camel-colored sport coat.

The other was a police academy graduation photograph depicting Stacy Shaw in her dark-green deputy's uniform, posing in front of the American flag.

"Someone's lapping up all the attention," Loomis muttered near Maggie's ear.

Andy Stucker had positioned himself at one side of the TV, acknowledging comments of condolence from his colleagues with a grim nod and the occasional thumbs-up. This was the first time Maggie had seen him since their run-in at the club yesterday, and she had questions, but she'd decided to allow him his space, for now.

It was hard not to notice his perfunctory smiles, or the trace of what she could describe only as boredom underlying his mechanical responses.

Is this shock? she wondered. *Or, something else?*

Depending on a hundred variables, she knew, everyone dealt differently with death. Some people imploded, shrinking into their shells, while others exploded, hitting out. Then there were those who embraced denial instead of acceptance, pretending that death had passed them by. Stucker's attitude didn't seem to fit into any convenient category. It was almost as though Clay's suicide had had little impact on Stucker, and he was behaving more in a way that was expected of him, rather than one that came from a place of grief.

Lieutenant Laremy Dunbar, Smits's immediate superior, stood beside Stucker, shaking hands with each newcomer as they joined the gathering. Dunbar looked overheated and slightly breathless, like his shirt collar was buttoned up too tight. There was a valid reason why his expression was bleaker than most. Dunbar wasn't just Smits's line commander; he was also Clay's brother-in-law. His sister, Sasha, had lost her husband, and Dunbar's head was hung,

149

his hands clasped together, like he was in church and praying for redemption.

Maggie wondered how Sasha had coped overnight without Clay at her side. The first night was always the worst, followed by the next and then the next, and so on. She knew that Sasha's boys had collected her from Smits's condo late yesterday afternoon, and that the family had been allowed access to their home again. Maggie could only imagine what kind of night she'd had, her thoughts tormented, not just with grief, but also by the possibility that Deputy Shaw had died at her husband's hand. It was a heavy weight for anyone to bear, and Maggie was worried for Sasha's state of mind going forward if it did turn out that Clay had built the bomb.

She made a mental note to get in touch, help out where she could, or at least make the offer. Sasha wasn't the world's most affable person. She didn't let many people get close. Her instinct was to draw herself into her shell at the first sniff of trouble. But Maggie wanted to speak with her. Despite Smits's command to the contrary, Maggie needed to quiz Sasha about the arguments that she and Clay had been having lately, loud enough for their neighbor to hear.

Maggie realized Dunbar was staring directly at her, and she held his gaze until he looked away.

"Starting to whiff a little in here," Loomis whispered.

"I've a feeling the stink is only going to get worse," she whispered back.

According to the clock on the wall, it was exactly 10:00 a.m.

The door opened, and Smits entered the room. His big frame seemed slightly stooped, as though he bore the weight of the world on his shoulders. His arrival signaled the end of the chatter, and an expectant hush settled over the proceedings. Like most of those present here, Smits's somber attire matched the mood.

He shared a cool handshake with Stucker and then a stiff hug with Dunbar. A professional nod toward Major Oysterman and Captain Velazquez, both sitting a few chairs back, and then a reluctant glance at the portraits of the fallen officers blazing away on the TV screen.

"Thanks, everyone," he began as he surveyed his audience. "I appreciate the turnout. It's a dark day for all of us, and I'm conscious of the fact that each of you has other places you need to be today. So I'll keep this as tidy as possible." He paused a moment to take a breath.

"This holiday weekend we lost a brother and a sister. Detective Clayton Young of Homicide Squad, and Sheriff's Deputy Stacy Shaw of Patrol Division." He raised a hand to the screen behind him. "Saturday evening, Detective Young, a seasoned investigator with over thirty years on the force, unexpectedly took his own life. Those close to him are still reeling from the shock."

Not Stucker, Maggie thought.

Stucker's expression was the least tense in the room, his posture far too relaxed for a man whose best friend had just died.

"His loss," Smits said, "to those who knew him, and to the Orange County Sheriff's Office as a whole, is tragic in itself, but that tragedy is doubled by the fact that his actions also led to the death of one of our newest recruits, just two weeks on the job. At this time our deepest sympathies are with the family of Deputy Shaw." He took another breath.

Maggie realized she was holding hers, and let it go.

"Over the years," he said, "many of you had the privilege of working with Detective Young. Forming good relationships and strong friendships. And despite what happened yesterday, he'll be sorely missed. Rest assured, we are doing everything we can to understand why these terrible events happened." He turned to Stucker.

"At this point," he said, "I think it only appropriate if Detective Young's partner of the last ten years, Detective Andrew Stucker, says a few words in tribute." Smits stepped aside, gesturing at Stucker to take center stage. "Detective."

Stucker cleared his throat and spoke up. And as he began to drone on about how he considered Clay a brother-in-arms and a team player of the highest caliber, Maggie tuned out his voice.

She thought about her father instead—about his nighttime trip to the Sheriff's Office, and how odd it all seemed in the bright light of day.

Still, she couldn't fathom why he'd told Deputy Willits that he lived at her address. She'd brought it up in the car on the ride home, but her father had insisted the deputy had misunderstood him. He'd given him the address on purpose, to see Maggie. But Maggie wasn't sure.

Granted, her father had lived in the house on Wineberry a long time ago, for decades, raising his family and carving out a life. But not for the past ten years. After Maggie's parents had divorced and sold her the family home, he'd downsized to a property at Red Bug Lake, to be closer to his lecturing job at the university. Her father was an intelligent man, a retired physics professor of some repute. His mixing up information was like a calculator suddenly computing that two and two equaled five.

Something was off with him.

After giving the incident more thought, Maggie had decided there had been other behavioral inconsistences, too, over the last few months. A handful of things she'd noticed, but never connected. Nothing that meant anything particular in isolation—inconsequential stuff, like his leaving the shower running, or wearing a dress shirt with sweatpants—but when all the dots were connected, it drew a disconcerting picture.

Of course, Maggie knew her father wasn't getting any younger. Since his retirement from lecturing the year before last, he'd more or less lived the life of a hermit. Retiring from the university had pulled in his horizons, and it had taken him quite some time to adjust to having too much time on his hands. Some behavioral issues were expected. Even so, she couldn't ignore the feeling that there was *something* underlying his sometimes-odd conduct.

Perhaps the first step would be to speak with Steve about it when he got back from his conference next weekend. Get his opinion before she broached the subject of a medical checkup with her father.

A rumble of expectancy rose in the crowd, and Maggie refocused on the here and now as Jasper Carmichael made his way to the front of the room. She saw him slot a flash drive into a laptop at the head of the conference table, and the portrait photos on the TV screen disappeared.

"Bear with me, folks," he said as he tapped at the keyboard. "All right. Here we go."

An image lit up on the screen. It was a photo of the back seat of a car—*Clay's* car—crystal clear in fifty inches of high definition.

A wave of unease rippled through the room.

Central in the image was a silvery metal cylinder lying on the black leather, surrounded by glass crumbs. It looked like a short length of heating pipe, about a foot long, one end capped and the other buckled, blackened, the rim torn outward to form jagged petals.

"As you can see," Carmichael said as he glanced at the screen, "the improvised explosive device was of the standard pipe variety, as evidenced here. Aside from the missing cap, most of the casing appears to be intact. This is something you don't see all too often. Normally, concussive force reduces the entire pipe to tiny fragments."

"Does that signify a low yield?" someone asked.

"It does. My first impression was that it had likely malfunctioned. But now we know it wasn't a failure. This device isn't a dud. It definitely exploded, just not massively." He demonstrated with his hands. "For those of you unfamiliar with the process, as the explosive material expands and the internal pressure builds up, the metal crystalizes. Then it ruptures, suddenly, and the shrapnel flies out in all directions."

"What went wrong here?" someone asked.

"At this stage, it's difficult to say if the bomb detonated as intended, or if the maker miscalculated the payload."

"In other words, it's possible he didn't use enough explosive material?"

"Correct. Once they run the tests, Forensics will confirm either way. Right now we're confident he used smokeless powder. Otherwise known as common over-the-counter gunpowder. The kind you can pick up at most outfitters and ammo supply stores."

"You can get a pound of smokeless powder for as little as fifteen dollars," someone said.

Carmichael nodded. "For the majority of homemade IEDs, it's the material of choice." He tapped a key on the laptop, and the image on the screen switched to one showing several gray streaks on the car's red bodywork. "Even though there was a general lack of smoke noted during the explosion, these powder burns appear to emanate from the flash point, located, we believe, just inside the driver's door."

He tapped another key, and the image changed to a photo of the inside of the door itself. The plastic inner skin could be seen hanging off the metal frame at an angle, its dark-gray surface cracked and broken. Bits of it missing. The door pocket was completely gone, and there were holes all around the skin where the force of the blast had ripped it off its retaining studs.

"Right off the bat," Carmichael said, "we're siting the bomb either in the pocket, or wedged between the seat and the door itself."

He tapped the keyboard, presenting his audience with a side view of the driver's seat, taken from level with the inner sill. The view was angled slightly upward, so that it was possible to see the inside roof in the background, the beige headliner covered in a fine spray of blood.

Maggie focused on the seat itself.

Apart from a few leather shreds still attached to the sewn seams, most of the upholstery was gone, the foam hanging out, cratered and streaked with dust.

Someone asked about the trigger mechanism.

"The trigger appears to be mechanical and not electronic," Carmichael answered. He pressed a key, and the photo on the screen was replaced with the close-up of a frayed strand of metal wire, about six inches long, dangling from a plastic hoop near the roof of the car. "We found this wire fixed to the grab handle above the driver's door. We believe it was connected to the initiator, probably a blasting cap."

"Like a trip wire," someone said.

"Yes, exactly like a trip wire. When the door opened, it pulled the cord and activated the initiator."

Someone said, "So the IED was rigged to harm the first person to open the door, probably a first responder?"

Maggie saw Carmichael glance at her. "That certainly appears to be the case, yes."

The murmur of unease surged again.

"How easy is it to build one of these IEDs?" Captain Velazquez asked.

She sat beside Oysterman, quietly listening until now. Ordinarily, a uniform patrol section commander such as Velazquez would never sit in on a Major Case meeting of this nature, and especially not one involving Incident Command. But one of her deputies had died in the line of duty, and no one was batting an eye at her presence.

"Unfortunately," Carmichael said, "building one of these things is way too easy." He tapped a key, and the image of the ruptured pipe reappeared on screen. "Rudimentary IEDs like this can be manufactured at home. There's no special equipment needed. Anybody with a workbench and access to the internet can put one of these things together. That's the frightening part. Improvised explosive devices are just about unpoliceable."

It wasn't a real word, but everybody understood its meaning.

"So, just to be clear," Velazquez said, sounding slightly dumbfounded and in need of confirmation. "Literally *anyone* can build one of these?"

"Just about. That said, it takes skill not to blow yourself up in the process." Again, his hands demonstrated while he spoke. "Actuators in the trigger mechanisms are renowned for being sensitive. They're notoriously fiddly. Amateurs blow their fingers off all the time. It's one thing to purchase the components; putting them together safely is a whole other ball game."

"You need a strong nerve and a steady hand," Smits said.

"For sure."

"How soon will we have the full picture?" Smits asked.

Carmichael pulled the flash drive out of the laptop, and the TV screen went blank. "I'm told Forensics will start working on the reconstruction today. Realistically, I'd say we're looking at end of the week before we get the comprehensive evaluation."

Smits thanked Carmichael, and the Bomb Squad commander returned to his seat.

"Even though it's business as usual," Smits said to his audience, "everyone needs to be aware of two instructions coming down the chain from Captain Corrigan."

"How is he?" Oysterman asked.

"Home tomorrow, I hear. He's doing good, sir. Learning to use a patch like a one-eyed pirate. Knowing the captain, he'll be back on duty the same day."

Smits's comment seemed to break the tension in the room, and the release was palpable.

He waited for everyone to settle down again before saying, "Okay. Here're the captain's two wishes. One, the press. It goes without saying. No talking under any circumstances until after we've made the official statement. We want to make sure we have the complete and true story before they print their version of it. No leaks, ladies and gentlemen. Remember, what happened yesterday reflects on each and every one of us. Let's keep it professional.

"Two, be alert. Right now we have no way of knowing if this is a solitary incident. For all we know, there could be other IEDs out there, armed and waiting for you to pull the trigger. Until we know otherwise, we treat every public call, every visit outside of this office with extreme caution. Uniformed patrol has been apprised likewise." His gaze roved the room. "Any questions?"

"Do we know why Detective Young built the bomb?"

The question came from Major Oysterman.

Smits rubbed at his jaw. "Theories aside, sir, it's probably best if I pass your question over to our lead investigator." His gaze found Maggie. "Detective Novak, can you shed any light for the major and for the rest of us?"

Oysterman swiveled in his chair to face her, followed by every eye in the room.

Maggie had learned long ago never to hesitate. Hesitation suggested uncertainty, and uncertainty implied incompetency.

"I believe the intention was to kill Detective Stucker," she said to gasps from the crowd.

"That's a crock of BS," Stucker said, loud enough to silence the room. "You're the one he wanted dead."

Chapter Seventeen

CROSSHAIRS

Shouting over the ensuing uproar, Smits called an end to the meeting, and as the conference room emptied, he pointed in turn at Maggie, Loomis, and Stucker, his cheeks glowing blood-red. "You three. My office. Now."

Maggie went to stop Stucker from leaving the room after Smits. She wanted to set her colleague straight, to shout him down and put him in his place. But Loomis caught her by the arm, preventing her from following Stucker into the hallway.

"Let him go," he said.

Maggie twisted out of his grasp. "Since when did you become a Stucker fan?"

"Never. But the dude is in grieving mode. Cut him some slack. Trust me, Novak. The last thing you want is to inflame a sensitive situation right now."

Maggie's blood boiled, but she knew Loomis was right. Allowances had to be made for extenuating circumstances. She had to remember that she had no way of knowing how she might react if the roles were reversed. Making a scene might release her own tension and feel rewarding in the moment, but beyond that, it wouldn't achieve a thing.

By the time they got to Smits's office in the corner of the Major Case suite, Smits was already installed behind his big desk, his jacket off and his sleeves rolled up, looking like he was spoiling for a fight. Stucker had perched himself on the rim of the windowsill, his arms folded and his mouth a hard line.

"Somebody, please tell me, what the hell was that?" he said, then pointed at Maggie. "You first."

"The major wanted to hear my opinion," she said. "I gave it."

"And effectively opened up a can of worms in the process."

"Sir, I didn't—"

He raised a silencing hand. "Save it, Detective. Your comment implied division in the ranks. This situation is a finely balanced mess as it is. I shouldn't have to remind you of that. Now, more than ever, this department needs to present a show of solidarity. Not a mudslinging match in front of the entire unit." He pointed at Loomis. "You. What's our first in-house rule?"

"No incendiary comments in front of the top brass."

"Wonderful. At least somebody read the memo. What makes you 100 percent sure Detective Stucker was the intended target?"

Loomis pulled out a chair and began to speak.

Smits raised the hand again, cutting him off. "Not you. I was asking your partner. And don't sit. You won't be here that long."

Loomis pushed the chair back under the desk and retreated.

Maggie said, "Right now it's the only theory that fits the facts."

"I take it you're referring to the text messages."

"Yes, sir. It's right there in black and white. Clay summoning Andy to the Walmart parking lot, knowing full well he would open that car door the second he saw Clay sitting there dead. The text was a lure."

"He wanted Detective Stucker to die."

"I believe so."

Stucker let out a moan. "Only, it didn't work, did it? I didn't even read the messages. So it wasn't a very smart plan, was it?"

Smits rotated his gaze to Stucker. "Your phone was off."

"Yes, sir. All night. Like I told Novak here. I have a policy of turning off my cell during the holidays. If Clay wanted to kill me—which I know he absolutely did not want to do—the easiest way would've been for him to come out to Titusville and do it in person."

Smits's gaze came back to Maggie. "He has a point."

Maggie drew a breath. "Sir, Andy's theory only works if we assume Clay was thinking rationally. The fact he committed suicide suggests he wasn't, at least not right then and there. None of us know exactly why Clay chose that particular kill method. We might never know. But I'm confident I wasn't the target."

Smits seemed to accept her argument, at least for now, and Maggie saw his gaze move back to Stucker. "Well?"

"Sir?"

"Have you forgotten your own little bombshell you dropped in front of the major just a minute ago? Explain to me why you think Detective Novak was the intended target."

"In my defense," Stucker said, "I was only repeating what I was told."

"By whom?"

"By Clay. Right after the fight they had."

"You weren't there."

"No. But he called me after. He was angry and needed to vent."

"I thought your phone was off?"

Stucker hesitated before saying, "He used the club's landline."

"You mean, the strip joint? Don't get me started on that one, Detective. What exactly did your partner say?"

"That Novak's attitude stank and it would get her killed some-day. And if it did, she deserved it."

Silence fell, and all eyes looked at Maggie.

"Harsh," Loomis said.

Maggie's flesh was on fire, her heart suddenly racing. "It's okay," she said. "Clay was angry; that's all. Everybody says things they don't mean when they're angry. He was just sounding off. We all do it. I know he didn't mean it."

"Either way," Smits said, "our infighting doesn't look good in front of the top brass. What we absolutely don't need is them asking you to recuse yourself. Do we, Detective Novak?"

"No, sir."

"So starting right here, right now, we all sing from the same hymn sheet. Understood?" He looked at each of them in turn, only moving on when he received their nod of confirmation. "All right," he said. "I'm glad we all decided to be grown-ups." He turned to Stucker. "One last thing before I let you go. And I need you to be completely up front with me, Detective. Is there any reason, any reason at all, why Detective Young might have wanted to cause you physical harm?"

"None whatsoever." His reply came without hesitation. "I would've died for the guy, but not that way."

Smits seemed to debate Stucker's response for a second; then he flapped a hand at him. "Okay. Good. You're excused. Get out of here. Go resume your vacation days. We'll call if we need you."

Stucker pushed up off the windowsill and crossed the office.

Maggie said, "Sir, I have a question for Andy before he leaves."

Stucker paused at the door. "What?"

"Do you know if Clay rented space somewhere?"

Stucker shrugged. "If he did, he kept it from me."

"Why do you think that was?" Loomis said. "Seeing that the two of you were so tight and all?"

"At a guess, Ed, because he was building a bomb." It would have been the perfect sarcastic comeback had Stucker finished it with a *duh*.

He cocked an eyebrow at Maggie, then went through the door and closed it behind him.

Smits waited until Stucker was out of earshot before leveling his gaze on Maggie. "You think he's hiding something."

"I think Andy is doing what Andy does best, sir, which is keeping his cards close to his chest. I'm not sure if he's being deliberately cagey because we intruded on his private life yesterday, or if there's something pertinent to the case he's choosing to withhold."

"Any ideas what that might be?"

"In all honesty, I wouldn't care to hazard a guess right now. I need to do more digging. With everything that's happened, it's possible I'm picking up mixed signals."

"But your gut insists there's *something*."

Maggie nodded. Speaking with Stucker yesterday at the Orbit Club had sparked more questions than answers, and she'd come away feeling dissatisfied with the outcome. Several hours later, staring into the flames inside her firepit, Maggie had thought long and hard about Clay and Stucker's working relationship, as well as their personal friendship, trying to recall any instances of her witnessing tension between them, or signs pointing to a future breakup. She'd struggled to come up with a single example of them butting heads, never mind falling out.

"What about you?" Smits's question was directed at Loomis.

"Me?" he said. "Let's just say I know better than to go up against Novak's gut instinct."

Smits laced his fingers and tapped them against his chin, deep in thought for a moment. "Okay," he said at last. "At some point, I'm going to have to talk to the press and put a lid on the rumors. When I do, I need to go in there armed with all the facts. I need you to go back over what we already know. Check the evidence, the timelines, the stories. Find out where Clay built that bomb, and why that was his preferred kill method. If Detective Stucker was indeed his intended target, I want to know what he did to piss Clay off to the point of wanting him dead. I need reasons, not just theories. Now get out of here. I've got a call to make."

Chapter Eighteen

COLD HARD FACTS

Nothing about the single-story, two-toned, windowless building on Thirty-Fifth Street in the city caused it to stand out from its neighbors. About the size of a chain restaurant, the evidence storage facility was a flat, nondescript square box situated between an office block and a broadband supply company. Anonymous in its blandness, with no signage in sight.

Maggie suspected the architect had watched one too many dystopian movies.

Partly obscured behind a row of strategically planted trees, a small parking lot stretched along the front. Maggie parked the motor pool sedan alongside a sheriff's cruiser in the shade of a palmetto and climbed out.

After yesterday's above-average temperatures, today was moderately warm. Vapor trails crisscrossing an electric-blue sky.

Maggie pulled off her sunglasses as she went through the glass doors at the corner of the building. Inside, the Orange County Sheriff's Office property and evidence storage facility smelled pine fresh.

She handed her ID and gun to the administrator sitting behind the reception counter, then signed herself in, noting down the time and reason for her visit. The administrator put Maggie's Glock in the safe bolted to the wall behind the counter and then handed back Maggie's badge.

"Happy New Year, Detective Novak," she said with a smile.

The truth was, it couldn't be further from happy, but Maggie returned the warm smile nonetheless.

Life goes on, she told herself, *even when death stops everything dead.*

A glass-walled corridor led to Evidence Storage. Maggie passed a suite of brightly lit offices and sterile examination rooms. Technicians in white lab coats processing evidence and analyzing data on their screens.

She said *hello* to each member of the Evidence Unit she encountered on the way to her destination, and at the end of the corridor, she passed through a sealed door into the climate-controlled part of the facility responsible for housing the actual evidence. It was noticeably cooler in here. Everything high gloss and dust-free. The walls, the floor, the ceiling—all crisp white and featureless.

Like something out of a science fiction film.

A male clerk, seated on a stool at a tall desk with a computer terminal on its top, checked her ID again and asked her to sign the visitor log.

"Smile for the camera."

Then she filled out an evidence request form, and he directed her to wait in a small side room. The room had no door and, except for a stout glass-topped table in the middle, no furniture. The table was lit internally, lighting up as she entered the room, its surface glowing white.

On the corner of the table, a box of vinyl gloves and an evidence tape dispenser were positioned side by side. Maggie extracted a pair of gloves and snapped them on.

Her eye caught the camera pointed at her near the ceiling.

After she and Loomis had left Smits's office, Maggie had suggested they start with Clay's personal effects collected at the crime scene and work outward from there. Loomis had opted to check Clay's workstation and locker while Maggie drove five minutes down the road to the evidence facility.

Maggie wasn't sure what they would find, if anything at all. In her experience, people who committed suicide tended to get their business in order first, leaving no major loose ends. Add to that the fact that Clay had premeditated a murder, and it wasn't hard to envisage their searches coming up empty handed.

The clerk reappeared holding an evidence box and placed it on the table. Maggie thanked him, and he returned to his desk duties, telling her that if she needed anything else, for her just to call out.

Maggie took a beat to look at the box, her belly curling into a ball as she saw Clay's name next to the case number.

How did it come to this?

She thought about the last time she had seen Clay alive and in person during their argument two days ago. He'd been dynamic and loud, incensed over Nick's article. Embarrassed, she remembered, because of Nick's assertion that Lay-Z Creek's death was a direct result of Clay's negligence.

Without doubt, Nick's exposé would have reopened painful wounds in the public memory this week, prompting negative reactions. And Clay, having already lived through the backlash once, had expressed to her his fear of living through it all again.

Was it enough to tip him over the edge? she wondered.

It suddenly occurred to Maggie that if Clay had secretly felt that he and Stucker were responsible for Creek's death, and he couldn't live with the guilt, then it could explain both his suicide and his attempt to kill his partner.

One thing was for sure: her task would have been a whole lot easier had Clay simply left a suicide note explaining everything.

She returned her attention to the evidence box.

A large white label was stuck to the cardboard, listing items and collection details. A series of words and numbers that were meaningless in isolation, but together formed a unique crime scene fingerprint. Contents included a cell phone, a bunch of keys, a brown leather wallet, a police badge, a .45-caliber Glock 21 Gen4, and a bullet casing. But no clothing—she assumed Clay's clothes were still at the ME's office.

Half the label formed an in-and-out log, used to record items that were removed temporarily, in the case of extra forensic processing or evidence presentation at trial. Already, there were two entries in the log, and Maggie recognized the handwriting as belonging to Robbie Zeedeman, OCSO's resident firearms specialist. At 8:07 a.m., he'd signed out Clay's gun and the bullet casing, presumably for ballistic testing and comparison.

Using the penknife on her key ring, Maggie sliced the red evidence tape sealing the box. Then, taking a deep breath, she removed the lid.

There was a bunch of brown kraft paper packets stacked inside, each one labeled with its contents.

She reached in, taking each packet out in turn and placing it on the illuminated table. She started with the packet marked **WALLET**, carefully undoing the string fastener and emptying its contents onto the glowing surface.

A handful of coins and Clay's billfold slid out onto the table. She opened the wallet, finding several credit cards and a wad of banknotes as thick as her little finger. Mostly, the notes were one-dollar bills and just a few higher denominations, adding up to much less than she thought at first glance. The label on the packet noted the paper money content as seventy-six dollars.

Tip money, she assumed.

Several business cards were tucked inside a series of slots. Maggie spotted something that looked familiar, and she removed a jet-black card with the words THE ORBIT CLUB in pink on the front.

Aside from the obvious, she wondered what Clay's connection was with the Titusville strip club.

Clearly, he'd known of its existence, and presumably he was equally aware of Stucker's role in its day-to-day management. Had he been there, not just to socialize with Stucker, but as a client? Was that why he kept the business card in his wallet? Was there more to the operation than Stucker was letting on to?

She turned it over in her gloved hands. A cell number was written on the card's reverse. Out of curiosity, she dialed it, and after a few seconds, the call was picked up, but no one spoke.

"Hello?" she said into the silence. "My name's Detective Novak, and I'm with the Sheriff's—"

The call disconnected.

Maggie tried the number again. This time, hearing it ring continuously without anyone picking up.

"I wonder who you are?" she mused out loud.

She added the number to her Contacts, labeling it Clay's Orbit Card, intending to call it again later. Then she took photos of the card, front and reverse, before returning it to the wallet.

Next, she undid the packet labeled PHONE and tipped Clay's cell into her hand.

Luckily, it still held a charge, and the screen brightened as she pressed the power button, presenting her with the text message conversation between Clay and Stucker that she had seen yesterday: the final two texts sent December 31 at 10:48 p.m., containing the ominous warning *they know*, standing out like a danger sign.

Maggie scrolled back through the conversation, not knowing what she might find.

A clue, hopefully, to point to Clay's state of mind?

She scrolled back over the last several weeks, seeing mainly boyish banter and the occasional silly GIF. Nothing to indicate that Clay's mood was anything but *normal*.

Maggie skipped back to the final two messages and stared at the words *they know*.

In one sense, Stucker had confirmed her thoughts. Clay had known before the holiday that his partner was spending New Year's in Titusville. He'd known Stucker was an hour's drive away. He'd chosen to lure Stucker back to Orlando with a text message, gambling on him arriving at the car in the Walmart parking lot before anyone else happened to chance on his suicide. Maggie had established that Clay liked to gamble, but relying on Stucker picking up the message and then rushing to the scene before anyone else opened the car door was dangerous odds, especially when he knew that Stucker had a bad habit of not answering his cell during the holidays.

What was she missing?

Maggie closed the text conversation and studied the list of contacts that Clay had been texting recently, recognizing the names of some of her coworkers, as well as Sasha and other members of Clay's family.

How had Sasha broken the news of their father's death to her sons? she wondered. Was there any less damaging way other than sitting them down and telling them the truth?

Maggie spotted the number from the back of the Orbit Club business card, the one she had just called, and she tapped it, opening the conversation.

This was no ordinary chat, she realized as she scrolled through the texts. That much was obvious right away. The "conversation" sent to Clay from the mysterious number consisted of a series of dates, times, and hotel names, and no actual *conversation*. After each received message, Clay had replied with either a thumbs-up or a thumbs-down. Two, sometimes three texts each week, spelling out rendezvous information for various locations spread across the county.

Maggie experienced a sinking feeling.

She had seen text conversations similar to this before, although none quite this clinical. Usually, in her experience, these kinds of text conversations were associated with one of three situations: innocent business meeting arrangements, regular drug buys from a dealer, and extramarital affairs.

Maggie knew that unless Clay had been meeting with an informant on a regular basis, he had no reason to conduct innocent business meetings this often and at all these different hotels.

At Smits's apartment, Sasha had sworn that Clay hadn't been using recreational drugs of any kind. He was a fitness freak, she'd said, and she'd be able to tell if Clay had abused drugs. Therefore, no dealer. But spouses could be deceitful, deceivers adept at hiding habits.

But evidence didn't lie.

Maggie knew that Elkin's autopsy would reveal the truth. If Clay had had a chemical dependency, he would find evidence of it.

Maggie frowned at the text conversation on the phone.

Was Clay having an affair?

The thought made Maggie feel bad for Sasha.

She could still remember vividly the moment she'd first learned of her mother's affair a decade ago—the one that had finally ended her parents' marriage—and the feeling of being betrayed even though the cheating had been on her father. Like part of her life had been a lie. Her initial confusion giving way to disbelief after learning that her mother had had multiple affairs, dating back to

171

before Maggie had been born. Then her disbelief turning to frustration as Bryan and Nora had sided with their mother. Their father had always chosen his profession over them, they'd argued. But Maggie had seen the effect the breakup had had on her father, seen the way her mother's cheating had made him feel unworthy and somehow less of a man, and she'd decided then and there to stand by him despite his flaws.

Her father had once said, "When affairs blow apart the nuclear family, the fallout makes everyone sore."

Maggie took a breath.

The Youngs' neighbor had mentioned Sasha and Clay arguing more than usual lately.

Could an affair be the explanation?

Maggie needed to know who the mystery number belonged to.

For that reason, she phoned Donna Krick in Digital Forensics Squad.

Krick specialized in the forensic analysis of mobile devices, particularly in the retrieval of crucial data from locked phones and computers.

"I need you to trace a private cell number," Maggie explained.

"I'll do my best," Krick answered. "It might take a couple of hours, though."

Maggie gave Krick the number, then called it herself again, only to hear it ring unanswered for a second time.

Someone didn't want to speak to her.

Maggie checked Clay's recent call log.

As expected, there were dozens of incoming and outgoing calls placed and received over the last week or so. Again, many to and from people saved in Clay's Contacts list. Names and numbers familiar to Maggie. Nothing that leaped out at her. In fact, the list didn't read much different from her own call log. At the office, a large part of Maggie's time was spent on the phone, speaking with other agencies or chasing case queries. Some days it was all she seemed to do. The same could be said for her fellow investigators.

She looked for the mystery number, but didn't see it. She scrolled back over the last several weeks, through a hundred or more calls, without success.

The fact that it wasn't there suggested to her that Clay and this particular person never actually spoke on the phone, or at least not on *this* phone. Text messaging only. It reaffirmed to her that the number was linked to some kind of clandestine activity.

Did it contribute to his suicide, though?

The most recent incoming calls were all from Sasha. At least thirty placed one after the other, some separated by minutes, some by seconds, all made between 10:52 p.m. and 11:55 p.m. on New Year's Eve. It was the call log of a wife trying desperately to contact her missing husband.

The memory of Sasha calling Maggie two minutes before midnight on New Year's Eve floated into her mind, and Maggie chided herself for failing to act then and there on Sasha's call.

Maggie focused on the most recent call entry made before Sasha's persistent telephoning.

According to the log, at 9:48 p.m. on New Year's Eve—minutes before Clay had left home for the store—he had picked up his last-ever phone call, from a cell number not listed in his Contacts. The call had lasted one minute and thirty-six seconds.

Shortly after receiving it, Clay had told his wife he was going to the store for milk, never to return.

Maggie picked up her own phone and dialed the number.

Almost immediately, she heard a recorded message advising her that the number was "no longer in service."

She stared at the screen, wondering.

Then the phone rang in her hand, the caller ID reading *Donna Krick*.

"I'm impressed," Maggie said. "That must be an all-time record."

"Sheer luck," Krick answered. "The ping came back quicker than expected. I think the cell networks are all quiet after yesterday's mayhem. I'm afraid it's not good news, though. The number is unlisted."

Maggie's hopes nose-dived. "So it's a burner phone?"

"Yes. In all likelihood it's a throwaway. Not many people register disposables on their mobile plans."

"Is there any way we can trace its location?"

"Typically, no."

"But you'll give it a try?"

"Um . . . I guess I will."

"Donna, I owe you a drink."

"Maggie, that's what you always say."

"At least I'm consistent." She heard Krick laugh. "Listen," she said, "before I let you go, I've got one more number I need you to run."

"Okay. Fire it at me."

Maggie read out loud the number she'd just dialed—the last call that Clay had picked up on New Year's Eve.

"Sounds like it's probably another throwaway," Krick said after reading it back to her. "Leave it with me?"

"Sure thing, Donna. Thanks."

Maggie added the number to her own Contacts, labeling it Clay's Last Call.

Then she accessed the Photos app on Clay's phone and scrolled through a mosaic of pictures, looking for anything *unusual*.

Maggie had no idea what that might entail. In the course of investigating suicides, she had found unusual photos on phones quite a few times. Weird selfies of the suicide victim staring at their reflection in a mirror. Photos of family tombstones. And, once or twice, close-ups of the scars left behind from failed suicide attempts.

For the most part, the images on Clay's phone were crime scene snapshots—her own Photos app contained similar sets—with only a handful of personal pictures: Clay spending quality time with his sons at Universal Studios, selfies of them eating towering burgers in a restaurant at CityWalk, the three of them looking happy and . . .

Glad to be alive.

A pang of sadness broke inside her.

Visually, Clay's boys were a good mix of him and Sasha. Tall and strong, with face-splitting grins and gleaming eyes. Heroic smiles that emphasized the sadness rising inside her.

With a lump in her throat, she skimmed through the last few months of Clay's life, finding photos of Clay and Stucker together, but strangely, no pictures of Sasha.

Were things less than rosy in the Young household?

Finally, finding nothing that could be described as unusual, Maggie powered down the phone and turned her attention to the packet marked **KEYS**.

The keys jangled as they spilled onto the table. Half a dozen jagged slices of metal attached to an electronic fob. Five keys that looked like they belonged to regular house locks, and one that didn't.

The exception was a long padlock key, with a red rubber cap covering its head.

Maggie took a closer look.

Printed in white on the front of the cap was the number 402, with the head of a cartoon beaver stamped into the reverse side.

"Bingo," she said.

Chapter Nineteen

FACTORY SETTINGS

Maggie rolled down the car window and took a photo of the tall billboard sprouting out of the roadside grass a few yards away. Sunlight running like liquid gold on its metallic edges.

HECTOR'S SELF-STORAGE

Then she exchanged her phone for the padlock key she'd logged out of Evidence, holding it up in her gloved fingers so that she could visually compare the cartoon beaver head on its reverse to the larger-than-life logo on the billboard.

The two images were identical.

Just as she'd thought, the key came from this storage facility.

She swung her gaze to the business premises itself, made up of a series of long, low buildings with beige walls and red roofs, set back from the street behind a wall and trees.

Not much had changed in the years since she had last been here. The facility in Oak Ridge had formed the scene of one of her first cases after joining Homicide Squad: a homeless man riddled with cancer had accessed an unlocked unit, crawling into the dark space to die. It had been the height of summer, with soaring temperatures, and Maggie had been called to investigate a week later, when the smell had gotten so bad that it had started to affect business. Until that day, she hadn't fully appreciated what heat, humidity, and time could do to a corpse.

Her gaze stopped on the big roller gate at the end of the short driveway leading in from the street. Tied to the bars with nylon rope, a sun-faded vinyl sign advertised AVAILABLE UNITS FROM AS LITTLE AS $50/MONTH.

She heard the sound of a vehicle pulling into the driveway behind where she had parked, and she got out of the sedan.

It was a sheriff's cruiser, with Loomis sitting in the passenger seat, his Wayfarers teetering on the tip of his nose.

"Thanks for the lift," he said to the deputy as he climbed out. He slammed the door, then loped toward Maggie as the cruiser reversed back out.

"What's up, Novak?" he said. "Been waiting long?"

"Ten minutes, tops."

In fact, almost an hour had passed since she'd called Loomis from the evidence facility on Thirty-Fifth Street. While it had taken him thirty minutes to get here from the Sheriff's Office on West Colonial, she had repacked Clay's effects and signed the padlock key out of Evidence, driving to the self-storage facility in Oak Ridge with minutes to spare.

On the way, Maggie had called Jasper Carmichael, placing him and the Hazardous Device Team on standby should the location turn out to be the place where Clay had built the bomb.

She handed Loomis a bulletproof vest from the trunk of the sedan. She was already wearing hers, tight enough to cut off circulation.

"Find anything interesting in Clay's locker?" she asked as they made their way to the gate.

"The usual stuff," he said, fastening the vest. "Including two full clips. But nothing extraordinary. Unless you count these." He got out his phone and pulled up a picture.

Maggie stopped to take a look. She cupped a hand over the screen and shielded her eyes against the afternoon sunshine. The image showed what appeared to be several sealed condom packets on a locker shelf.

"Are you thinking what I'm thinking?" he said.

"That, if nothing else, at least Clay believed in birth control?" She went up to the gate and pressed the buzzer. "To be perfectly honest, Loomis, I'm not surprised. The possibility of Clay having an affair had already crossed my mind. I found an anonymous number in his phone, as well as a whole series of text messages listing rendezvous times and meeting places."

Loomis blew out an expletive. "The old scoundrel."

"I can think of more appropriate nouns."

A clunking noise sounded as the lock mechanism disengaged. Maggie rolled the gate aside, just enough to allow them to slip through.

A rotund Hispanic man wearing a straw hat and an oversize bowling shirt came out of the office to meet them. Gold chains swinging from his neck.

"Welcome to Hector's Self-Storage," he announced. "I'm the manager. What can I do for you good folks from"—he peered at the white logos stenciled on their vests—"the Sheriff's Office?" All at once he didn't look quite as jovial.

"We'd like to take a look at one of your storage units," Maggie said.

"Sure thing, Officer. No problem. Soon as I see the warrant."

She held up the padlock key. "I don't need one. Just directions to unit 402."

The manager didn't protest any further. He pointed out the general location of the unit in question and then muttered something about disclaimers and lack of liability. Loomis told him they'd take it under advisement, and to give them some space.

Underfoot, the concrete was sun bleached and cracked. Red roll-up doors on either side, the paint touched up here and there with a slightly lighter hue. Above each closure, a small plate with a number engraved in it.

They arrived at a door marked 402. The blood-red paint on the corrugated metal was flaky and scratched, with patches of the aluminum peeping through.

Maggie handed Loomis a pair of vinyl gloves.

"Okay," he said. "What's the game plan here?"

"First and foremost," she said as she inspected the door, "we avoid blowing ourselves up."

"You don't say."

Maggie had voiced her concerns to Loomis over the phone before coming down here. Basically, if this self-storage facility did turn out to be the location of Clay's bomb factory, then they had to be mindful of further booby traps. They were working under the assumption that Clay had already set one explosive trap. His rigging another IED to detonate the second someone raised the roll-up door was a possibility they ignored at their peril.

Alternatively, the unit could just be full of old furniture and bric-a-brac collected by Clay and Sasha over the years, and the storage unit could be a dead end.

"We should've run it past Sasha," Loomis said.

"Too late for that now." Maggie studied the disc-shaped padlock looped through the latch. "If you'd rather retreat to a safe distance, now's the time."

"Over my dead body."

Maggie slid the key into the lock. The way she saw it, Clay couldn't booby-trap the door from the outside. Not after he'd pulled down the door. And there was only one way in and out.

She turned the key, and the clasp sprang open with a clunk.

"Heart just missed a beat," Loomis said.

Maggie unhooked the lock and handed it to him. "It's possible there could be some kind of trip wire attached to the door itself from the inside. Clay would've still needed enough room to get out himself after setting it. My thinking is, we should at least be able to lift the door enough to see if there's a trigger."

She dropped to her knees, hooking her gloved fingers under the bottom edge of the roll-up door. "Ready?"

"With you to the death, Novak."

She glanced up at him. "Really? You want to tempt fate like that right here, right now?"

"I'm just saying . . ."

Maggie raised the door to a foot above the ground, causing Loomis to flinch and step back.

"Careful," he warned. "I have a delicate constitution."

Maggie retrieved a flashlight from her pocket, then lay on her back on the hard concrete, lining up her eyes with the bottom edge of the door. "Okay," she said, peeping under. "Let's see what we have here."

The beam lit up the door's rippled inner skin, its silvery finish dulled and scuffed with years of use. Holding the flashlight level with her head, Maggie examined the metal tracks screwed to the doorframe on either side, checking for triggers.

"Looks clear," she said.

She could see no telltale wires, or anything physically attached to the roll-up door. She pushed with her heels until her head was far enough inside to allow her a clear view of where the roller mechanism was bolted to the roof above the door.

"Feedback?" Loomis said from outside.

"Can't see any wires," she said.

"What about deeper inside?"

Maggie rolled onto her side, straining her neck so that she could peer into the darkness beyond the door.

Daylight leaking under the door illuminated a wedge of poured cement stretching away from her. Maggie swept the flashlight across the dark. Its beam struck bare cinder-block walls, an AC vent blowing cool air into the unit, and then a trestle table standing against the back wall. Oblique shadows reaching for the roof as she moved the flashlight side to side.

"I can see a folding table at the back," she said. "Looks like it's been used as a workbench. Otherwise, the unit seems empty."

"Any signs of bomb-making equipment?"

Maggie focused the flashlight on the table. She could make out a few shapes on its surface, but from her perspective, it was hard to say exactly what the objects were.

She extracted herself from under the door, and Loomis helped her to her feet.

"What's the verdict?" he asked.

"I think we're good to go."

He flexed his gloved fingers. "So we're doing this?"

"We are."

"All right then. Do you want to stand back, just in case?"

"Nope."

"Sure?"

"Sure."

"Okay." He nodded. "Your funeral, Novak."

Maggie gave him a fake smile. "You say the sweetest things."

Loomis bent down. He curled his gloved fingers under the door's rim and hoisted it all the way up.

Unobstructed daylight flooded into the unit, throwing a long panel of light across the cement floor and up onto the back wall.

Maggie directed the flashlight at the objects on the workbench. "I can see pliers, cutters, a hacksaw, and what could be a reel of wire. Looks like we just found the bomb factory."

Loomis reached around the doorframe for the light switch.

Maggie grabbed his forearm. "Let's leave it off," she said, "just in case it's a trigger."

She saw his eyes grow wide.

Inside the unit, a fluorescent bulb crackled and spluttered into life on the ceiling.

"I pressed it already," he said. "No harm, no foul, I guess."

Then the light went out.

And Loomis reacted first. The flat of his hand came up and struck her on the sternum, near the top of her bulletproof vest, pushing her off balance.

The blow took Maggie by surprise. She grabbed for the doorframe as her feet went out from under her, but her fingers missed it by an inch. She twisted as she fell, realizing that Loomis was falling, too, in the opposite direction, his long arms wheeling as he threw himself backward. And she hit the ground on her butt, hard enough to jar her spine.

Inside the storage unit, the fluorescent light crackled again and came back on.

"Someone's jumpy," she said.

Loomis blinked at her. "It's the thought that counts, right?"

While Loomis called Carmichael, Maggie went in search of the facility manager. She found him pacing around outside the small site office, chewing on his fingernails.

"Bad news," she told him. "We're closing you down for the day."

He stopped in his tracks, his fleshy jaw dropping. "What? No. Seriously?"

"Seriously. Unit 402 is a crime scene."

"But—"

"No buts, sir. I need to see the rental contract. Right now."

He began to protest about breaches of confidentiality and data protection, then gave up when Maggie mentioned the words *possible links to terrorism*. Her words propelled him into the office, and he returned a few moments later looking sweaty, a bunch of paperwork in his hand.

"Here," he said, handing it over. "All three contracts."

Maggie frowned at the papers in her hand. "What's this? He rented *three* adjacent units?"

"Sure. All paid for in advance."

"Your cooperation is appreciated," Maggie said. "Now please lock the front gate. And don't go anywhere. I may need you to answer further questions."

The manager looked like he was going to vomit.

Maggie glanced through the paperwork as she made her way back to Loomis.

Three separate rental contracts, in which the small print essentially insulated the storage company against any affiliation with the renter and what they stored here. Probably, none of it able to hold water in a court of law. At the back of each contract she found the same handwritten details: the date of agreement, the amount paid in advance, a contact address, and a signature.

The trio of neighboring units had been rented at the end of October for a three-month period, with the rental fees paid up front, in cash. A total of $630.

On each contract, the signature was illegible.

But Maggie recognized the renter's address.

It was the Young residence on Wakulla Way.

Chapter Twenty

PROOF POSITIVE

"All clear," Jasper Carmichael announced as he pulled off the bombproof helmet. He ducked under the police tape. Like the rest of the law enforcement personnel gathered here, he wore a taut expression and a tactical vest, the only difference being Carmichael's armor was twice the thickness of everybody else's and came with a large upright collar to protect his neck. "We found tools and components, but no bombs."

"Do we know if more than one was made?" The question came from Smits.

Maggie had called her sergeant the second she'd shown Loomis the rental contracts, and Smits had arrived hot on the heels of Bomb Squad.

"Hard to say," Carmichael said. "We found a couple of one-pound powder kegs. Both empty. The weight looks about right for the single IED we saw yesterday. If he built another, I'd expect to see more empty kegs."

"Unless he threw them in the trash," Loomis said.

Carmichael's face seemed to creep up a little higher on his skull. "There's always that," he agreed. "We can never be 100 percent sure. But in my opinion, and that's what counts here, I believe we're looking at a solitary device."

Smits breathed an audible sigh of relief, an action shared among all those within earshot. "What about the two units on either side?"

"Again, both empty," Carmichael said.

"Do we know what he was doing with them?"

"He used them as exclusion zones," Maggie said. "Renters come and go around here at all hours of the day. My thinking is he didn't want any neighbors noticing what he was doing."

Smits nodded. "Okay. Sounds feasible." He rubbed his jaw. "This is good work. Well done, everyone." He patted Carmichael on the shoulder. Then he waved a hand at the team of CSIs grouped with their equipment bags about thirty yards away in the shade of the building. They had been waiting patiently for the last thirty minutes while the Hazardous Device Team swept the units. They cracked open their bags and began to suit up in white papery coveralls.

"I spoke with Detective Stucker on the way down here," Smits said as Carmichael left them to rejoin his team. "He says he doesn't know anything about Detective Young renting any units."

"Where is he?" Loomis asked. "Shouldn't he be here?"

"He's back in Titusville. On his own time. We can't force his participation. He has vacation days booked in." He looked at Maggie. "What's this about Detective Young having an affair?"

Maggie had briefly mentioned it on the phone. Now, she explained in full about the condoms Loomis had discovered in Clay's locker at the Sheriff's Office, and the clandestine text messages she had found on Clay's phone.

"An affair neatly explains both," she said. "I think we should consider telling Sasha."

Smits didn't look happy with her suggestion. Maggie thought he hadn't looked happy since she had seen him at his apartment yesterday morning.

Is that how we all look right now?

"The world has already been upended for Mrs. Young," he said. "I'm not sure right now's the best time to break the news that her suicidal and murderous husband was also cheating on her. Do you, honestly?"

Smits had a point, but Maggie knew that if this was about her and Steve, and he was the one fooling around behind her back, she would want to know, even if she was grieving. Who wouldn't?

"Besides," Smits continued, "even if he was having an affair, do we think it has a bearing on the case?"

Maggie watched the CSIs duck under the tape and make their way to the storage units. "Right now, I don't think we should rule anything out. For all we know, the affair might've ended badly for Clay, and it helped push him over the edge."

Smits nodded thoughtfully. "He couldn't go on living without her."

"Possibly. Plus," Maggie said, "cheating husbands confide in their mistresses all the time. If Clay did have issues with Andy, she might know what it is."

"In other words, you need to talk with her."

"Yes, sir."

Smits rubbed at the fine stubble on his jawline. "Do we have any idea who this mistress might be?"

"No. But I know someone who might."

"Sasha," Loomis said.

Smits rolled his eyes. "Wasn't I clear enough about that?"

"Crystal," Maggie said. "But women are intuitive. If there was an affair, I think there's a strong chance Sasha already knows about it. Not only that, she might've figured out who it is."

Maggie's phone rang. She excused herself to take the call. The caller ID read *Zee*—short for Robbie Zeedeman, the principal fire-arms analyst at the Orlando Crime Lab.

"Howzit?" he asked after she answered.

Regardless of the circumstances, this was Zeedeman's standard salutation. Born in Cape Town, Zee had a clipped South African accent and a proclivity toward laughing at all the wrong moments. No one knew if his inopportune laughter was the result of nerves or a weird sense of humor. Either way, it raised eyebrows.

"Hey, Zee," she said. "I'm good, thanks. Howzit yourself?"

"Enjoying oxygen," he said with a laugh. "We have things to discuss, Mags. When can I expect you?"

Maggie looked around her at the crime scene activity: the CSIs beginning to assess the storage unit; the Bomb Squad clearing out; Smits drifting away, speaking on his own phone. "I'm kind of busy right now."

"Trust me. You will not want to miss this."

"The results on Clay's sidearm?" Maggie was already aware that Zee was processing both the gun and the bullet casing collected at yesterday's crime scene.

"It's much more complicated than that," he said dismissively, as though the results were trivial. "Come and see me, Mags. And as if by magic, all will be revealed." He hung up before she could say otherwise.

Maggie saw Loomis looking questioningly at her.

"That was Zee," she said, going over. "He needs us at the Crime Lab."

"Problems with Clay's gun?"

"Maybe."

"You go," he said. "I've got this."

"You're sure?"

"Piece of cake. If we're finished before you get back, I'll catch a ride. Now get outta here, Novak. It's midafternoon, and daylight's burning."

Chapter Twenty-One

FULLY LOADED

The Florida Department of Law Enforcement building on Robinson Street, with its carpet-tiled hallways and its foam-tile ceilings, always reminded Maggie of a throwback to the 1980s. It had undergone a major technical refit a few years back, introducing state-of-the-art technology, but the old bones of the building still poked through.

Maggie parked the sedan on the street and made her way inside. She signed in at the Crime Lab reception desk and then navigated the maze of corridors to Ballistics, formally titled **FIREARMS**.

She found the emaciated figure of Robbie Zeedeman in his glass-walled office, sipping at a carton of fruit juice through a straw. Zee was in his midforties and looked like he hadn't eaten a nutritious meal his entire life. Bloodless skin draped over spindly bones, like a bedsheet on a drying rack. Zee didn't get out much, which was why he insisted on speaking with people in person.

"You came," he said, leaping to his feet.

"You summoned," she said.

He let out a high-pitched laugh. "If only I had such magnetic power over all women." He handed her a file folder from his desk. "The ballistics report on Detective Young's firearm."

Maggie glanced inside at the half dozen pages. "What am I looking for?"

He leaned against his desk, nursing his juice. "The three anomalies."

"You mean you're going to make me find them?"

He winked. "You're the detective."

While Zee sipped his drink and watched her with his sky-blue eyes, Maggie skimmed through the file. As expected, the report was a comprehensive breakdown of ballistic testing and slug analysis, containing five-syllable words and technical phrasing Maggie only ever read in one of Zee's reports. His complex style of writing made string theory seem like child's play.

"Clay used his service weapon," she noted.

"Correct."

"And the slug recovered from the roof of the car matches the shell casing recovered from the floor of the vehicle."

"Correct again. Keep reading."

She read some more, noting the type of bullet. "It was a hollow point."

"Which is odd, don't you think? I've seen Clay at the range many times. He was old school. He didn't care much for hollow heads."

In law enforcement, hollow points were both the recommended and the preferred type of ammunition. Although using them was not compulsory, most officers favored them because of their accuracy and their ability to stop a suspect dead in their tracks.

But some officers preferred traditional round-headed bullets, and Maggie also knew that Clay was one of them.

"Anomaly number one," Zee said a little too cheerfully. "Keep reading."

Maggie did, scanning through more technical information. At the bottom of the second page, she noticed the words *empty magazine*, and looked up. "There were no other bullets in the clip?"

"None," Zee said. "And congratulations, you found anomaly number two. Let me ask you a question, Mags. How often is it you fully empty the magazine in your Glock?"

"Aside from at the shooting range, or for cleaning, I suppose the answer is never."

"Exactly. I assume you fully reload it again after?"

"I do."

"Good. Because you never know when you'll need every one of those thirteen bullets. Right?"

"Right."

For the most part, in movies and on the TV, police characters were portrayed with a *shoot first, ask questions later* mentality. Gun-toting defenders of the peace, happy to empty one clip after the other in the name of justice.

Always, multiple spare magazines in their pockets.

Maggie had never fully unloaded her Glock in the line of duty. Not once in eighteen years. In reality, run-ins with criminals rarely ended in an exchange of bullets. And on the rare occasion when rounds were fired, normally no more than two shots on target were needed to neutralize the threat.

Shoot-outs at the O.K. Corral were the stuff of Hollywood.

Slurping juice, Zee pointed to the report in her hand. "Take note," he said. "The magazine in Detective Young's firearm was completely empty. According to the evidence inventory, no intact bullets were recovered from the crime scene."

"He only needed one to kill himself."

It was a dark and impactful thought, but Zee laughed.

"Yes," he said. "Great observation, Mags. But why did he take the time and the trouble to unload the remaining twelve bullets?

What was the point? And what did he do with them? It's strange behavior."

"Suicide is." Maggie thought about her search of the Young residence yesterday, and the absence of bullets in Clay's gun safe. Loomis had been more successful. He'd found two full clips in Clay's locker, each filled with regular 9 mm rounds, but no loose bullets, and definitely none that were hollow points.

"Anyway," Zee said, "that's the second mystery pinned down. Nice job. Now for the third . . ."

"Let me find it." Maggie turned more pages, scanning the notes as she did so. Halfway through, she came to the fingerprint analysis and an attached sheet containing a series of black-and-white images. Pictures of dusty prints on the black Parkerized surface of Clay's handgun. According to Zee's notes, he'd recovered three partials and part of a palm print on the grip, as well as one partial on the trigger. Maggie looked up. "Only four partial fingerprints?"

Zee smiled. "Weird, right? It's inconsistent with general usage." He pointed at the page of images. "Under normal circumstances, we should see random prints scattered all over the firearm—dozens in fact, especially on the slide."

To load the bullet into the chamber, Maggie knew that Clay would have needed to use his free hand to rack the slide. The action would have left smudged prints on both sides of the gun.

"But there aren't any," Zee said. "What you see here is the bare minimum number of prints produced by someone holding the gun and firing it." He demonstrated with an invisible gun. "Also, the magazine and the bullet casing both lack prints. Not a single one. In my opinion, it's all very weird. I rang Evidence. They confirmed no gloves were found at the scene."

Maggie waved the folder. "All this could be explained by Clay keeping his gun meticulously clean."

Zee took a sip of his juice. "Is that what your intuition tells you, Mags?"

"No."

"Exactly."

Maggie knew that for this setup to exist, Clay would have needed to empty the magazine and wipe the gun down, then load one bullet into the chamber—all before setting off to commit suicide. Zee was right. Even considering the fact that suicidal people sometimes behaved irrationally and erratically, it was odd behavior.

Unless there's more to Clay's death than we presently know, she thought. Something that went beyond a case of simple suicide.

She waved the report at Zee. "Can I get a copy?"

Zee smiled. "Take it. It's yours."

Chapter Twenty-Two

GREASEPAINT

Maggie's phone vibrated in her pocket as she drove south on Orange Avenue. She waited until she had slowed to a stop at the intersection with Michigan Street before taking it out and checking the screen. It was a text from the county's colorful medical examiner, Maury Elkin, his message informing her that he had completed the autopsy on Clayton Young.

Maggie's breathing quickened as she read his words.

She knew the postmortem would have been a difficult operation for Elkin to perform. Elkin was a hands-on ME. He insisted on close working relationships with all the homicide detectives who kept him in work. Whenever there was a special occasion to celebrate at the Sheriff's Office, he was the first to put his name on the list of attendees.

Not just to Clay's fellow detectives, but to Elkin as well, Clay's death was the equivalent of losing a member of the family, and Maggie couldn't begin to imagine the level of mind control that Elkin must have employed even to cut into Clay's chest, never mind remove his organs one by one for analysis.

For a moment she contemplated delaying the inevitable, postponing her visit to the District Nine Medical Examiner's Office until after the processing of the bomb factory was complete. That way she could take Loomis with her, perhaps distract herself with his gallows humor, using his fear of dead bodies to depressurize what she knew would be an extremely tense viewing for all.

But Maggie was protective of Loomis, in the same way that he looked out for her best interests. Even though there hadn't been an ounce of brotherly love between him and Clay for a long time, she couldn't put him through a trip to the morgue.

As the light changed, Maggie skipped lanes, going left through the intersection. Butterflies wheeled in her belly. Not the giddy vibrations of happy anticipation, but rather the ripping razor wire of dread.

She distracted herself with thoughts of Clay's timeline, visualizing the series of events that had led up to his death. For Clay to have built the bomb, Maggie knew he would have needed a clear mind. Not one polluted with thoughts of escapism. It jarred with the idea of suicide. He'd rented the self-storage units two months ago—eight whole weeks before meeting his end. During that time he'd been focused on the task at hand and acting methodically. Going about his business as usual, his work colleagues oblivious to his game plan. Then, from nowhere, he'd acted like a crazy person and killed himself. Just like that. No one around him even aware he'd been building a bomb in his spare time.

At least for the past two months, Clay had had the foresight and the lucidness to plan his own death and that of his colleague. How did that fit with someone whose mind must have been in a state of constant torture? Was it possible to reconcile the two?

Had building the bomb given him purpose? she wondered. Is that what had kept him sharp and in control right to the end?

While his outlook must have been grim, a "sense of purpose" explained his ability to function seemingly as normal. But it didn't explain Zee's ballistics findings. And Maggie wasn't a fan of anomalies.

Maggie parked the sedan outside the nondescript beige building on the corner of Bumby Avenue, and signed herself in at the counter. The receptionist informed her that Dr. Elkin was having a late lunch in the courtyard—a quiet leafy space squirreled away between the busy administration hub of Building One and the chilled autopsy suites of Building Two—and Maggie made her way there with her butterflies doing somersaults.

This is crazy, she told herself. *Relax. You've done this hundreds of times before.*

But this was the first time she'd ever come here because of a fallen colleague.

She found Elkin sitting on a metal bench under a sprawling tree, eating sushi from a Tupperware container. He had on olive-green chinos and a pink short-sleeved shirt open at the collar. He was in full shade, but his vitiligo made it appear like he was in dappled sunlight, one of his eyelids wilting in the afternoon heat.

"Maggie," he said with a smile when he saw her. "I didn't expect you to drop everything and come running right away." He began to stand, but Maggie waved him back down.

"Please," she said, "finish your lunch. I was passing by and figured it would be more efficient to do this now."

"You mean to get this over and done with."

She smiled. "In not so many words." She sat down next to him.

Several other city employees were scattered across the courtyard, sitting at the metal tables, recharging in the afternoon sunshine. Some chatting, some stooped in silence over their phones. It was a pleasant spot—if you ignored the fact that mere yards away dozens of dead bodies lay on gurneys in the huge coolers.

Elkin tipped the plastic container toward her. She shook her head.

"I agree," he said. "Sushi is just not the same without sake."

"I think you mean it's not the same without being cooked," she said with a slight chuckle.

Elkin put the lid on the container and stowed it next to him on the seat. "Are you good," he asked, "talking out here?"

"Sure. If you are. I wasn't sure if you needed me to see—"

"Not necessary," Elkin said, holding up a hand and halting her in her tracks. "It's not something anyone should see unless there's no other choice. Maybe once the mortician has fixed him up like new. Do you know if Sasha's having an open casket?"

Maggie shuddered at the thought.

"It's not exactly something that's come up in conversation," she admitted.

Maggie had seen the *before* and *after* photographs of people with nonsurvivable gunshot trauma to the head many times before. She knew the complex work entailed in reconstructing skulls, adding latex flesh and synthetic hair, installing fake eyeballs with iris colors to match the victim's originals. Mortal wounds masked, and none of it *real*. Rebuilding a person's exact facial features and bone structure from photographs took skill and a good eye for detail. Years of fine-tuning. Most morticians were artists in their own right, and they deserved much more credit than they were given.

When Sasha and her sons saw Clay again, rebuilt after blowing his brains out, they would have little idea of the work involved just to make him look *normal*.

As for Maggie, being privy to the *before* made the *after* seem totally unreal, no matter how skillful the restoration work.

There was always something added and something taken away. Skin too flawless. Hair too rich. Lips too full.

It was as though the victim had become perfect in death, visually a better version of themselves.

"Extreme and nonsurvivable brain trauma as the result of a self-inflicted gunshot wound," Elkin said, forcing her thoughts back into the moment.

She blinked. "The cause of death."

"Exacerbated by irreparable tissue damage leading to acute hypovolemia."

Now she gaped.

It wasn't quite a technical description of the bullet burrowing through Clay's brain, but it sufficed to illustrate the outcome.

"Of course," he continued, "it doesn't explain the cause of death, just the mechanism."

Maggie had been here a hundred times. She knew the drill.

In coroner speak, the *mechanism of death* wasn't always the same as the *cause of death*. Especially in cases of suicide, the actual *cause* was usually the psychological *reason* behind the unlawful killing, while the physical process of the death itself was referred to as the *mechanism*.

Maggie knew that the bullet had ended Clay's life, but it wasn't what had *killed* him.

She'd known this from the second she'd seen his slack and bloody face through the glass of the driver's window. Clay had jammed his sidearm under his chin and pulled the trigger for a reason she had yet to determine. It was this motive that was the cause of his death. Everything else was a matter of biology.

"Otherwise," Elkin said, "Clay was in good physical shape."

"You're right. He worked out and ate all the right things." Maggie's words sounded a little inane to her, and she wondered how they came across to Elkin.

In Sasha's own words, Clay had been a fitness freak, obsessed with his health. Maggie knew from conversations she'd had with him—his aim had been to live deep into old age, retiring in the next few years and taking a world cruise, sailing off into the sunset with Sasha. The irony of Clay being fanatical about staying in shape and then possibly ending his life prematurely was a cold slap in the face.

And all the effort now seemed a waste of time and energy.

Unless, she thought, *he didn't kill himself.*

"Did you find anything else?" she asked Elkin.

"Such as anything in particular?"

"Unusual readings in his blood work."

"If you mean did he have any underlying medical conditions . . ."

"I don't."

"In that case, I can only think that you're referring to the existence of illegal compounds. The answer is no, Maggie. I didn't find any unusual drug activity. The blood work was all clear."

Maggie felt only slightly relieved at the news; a lack of drugs confirmed to her that the anonymous text conversation she'd found on Clay's phone wasn't with a dealer—at least, not one supplying Clay for his personal use. It did, however, increase the likelihood that Clay had been having an affair behind Sasha's back.

Maggie wasn't sure which was worse.

"Did you find a suicide note?" Elkin asked.

"We didn't."

Maggie had looked, both at the Young residence during the search of the property and among the evidence collected at the crime scene. Aside from the ominous text message—that could be interpreted as a suicide note in itself—she had found nothing on his phone either.

"Odd," Elkin said. "No note—especially when Clay was programmed to write reports on a daily basis. It wasn't like he was ever short of something to say."

"No, you're right. Clay liked being heard; that's for sure. He always had to have the last word. But an absence of a note isn't that unusual. At least half of all suicides don't leave any kind of written explanation."

"And those they leave behind are left scratching their heads."

A blackbird landed on the end of the bench next to Elkin, its shiny black eyes examining the Tupperware container. Elkin clapped his hands, and it retreated into a nearby tree, squawking noisily.

"What about gunshot residue?" Maggie asked.

"Swabs confirmed the presence of GSR on the left hand, wrist, and forearm, as well as the clothing. All of it consistent with someone doing this." Elkin mimicked the action of putting a gun up under his chin and pulling the trigger.

Maggie's stomach bottomed out.

Elkin got to his feet and stretched. "Come on," he said. "Let's get you that autopsy report, and a strong cup of coffee. You look like you could do with a double shot."

Chapter Twenty-Three

BRIEF ENCOUNTER

On her way back to the bomb factory at Hector's Self-Storage, Maggie took another detour, this time dropping by the Walmart Supercenter on Orange Blossom Trail. She parked the sedan on the crosshatching outside the main doors and posted her police notice on the dash. Then she paused to take in the scene.

A day had passed since the incident had closed off public access to the store, putting it in the media spotlight, and yet it was business as usual, as though none of it had happened. The parking lot brimmed with customer vehicles, and the entranceway was a cattle market of people pushing shopping carts.

Everything ordinary, with no hint of yesterday's disruption. No leftover bits of police tape fluttering in the trees. No tense faces expecting the worst. Nothing to suggest that something terrible had happened here just hours earlier.

How many people had already trampled over Deputy Shaw's bloodstain without even noticing it?

Maggie hung her sunglasses from a shirt button and went inside, making a beeline for the back of the store. She'd called ahead, and Jeff Willoughby, the store manager, was waiting for her outside the security door leading to his office.

"You owe me a hundred grand," he said as he held out a USB flash drive to her.

She plucked it from his grasp. "For this?"

"In missed revenue," he said. "That's how much we lost here yesterday."

"Some people lost a whole lot more," she countered.

Willoughby smiled. "You're right. Put in that kind of context, I don't have a leg to stand on." He looked at her, his smile warm and genuine.

"I appreciate this," she said, waving the flash drive. She turned to leave, but Willoughby wasn't finished.

"Before you go," he said, "there's something you need to see."

Maggie rotated back on her heel. "Okay. But it'll have to be quick. I need to be someplace else, like an hour ago."

"I promise you won't be disappointed." Willoughby tapped an entry code into the door's keypad and pushed the door open. He went through, holding the door open for her.

Maggie accepted his invitation, then followed him down the hallway to his office.

Willoughby hadn't mentioned anything extra on the phone when she'd called on her way out of the ME's office, and she wondered what she might be walking into.

The computer monitor on Willoughby's desk had been spun around so that the screen was visible as they entered the office. Willoughby had set it up to display a freeze-frame image of Clay leaving the dairy section, a carton of milk in hand. It was a similar image to the one Maggie had seen yesterday morning: Clay in his white polo shirt that she had last seen drenched in blood.

A chill blew over her skin.

The time stamp on the image read 10:08:56 P.M., 31 DEC.

Willoughby rolled a swivel chair over to her. "Please," he said. "What did we miss?" she asked as she sat down.

Willoughby rolled up another chair beside hers and pressed a button on the computer keyboard. "You'll see," he said as the video resumed playing.

Maggie's breathing was shallow as she watched Clay move through the dairy section. After seeing him cold and dead, his brain sprayed across the ceiling of his car, the sight of him warm and alive and animated seemed to grate with reality, tightening the muscles around her diaphragm. This was the first time she'd reviewed this footage since finding him dead, and it was unnerving. She looked for telltale clues in his face, any kind of giveaways to indicate he was minutes away from following through on the biggest decision of his life.

No doubt about it, Clay's suicide was still raw, and this was like pouring salt in the wound.

Even so, she didn't even blink.

She watched as Clay came to a freestanding freezer, where he paused to glance inside before picking up his pace again and heading out of the dairy section. His actions seemed unaffected by what he knew must surely be coming, each step appearing light and carefree.

Maggie wondered how typical this behavior was in instances of suicide. As a psychotherapist, Steve would have an idea, or at least some industry statistics he could share. But she hadn't discussed Clay's death in detail with him yesterday evening at Nora's house. Still stunned by the day's events, she'd brushed over it when they were alone. But now that Clay's death had started to sink in properly, it would be interesting to hear Steve's professional take on the psychological slant.

That's if Clay really did commit suicide.

The concept had been gnawing away at her, increasingly, with each new irregularity she uncovered. Given the facts as they stood, it sounded counterintuitive. But her gut instinct was whispering that something wasn't quite genuine about the whole deal. Of course, she was the first to admit that the tangible evidence confirmed suicide, enough to satisfy a court of law on the verdict in any case. But it was just the small things that kept prickling Maggie's subconscious. Like the fact that Clay had used his going for milk as an excuse to be out of the family home when he killed himself, but then actually went ahead and bought the milk before performing the act. It was odd behavior in anyone's book.

If Clay wasn't responsible for his own death, then who was?

Right now, she couldn't explain why Clay had switched out his usual 9 mm round for a hollow point. She couldn't explain why he'd wiped the gun down. She couldn't explain why he'd sent the two urgent text messages to Stucker, knowing full well he was an hour's drive away in Titusville. She couldn't explain away any of the anomalies wholly within the context of suicide.

Willoughby cleared his throat, interrupting her train of thought. "To make life easier," he said, "I edited the feeds together."

Maggie blinked, coming back into the present. On screen, the point of view switched to a different camera, this one looking down at the grocery department from a central location. "You didn't have to do that."

"I had a free afternoon yesterday. Remember?"

This was a new viewing angle that Maggie hadn't seen before. Yesterday, under her instruction, Willoughby had skipped the feeds, jumping the playback from the grocery department to the parking lot and effectively bypassing the recording of Clay at the checkouts. The jump had also spun the feeds forward by almost half an hour.

At the time, Maggie had wondered aloud about the long interval between Clay picking up his milk and his leaving the store, and Willoughby had postulated that checkout operator levels, at a minimum on New Year's Eve, probably accounted for the delay.

Hours later, Willoughby had tracked Clay's progress through the recordings, editing the feeds together for Maggie's convenience, and the missing time was unfolding before her eyes.

Less than an inch tall on the screen, Clay was visible at the top of the picture, growing larger as he walked toward the camera along an aisle stocked with soda. His gait remained uncomplicated, as though he didn't have a care in the world.

He didn't look like a man who was revving up to blow his brains out.

"Here we go," Willoughby said.

Still approaching the camera, Clay began to cut through the clothing department.

As he did so, a figure in a gray hooded sweatshirt appeared in the bottom of the frame, their back to the camera. The hood was pulled up over a black baseball cap, so that the brim protruded like a beak.

Clay seemed in a world of his own, unaware that the person in the hoodie was on an intercept course. In fact, he didn't seem to notice the person blocking his path until the last second, almost colliding and trying to sidestep. Then a look of recognition descended over his face, and he stopped, clearly speaking with the newcomer.

Maggie sat forward. "Does this feed come with sound?"

"No such luck," Willoughby said. "But if you need someone to interpret, my sister's a trained lip-reader. I can recommend her."

"Good to know. Can you zoom in now that you've edited?"

"I believe so." Willoughby clicked some keys, and the image expanded so that Clay and the newcomer filled the screen. "There you go."

Maggie leaned closer to the monitor, studying the silent conversation for several seconds before saying, "It's a woman."

"How can you tell?"

She pointed. "The red nail polish is a dead giveaway."

Even though Maggie couldn't see the woman's face, she could deduce certain basic dimensions, such as she was at least a full head shorter than Clay, slimmer and with an overall smaller body frame. Dark skin on the backs of the hands, pointing to her being African American. Red nail polish, and what looked like a black ring on her right thumb. Definitely a woman.

"Out of interest," Willoughby said, "I tracked her through the store, before and after they talked. Not one camera caught a glimpse of her face."

"Did she buy anything?"

"No. And after they talk, she leaves right away. I tried to get a fix on which way she went once she was outside, but I lost her in the dark. What do you suppose they were talking about?"

"Whatever it was, it wasn't an easy conversation—that's for sure."

Maggie didn't need to hear the audio to pick up on the gist of what was being said in the recording; their body language spoke volumes. While Clay's expression revolved through several emotions, mostly heavyhearted, the woman in the hoodie expressed herself with sharp hand movements, sometimes gesticulating in Clay's face. Clearly, she was unhappy with something and wanted Clay to know about it.

Willoughby pointed at the screen. "By the way, this goes on for the next ten minutes. Would you like me to fast-forward to the interesting bit?"

"If you don't mind."

He leaned over and hit a key on the keyboard. The image returned to its normal size, and the playback sped up, Clay and the unknown woman talking at a hundred miles an hour. "Can I be blunt?" he said.

"Sure."

"Are you involved with someone?"

Maggie was momentarily taken aback by his question.

"I noticed you're not wearing a ring," he continued before she could answer. Then he laughed nervously. "Oh my God. Did I just say that? I have absolutely no idea what's come over me. I don't normally do this kind of thing."

"You mean like pry into a person's private life?"

"No." He flashed a smile, his whole face lighting up. "No. Not that at all. I mean"—he took a breath—"asking if I can take someone like you out for a drink sometime."

"Like . . . me?"

"You know? Someone who is higher up the food chain than I am."

Maggie made a face at Willoughby questioning his own self-esteem. She was used to male attention, both good and bad. In some ways, it came with the job. But it wasn't every day someone she barely knew asked her out for drinks. "For real, Jeff? You're asking me out on a date?"

"Sure." He looked slightly hopeful. "Why not? My mom always told me to shoot for the moon."

"Maybe she wanted you to work for NASA."

He laughed, this time with fewer nerves. "Maybe she did. That would've made her day, for sure." He reached over and tapped the keyboard again, dropping the playback to normal speed.

On screen, the conversation had become fiery. Lots of wide eyes and hand gestures. Clay seemed to be in the middle of saying something when the woman put her hand against his chest, silencing him.

"Jeff," Maggie said, "I'm flattered you asked. But if we're being blunt, you need to know I'm *with* someone." She almost said *engaged*. It was on the tip of her tongue, but her subconscious switched it out at the last moment.

If Willoughby was disappointed, he didn't show it. "Well, all I can say is he's a lucky guy. And if he ever fails you, my offer still stands." He pointed at the monitor. "Here it comes."

On screen, the unknown woman raised her hand again, this time swinging it at Clay's face and slapping him across the cheek, hard enough to knock his head to the side.

Then, while he was still recovering from the blow, she pushed him in the chest, forcing him to take a backward step. As he checked his balance, grabbing out at a nearby clothes rack, the woman headed out of view, leaving Clay looking stunned and slightly shaken.

Willoughby paused the playback. "That's it," he said. "Like I say, I tracked her all the way outside, but didn't see her get into any vehicle."

Maggie was still processing what she'd just seen. "And all this is on the flash drive?"

"Both the edited and the unabridged versions. The complete timelines from all feeds, between ten and eleven."

"Thanks, Jeff."

"You're very welcome, Maggie."

Willoughby escorted her back to the shop floor. "Look," he said as he held the security door open for her, "I didn't mean to freak you out back there. The last thing I want is to come across as a weirdo. I'm just a straitlaced guy who recognizes good people when he sees them. I'm sorry if I made you feel uncomfortable in any way. Believe me, asking strange women out on a date isn't what I normally do."

Maggie raised an eyebrow. "*Strange* women?"

209

He laughed. "There I go again."

Maggie smiled. "Thanks again for the footage, Jeff. I'll be in touch."

As she drove out of the Walmart parking lot, she called Loomis, bringing him up to speed on her discoveries. In return, he told her that the storage facility in Oak Ridge had been processed and released, and that everybody was clearing out. Now that the emergency rush to find the bomb factory was over, Smits had given his blessing for her and Loomis to finish their shift an hour early. It was to help compensate for their working New Year's Day, he'd said.

"I'm taking advantage and heading home," Loomis told her over the phone. "This dude needs to spend some quality time with his beautiful family. What about you, Novak?"

"I have plans," she said, knowing that none of them involved spending any quality time with anyone.

Chapter Twenty-Four

THE SPARK IN THE TINDERBOX

Mid-November, a couple of weeks after his renting the storage unit in Oak Ridge, he got a visit from the straw-hat-wearing facility manager.

Swapping out the unit's padlock with one of his own had put the manager's nose out of joint, and he was attempting to gain entry under the guise of what he called a *quality assurance check*.

Of course, they both knew it was an excuse to pry, for the manager to see why he was spending so much time inside the unit, sometimes for hours on end, sometimes late into the night.

What was he working on in there?

And that's why he'd taken suitable precautions to keep the manager out of his business, including substituting the padlock for one of his own. He had plans to switch it back when he was done, and he'd told the manager as much, but it didn't stop him from snooping.

"Don't think this is my choice," the manager called from outside the unit. "It's for fire safety compliance."

Sure.

The roll-up door was pulled halfway down, an afternoon breeze circulating the stale air. As always when he was inside the unit, his truck was backed almost right up to the open doorway, leaving a gap just wide enough to squeeze through, but far too narrow for the portly manager to get past. Not without surgery or a year of serious calorie counting.

"It's to satisfy city permits," the manager added. "Last thing I want is my license revoked."

He was nothing if not persistent.

Inside the unit, he put down the welding nozzle and tore the tinted goggles off his face, blinking as sweat ran into his eyes. "It doesn't say anything about a safety check in the rental contract." He wiped the sweat away with the back of his hand, smearing grime across his face, like jungle camouflage. "I'm busy here. You're inconveniencing me. Come back another time." He took out his phone and connected it wirelessly to the Bluetooth speaker on the workbench.

"Okay, amigo," the manager called. "You win. For now I'll give you your space. But I'll be back. You can count on that."

No doubt.

"Make sure you fetch the proper paperwork when you do," he called back. Then he turned up the volume on the phone until music boomed from the speaker and bounced off the walls.

The manager was a nuisance, but nothing he couldn't deal with. He'd handled far worse stresses over the last few months. Events that had driven a serrated knife deep into the heart of his family. Daily, he'd seen those he loved crippled with pain, unable to pull themselves out of their emotional quagmire. Crushing pressure squeezing every last drop of essence out of him until it had left him as insubstantial as a shadow.

But he hadn't let anyone see the damage. None of his work colleagues. No one in his family. He'd worn a granite mask, sunny on the outside while dark thunderstorms raged within.

Over time, hurt hardening into rage.

At first he'd taken his temper out on inanimate objects. Hammering six-inch nails into blocks of wood, beating them into the grain until the timber cracked and splintered. Pummeling the punching bag in his garage until the blood in his muscles turned to lead. Thinking that if he got the darkness out, the light would come back in.

He was wrong.

Lately, things had gotten worse at home. The atmosphere becoming grimmer, darker. Nothing he could do was good enough anymore. Everything that went wrong was his fault. And what was he going to do about it?

Then salvation had come from an unexpected source. A throwaway comment giving him fresh insight into a new purpose. One that would reset everything.

Personally, there would be a high price to pay. But wasn't that the way of the world these days?

Repositioning the goggles over his eyes, he picked up the welding nozzle again and went back to his work.

Chapter Twenty-Five

THE OTHER WOMAN

Maggie pulled open the fridge door and stared at the meager offerings on the shelves inside. She wasn't particularly hungry, and she couldn't remember the last time she had stocked up on groceries. She reached for the opened bottle of wine in the door and poured herself a glass of chilled grenache.

She had no idea why she had told Willoughby that she would *be in touch*.

What did it even mean?

Now that he had supplied her with the video surveillance footage, any further dealings between them were unnecessary. Purpose served. And yet, in closing, on departure, she had made a point of saying that she would contact him again in the future.

"Why did you even do that?" she asked herself as she returned the wine to the fridge. "Why would you go and leave him with a glimmer of hope?"

Was this her ego's way of fighting for its freedom?

Perhaps the true answer came from a place of fear, she realized— her response to Willoughby coming as a result of her rebellious subconscious striking out in the wake of Steve's marriage proposal. The thought of having her wings clipped, unthinkable.

Did the whole concept of wedlock scare her *that* much?

Maggie had witnessed her parents' sham of a marriage for years. Living through it as a bystander, watching from the sidelines, seeing the daily dysfunction, the antipathy, the creeping rot that had consumed the family from the inside out.

Maggie had never mentioned it to Steve, but she had always viewed matrimony as a compromise.

She knew it was a myopic viewpoint, but she couldn't deny that the idea of tying the knot instantly aroused a feeling of being *trapped*.

And claustrophobia was a real problem for Maggie.

As a child, she had once gotten stuck in a small space, fear of being unable to breathe blazing through her until rescue had arrived.

When Maggie thought about marriage, *that* was the feeling that engulfed her.

She carried her wine through to the den, the mauve mood lighting coming on automatically as she entered. It was after nine p.m., and, despite a bellyful of leftover takeout and a long soak in the tub, she was finding it difficult to unwind. She should have felt at least a modicum of closure—they'd found the place where the improvised explosive device had been made—but instead she'd rattled around at loose ends all evening, uneasy, with more questions than she had answers for.

She dropped into the corner of the couch and tucked her legs underneath her.

The den was a legacy from the days when the house had belonged to her parents. Originally her father's chaotic office—crammed with science books and dog-eared copies of *Sky & Telescope*—Maggie had painted the faux wood paneling and

215

converted the traditional professor's study into a cozy hideaway softened with plush furnishings. She often hid herself away in here when she needed a quiet place in which to think, or escape.

Her gaze caught the hibernating laptop on the small accent table next to her.

She needed to take a minute to reassess.

She couldn't carry on pussyfooting around the marriage issue with Steve as though it was a choice between imprisonment and independence. Who *thought* like that? She needed to grow up and make a commitment, one way or the other. Stop avoiding the subject and get *real*. Her being anything less than candid with Steve was unfair to them both, and it was shortsighted of her to base her entire future on a past that wasn't even hers. Just because her parents' marriage had failed, it didn't necessarily follow that hers would, too. Plus, she wasn't getting any younger. Time was passing her by, seemingly swifter with each passing year. Did she really want to miss out on what could be a happy union and the best years of her life?

Was *fear* a reason not to marry?

Was fear a reason *to* marry?

Maggie took a sip of the wine.

On reflection, her ping-ponging indecision all sounded a little bit pathetic.

Her phone chimed.

"Speak of the devil," she said as she checked the screen.

It was a text message from Steve:

At a bar in Atlanta with a bunch of like-minded conventioneers. Postseminar brainstorming session promises to last deep into the night. Already getting loud. Call you in AM. Stay safe.

He'd ended the message with a heart. Maggie typed back:

Have fun.

She ended her message with a smiley face, and sent it, staring at the phone for a full minute, waiting for Steve to text back, but he didn't.

Maggie nudged the laptop awake and narrowed her eyes as the screen brightened. She fished the flash drive from her pocket and slotted it into a USB port.

By the looks of it, Willoughby had copied half a dozen video files to the drive, recorded from various security cameras dotted across the Walmart property, and each containing an hour of raw footage from 10:00 p.m. through 11:00 p.m. on New Year's Eve.

She clicked on a file labeled Prime Edited Version, knowing that it was the video Willoughby had shown her earlier, the one containing the combination of camera angles he'd thoughtfully stitched together.

Willoughby had gone out of his way to make a good impression.

As the video began to play, Maggie expanded it to full screen and set the playback to ten times normal speed. Then she sat back, sipping wine as her thoughts rewound to the events of the afternoon.

After speaking with Loomis from the Walmart parking lot, Maggie had driven back to the Sheriff's Office on West Colonial Drive, where she had brought Smits up to date on her conversations with Elkin and Zeedeman.

Despite Maggie's growing reservations, their overall findings supported the suicide angle. But there were irregularities. Anomalies that Maggie was yet to explain, and part of her couldn't settle on the basic idea that Clay had left home on New Year's Eve armed with a single hollow point round, intent on taking his own life. It didn't make sense, and it nagged her—that she was missing something crucial. Something that was hiding just around the corner.

Was the woman Clay met in Walmart connected to his death?

Maggie had told Smits about her, and they'd debated for a while over her identity and any role she might have played in what had happened with Clay.

Was she Clay's mistress? Was his need to go for milk that night simply an excuse to meet her in secret?

If so, what went wrong? What were they arguing about?

More importantly, was it the deciding factor, the catalyst that had caused Clay to end his life then and there?

Maggie could still remember occasions in her early teenage years when her own mother had left the house at unusual times, or arrived home later than planned, never once connecting her odd behavior to her cheating on Maggie's father. Even though Maggie had been old enough to understand relationships, it was only years later, when her parents had announced their separation, that Maggie had put two and two together, recognizing that many of her mother's excuses had been nothing but obfuscations to hide her adultery.

Her mother had had affair after affair after affair, obscuring her infidelity with lies stacked on top of lies.

How many untruths had Clay used to cover up his deceit?

Around six o'clock, while Maggie had been writing up her report, Donna Krick had telephoned her from Digital Forensics regarding the cell phone numbers Maggie had asked her to run through the system: the last number that had called Clay that fateful night, and the number she'd found on the reverse of the Orbit Club business card. Despite a valiant effort, Krick had been unable to pinpoint a location or further information on either.

Her verdict: either the phones had been powered down, or the SIM cards had been removed.

Krick had explained that she could put red flags on the numbers, alerting her the second they logged back into the cellular network, but not without a court-issued warrant.

Maggie hadn't asked how Krick had managed to circumvent the phone company and a whole bunch of FCC regulations just to get the information she had done. Maggie knew Krick worked in conjunction with her counterparts at the FBI, but Maggie had never gone into the specifics of the relationship.

A good magician should never reveal her tricks.

On the laptop screen, Clay was deep in conversation with the mysterious woman, his body language defensive.

"Who are you?" Maggie wondered out loud.

Something was bugging her, and she couldn't pin it down.

She picked up her phone and called Loomis on FaceTime.

"Everything okay?" he asked as his image appeared on the screen. He was in his living room, a bottle of beer in his hand. The room was dimly lit, cozy.

"Sorry if I'm interrupting anything," she said.

"Sure. Abby's just this second scooted upstairs to see to one of the babies. Believe it or not, we're trying to have a date night." He turned his phone around so that Maggie could see a big flat-screen TV with the picture paused.

"Pretty Woman," she noted. "Abby's choice?"

"Mine," he said, coming back into the frame. "It's her favorite."

"You're such a romantic."

"We try to please. What's up, Novak?"

"We need to find out who she is. The woman in Walmart. Whether or not she's Clay's mistress, we need to know what part she played in Clay's life *and* his death. Apart from the cashier, it's likely she's the last person he spoke to before killing himself. We need to know what they were arguing about."

219

A smile broke out on Loomis's face. "Novak, don't you ever take a break?"

"I guess I don't have babies to keep me distracted."

He tipped the beer bottle at her. "Your choice, partner."

"Let's not go there."

"You brought it up. Besides, it'll happen. Watch this space. I'm speaking from experience here. Marriage is just the start."

Maggie made a face. "I'm too old for kids."

"That's what I said. Look at me now. Couldn't be happier."

"Anyway," Maggie said, keen to steer the conversation back on track, "this woman, I'm thinking if she is Clay's trigger, it's all the more reason we need to speak with Sasha as soon as possible. See if she knows who she is."

Loomis's smile vanished. "Wait a minute, Novak. You do remember Smits banning us from broaching the subject with Sasha, right? As far as he's concerned, it's a danger zone we enter at our own risk."

"Smits is wrong. I agree; it's noble of him to want to protect Sasha. I get that. But he isn't doing us or her any favors. Besides, I've had a feeling right from the start that Sasha knows more than she's saying. If you ask me, I think she knows all about Clay's affair. And I think she knows who this other woman is. I've decided. First thing tomorrow, I'm going to talk with her."

Maggie saw Loomis look off to the side.

"Abby's coming down the stairs," he said. "Sounds like this date night is back on." His gaze swung back to the phone. "Time to go, Novak. Anything else?"

"Nope."

"In that case, please don't call me again tonight unless the world's about to end."

Smiling, Maggie disconnected the call.

The playback on the laptop had reached the point where Clay was outside the store, his blurry image skittering through the pools of lamplight toward his red Sentra. She saw him open the driver's door and disappear inside.

She tapped the touch pad, dropping the playback to normal speed.

Her heart was suddenly thudding against her ribs.

This was the first time she'd reviewed this part of the footage since first seeing it yesterday morning, she realized, and the knowledge of what was to come had goose bumps breaking out on her arms.

The time stamp in the corner read 10:37:01 P.M., 31 DEC.

Maggie drained her wine, then swapped the empty glass for the laptop so that she had a better view of Clay's car. Then she peered closer, trying to see any real detail in the car itself.

The driver's window was smaller than her littlest fingernail and as black as night. She used pinch-to-zoom to enlarge the image, but the magnification increased the overall blurriness as well, the weak ambient lighting in the shot and the car's distance from the camera combining to make proper detail impossible. If she hoped to see Clay through the glass, she was mistaken. She couldn't even make out the shape of anyone inside the vehicle, never mind pick up any movement. But it didn't stop her eyes from searching for even the smallest glimpse of Clay's last movements, no matter how fleeting.

She resumed the playback at ten times speed, one eye on the time elapsing in the corner of the image.

Eight minutes from this point, she knew, Clay would shoot himself fatally in the head.

Her breath caught in her throat at the thought of it.

Watching the video a second time around, knowing the inevitable outcome, was macabre. It reminded Maggie of certain kinds of evidence footage: principally, dashcam recordings of traffic

221

accidents in which innocent-looking situations had turned into bloodbaths in the blink of an eye. It was unsettling, and she wanted to reach out and close the screen. But as much as it repelled her, she was on the edge of her seat, hooked, her heart rate speeding up as the fatal moment approached.

As the time stamp reached exactly 10:45:00 P.M., Maggie touched the keyboard, reducing the playback speed to normal again.

Her skin crawled. She knew what was about to happen at any second. She was expecting it, psyched up for it, prepared. But when the car's windows briefly turned fuzzy white, it still startled her for a second time, making her recoil from the screen.

With her heart racing, she paused the video. Then she took a deep breath before rewinding it by a few seconds, pausing it again at the precise moment in which the Sentra's windows lit up—the last second of Clay's life.

The time stamp read 10:45:14 P.M., 31 DEC.

Maggie stared at the image of the Nissan Sentra in the middle of the picture, a cold breath moving across her skin.

Then something caught her eye, and curiosity drew her even closer.

She hadn't noticed it when she'd first watched this footage in Willoughby's office. But now that the video was paused and zoomed in, she could just make out an indistinct shape in the enlarged driver's window. A slightly darker blur, highlighted in the muzzle flash. And she realized with horror that it had to be the ghostly image of Clay's face as the bullet burst through his brain.

Much to her frustration, Maggie couldn't sleep. It was a sapping pattern that repeated itself whenever things preyed on her mind.

Essentially, each time she began to nod off, a sudden revelatory thought would come crashing into her mind, knocking her wide awake again.

According to the digital alarm clock on the nightstand, it was a few minutes after one in the morning.

Maggie had been tossing and turning for the last couple of hours, stewing over everything she knew about Clay and Sasha and the whole big mess of things that his death had churned up.

She envied people who could switch off and sleep soundlessly for eight hours straight. She couldn't remember the last time she'd slept all the way through to her wake-up alarm. Maybe in her teens? A long time ago, at any rate.

Steve said that sleepless nights were a byproduct of her job, and that he could teach her techniques she could use to train her mind to power down after dark. But Maggie did a lot of her intuitive thinking between the sheets, even figuring out critical case scenarios, and if it meant cracking a case, the occasional bout of insomnia was an acceptable trade-off.

She gave up and got out of bed, suddenly compelled to watch the entire Walmart surveillance footage from start to finish. It occurred to her that she hadn't seen Clay arrive at the store, or if anyone had approached the car after he'd pulled the trigger, drawn by the sound of the gunshot or the muzzle flash.

She started to get dressed, then paused as a white light lanced into the bedroom, slicing through the blinds.

Curious, she padded over to the window and peeped out.

The cul-de-sac was asleep, the bright light coming from a car as it reversed into Nick Stavanger's driveway across the street. She saw Nick emerge from the passenger seat, waving at the driver as he shut the car door.

Does Nick know the outcome of Steve's proposal the other night? she wondered.

223

She recalled him being there at the rooftop party right before she'd gotten the phone call from Sasha, but not if he was still within earshot when Steve had dropped his bombshell. Nick was the neighborhood night owl, but the title didn't simply refer to his habit of staying up late. Both his eyesight and his hearing were impeccable. If anyone had picked up on her reaction to Steve's question and recorded it to memory, it would have been Nick.

Across the street, the car pulled out of the driveway, its headlights momentarily dazzling her. Maggie glanced away, and when she looked back, she realized Nick was looking directly at her.

Maggie let the blinds snap back in place, leaving a kink. Automatically, she withdrew from the window, even though she was pretty sure he couldn't see her standing here with nothing on in the dark. Not that it would mean anything if he did see her nude; Nick was about as sexually interested in her as she was in him.

Through the kink in the blinds, she saw him start to cross the street toward her house.

She pulled on leggings and a tank top and made her way downstairs.

"Been somewhere nice?" she asked as she opened the front door.

Nick wore a dark five-o'clock shadow, jeans, and a black velvet jacket over a white Scissor Sisters T-shirt.

"Cinema," he said, coming to a stop a yard from the door.

"Anything worth watching?"

"Nope." He fished a pack of cigarettes from his jacket pocket and shook one out. "I saw you peeping and wanted to make sure you weren't being held hostage."

Maggie smiled. "My knight in shining armor."

He lit the cigarette. "Sarcasm doesn't suit you, Maggie." He sucked hard and blew a cloud of smoke into the night.

"Those things will kill you," Maggie said.

"Duly noted. Anyway, about what happened with your colleague, I just want you to know I'm sorry, Maggie. Suicide's a nasty business. Despite what I wrote about him, I liked the guy. The city is a little less safe without him around."

"That's for sure."

"If you need a shoulder to get teary on . . ."

"I'll be sure to call Steve."

"Speaking of which, how is lover boy?"

"He proposed."

Nick didn't look surprised in the slightest.

"The other night," Maggie said, feeling the need to explain. "At the party. On the stroke of midnight."

"How vanilla."

"Now who's being sarcastic?"

"I'll give him credit for one thing, though. The guy has great timing. Not like me. My timing is lousy. It isn't even as good as Detective Young's. Now *his* timing couldn't be more perfect if he'd planned it that way."

Maggie stared at Nick, a sudden thought occurring to her.

"What?" he said. "You look like you've seen a ghost."

"Nick, I have to go. I need to check something out."

"Okay." He pointed at her with the two fingers holding the cigarette. "But don't forget our exclusivity deal, Detective. I don't just love you because you're you. We're friends with benefits, remember?"

Maggie told Nick to scram, then locked the front door and hurried through to the den.

Her laptop was still on the small accent table, together with her cell phone. She opened the computer's lid, and the screen lit up, throwing shadows around the room. The video was still paused at the point where she'd left it: Clay's ghostly image illuminated in the muzzle flash.

The time stamp reported Clay's exact time of death as 10:45:26 P.M., 31 DEC.

But something was *wrong*.

And Maggie realized it was the *timing* that had been bugging her all evening.

She picked up her phone and opened the Photos app, scrolling through the batch of recent crime scene pictures until she came to the photo she'd taken of the last two text messages on Clay's phone, including the words *they know*.

Both messages had been sent within seconds of each other, at approximately 10:48 p.m.

Maggie scooted her gaze back at the laptop, to the time stamp displaying Clay's exact time of death at 10:45:26 p.m.

At least two-and-a-half minutes of difference.

The heat lingering inside Maggie seemed to intensify, a strange sense of *I told you so* settling over her.

With her gaze glued to the screen, she dialed Willoughby's number, letting it ring and ring until he picked up.

"Hello?" He sounded sleepy. "Maggie? Is that you?"

"Quick question," she said. "The time stamp on these video recordings you gave me. How accurate are they?"

"You do know it's the middle of the night, right?"

"Jeff, please focus. This is important."

She heard him stifle a yawn. "All right. Here's how it works. The machines time sync each morning with the internet. They couldn't be any more accurate." He started to ask her why she needed to know, but Maggie thanked him and ended the call before he managed to get it out.

The heat in her chest was making her heart skip.

She compared both time stamps again, knowing that what she saw was impossible.

Unless . . .

Hardly breathing, she resumed the playback on the laptop, her lungs burning as she stared at the shadowy image of Clay's red Sentra. Seconds creeping into minutes.

She thought about Clay slumped behind the darkened glass, his head tipped back, blood oozing from the hole under his jaw while bits of brain matter dripped from the roof. She thought about him sitting there all night, his flesh cooling, his muscles hardening, his skin warming as sunlight poured through the windshield, drying his blood and turning the car into an oven. She thought about the pipe bomb primed and waiting for her to open the driver's door. A controlled explosion that had peppered the watching crowd with lethal shrapnel, pulverizing Captain Corrigan's eyeball and ripping a fatal hole in Deputy Shaw's femoral artery.

The time stamp read 10:48:01 P.M., 31 DEC.

Her throat was as dry as a tinderbox.

She leaned closer to the screen, her heart banging wildly as she tried to see detail through the car's dark windows, hoping to glimpse something to explain the two-and-a-half minute time discrepancy.

But even on full magnification, there was nothing to see.

An uneventful minute passed, followed by another, and then another. No noticeable change in the scene whatsoever. It was as though she were staring at a freeze-frame.

At 10:54 p.m., the progress bar at the bottom of the video had almost reached its limit.

Could Clay's phone be set to the wrong time? she wondered.

What was she missing?

Then, as the time stamp changed to 10:55:00 p.m., the unbelievable happened, and Maggie's heart almost stopped beating altogether.

The Sentra's rear door opened, and somebody climbed out.

Chapter Twenty-Six

BOMB IN A BAG

Maggie's lungs burned, and she remembered to breathe, sucking in air through her teeth and quelling the flames. In the same instant, she reached out and hit the pause button on the laptop, freezing the image of the person exiting the vehicle.

She'd been right all along to question the suicide.

Clay hadn't been alone in his dark place when he'd killed himself. This person had been sitting in the back seat all the while.

Maggie was shocked, but in no way was she surprised. She had suspected for some time now that there was more to Clay's apparent suicide than met the eye. A number of inconsistencies conflicting with the presented evidence. And this new discovery confirmed her suspicions.

But the sight didn't fill her with celebratory feelings, only a cold kind of sickliness, deep in her core.

The figure looked like that of a man, dressed in black. Gloves, pants, and a hooded sweatshirt with the hood pulled up over his head, his blurry face deathly white.

Unnaturally white, she thought.

Maggie peered closer.

He was wearing a mask, she realized. By the looks of it, a white plastic hockey mask—the kind with eye sockets and breath holes that teenagers sometimes used to scare their friends on Halloween.

She let the video play for another second or two before pausing it again, this time with the man in the mask glancing toward the camera as he closed the car door. There was something tucked under his arm, she noted. It looked like a folded bag of some sort. She took a screen grab and then restarted the video, watching as he disappeared in the darkness, gone from sight within seconds.

Maggie picked up her phone to call Loomis, then saw the time and changed her mind.

Although this new turn of events was a game changer, the news of it would have to wait until the rest of the world was awake.

In the meantime, nothing was stopping her from poring over every second of surveillance footage.

Maggie minimized the video and clicked on another of the files Willoughby had copied for her, this one labeled Unedited Parking Lot Feed.

She let it play from the beginning, from 10:00 p.m., curious to see at what point the killer had entered Clay's car. Approximately five minutes in, she saw the Sentra appear at the top of the image and park. Seconds later, the headlights went off, and Clay climbed out. He looked relaxed, his gait easy. She watched him stroll toward the camera, his image growing bigger in the frame as he made his way into the store. A minute later she detected movement near the Sentra, and she used pinch-to-zoom to magnify the scene.

Then she paused the video, squinting at the screen and trying to smooth out the graininess of the image.

His face was hidden behind the hockey mask, and in his gloved hand, he held a black sports duffel bag.

And in the duffel bag, Maggie knew, there was a pipe bomb.

Clay hadn't built the IED.

With a shaky finger, she took a screen grab.

Chapter Twenty-Seven

THE OTHER MAN

Forget everything we thought we knew," Maggie said. "We were dead wrong. Clay didn't commit suicide. He was *murdered*."

Her words cut through the silence in Smits's office like sniper bullets, each one hitting their target and deadening the air.

Together with Loomis, Maggie was sitting at Smits's desk, her brain in overdrive after one too many strong coffees, her thoughts pin sharp despite the missed sleep.

Following her discovery of the masked man inside Clay's car, she'd spent a good deal of the night going through each video file in fine detail, taking screenshots. At around four in the morning, she'd managed a miraculous couple of hours' sleep, slumped on the couch in the den. But the sleep had been plagued with the same nightmare as the night before: Clay sitting in her Mustang, staring at her as the car filled with bright-red blood.

Just before sunrise, Maggie had given up on sleep altogether and gone for her daily run, hoping to burn off some of her excess energy. But the metronomic beat of her footfalls had brought even greater clarity, focusing her to the point that her mind seemed ablaze.

A dilemma existed.

Clay had killed himself. The autopsy results and the GSR on his left hand confirmed he'd pulled the trigger. But Maggie was now certain he hadn't gone out of the house that night with the intention of committing suicide.

Someone else was involved in Clay's death.

Someone who had probably forced his hand.

And *that* was the real shocker.

On its own, the possibility that her colleague hadn't willfully ended his life completely turned the investigation on its head. Add to that the probability that he hadn't planted the bomb, either, and the whole case wasn't just upended; it was blown wide open. Everything she'd learned about the incident, everything she assumed to know, all of it was now scattered to the four winds.

And Maggie was on fire.

"Tell me again," Smits said. "What do we know about this masked man with absolute certainty?"

Like Maggie, he was still trying to wrap his head around the new information that had catapulted the investigation back to square one.

"For starters," she said, "the suspect is male."

Maggie drew Smits's attention back to the 8 x 10 color photograph she'd placed on his desk a few moments ago. It was one of the screenshots she'd taken last night, from the unedited Walmart video feeds.

The time stamp read 10:07:39 P.M., 31 DEC, a minute *after* Clay had parked and gone into the store.

The image showed the unknown subject standing outside the Sentra, about to open the rear passenger door and climb inside.

Smits put his readers on and peered at the photo.

"Using the Sentra's dimensions as comparison," she said, "I put his height at around six foot. Medium build. Healthy posture.

He's carrying the bag in his right hand, so the likelihood is he's right handed."

"And at this point, the bomb is in the bag?"

"Yes, sir. There's a ten-minute delay between the muzzle flash and the killer exiting the vehicle. In that time, I believe he sent those two text messages to Andy's phone and then planted the bomb."

Smits swore under his breath. "Just when things couldn't get any worse. How did we miss this?"

"Simple," Maggie said. "We were distracted. The killer set the scene to make us believe Clay had acted alone. None of the evidence indicated a second-party involvement. Granted, there's a number of small anomalies. But everything we have that's concrete confirms the suicide angle. Until now."

"In other words, we were duped."

"That's one way of putting it," Loomis said. "The thing is, Sarge, if not for Novak finding this, we'd still be in the dark and chasing shadows. Credit where credit's due."

Smits looked like he was going to throw Loomis out. "You know, I'm surprised at the two of you. This is lazy police work. Right here. These recordings should've been thoroughly checked."

Loomis went to speak again, but Maggie cut him off. "You're right," she said. "It's my fault. I messed up. I saw the muzzle flash, and I went off like a rocket. If you recall, at that point in time, we still had Clay down as missing. My only reason to view the Walmart security footage at all was to confirm he'd visited the store. There was no urgency to check the rest of the recording beyond the muzzle flash. It was my mistake. Willoughby—"

"Willoughby?"

"The store manager. When I arrived there, he brought up the internal feed showing Clay already in the dairy section. I asked him to jump the feed to the moment Clay returned to his vehicle. Then

233

I saw the muzzle flash and had no reason to look any further. But you're right. I should've been more thorough."

"I suppose it's been hard on all of us," Smits said. "But if the press get hold of this . . ." His complexion paled at the thought.

"They won't," Maggie said. "Right now the three of us are the only ones who know. We still have time to get in front of this. Fix it. But we need to act fast."

Smits jabbed a finger on the photograph. "Where was Detective Young when this was happening?"

"Inside the store. See the time stamp in the corner? The suspect got in Clay's vehicle one minute after Clay got out."

"He lay in wait for him?"

"Yes, sir."

"Do we know where he came from?"

"It was one of the first things I looked for. But the camera range is limited, and it's just too dark. Honestly, the lighting in the parking lot leaves a lot to be desired. It's possible he came from another vehicle parked somewhere else. But it's equally possible he arrived there on foot. I'm hoping Digital Forensics might be able to perform a miracle and pull out more information."

"You've sent them the files?"

"Yes, sir. Marked *urgent*. But you know how this goes. It could be days before they come back with anything."

Smits leaned back in his chair, as though distancing himself from the glossies on his desk. "You realize this is a complete mess?"

"I do, sir."

He laced his fingers together, going silent for a moment as he tapped them against his chin. "Okay," he said at last. "Let's be positive here and move forward. You've had all night to think about this. What's your new theory?"

Maggie drew a deep breath. "This person"—she motioned to the masked man in the picture on his desk—"the true *killer*, he planned this in advance. The suicide, the bomb. In all likelihood, he probably watched Clay for some time, noting his routines and working out the best time to get to him."

"When he was on his own."

"Yes. Both Clay's work schedule and his homelife kept him busy. For Clay, the Walmart parking lot was probably as alone as he ever was. Plus, as I've pointed out, the lighting there is pretty dire at night."

"And there's no direct line of sight to the Trail."

"No, sir. Or, to any of the other businesses close by for that matter. This kind of location is just about as isolated as it gets in the city."

"The perfect place."

Maggie nodded. "So my thinking is, the killer planned to attack Clay in that location. Maybe not that night. But he was prepared for it. If it didn't happen New Year's Eve, then maybe one night this week, or next. Sasha said Clay's late-night trips to the store were a regular occurrence. From observation, the killer would've known that. Willoughby said that customer foot traffic was lighter that evening because of the holiday. That meant fewer potential witnesses. I'm guessing the killer saw his moment and pounced."

"He shot Detective Young and faked the suicide."

"Not quite."

Smits's eyes narrowed. "Come again?"

"Bear with me, and all will become clear." Maggie placed a printout on the desk in front of him. "According to Zee's ballistics report, Clay's fingerprints were the only ones found on the gun."

"Easy," Smits said without even glancing at the report. "You can see from the video the suspect wore gloves."

Maggie placed another 8 x 10 on the desk, this one showing a magnified view of the bullet casing and the mushroomed slug recovered from Clay's vehicle. "Plus, there was only one bullet in the gun."

"A hollow point. Yes, I see that. What's your point?"

"Like the rest of us, Clay carried his sidearm with him wherever he went, and he kept it fully loaded at all times. As you know, the magazine holds thirteen bullets. We didn't find any stray rounds anywhere in the car, or at Clay's home address."

"What about his locker?"

"Two full clips," Loomis said. "But no loose bullets."

Smits's eyes were on Maggie. "Detective, I'm not sure I see where you're going with this."

"The bullets Loomis found in Clay's locker were all round heads. Clay was killed with a hollow point. We haven't found any other hollow points anywhere. I think the killer switched them out, substituting the regular nine mils for the single hollow point."

"Why?"

"It gets the job done."

It was rare, Maggie knew, but with regular rounds, people sometimes survived gunshot wounds to the head. The skull was thicker in certain parts, and scalp muscles could tangle up a glancing shot. A hollow point bloomed on impact, causing significantly more tissue damage. The chance of someone surviving a close-range encounter with a hollow point was probably zero.

Smits spread his hands. "So Detective Young didn't kill himself after all."

"Well," Maggie said, "that's not technically true either. And this is what I'm getting to. Although I have no doubt the killer is responsible for Clay's death, I don't think he physically held the gun under Clay's chin and pulled the trigger." She pointed at the autopsy report on his desk. "According to Elkin, the presence of GSR on Clay's left hand proves he fired the gun."

"Plus," Loomis said, "the logistics are all wrong. Allow me to demonstrate." Noisily, he got to his feet and dragged his chair behind Maggie's. "Pretend I'm the killer sitting in the back seat." He made the shape of a gun with the fingers of his left hand and dropped his arm over Maggie's left shoulder. "Be nice," he said to her.

"Be gentle then," she replied.

Loomis pressed two fingertips to the soft tissue under her jawbone. "See the body positions?" he said to Smits. "Even though I'm using my left hand, the angle places my head slightly higher than hers. Plus, I have to lean over quite a bit to see what I'm doing. My head ends up exactly where the bullet exited Clay's skull."

Smits nodded. "In other words, the killer would've shot himself in the face."

Loomis pulled the imaginary trigger and threw his head backward.

Smits rolled his eyes at Loomis's theatrics and told him to sit. "Back over there," he said. "Where I can keep an eye on you."

Looking sheepish, Loomis returned his chair to its original position and sat down again.

"At the very least," Maggie said, "the killer would've been hit by blood spatter. You've seen the crime scene photos, Sarge. There's a fine spray all over the inside roof of the car and no void in the spatter pattern. I believe the killer coerced Clay into killing himself."

Last night, after watching all the surveillance videos, Maggie had come to the conclusion that whatever the killer had used to convince Clay to take his own life, it had to be highly explosive. Not just a case of *your world will end if you don't*, but rather *your whole family's world will end if you don't*.

Smits was looking baffled. "How does something like that happen?"

"I'd imagine, not very easily. Coercion only works if the victim has something to hide. We know Clay had gambling debts. And there's the possibility of an affair. But I'm thinking, for him to go along with this, there has to be a real nasty skeleton in his closet. Something he couldn't live with if it came to light."

"Any ideas what?"

"Not yet. But I intend to find out." She would make it her mission. Not just to wrap the case up neatly, but also for Sasha's sake. Sasha needed to know that her husband had taken his life under extreme duress, probably to save her and his sons from public humiliation. She had a right to know.

Smits picked up one of the photographs from his desk and studied it. "What I don't get is why Detective Young didn't use the gun on the suspect."

"That can be explained away with an accomplice," Loomis said. "Someone with orders to hurt Clay's family if he didn't play ball."

"Fear is the best kind of insurance policy," Maggie said.

Smits seemed to deliberate on their comments for a few seconds, lacing his fingers together and resting his chin on them. "Somebody went through a whole bunch of trouble to make us think this was suicide. The question is why?"

"Because suicide stops us looking for a killer," Maggie said. "And the killer walks away scot free. It was a complex plan, but it had to be. For the killer to get away with it, we had to buy it hook, line, and sinker. We had to believe that Clay wanted to kill himself as well as Andy. And we did, for a while. We bought it. I'm telling you now, this person knew how to play us. Whoever it is in that hockey mask, he has a good grasp of police procedures. He knew exactly what to do to throw us off his scent and send us in the wrong direction."

"You think this is an inside job?"

"Right now I think anything's possible. I'm certainly not dismissing it."

"What about motive?"

"Off the bat," Maggie said. "Money. We know Clay had huge gambling debts. He also had life insurance. Private cover as well as county death benefit. He owed Andy forty grand."

A look of incredulity descended over Smits's face, but not because of the enormity of the figure. "You've got to be kidding me."

"Sarge, I wish I was. But Andy's been acting cagey since the get-go. When we spoke with him in Titusville, he didn't offer up where he was on New Year's Eve. In fact, he went out of his way to avoid the subject, saying he was busy and it was none of our business. I'd like to interview him on record. Rule him either in or out of the investigation. One way or another, we need to know if Andy Stucker is the man in the mask."

Chapter Twenty-Eight

BRICK WALL

Interrogating a colleague and fellow homicide detective in connection with the murder of another officer wasn't simply a case of securing Smits's consent. Due to the rank structure within the Sheriff's Office, permission for any such request had to be sought from a line commander of at least two ranks above the officer to be questioned. That meant speaking with Smits's immediate superior, Lieutenant Laremy Dunbar, and Maggie had reservations about it right from the start. Not only was Dunbar the brother of Sasha Young and therefore close to Clay, but he and Stucker were as thick as thieves, with Dunbar being the third wheel in Stucker's and Young's adventures outside the Sheriff's Office. Some degree of bias was inevitable.

It was also proving to be an obstacle, with Dunbar blocking every attempt she and Smits made to move forward with interrogating Stucker.

"It's as simple as this," Maggie said to Dunbar. "Andy has a duty of responsibility to eliminate himself from the investigation. At the very least, he needs to provide an alibi." She'd spent the last few minutes saying more or less the same thing in various different ways, each attempt rejected with equal amounts of negativity and vigorous hand waving from Dunbar. The air in his office wasn't exactly blue, but it was electrified. "It's incumbent on him to step up and cooperate. We need to bring him in."

"Never going to happen," Dunbar said, reinforcing his words with hand gestures. "Not today. Not tomorrow. Not any other day. Andy is innocent."

It had been a sight to see: Dunbar collapsing into his chair with shock as Maggie had explained her latest theory—that Clay's suicide had been coerced and that they were now looking for a killer. A killer who could be one of their own.

"Let's not forget he has experience with explosives," Smits said.

Inasmuch as Maggie had been trying to keep a lid on her frustration, Smits had kept his arguments rooted in diplomacy, seemingly without effort.

"Before Carmichael took the job," he said, "Detective Stucker spent five years overseeing Bomb Squad."

Dunbar's frown turned into a look of amazement. "Seriously? That's the best you've got?" He shook his head. "Take note, people. I will not sit quietly by while you two go about assassinating Andy's character. He's good people, and he just lost his best friend. The least we can do is be supportive, give him some space. Andy is the innocent party here. Novak, you are not to pursue this. Do I make myself clear?"

"With respect, sir," Maggie said, "that's a mistake."

Now Dunbar glared. "Excuse me?"

Smits stepped forward. "What Detective Novak means is—"

"We don't compromise the investigation," she said, stepping forward herself. "Just because Andy is one of our own doesn't automatically give him a free pass. That's not how we operate. If he is involved and we turn a blind eye, how is that justice for Clay?"

There was a moment in which no one spoke or moved. Then Dunbar rose in his chair as though hoisted up on strings. He planted his curled fists on the desk and leveled his gaze on her. "Detective Novak," he said quietly, his voice controlled, but his breathing quickened, "listen to me very carefully. My dear brother-in-law is not yet interred. As a family, we are all in a state of grief. His loss is unbearable. This situation calls for restraint and a light touch. Running around accusing our friends of heinous crimes just because it's convenient to do so is a disservice to his memory. I can personally vouch for Andy. May I suggest, instead of trying to sully his good name and disrespect Clay in the process, you should try exercising a little sensitivity. Consider this your one and only warning. Venture down this path, and there will be consequences. Now get out of my sight. I've got a funeral to help organize."

Maggie was dumbfounded.

Dunbar had pressed every one of her emotional buttons, and it demanded a concerted effort on her part not to say something that would see her immediately removed from the case.

"What now?" she asked Smits as they left Dunbar's office.

"Leave it with me," he said. "I'll fix this. Meanwhile, go speak with the self-storage manager again. Show him some pictures. See if he can positively ID who rented those units. If Detective Young didn't build that bomb, somebody else did."

Chapter Twenty-Nine

STANDING ROOM ONLY

Maggie scowled at the sky. It was the color of wet cement. Cloying clouds dimming daylight. According to the TV meteorologists, a nor'easter was battering the Eastern Seaboard, dumping heavy snow as far south as the Carolinas, and over the next twenty-four hours, Florida was in for stormy weather.

And Maggie hadn't packed an umbrella.

She parked the motor pool sedan outside Hector's Self-Storage on Oak Ridge Road and checked her phone.

One unread text message, from Loomis:

Needle in a haystack

Under Smits's instruction, she had left Loomis back at the office, poring through case files, specifically every homicide investigated by Stucker and Young in the past twelve months.

Although she and Loomis were both convinced that Stucker knew more than he was saying, they couldn't overlook the possibility that the killer might originate from a current, cold, or closed case.

Someone with a grudge. An aggrieved third party with a score to settle, or the agent of somebody Stucker and Young had helped put on death row.

These things happened.

In the five years Maggie had worked Major Case, she had received a number of death threats, not just from convicted killers, but also from associates of murderers serving life in supermax. The majority of threats were knee-jerk reactions, and she'd taken them with a grain of salt. But one or two remained real, giving her continued cause to be alert. So far, no one had attempted to follow through on their dark promise. But Maggie was conscious of the law of averages, knowing that the prospect of someone coming after her someday was one she would be foolish to ignore.

Loomis, she knew, had his work cut out for him.

With seventeen million annual visitors, Orlando was Florida's undisputed tourist capital. But it was also a working city, with crime and poverty and an average of two new homicides every week to add to the Squad's workload. As such, there was a mountain of material for him to go over, and faced with the task of looking for persons of interest across dozens of murders, Smits had reassigned half of the Squad to help Loomis in his uphill quest.

Not only was there a sense of renewed conviction within the unit to solve the riddle of Clay's "suicide"; now that the investigation had taken a completely new direction, there was also a rekindled sense of urgency, with Major Case pulling out all the stops to apprehend the masked man seen in the Walmart surveillance video, as well as to identify the unknown woman seen arguing with Clay.

Maggie heard laughter outside the car, and she looked through the passenger window to see two young women strolling along the sidewalk, dressed in running gear. They were taking a break from their run, sharing a funny story and laughing out loud. One of the women reminded her of Deputy Shaw; she had the same short haircut, the same boyish figure, about the same age, too. Maggie watched her as they passed the car, suddenly overwhelmed with a compulsion to hear how Deputy Ramos was holding up.

She put a call through to Dispatch, requesting that he call her back. The dispatcher informed her that Deputy Ramos had taken sick leave and wasn't on today's duty roster. Maggie contemplated calling Human Resources and obtaining his cell number, then decided against it.

He had enough on his plate at home, dealing with his son's health issues, without her invading his privacy and dredging up his grief.

She climbed out of the sedan and buttoned up her jacket as she crossed toward the entrance gate. There was a strong feel of imminent rain in the air, and a cool wind was whipping up. Palm leaves flapping like flags.

She'd wait till Ramos was back on duty. Speak with him then.

Maggie buzzed through the gate and found the facility manager sitting behind the reception counter in the small office, hunched over his cell phone and chuckling to himself. She hadn't called ahead; she wanted to see a fresh and unrehearsed reaction from the manager when she presented him with Clay's photograph.

"Sounds like fun," she said as she stepped inside the small office.

The manager's smile faded as he recognized Maggie and the police badge in her hand. He put the phone facedown on the counter and folded his fleshy arms. "What now?" he asked.

"I'm conducting follow-ups," she said. She glanced around the office. "Does this place have surveillance cameras? I didn't see any when I was here the other day."

"That's because there aren't any. Our clientele value their privacy. We take it very seriously."

"Yes, we noticed." She looked back at him. "After what's happened here, and for your own security, perhaps installing a closed-circuit TV system wouldn't be the dumbest thing."

Uncertainty rolled around the manager's face. The tug-of-war between progress and inertia.

"The man who rented those three units," Maggie said. "Can you describe him?"

The manager shrugged. "Maybe."

"What if I show you a picture?"

"Okay."

Maggie found the stock image of Clayton Young on her phone, struck anew, as she glimpsed his confident smile, that life was incredibly fragile.

She showed the manager the image. "Is this the person who rented those units?"

She saw his gaze stay on the screen for less than a second. "No," he said.

"Please. This is important." She held the phone a little nearer to him. "Look closer. Take your time."

"I don't have to," he said. "That isn't him."

"How can you be sure?"

"Because he wasn't a black guy."

"He was white?"

"Put it this way: he definitely wasn't *black*."

Maggie substituted Clay's picture with the press image of Andrew Stucker she'd downloaded from Major Case's secure cloud storage. In the publicity shot, Stucker looked relaxed in his red button-down shirt and his brown tweed jacket, subtle makeup minimizing the sheen on his bald scalp.

"How about this man?" she asked, leaning on the counter. "Again, take your time."

She watched his reaction, looking for telltale signs of recognition. But the manager's expression remained impassive.

"You know," he said as he squinted at the screen, "I can't be sure. Maybe. Maybe not. I mean, the guy, I remember he wore sunglasses whenever he was here, and one of those hoodies with the hood up. I don't think I ever saw his whole face."

Maggie felt slightly disappointed. "What about distinguishing features, or an accent of some kind?"

"Not that I remember. We didn't speak much. He kept himself to himself. I do remember he said he was local, though."

"What about his vehicle? I'm assuming he had one."

"Pickup truck."

"Make and model?"

The manager shrugged. "I'm not good with cars. I remember it was a dark color. To be honest, I got bad vibes from him from the start. I kept my distance."

Maggie leaned off the counter. "We're not making great progress here, are we?"

"He played music." The manager said it as though he were offering her a consolation prize. "Whenever he was inside the unit. He had it on loud, too. I complained, but he kept it turned up."

"What kind of music?"

"Rap. Mostly that local kid who you guys killed a while back."

Maggie felt her surprise erase the frown on her face. "You mean Lay-Z Creek? Are you sure it was his music?"

"I'm a fan. He wrote some sweet songs."

Maggie put her phone away "Do you think you'd be able to describe the man who rented those units to our sketch artist?"

"I can do better," he said. He picked up his own phone and tapped at the screen. Then he presented her with a picture from the internet.

Maggie stared at the image. "Are you sure he looked like this?"

"Minus the moustache, more or less. Sure."

The picture on his phone was the famous black-and-white police composite sketch of Ted Kaczynski, the Unabomber, in his hood and aviator sunglasses.

"There's something else as well," the manager said.

Maggie looked up from the screen. In the few seconds she'd looked away, his expression had become anxious, his skin sweaty.

"Are you okay?" she said.

"I might need your protection."

"My *protection*?" She let him see her frown. "Why?"

She saw him glance from side to side, as though checking to see if somebody might be eavesdropping on their conversation. Then he leaned forward on the counter. "I know what happens," he said quietly.

"Happens?"

"To informants. I know what *happens*."

Maggie's frown stayed put. "Okay. Tell you what. Why don't you just say what it is you're trying to say."

The manager stared at her for a moment, like she'd asked him to walk through fire.

"Well?"

He took a big breath. "This guy. I think he's a cop."

"What makes you think that?"

"For starters, the way he acted. Like he was superior or something. I've dealt with plenty of cops in my time. After a while, you recognize the signs." He leaned forward on the counter again, sweat beading on his jowls. "So tell me. How does your protection work exactly?"

Chapter Thirty

BLOOD IN THE WATER

I t definitely wasn't Clay who rented those units," Maggie told Smits on speakerphone as she drove away from the storage facility in Oak Ridge. "And before you ask, the manager couldn't positively identify Andy either." She heard Smits thank God for small mercies. "But that doesn't automatically exonerate him," she added. "The manager is convinced it's a cop."

"What?"

"He has no direct proof. Right now it's just a feeling."

"A cop?"

"And get this. The manager is a Lay-Z Creek fan. He said he heard the suspect playing Creek's music inside the unit. Loud enough to hear all the way to the main office."

"What do you think?"

"That it's probably 99 percent coincidence."

"But it's the 1 percent that piques your interest."

Smits knew her well. "Put it this way," she said. "I think it would be the sensible thing to take a good look at the Creek incident, just in case. There were plenty of unhappy characters surrounding that episode, including several death threats made against Andy and Clay."

"And if the manager's hunch is right about him being a cop . . ."

"It corroborates the inside job theory, which still means it could be Andy."

She heard Smits make a sound like he was grinding his teeth.

"I'm having a hard time accepting that, Detective," he said.

"Well, whoever it is, it sounds like he deliberately disguised his appearance. The manager said the suspect wore sunglasses and a hoodie each time he visited. I checked the duty roster before coming down here. It was Andy's day off the day the units were rented. Plus, the manager said the suspect drove a dark-colored pickup truck. Andy drives a black Ram. I still need to speak with him in an official capacity."

"About that," Smits said. "I've just this minute spoken with Captain Corrigan."

A postexplosion image of the captain came into Maggie's mind: Corrigan lying on his back in the parking lot, unmoving as paramedics worked on him. "How is he?"

She heard Smits let out a long and weary breath. "As good as it gets for a guy who lost an eye. No doubt about it, it's going to be an uphill struggle. He'll have to adjust to seeing the world in two dimensions. I wouldn't want to trade places; put it that way."

"The captain's a strong character," Maggie said. "He'll be okay. I don't mean to downplay his injury in any way at all, but it could've been much worse." She imagined Deputy Shaw lying on Elkin's steel autopsy table, her face ashen, her skin bloodless as he cut into her chest and peeled back her dead flesh. "You went over Dunbar's head, didn't you?"

"I did. The captain agreed with me. Lieutenant Dunbar is too close to this case to act impartially. He needs to recuse himself."

"Thanks, Sarge."

"Don't thank me, Detective. I have no doubt leapfrogging the lieutenant like this will come back and haunt both of us."

Maggie was grateful for Smits going out on a limb for the investigation, but she knew that Dunbar would see *her* as the real instigator. And making an enemy of a senior commander wasn't recommended.

"The press sharks are on the prowl," Smits was saying. "I've got instructions to release a statement later today, either to quash the rumors of foul play, or to confirm them. I've got a four o'clock sit-down arranged with Amanda Franz from WESH-2 News. Any pearls you can find in the meantime will go a long way to calm the waters. More than anything else, I need to say something other than this is all an inside job."

Chapter Thirty-One

ANY PORT IN A STORM

Maggie switched on the Mustang's headlights as the first big drops of rain marbled the glass, the windshield wipers coming on automatically. Dark clouds gathering in the north and a detectable drop in air temperature.

A storm was on its way, and she hadn't brought a raincoat.

She signaled at the next intersection, leaving Orange Blossom and heading east on Sand Lake Road.

After yesterday's bugle call meeting, and with another week of vacation days saved up, Stucker had returned to Titusville. He'd told Smits he wouldn't be back in Orlando until the day of Clay's funeral.

Maggie was having a hard time getting over his blasé attitude.

Before setting out for the storage facility, and despite Dunbar's wishes, she'd placed several calls to Stucker's cell phone, hoping to save herself the trouble of driving out to the coast. Each had gone straight to voice mail. She'd left messages, explaining the importance of him phoning her back. No response. She'd even telephoned the Orbit Club landline, explaining to a disinterested man on the other end of the connection that she needed to speak with his boss as a matter of urgency. He'd told her Stucker wasn't expected at the club until later in the day, but he would pass along her message at the soonest opportunity. That was an hour ago, and Stucker still hadn't returned any of her calls.

Maggie's patience with him was wearing thin.

She accelerated onto the Beachline as heavier rain pebbled the windshield. Wipers sluicing off water. She turned down the air-conditioning, and called Loomis on speakerphone.

"Hey," she said. "Quick update. I still can't get hold of Andy. So I'm en route to Titusville. Any progress at your end?"

Loomis was still sifting through case files, looking for anyone who might have a grudge against Stucker and Young.

"A couple of mediocre hitters," he admitted. "But none that could knock it out of the ballpark. I know I'm stating the obvious here, Novak. But the thing about murder investigations is, they're full of suspicious characters."

Maggie found herself smiling. "While I remember, take a good look at the Creek incident. The manager at the storage facility remembers the suspect playing Creek's music. I know Nick's article brought the incident to everyone's attention again. People still believe his death was preventable, and that Clay should never have used a Taser on him. Not with Creek's heart condition. People were pretty mad at the time. There were lynch mobs with placards outside the courthouse. Emotions were running high. Maybe there's something there."

"Like a vengeful superfan."

"Or a disenchanted family member. Look at anyone with police or military connections. The person who did this, he didn't learn how to build that bomb from watching a YouTube video. We need to look for someone not just with the motive, but also with the know-how."

"Consider it done," he said. "I'll get right on it. Enjoy your trip to the Space Coast, partner. But stay safe. The forecast is pretty bleak."

◆ ◆ ◆

Gusting wind and hammering rain were no fun. Maggie used the drive time to think about the case and what she knew so far, but her mind kept wandering to Steve and his proposal on New Year's Eve.

Like it or lump it, she was going to have to sit down with him at some point and talk about *the question*. He was back from his conference in Atlanta this weekend. Just a few days. Maybe then? Any later and it might look like she was deliberately avoiding the subject.

"It would help if you could remember your answer," she told herself. "Save yourself the heartache."

Was it *yes*, *no*, or *maybe*?

One thing was clear: her inability to recall her response to his question was a poor excuse for her silence. It made a mockery out of Steve's sincerity, and it was simply unfair of her to act dumb. She couldn't keep tiptoeing around the subject—and *him*—for fear of being embarrassed. She owed it to Steve to be up front, honest. She owed it to *herself*.

Yes, no, or maybe?

Maggie mulled over the options, trying to be realistic as well as objective.

A *yes* would take her along a route that led to the ultimate commitment. At some point she and Steve would move in together. His place or hers, or somewhere new to them both? That, in itself, presenting a frightening concept. It would mean giving up certain liberties. They would marry, and she would become Mrs. Kinsey. It would mean compromise on a scale she'd never experienced before.

Perhaps they would plan a family. Again, another terrifying thought that would mean more restrictions and greater responsibility. *And impact on her work.* They would settle down and grow old together. Hopefully, happily ever after.

"Isn't that what everybody wants?"

Is that what *she* wanted?

No question, a *no* would place an expiration date on their relationship. She and Steve would probably continue as is in the short term. But with no real future for them in sight, they would eventually drift apart and go their separate ways.

Yes or no?

The question, she realized with a start, wasn't just whether she wanted to be married, but whether she wanted to marry *Steve*.

Maggie spotted signs for KENNEDY SPACE CENTER and TITUSVILLE, and she slotted the sedan into the left-hand lane.

"Why are you being a pain, Andy?" she asked out loud.

She visualized the masked killer sitting in the back seat of Clay's car on New Year's Eve, talking with Clay for those eight minutes, coaxing him into blowing his brains out.

How did something like that *happen*?

How was it possible for somebody to persuade someone else to end their own life?

"Was that you in the back seat, Andy?"

Is that why Clay didn't retaliate, because his best friend was the one forcing his hand?

Maggie drove for a while with her thoughts skipping from one scenario to another.

Then, as she followed the right-turn filter lane onto Columbia Boulevard, she called Nick Stavanger on speakerphone. To get a fuller picture of events, she wanted to review the entire TV footage shot at the Walmart crime scene, and not just the edited bits already broadcast on the local TV news. But she knew an official request would take time to work its way through the red tape. Working at the *Orlando Chronicle*, Nick had high-profile media connections.

"Hey, you," he said as he picked up. Maggie could hear chatter in the background. "I'm on a tight deadline here," he said. "No time for chitchat. What do you need, Detective?"

"What makes you think I'm calling with a favor to ask?"

"Besides history? Let me see. Oh, yes. It's the middle of a workday, and as a rule, unless it's an emergency, we never make social calls in the middle of a workday."

"I guess you're right."

"I know I'm right. Is it an emergency?"

"Kind of."

"Okay. Good. Ask away."

"Do you still have friends at the TV networks?"

"I do."

"Can you get me an unedited copy of the live TV coverage from New Year's Day?"

"Of the Walmart suicide scene?"

"Yes."

"Can't you request it yourself?"

"I can. But you're about a week quicker."

Nick was quiet for a second or two, and Maggie knew that her unexpected phone call had gotten his mental gears whirring, the journalist in him sniffing something fishy.

"Maggie, is there more to this story than a simple suicide?"

"There's no such thing as a simple suicide."

"You know what I mean."

"And you know I can't tell you, even if there is. Let's just leave it at that."

"Now I'm intrigued. Okay. Look. I'll get you those tapes. But throw me a bone here. Give me the scoop."

"Nick, I can't. Not this time. Smits has already scheduled a sit-down with Amanda Franz, and he won't budge on it."

She heard him sigh.

"Look," he said, "if this is about the article—"

"It is."

"Traitor."

Maggie smiled. "Sorry, Nick."

She heard him laugh it off, but she knew the blow had hit him where it hurt.

◆ ◆ ◆

Maggie drove slowly through the deep puddles collecting on Riverside Drive, rainwater pummeling the fenders. It was dim as dusk in Titusville. Squally conditions. Roadside trees leaning over, and power lines jangling.

Out on the river, the storm was whisking up white-crested waves and reducing visibility down to yards. A thick rain-mist hanging over the water. It looked inhospitable out there, choppy, and yet she could see several white gulls suspended in the dusky sky, their wings unmoving, as though they were pinned in place.

After yesterday's debacle, Stucker would resist cooperating, she knew. And if she did insist he return with her to Orlando for an official interview, there was no way he would do so willingly.

Stucker's riverfront residence was hidden behind a curtain of rain.

Maggie swung the sedan into the crescent-shaped driveway; then she sat in the car for a minute, waiting for the downpour to subside.

She knew, even if she could bring him in, interrogating Stucker would be akin to squeezing blood from a stone.

It was a sad-but-true fact that members of law enforcement suspected of wrongdoing were given privileged treatment. There was no written rule. No handbook on how to treat colleagues connected to crime. The "special arrangement" existed in the quiet space between trust and betrayal. Unlike most persons of interest required to attend the Sheriff's Office for questioning, fellow officers were offered a variety of appointment times, with the whole operation handled by senior management wearing kid gloves. Suspect officers were also encouraged to have a union rep present as well as an attorney.

Realistically, Maggie wasn't interested in taking her conversation with Stucker that far.

Whatever he was hiding, she'd find her answers *here*.

A minute passed, and the rain didn't ease off. Maggie braved the weather, using her jacket as an umbrella as she ran across the waterlogged gravel to the canopied front door.

The din of the downpour was louder here under the porch, thundering on the roof. Maggie rang the doorbell, shaking off raindrops and wishing she'd had the foresight to bring a raincoat with her, and maybe gloves.

The storm was sucking up every bit of warmth, even from her skin.

The door opened to reveal Klementina wearing a hooded sweatshirt and skinny jeans. Her bright-red lipstick made her mouth look like a bloody slash. "You again," she said. "This time you bring storm. Normal people bring booze." She glanced side to side and around Maggie. "Okay. Where is handsome?"

"If you mean Loomis, I left him back in Orlando, snowed under."

Klementina made a face.

"With paperwork," Maggie explained. "May I come in?"

"No, you may not. I have mopped. You will dirty floor." She kept hold of the door, denying Maggie passage.

"Listen," she said. "I need to talk with Andy. I drove by the club on the way here, but didn't see his truck. I notice it's not here either. It's an emergency. Do you know where he's at?"

"Of course. He is consumed with capturing fish. I say to him, look at weather. It is dogs and cats outside. I tell him he is crazy person."

Maggie sighed. "Klementina, I don't have time for your dishonesty. You told me he was fishing the other day, when he was in fact at the club, and you knew it. That kind of obfuscation is called lying to a police officer. It's classed as making false statements. It's against the law."

Klementina made an innocent face. "I swear on your life, Novak. This is truth. My husband, he is on fishing expedition." She must have seen the doubting look descending over Maggie's face, because she dug out her phone and showed Maggie her last text conversation with Stucker. "See with your own eyes. He was visiting with his mother. But then he had to take urgent trip to marina. You will find him out there, in lagoon. *Fishing.* Crazy, I know."

◆ ◆ ◆

Maggie was wet. Despite the blowers set to maximum, the car's windows were steaming up. She added heat into the mix as she drove north, but still had to wipe away some of the excess condensation from the inside of the windshield with the cuff of her sleeve. The inclement weather was closing in. Black clouds transforming midday into midnight. Hardly any other vehicles on the road and absolutely no one out on foot.

Klementina had provided directions to a marina located less than a mile away. Apparently, Stucker had left his mother's nursing home on Merritt Island thirty minutes ago. Maggie was thinking that if she hurried, she might catch him still at the marina.

Who in their right mind goes fishing in this weather? she wondered as a palm frond blew into the road, causing her to swerve.

"Andy's not the only crazy person," she murmured to herself.

Up ahead, she spied a bunch of boat masts appearing through the incessant rain. She slowed the sedan, following a side road into the marina access point. The road ran parallel to the highway, opening up into a visitor parking lot with a couple of vehicles facing the riverfront, including Stucker's pickup. Maggie parked alongside it, and peered at the myriad boats bobbing up and down in the marina.

There must have been a couple of hundred in all shapes and sizes. Big yachts with tall masts and sails safely stowed. Sleek powerboats locked down against the gale. Maggie couldn't see any signs of life, or any lights piercing the gloom.

She could see an endless barrage of frothy waves rolling into shore, though, lifting the boats and rocking them from side to side. Tarps flapping. Antennas bending. Waves crashing against the piers and throwing up spray.

"You couldn't have picked a worse day to be down here," she told herself.

Even from inside the car she could hear the constant dull thuds of boat fenders banging against the docks. The creak of timbers and the clanking of bells. The place looked treacherous, sounded dangerous. Planking slicked with rain. One misstep and she would be in the water before she could blink.

"You're going to get drenched all right."

Of course, there was nothing stopping her from waiting it out, sitting here listening to the radio until Stucker came back to his truck. She'd come all this way. It would be pointless turning back now, empty handed. According to Stucker's last text message to Klementina, he said he could be gone awhile.

Did Maggie really want to sit here twiddling her thumbs for the next several hours when there was a chance that Stucker's boat hadn't yet left the marina?

Maggie made up her mind. She tied her hair in a ponytail, fastened her jacket, then braced herself as she pushed open the driver's door.

Right away, the squall tried to rip it from her hands. She held on as she climbed out, cowering for a second in the lee of the car, the gust trying to lift her off her feet. She waited for it to switch directions, then slammed the door shut and stooped her way into the marina. Cool rain blasting her skin, running down her neck and under her collar.

Klementina's directions included the specific dock location and the name of Stucker's boat—*Celestial Body*—as well as a brief description of the medium-size cabin cruiser. Maggie didn't know much about boats. Klementina had said that Stucker's reminded her of a wedding cake, and that Maggie would know what she meant the moment she clapped eyes on it.

Maggie spotted the marina office block and hunched her way in that direction. Rain stung her face, reminiscent of the glass wounds she'd suffered during the car bombing. She kept her head bowed, her eyes scrunched, her arms wrapped around her as she fought to make progress against the switching wind.

Unsurprisingly, the office was closed. No lights on. She continued past, following the canopied walkway running along the dockside.

Rain ran into her eyes and dripped off her nose.

She came to a pier access point, closed off with a chain-link gate. She tried it, finding it locked. It didn't stop her. She hooked her fingers on the top and climbed over, dropping onto the wet

261

timbers on the other side. Swaying boats, both left and right. Taut lines and buoys bouncing. With the wind buffeting her, she made her way along the dock, every now and then reaching for a piling to steady herself against the storm.

According to Klementina, Stucker docked his boat at the far end of this pier, where the wooden walkway split to form a T.

Maggie was half expecting to see an empty dock and no trace of either the boat or Stucker.

But it seemed luck was with her.

Through the driving rain she glimpsed a white three-tiered cabin cruiser rising and falling at the end of the dock. With its distinct layers reducing in size with height, she could see why Klementina had likened it to a wedding cake. To support the analogy, she could just make out the dark shape of a man standing on the flying bridge, like the model of a groom without his bride.

Andy Stucker.

Maggie hollered his name. But the wind snatched it away. Automatically, she fell into a jog.

He seemed engrossed in the boat's control console, pushing buttons and pulling levers.

"Andy!"

She was still about fifty feet away when she realized that the boat was powered up and beginning to edge away from the dock.

"Andy!"

The thought of being so close and yet so far away squirted hot adrenaline into her chest, and her jog became an all-out sprint, her arms pumping in rhythm with her legs.

Did she think she could catch the boat?

"Andy! Hold up!"

She could see the cruiser begin to pivot away from the dock, a gap opening up. She knuckled down, knowing she was committed and moving too swiftly to stop herself from sliding into the water even if she put the brakes on *now*. She didn't slow. She increased her speed, the end of the pier coming up fast.

Are you really going to do this?

She glimpsed a swimming platform jutting out of the boat's stern at water level, and then she was at the end of the dock, leaping with all her might, launching herself at the boat like an Olympic long jumper.

It was as if time stood still.

Maggie sailed through the air, arms wheeling, legs cycling, willing herself to clear the choppy water opening up beneath her.

For a second she believed she could make it.

But the gap was already several yards wide, and it was clear she was going to miss.

Chapter Thirty-Two

ASK QUESTIONS LATER

Maggie realized her mistake in the same moment that a fierce gust hit her from behind, hurling her headfirst at the boat. The stern came up faster than expected, and she crashed awkwardly and without any grace into the fiberglass, slamming against the words *Celestial Body* emblazoned on the hull. The impact pancaked her lungs, and she collapsed heavily onto the swimming platform, jarring bones and unable to breathe.

Stunned, she snatched at her bearings, blinking and trying to suck in air as brackish water sprayed across her face.

The boat tipped, and water surged over her, taking what little breath she had.

Then she was sliding off the platform, slithering feetfirst into the water. Instinctively, she twisted, grabbing out at the hull as it slipped by, her hands squeaking against the white fiberglass. The boat bucked like a mule, and water deluged her again. She clamped her mouth shut as it swamped over. Somehow she managed to grasp a nylon tether attached to the gunwale, wrap her fingers around it, and cling on. Her slide stopped. She swung her other arm around and curled her fingers around the rope, lifting her face clear of the water and *breathing*.

Her voice was cursing in her head, over and over.

She took a second to assess, blinking water from her eyes.

She was on her belly on the swimming platform, up to her waist in the brackish water, her legs trailing out behind as the boat accelerated out of the marina. Soaked to the bone, her sodden boots weighing her down. The knuckles on both hands pink-white, the nylon rope biting into her skin.

She could feel the engines thrumming through her chest, feel the lagoon water being churned up around her.

What had she been thinking?

Teeth gritted, she heaved with all her strength, dragging herself fully onto the platform and then scooting up into a seated position against the stern. Sucking in damp air. Behind her, the engine kicked up a gear, submerged propellers spinning faster, waves thumping against the hull and vibrating through her spine.

Was she out of her mind?

Riding the swells, the boat began to distance itself from the marina, until both it and the shoreline were swallowed up in the mist. No land or reference points visible in any direction. No brightly colored channel buoys in sight. Only the weather and the water. Both intimately connected and seemingly inseparable.

She could have been a mile from shore, or a hundred.

"That was a stupid thing to do," she told herself.

She realized she was shivering. She couldn't remember the last time she had shivered in the middle of the day.

Still slightly dazed, she stayed there for almost a minute, catching her breath and chastising herself for being impulsive. Ask anyone, and they'd say the same thing. Throwing herself headlong at a moving boat was, in a word, reckless, and it could have resulted in a serious injury. As it was, the collision had rattled her bones and reawakened the ache in her shoulders. The palms of her hands stinging, again. Otherwise, she was lucky she hadn't snapped a leg, or her neck. Punctured a lung or knocked out her teeth.

Stucker had no idea she had jumped onboard.

Dripping water, Maggie got to her feet and clambered over the gunwale into the canopied afterdeck.

The flying bridge piggybacked the main cabin and jutted out halfway over the stern area. The other half of the roof was composed of a brown canvas canopy billowing in the wind. At one side, an aluminum ladder with wooden steps led up to a hatch in the flybridge floor.

Maggie squelched her way over.

"Andy!" she shouted into the wind. "Andy, it's Maggie. We need to talk."

The flat rungs were holding water, slippery, the soles of her boots barely gripping the wood as she climbed. She lifted up the hatch lid and poked her head through.

Stucker was standing side on to her, a few feet away, preoccupied with steering the boat. He had on a knee-length raincoat with the hood pulled up, rain pelting the oilskin and running off.

Maggie blinked against the spray lashing her face. "Detective," she called. "You deaf or something?"

He seemed to hear for the first time; she saw his head twist inside the hood, his frame stiffen. Then he did something she wasn't expecting. He kicked out, his boot coming up at her face. She drew back. But he wasn't aiming for her. His foot connected with the hatch instead, knocking the lid back down on her head.

It wasn't heavy, and it didn't hurt, but the impact was enough to weaken her already tenuous grip on the ladder, and she slipped off, falling back down and landing in a heap on the afterdeck.

Dazed, Maggie rolled onto her back.

Then she heard thunder clap, and a small hole appeared in the canvas roof above her head.

Maggie stared at it, her sluggish thoughts taking a second to work out what she was staring at.

Then a second bang sounded, and another hole appeared about a foot from the first. A third and a fourth followed—random holes bursting open in the acrylic.

Adrenaline exploded through Maggie's chest.

Stucker was shooting at her.

Was it any surprise? She'd insinuated that he and Clay had been up to no good. She'd questioned the reputation of his family business. More or less, she'd accused him of being a murderer. Then she'd boarded his boat, armed and uninvited, and his defense would be *trespassers will be shot.*

Maggie reacted exactly as her training had taught her. It didn't matter that it was one of her colleagues doing the shooting. Friend or foe, a police officer was trained to defend herself, sometimes to the death.

Flat on her back, Maggie raised her own gun above her head, mentally triangulating Stucker's location.

A fifth bullet broke through the roof and burrowed into the deck an inch from her head. An alarm bell ringing in her ear. The next one would hit her square in the face, she was sure of it.

Without a second thought, she aimed at the spot where she judged his legs to be, and squeezed the trigger, twice, in quick succession.

Chapter Thirty-Three

BLUE MURDER

Maggie's double-tap gunshots reverberated around the afterdeck, bringing an abrupt end to Stucker's shooting.

Hardly breathing, she stared at the handful of bullet holes in the canvas roof above her, disbelieving the events of the last few seconds. Except for the rainwater beginning to drain through the holes, there was no sign of movement on the flying bridge.

Was he reassessing, or had she winged him?

Her answer came a second later in the form of heavy footfalls thudding across the flybridge. She tracked the movement with the Glock, wondering how badly she might have hurt him, if at all, and the consequences for her career if she had. Either way, she'd willingly opened fire on a fellow officer, the reward for which would be a permanent black mark on her record, even if she'd acted in self-defense.

No one liked cop killers, especially cops.

The thudding stopped at the edge of the roof.

Maggie held her breath, staring down the iron sights.

In the corner of the roof, the hatch lid was still closed. She aimed the Glock at it, watching for a crack of light that would denote it being opened and Stucker coming through.

It stayed shut. Idle seconds ticking by.

What was he doing?

Then she saw movement at the edge of the canopy. The dark silhouette of a man falling from above, dropping vertically past her point of view and into the water. A dull splash as he hit the undulating surface.

Fear flashed through Maggie's chest.

She rolled to her feet, holstering the gun as she rushed to the side of the boat.

She scanned the surface, squinting against the sea spray, frantically trying to spot Stucker in the craze of overlapping waves.

"Andy!"

She thought she saw an arm roll up out of the choppy water, several yards behind the boat, bent at an angle, imitating a shark fin, but then it disappeared again, and she couldn't be sure of what she'd seen.

"Andy!"

For a second she contemplated jumping in.

On the whole she wasn't a bad swimmer. Her father had insisted each one of his children learn how to swim when they were young. The ability had saved her life several times. At a push, she could even swim the length of an Olympic pool underwater.

How deep was the lagoon? Four or five feet on average?

Maybe if she removed her jacket and boots, she might be able to find him, walk on the bottom, and tow him back to the boat.

But then she dismissed the idea as lunacy.

There was no sign of Stucker anywhere. And she had no idea what kind of undercurrents were being roused by the storm, or if the boat was still following the deeper boat channel. Even if Stucker wasn't wounded, she knew, the chances of him being able to stay afloat in these conditions long enough to be rescued were woefully slim.

Every second counted. And she'd used too many up already just thinking about it.

"Andy!"

The terrifying probability was that he'd already gone under, dragged to the sandy bottom by the weight of his garments. If not drowned, then soon to be.

Fire swept through Maggie's chest, searing her lungs.

Had she just killed Andy Stucker?

Chapter Thirty-Four

A PLEA OF SELF-DEFENSE

Maggie's mind whirled into overdrive. It took effort to push her personal emotions aside, to tell herself that she had to *think* and act *fast*.

The boat was still moving, she realized, distancing itself from Stucker with every passing second.

She spun around and scrambled up the ladder, throwing back the hatch and hauling herself up into the flying bridge.

The boat's motion was emphasized up here, the whole deck swaying precariously from side to side. It was a struggle to keep her balance and stay on her feet.

Streaks of blood pooling in the rainwater, stark against the deck.

Maggie's stomach clenched.

She tasted bile in the back of her throat and swallowed it down. Now was not the time to be squeamish.

"He gave you no choice," she told herself as she examined the control console. "It was either you or him."

It didn't make it any easier.

Maggie had never steered a boat of this size before, but the controls looked fairly straightforward. A few dials, buttons, and levers. Everything labeled. How hard could it be?

She located the shift lever and threw it in neutral. Then she pulled the throttle all the way back. The boat began to decelerate, sharply. Oncoming swells slapping against the hull and sending shock waves up her legs. She held on, knocking the shift into reverse and then moving the throttle forward halfway. It took a moment for the propellers to start spinning in the opposite direction.

"Come on; come on," she implored as the boat started to crawl backward.

Without a frame of reference, it was impossible to tell if the boat was retracing its course exactly. Maggie had to hope that it was, or close. She counted out thirty seconds—the approximate duration between Stucker falling in the water and her stopping the boat—then she knocked the shift into neutral again and shut the power down completely.

The engine sputtered and went silent. Adrift, the boat rocked and rolled as waves thumped the hull.

Half blinded by driving rain, Maggie peered over the handrail and scanned the turbulent water.

Visibility was down to yards.

She called Stucker's name again, cupping her hands together and hollering as loudly as she could. Waiting, listening, her eyes searching the waves. Then she yelled again, over and over for the next minute. But all she could hear was the raging storm and the wind whistling through the bullet holes in the canopy.

Maggie felt a quiver run through her, and an unexpected sob sounded in her throat. Suddenly light headed, she gripped the handrail, going with the motion of the boat.

A sense of dread pluming within her.

She pictured Stucker as he tumbled into the lagoon, rolling in the water, the boat receding into the mist as the waves crashed over him, one after the other without letup. Gasping for breath as his system went into shock. Blood clouding from his bullet wound as the weight of his clothes pulled him under, a stream of bubbles rising from his lips. Brackish water flooding his mouth and throat, suffocating, strangling. His pupils dilating as his battle to stay alive was lost.

Hard rain stung her face. Maggie wiped her eyes and quivered some more.

Stucker had probably drowned.

And it was all her fault.

◆ ◆ ◆

Another painful minute crept by before she was able to snap herself out of her stupor. Sick to her core. A hornet buzzing in her head. Everything foggy.

"Think," she told herself.

She had to tell someone. Call for help. There was a small chance that Stucker had survived and he was clinging to a buoy somewhere, hanging on, his strength slipping. Time was of the essence. She needed to alert the Coast Guard—*now!*—throw all hands on deck.

She reached for her phone, then realized with alarm that her pocket was empty. She patted her other pockets, finding each one empty, the phone missing. It must have fallen out during her acrobatics, sinking to the bottom of the lagoon.

A frustrated scream worked its way free of her lips.

She glanced behind her at the boat's control console, looking for anything that resembled a two-way radio, but not seeing it. Maybe there was one down below, in the cabin?

Her head spun.

"Breathe," she told herself.

Shaking, she descended the ladder, clutching onto each slippery rung as the boat tipped one way and then the other.

Nausea rising in her belly.

Ordinarily, Maggie didn't suffer from seasickness, but right now she could gladly throw up. It was psychological shock, she knew. Trauma pushing her blood pressure through the roof and urging her to *run*.

Why did Stucker react like that?

Why had he tried to *kill her*?

The cabin door was secured with a padlock.

Maggie struck it with the handle of her Glock. The lock broke open after the third strike, and she let herself inside.

Then she stopped, dead in her tracks at the foot of the short steps leading into the cabin, unable to go any farther.

There was a man's body on the floor, wedged in the narrow walkway, blocking access to the main cabin. The bulky shape of a man in a sweatshirt and jeans, silvery duct tape covering his mouth and cable ties binding his wrists and ankles.

"Andy?"

Maggie's brain hit a mental brick wall.

Andy Stucker was staring up at her, his eyes bloodshot and wide. He waggled his manacled hands at her, prompting her to reach down and rip the tape from his mouth.

"Never thought I'd be so glad to see you," he said, spitting out sticky phlegm. "Please tell me you killed that son of a bitch."

Chapter Thirty-Five

DAVY JONES'S LOCKER

Maggie took a step back, momentarily lost for words as her mind tried to wrap itself around the fact that the man she'd shot at and perhaps fatally wounded wasn't her colleague after all.

Andy Stucker was very much alive.

And he was frowning at her.

"You look like you've seen a ghost," he said.

Maggie found her voice lurking in the back of her throat and forced it out. "I thought you were dead."

"You and me both. Like I said. Glad you decided to visit. You probably saved my life. Give me a hand?"

Maggie helped him into a seated position. He was heavier than he looked. She saw him shake his head, as though trying to clear smoke from his eyes; then he winced.

"Are you hurt?"

"A tad woozy is all. I'll live. He slugged me pretty hard on the back of my head. Tell you the truth—I was surprised when I came to, albeit here, trussed up. Thought I'd be singing with the angels by now." He waggled his hands at her again. "Scissors?"

"Where?"

He gestured over his shoulder. "Galley."

Maggie stepped around him, into the cramped kitchen/diner. She found the scissors slotted in a wall caddy. She snipped his bonds.

Stucker bounced to his feet, a little too quickly, and had to steady himself against the cabin wall with one hand while he clutched the back of his head with the other. "I'm fine," he snapped, even though Maggie hadn't asked. He took his hand away and inspected it, then showed it to her. "See. No blood. Always a good sign, right?"

"Unless the bleeding's internal."

He grunted something incomprehensible. "Well, aren't you a barrel of laughs." He squeezed past her, moving into the dining nook. He smelled of sweat and fear.

"Andy, what happened?"

"He called me," he said, lifting the long cushion on one of the bench seats. "Asking me to come down to the marina."

"He *called* you?"

"At the nursing home. I was visiting with my mom. He called me on their landline. Said he worked at the marina, and I had to get down here quick. The storm was damaging my boat. He knocked me out as I came onboard."

"And it didn't occur to you how someone from the marina knew where to find you?"

Stucker opened a trapdoor that had been hidden by the cushion. "Hindsight makes even stupid people seem clever," he said. "I was distracted. My mom's sick. He caught me off guard. I had no reason to think he wasn't for real."

"Did you get a look at him?"

"Nope." He reached inside the compartment and rummaged around. "But I did hear him mutter something right before he slugged me."

276

"Do you remember what it was?"

"Something like, 'This is for one.'"

"This is for *one*?" Maggie frowned. "That doesn't make any sense. One what?"

"Hell if I know."

"Are you sure that's what he said?"

Stucker paused his rummaging and stared at her. "As sure as anyone who got slugged over the head immediately after." His hand came out of the compartment holding a snub-nosed revolver.

Maggie's frown stayed put. "You keep a gun on your boat?"

"For protection," he said.

"From whom?"

"From backstabbers like your best buddy Stavanger. Clearly, that article of his stirred up a hornet's nest. Got people fired up. So much so that someone just tried to kill me." He flicked out the cylinder and inspected the bullets. "I heard gunshots."

"That's because he tried killing me, too." Maggie was still processing. "To be honest, I thought it was you."

He looked hurt. "Me?"

"Up on the flybridge. I thought it was you. I called out. And that's when he opened fire."

"And you shot back, thinking it was me?" Stucker flicked the cylinder back with a snap. "Thanks a bunch, Maggie."

"But it wasn't you," she said.

"Except you didn't know that at the time. Makes me feel all warm and fuzzy inside." He tried to squeeze past her again.

Maggie blocked his path. "You're wasting your time," she said. "He's gone."

"Where?"

"Overboard."

"He jumped?"

"I wounded him. He went overboard and under the water. I didn't see him come back up. We need to alert the Coast Guard." She glanced around the cabin. "Is there a radio we can use?"

Stucker's eyes narrowed. "You're sure he went overboard?"

"I'm sure. Radio?"

Stucker seemed to ponder her words; then he stuffed the revolver in his waistband and pulled open a kitchen drawer. He retrieved a handheld marine radio and switched it on. White noise burst from the speaker. He called the Coast Guard and outlined the situation in a few short sentences. "You going to explain what you're doing here?" he asked Maggie as he tossed the radio back in the drawer.

"I have questions."

"Don't you always?"

"There's been a development in the case," she said. "Someone else was in Clay's car that night. He was captured on video. Those texts to your phone, they were sent *after* Clay was already dead. I came here to find out where you were New Year's Eve."

"You thought it was me?" He looked more offended than annoyed. "Thanks for your vote of confidence, Maggie. We both just came *this* close to being killed by someone who, right now, looks pretty good for killing Clay. I think you can drop that line of questioning, don't you?"

"Even so, I'd still like to hear your alibi, to satisfy my own curiosity." She saw him clench his teeth, knowing that she was being an irritation, but couldn't help it. "I'm not letting this go," she added.

"Will it get you off my back?"

"For sure."

"I was out on the ocean that night." He said it with a sigh of resignation. "On my way back from the Bahamas."

"What were you doing in the Bahamas?"

"Why does it matter?"

"Because I'm curious. Plus, like you said, it'll get me off your case."

He let out a weary breath. "You're a royal pain, Maggie Novak. You know that?"

"I do."

"Can you keep a secret?"

"Can you be honest?"

The briefest smile happened across Stucker's face. "I've got this monthly face-to-face transaction with a guy in Freeport," he said. "He imports cigars from all over the world, and I pay him for his trouble."

Maggie let him see her dubious expression. "You sail all the way to the Bahamas for *cigars*. That must be the better part of a four-hundred-mile round trip."

"What do you want me to say? Our clients pay top dollar for the genuine article. It's not the kind of product you can ship via FedEx. It's no big deal."

"It's contraband, Andy." She shook her head. "I remember. Your wife. She offered Loomis a Cuban cigar the other day. That's where it came from, didn't it? From this *guy* in Freeport. You're importing them illegally. I know it's none of my business, but if OCSO were ever to find out you're smuggling cigars on the side . . ."

Stucker held up his hands in supplication. "Okay. You're right; you're right. It's none of your business."

He tried to squeeze past her, but Maggie didn't let him.

"Any witnesses?" she said.

"Do I need any?" His expression was challenging, his stale breath in Maggie's face. "I was with my wife. Okay? We were together, all night. Ask her to show you her phone. She took a billion selfies of us in Freeport."

"What time did you get back home?"

"About four in the morning. This boat has a GPS tracker. You can check those records as well."

He went to move past her, and this time Maggie stepped aside, allowing him passage. Stucker climbed the short steps leading to the afterdeck, and Maggie followed him outside.

The storm was throwing frothy spray across the boat as the hull rolled with the swells. Rain lashing and wind howling.

"Why didn't you just tell me this the other day?" she shouted. "It would've saved me coming all the way out here."

"And just think if I did," he shouted back. "I'd be at the bottom of the ocean right now. Your coming out here saved my life."

Maggie noticed something rolling around in the pooled water at her feet, and she picked it up. It was one of the suspect's spent slugs, mushroomed and splayed out like a flower.

"What's that?" Stucker said.

"A hollow point. Same as Forensics dug out of the roof of Clay's car."

Chapter Thirty-Six

LIFE PRESERVER

F orgive the pun," the granite-faced commander from the Coast Guard said to Maggie as they sheltered in the canopied walkway outside the marina's main office, "but until this storm passes, we're pretty much dead in the water."

Maggie felt her shoulders slump.

An hour had passed since Stucker had raised the alarm on the two-way radio and then, somehow beyond her comprehension, navigated *Celestial Body* through the mist and back to its berth at the marina. A frustrating hour in which the Coast Guard had pulled out all the stops to locate the suspect in what the commander was describing as *exotic conditions.*

"Could be we're looking at the morning before we make any headway," he told her. It wasn't what she wanted to hear. "We'll find him if he's out there. But right now, it's *challenging.*"

The passing hour had also seen no letup in the storm. If anything, the weather had deteriorated even further, hindering the search efforts and darkening the sky. No one was saying it, but Maggie could read between the lines. The odds of them finding anyone still alive in the water were rapidly diminishing with every minute that passed, and at some point the search and rescue mission would be downgraded to a recovery operation.

"What about PD?" she asked.

Acting on Stucker's distress call, the Coast Guard had notified the Titusville Police Department about the incident unfolding in the Indian River Lagoon, and the police had then contacted the marina manager, requesting he facilitate their immediate and unfettered access to all areas.

"A dozen patrol officers are already on-site," the commander said. "While we concentrate on the open water, they're checking vessels, looking for anyone caught up in the moorings. I'm told there's also a K-9 unit inbound. Should be here any minute."

"Tell them to check under the piers," Stucker called from behind Maggie.

Stucker was seated on a bench next to an ice machine, smoking a cigar in direct violation of the sign on the wall above his head. Klementina was sitting beside him, hooked onto his arm. A woolly blanket wrapped around them both.

Klementina offered Maggie a cold smile.

Stucker had called his wife the moment they'd made landfall, and she'd rushed down here, bringing comfort food in the form of grilled cheese sandwiches in aluminum foil.

Maggie had devoured her share, surprised at how hungry she was.

Shock, she knew.

To confirm Stucker's alibi, she'd asked Klementina to show her the photos on her phone. At first a little reluctant, Klementina had hesitated, finally giving in and allowing Maggie to look through a bunch of selfies, all showing the happy couple enjoying themselves in the Bahamas on New Year's Eve. Cuddles and kisses. Maggie couldn't decide if their clinginess was cute or cloying.

"The surge is pushing everything inland," Stucker called to the commander. "Under the piers is the first place I'd look."

"For your information," the commander said, "we're doing exactly that right now. I've also got response boats inside the lagoon and patrolling the canal. If your boy's here, sooner or later we'll find him."

The commander was the no-nonsense type who didn't come with a sense of humor. He'd rubbed Stucker the wrong way from the second he'd come over to update them on the search progress, and Maggie had found herself refereeing their *back-and-forth* with increasingly terse comments.

"You can appreciate," she said to him, "we just need confirmation either way. This fugitive is armed and dangerous. It's imperative we locate him."

"And I understand that, ma'am. Fully. I do. We're taking all necessary precautions. But these are demanding circumstances. We're doing the best we can."

Maggie sensed Stucker about to ruffle the commander's feathers a little more, and she quickly thanked the commander for his continued efforts, asking him to keep her updated. He nodded a salute and returned to his duties, hunching into the wind as he walked away.

"That guy couldn't find his ass with both hands," Stucker shouted.

Maggie rotated on her heels. "At least he's out there doing something positive."

"What's that supposed to mean?"

"That instead of taking your frustration out on the wrong person, why don't you put the energy into helping with the search."

Stucker just glared.

"My brave husband is victim here," Klementina said, squeezing his arm. "He should get medal."

283

Maggie resisted saying what she really wanted to say.

She wiped rain from her face with the corner of the blanket and let her gaze roam the marina.

Rightly so, Stucker's abduction had shaken him up. He'd stared death in the face, and that kind of reality check came at a price. Add to that the fact that the killer had caught him off guard, and it wasn't just the back of Stucker's head that had been wounded. His pride had taken a hit, too. And all at once he wasn't looking quite so invincible. He had good reason to be irritable. But it wasn't helping matters.

Maggie heard her name being called, and she turned to see the marina manager leaning out of the office doorway.

"It's for you," he said, holding a cell phone out to her.

With her own phone at the bottom of the lagoon and Stucker's nowhere to be found, Maggie had already borrowed the manager's cell to report back to base. Thirty minutes ago, she'd spoken with Loomis, recounting her confrontation on Stucker's boat, and then reassuring her partner that she was okay, and she didn't need him dropping everything and rushing out here. He'd told her Smits was in a meeting with Dunbar, and he'd have him call her back.

Maggie took the phone from the manager's outstretched hand and followed him indoors, peeling off into a side room so that she could talk in private.

It was Smits.

"Sorry I missed your call," he said in her ear as she shut herself inside what appeared to be a communal lounge filled with leather couches and information boards. "Things have been a little heated around here the last hour."

"Loomis said you were tied up, with Dunbar."

"Horns locked in battle would be more apt."

Maggie felt bad, knowing that Smits had taken flak over Dunbar being forced to recuse himself.

"What's the outcome?" she asked.

"Let's just say we won't be playing golf together for a while."

She heard Smits draw a labored breath.

"Anyway," he said, "that's for me to worry about. What about you, Detective? From what your partner tells me, it sounds like you made a difference today. Saved a colleague's life. That's a nice accreditation for your personnel file. What's the latest?"

Maggie filled him in.

"The all-important question," he said when she was done. "Did you get a look at the suspect?"

"No."

She heard him murmur a curse. It wasn't like Smits, and she could only put it down to his falling-out with Dunbar.

"He wore a raincoat with the hood over his head," she explained. "I saw him for maybe a couple of seconds." She visualized the killer standing at the boat's control console as rain ran off his knee-length oilskin. "I didn't have a great angle, but he looked about the same build as the suspect in the Walmart surveillance video."

"Same guy?"

"It's possible. Of course, there could be more than one person involved in this. But now that I've spoken with Andy, I don't think he's one of them. I've checked his alibi, and it seems legit. It looks like he was in the Bahamas with his wife on New Year's Eve. She took selfies of them both in Freeport. The photo metadata supports his alibi."

She heard Smits let out a breath. "Detective," he said, "you have no idea how relieved that makes me feel. What about Detective Stucker—did he see anything?"

"No. The suspect hit him from behind, knocking him out. But here's the interesting part. Right before the attack, Andy heard him say, 'This is for . . .'" Maggie's words trailed off as something occurred to her.

"For what, Detective?" Smits asked into her silence.

Maggie's heartbeat quickened. She told Smits to give her a second while she brought up an internet search page on the phone. "Andy thought he heard him say, 'This is for one.' But I'm now thinking the suspect said, 'This is for *Juan*.' They can sound pretty similar in the heat of the moment."

"You're losing me, Detective. Who's Juan?"

The search results came up, confirming her suspicions, and Maggie smiled to herself. "It's Lay-Z Creek's real name. Juan Acosta. I think this whole thing was a revenge attack, Sarge, done in Creek's name."

"And you believe Detective Stucker is telling the truth this time?"

Smits had a point. Maggie hadn't believed much of anything Stucker had said recently. In fact, she'd gone out of her way to try and prove that he had lied, or at the very least had had reason to be evasive. But when it came to this, to his hearing the attacker say what he did, Maggie had no reason to disbelieve him. His recollection had come without premeditation, and he hadn't named Creek directly; it had been her deduction just now, on the fly, that had made the link.

"Andy had no idea we were already looking at the Creek incident as a possible source for a disaffected character," she said. "He didn't need to offer up anything corroborative."

"He knew about Stavanger's article and your argument with Detective Young."

Smits was doing his job, Maggie realized. Double-checking her facts as well as her deductive reasoning. Making her question herself. Prove that her assessment was airtight, even though it might appear she was grasping at straws. She didn't doubt for one second that Smits thought Stucker was innocent on all counts. He was probing to see if she thought the same way, too, especially after her calling into question the integrity of one of his detectives.

"The Creek incident created a hotbed of public unrest," Maggie said. "Several anonymous death threats were made against Clay and Andy. I think Andy's testimony is a solid lead."

She hoped it was enough, at least to appease her sergeant.

"Okay," he said. "Let's shake this Creek tree and see who falls out. Meanwhile, what about prints—do you think Forensics can pull any from the boat?"

"I doubt it," Maggie said, glad to be moving on. "The suspect wore gloves."

"What about DNA? I heard you clipped him."

Maggie went over to the window and looked out at the boats jostling in the storm. "The thing is, sir, it's torrential rain here. By the time we made it back to the marina, all the blood was washed away. Titusville PD has taken swabs, but quite honestly, it'll be a miracle if there's any trace left."

"All the same," he said, "I'll tell the Crime Lab to expect incoming samples from the Brevard Field Office. While we're at it, what about the items he used to bind Detective Stucker?"

"Again, I'm not raising my hopes. You can pick up zip ties and duct tape like those at most dollar stores and just about every supermarket."

"What about the suspect's bullet casings?"

"All lost in the storm. Things were pretty rough out there. I did find one of the slugs, though. It was a hollow point."

"Which I guess strengthens the argument that the man in the mask and the man on the boat are both one and the same."

"Yes, sir."

"Good work, Detective."

Maggie saw one of the Titusville detectives walking past the window—a portly man with a gray goatee—and she knocked her knuckles on the glass. He slowed and looked, nodding an acknowl-edgment as he saw her. Then he changed course, aiming for the office door.

A moment later, he entered the lounge, dripping rainwater on the wood floor. "You better come quickly," he said. "Patrol made a discovery."

◆　◆　◆

Maggie shivered as she followed the Titusville detective along the dockside to a pier close to where she'd parked earlier. The daylight was almost gone. Streetlights glowing on the roadway. Cold rain needling her face, and damp boots starting to chafe.

Halfway along the dock, a pack of police officers in waterproof capes was gathered, rain drumming against their plastic ponchos. They held flashlights, their beams crisscrossing, their focus on the planking between two tall pilings jutting up through the pier.

"Make way," the Titusville detective ordered as they approached, and a gap opened up to allow them through.

Then Maggie stopped, a few feet short of a dark mass mounded on the wet timbers. At a glance it looked like a dead animal. A drowned black Labrador fished out of the marina. But in the beams of multiple flashlights, she recognized it as the killer's hooded oilskin.

One of the uniforms poked at it with a fishing gaff.

A sleeve flopped out to the side, slapping wetly against the wood, the sleeve knotted at the cuff.

"Is it his slicker?" the Titusville detective shouted to her over the gale.

"Looks like it," she shouted back. She bent down as the wind stormed around her, carefully unfolding the tangled mass with the tips of her fingers. The other sleeve appeared, also knotted at the cuff. "Where was this found?"

The uniform pointed with the gaff, directing her gaze and several of the flashlights to spools of rope coiled on the dock farther along a slip. "Bunched up," he said. "Over there."

"Snagged up on the line?"

"No, ma'am. Bundled up and stuffed inside the rope."

Maggie straightened. "You're sure it was on top of the dock?"

"Yes, ma'am."

The Titusville detective said, "Why ditch the jacket *after* climbing out? It must have weighed him down *in* the water."

"Because he no longer needed it," Maggie said. "See how the sleeves are knotted? He did that out in the lagoon. It's a survival technique. Tying the sleeves and trapping air under the coat turns it into a flotation device. He dumped it here so that it wouldn't slow him down on foot." A cold dagger pierced Maggie's gut. "Round up your people," she said as realization struck home. "We need to secure the perimeter right now. There's a chance he's still in the marina. We can't let him escape."

◆ ◆ ◆

The Titusville detective dealt out orders, and the pack broke up, going separate ways. Flashlights slicing through the twilight. *Look under tarps. Check inside any cabin not locked. Scour the boatyard next door.*

"K-9 on scene," someone shouted in the same moment Maggie heard a scuffling on the boards behind her.

She turned to see a police dog handler approaching, a black German shepherd with raindrops beading on its coat trotting obediently at his side.

"Move back," the Titusville detective shouted to those still remaining. "Give them some room." Everyone obeyed, stepping aside. He directed the handler to the oilskin. "The suspect's slicker."

The handler spoke into the dog's ear, then guided it to the raincoat. Gently, the dog sniffed at the mounded material, its snout hovering a hair's width from the wet fabric, going back and forth as it vacuumed up scent molecules.

"The suspect's wounded," Maggie shouted. "There should be blood."

Suddenly, the dog stopped sniffing and looked up at her. Brown eyes reflecting flashlights. Then it turned its back on the raincoat and began to sniff at the wooden planks leading away from the water.

"Scent acquired," the handler announced, and he set off at a jog, back along the dock, the dog straining at its leash ahead of him.

Maggie fell in behind. She heard the Titusville detective instruct everyone to *stay close* and *be alert*, and a dozen feet started to pound along the dock in her wake. Flashlights chasing shadows.

With the recovery of the raincoat, her hopes of a capture were suddenly renewed. Her thinking being that if the suspect's injury was debilitating and he hadn't gotten far, and if they looked hard enough, they would discover him in hiding.

Just waiting to be found.

And Maggie wasn't for giving up without a fight.

She took out her Glock as she ran, keeping the gun pointed at the ground and her arm straight, ready.

The handler passed by one docked boat after another, the dog moving like a panther stalking its prey. Head dipped, shoulders rolling, its tail at a right angle to its body, dead straight, its snout an inch above the rain-slicked wood. It seemed oblivious to the squall, scampering but totally focused.

The handler reached the end of the dock and went through the open security gate. Undeviating, the dog cut across the communal walkway, up over the roadside grass, and into the parking lot.

Maggie kept pace as it passed between two police cruisers, making a hard right after and moving behind several more black-and-whites parked helter-skelter.

The handler passed behind Maggie's motor pool sedan and Stucker's truck. Then the dog stopped, suddenly, and in the empty parking space on the other side of the pickup, it began to circle a small puddle on the concrete, its nose signposting the spot.

"Trail termination," the handler announced as everyone gathered around and half a dozen flashlights lit up the scene. "Looks like your boy flew the coop."

"He's gone?" the Titusville detective asked.

"He's in the wind," Maggie said. "Quickly. We need to widen the search. Get your men back in their cars and out on the streets. He can't have gone far. He's driving a dark-colored pickup, probably with Orange County plates."

But the truth was, the killer could have been halfway to Orlando, and without knowing an exact make and model of his truck, or better yet, a license plate number, he was as good as vanished without a trace.

Maggie was disheartened, but she didn't let it show.

Chapter Thirty-Seven

BUTTERFLY

Driving was proving an effort, and he had to pull over once or twice to attend to his bullet wound. Each time, he had to push the pain past the limits of his senses, forcing it to inhabit the sensory darkness beyond, where it could cause him the least harm. Numbness to everything was the only way to survive. He'd done it before, closing off his emotions so that he could function, cope. Get the job done. He could do it again.

It was the incessant bleeding that pained him now.

He angled the rearview mirror so that he could see his face.

"You've got this," he told his bloodied reflection. "Stay focused."

Deciding to follow his "purpose" to its conclusion hadn't been an easy decision to make. It wasn't like choosing a new car, knowing he could return it to the dealer if he changed his mind. Once he'd committed to walk this path, his fate had been sealed.

Before, and along the way, he'd evaluated the impact his actions would have on his family, balancing out the pros and the cons. Every step of the way, he'd had to remind himself, *this* was for *them*.

History books taught that sacrifice and bloodshed were the bones of every revolution, and that failing systems could only be fixed from within.

He knew that even if he got away with it, he wouldn't escape the internal persecution, the inner torment, the eternal damnation that came from knowing that he had taken an innocent life.

And if he failed, or if he got caught, then he would face the consequences like a man—what was left of him.

His reflection was unrecognizable in the mirror.

The irony was, he'd set out on this path to change things, but his journey had ended up changing *him*.

A new plan began to take shape as he drove back to the city.

Chapter Thirty-Eight

BIBLE STUDY

The wine tasted vinegary, and Maggie poured the rest of it in the kitchen sink. She contemplated opening another bottle, then looked at the lateness of the hour and decided against it. She wasn't in a celebratory mood anyway, and although the thought of pickling her brain in alcohol was tempting right now, ideally she wanted to remain sharp, focused; she had work to do, and it called for ice-cold clarity.

Something had bugged her the whole drive home.

She poured a glass of water from the fridge dispenser and dropped ice in it. Then she picked up the pizza box from the counter and went through to the den.

Mood lighting glowed as she settled onto a couch.

Maggie had done a ton of thinking on the drive back to Orlando, keeping to the posted speed limit and following her thoughts where they led.

Stucker's confirmation that the killer was linked with the Lay-Z Creek incident, and that he was targeting her colleagues as payback for the rapper's death in custody, had focused both Maggie and the investigation to a fine point. A concentrated dot as bright as the sun. And a motivation of revenge over Creek's death had become their go-to theory.

The investigation had gotten its legs and was sprinting for the finish line. They knew the *why* and most of the *how*. All that was left to learn was the *who*.

Of course, Maggie still wasn't ready to fully dismiss the possibility of Stucker knowing more than he was saying—especially when it came to the nature of the ambiguous texts sent from Clay's phone—but she recognized she had to give him the benefit of the doubt if she wanted to make any kind of headway with finding the killer's true identity.

In fact, she was convinced that she had most of the pieces already, at least to form a discernable picture, and that putting a name and a face to the killer was within her grasp. Teasing and tantalizing at the tips of her fingers. All she had to do was *reach*, and it was hers for the taking.

She took a slice of pepperoni pizza from the box on the couch next to her and tapped her laptop out of sleep mode.

Wet and cold, Maggie had remained at the marina until the steel sky had turned anvil black, lingering long after the cops and the Coast Guard had cleared out, pacing the parking lot, her cheeks ruddy from the wind, her hands numb, replaying in her head the shoot-out on the boat, and analyzing her proximity to her own death.

She'd lingered long after Stucker and Klementina had returned to their palatial home on the riverfront, reminding them to be extravigilant, that it was likely the killer would try to finish what he'd started. Stucker promising that if the killer did fancy another try, this time he wouldn't be so lucky.

She'd watched the storm bash boats in the marina, waiting to hear news from the Titusville detective if anyone had been admitted to any of the county's hospitals or medical centers with indications of a gunshot injury. She'd waited to hear if any of Brevard County's patrol units had stopped a vehicle with a fugitive at the wheel.

Finally, she'd thanked the marina manager for his time, and then she'd shipped out, getting back in the sedan and turning up the heat, driving barefoot to Orlando with the wipers on high.

It had taken her ten miles to stop shivering.

Maggie was the first to admit that she'd been disappointed with the afternoon's outcome. More than that, she'd been annoyed with herself for letting the killer slip through her grasp.

So close and yet so far.

His discarded raincoat was proof he had somehow been able to make it back to the marina—probably, as she'd speculated, using the oilskin as a float and going with the flow. Even with the wind whipping up waves, the lagoon averaged four feet in depth—six or seven feet if you counted the swells. If all else had failed, the killer would have even been able to wade back to shore. The blood trail leading to the parking lot proved he had then fled the scene.

Had they been minutes behind, already too late?

Several times on the drive back to the city, Maggie had recalled her arrival at the marina, trying to visualize the vehicle parked on the other side of Stucker's truck when she'd gotten there. But forcing her memory had proven pointless; she was only able to recall a glimpse of its rear bumper, Stucker's pickup obscuring the rest.

It niggled at her, the thought that the killer's car had been there all along, and she'd missed it. Their three vehicles parked side by side while the three of them had fought for their lives out on the water.

In all probability, Maggie knew, the killer had driven away before the police and the Coast Guard had arrived on the scene, while Stucker was still blindly navigating *Celestial Body* back to the marina.

With no surveillance cameras monitoring the parking lot, there was no way to form a workable description of the suspect's vehicle.

The killer had fled the scene and was now *anywhere*.

Maggie didn't like being beaten.

A few weeks into their relationship, Steve had let it slip that he saw her as competitive, not with him per se, but rather in her work environment. In fact, she was probably one of the most competitive women he'd ever met—in a good way, of course.

Maggie had had to politely disagree.

Being competitive wasn't in the running.

Law enforcement was a male-dominated environment, with a police officer ratio of six to one in favor of men, the disparity widening considerably with rank. A woman had to be two steps ahead of her male counterparts just to be on an equal footing.

What Steve called competitiveness, she called *survival*.

Maggie picked up her landline handset from its cradle on the accent table and called Steve's number. It was late, but all of a sudden, she wanted to touch base.

She chewed cold pizza, listening to his number ring.

Using the marina manager's phone, she'd called Steve earlier while she was still in Titusville, catching him between seminars and unable to talk at length. Just enough time to tell him she'd been in a scrape *again*, but that she was okay *again*. Steve had offered to cut short his Atlanta trip—no conference was more important than her welfare—but Maggie had urged him to stay put; he was guest speaking in several lectures over the next few days, and she didn't want to disappoint paying attendees who had traveled from all over the country.

Steve had called her back on her landline a couple of hours later, after she'd gotten home, allowing them to catch up in full, Maggie not realizing exactly how much she'd missed him until she'd heard him rave about the seminars he'd attended.

But he wasn't answering his phone now.

"Hey," she said as his voice mail came on. "I know it's late, and you're probably catching your beauty sleep. I just wanted to hear your voice. Don't worry. I'm okay. Everything's quiet here. I'll call you in the morning." She went to say, "I love you," but checked herself, not understanding why, then said it anyway.

Why did she falter when it came to spontaneously articulating her feelings for Steve?

Nick had called him "vanilla," implying that she could do better. But Maggie had no hunger for that. She was happy with Steve. His down-to-earth, soothe-talking normalcy was part of the attraction. It put things in perspective—doctor's orders after a long day of chasing murderers. That, and his capacity for holding on to a lightning bolt like her without burning himself.

Maggie knew she wasn't the easiest person in the world to live with, or to love. It took someone special to stay the course, to accept that she lived and breathed homicide. Steve wasn't perfect. He didn't check all the boxes. But he did check the ones that mattered. Maybe marrying him would be the making of her?

She hung up the landline and logged into Major Case's secure cloud server on her laptop.

Wired and exhausted, she had spent the early evening writing reports at the office—one for Smits and one for the Professional Standards Section.

No escaping red tape.

The first had been a relatively straightforward undertaking, printed out and left on Smits's desk. Smits was partial to printouts. He liked the feel of real paper in his hands. He'd read it in the morning, over coffee, perhaps raise an eyebrow, then file it.

The second had proved much trickier to put together. The Professional Standards Section was OCSO's equivalent of the IAD, the Internal Affairs Division, and Maggie had had to be mindful of her phrasing in compiling her account. Although the shoot-out on the boat was a clear case of self-defense, her use of deadly force had to be justified. There was no wiggle room. Her report couldn't raise doubt and call into question her decision-making capacity. It wasn't so much what she said, but how she said it.

She'd submitted the report, knowing she wouldn't hear anything anytime soon.

Then, before heading home, she'd looked through the documents that Loomis had left on her desk: the Creek files.

While she had lingered at the marina, Smits had instructed Loomis to look at persons of interest associated with the Creek incident. Her partner had circled names in reports and printed out a bunch of police mug shots of people who had caused a ruckus in the name of justice for the dead rapper—a list of troublemakers who had spoken out publicly, blaming and condemning Stucker and Young for Creek's death in custody. People with rap sheets as long as her arm. People known for violent crimes. Any one of them capable of killing Maggie and her colleagues.

None of them had looked remotely familiar—and Maggie had a knack for remembering faces.

Tomorrow would see them knocking on doors.

On her laptop, Maggie navigated to the folder labeled Creek Incident and scanned through the files on the server until she located the nine death threats that had come into the Sheriff's Office in the aftermath of the rapper's passing. One was a mailed letter, and eight were in the form of typed transcripts from incoming telephone calls.

The transcripts were short, mainly composed of one or two lines. Essentially, troublemakers using pay phones to shout abuse

299

at the switchboard operator. Making death threats against the lives of detectives before hanging up.

The scanned letter was altogether different.

It consisted of several typed paragraphs, all neatly justified. Not printed out to hard copy from a computer document, but *typed* the old-fashioned way: on a mechanical typewriter.

Maggie had never seen it before, which wasn't surprising; she'd heard about the death threats from her colleagues, but the Creek incident hadn't been within her purview at the time.

She expanded the scanned document to full screen.

Overall, the letter came across as a heartfelt plea for justice to be served on behalf of a grieving family. It talked about a young life robbed from them and the indifferent attitude of the authorities. It stated Detective Young's reckless use of a Taser on Creek when the rapper's heart condition was public domain, and the ME covering up foul play in his ruling accidental death. There were no direct threats to do harm per se, but both Young and Stucker were named as "facilitators" in the rap artist's death.

The letter concluded by stating that the family would never rest until those responsible for Creek's murder had paid in full for their crime.

Not surprisingly, there was no signature at the bottom. However, there was an underlined biblical reference:

Leviticus 24:19–21

Maggie knew less than a handful of Bible quotes by heart—this not being one of them. She opened a browser, typed the reference into the search bar, then sat back, mulling over the words that appeared on the screen:

19 Anyone who injures their neighbor is to be injured in the same manner: **20** fracture for fracture, eye for eye, tooth for tooth. The one who has inflicted the injury must suffer the same injury. **21** Whoever kills an animal must make restitution, but whoever kills a human being is to be put to death.

A little repulsed, Maggie clicked the quote away. She could appreciate the sentiments, but the essence went against everything she believed in as a police officer and as a public servant. In her eyes, there was no place for vigilante justice in a society hinged on the rule of law.

But the letter did affirm to her that the investigation was now on the right track. More than ever, she believed that Clay's coerced suicide and the attempts on Stucker's life were both because of the role they had played in the rapper's death.

An eye for an eye.

Maggie disconnected from Major Case's server and brought up her email app.

Straightaway, she spotted an email from Nick with the subject line Your Crime Scene Videos and a zip folder attached. She saved the attachment to her laptop, then unpacked the compressed files—half a dozen videos, each one marked as the "Property of WESH-2 News."

"I owe you, Nick," she said as she clicked on the first clip.

She chewed pizza as the video began to play.

The footage had been shot from a slightly elevated position, looking across the treetops and the Walmart parking lot. She could see the store in the background, and people crowding the edges of the shot. Maggie guessed it had been filmed from the camera situated on the roof of the news van. She could see a scattering of customer vehicles and red-and-blue police lights flashing. Walmart customers gathered in the store entrance area, not yet evacuated. The bomb yet to go off.

Clay's red Nissan Sentra was at the focus of the frame, dozens of officers corralled behind the yellow-and-black police tape. She spotted herself, standing with Deputies Ramos and Shaw a few yards to the side of Clay's car, and she discarded her pizza slice back in the box, suddenly not that hungry.

Seeing Deputy Shaw again, alive at the crime scene, brought a chill to Maggie's skin. The young deputy looked composed, hands on hips, talking with Ramos, unknowingly minutes away from her own death.

The world can change in a heartbeat.

Maggie muted the laptop's volume, then zoomed the picture in on the audience in the Walmart entranceway.

She was hoping she might spot the killer in the crowd.

Among law enforcement, it was a commonly accepted fact that some criminals revisited crime scenes after the event, often to get off on the spectacle of their handiwork, as well as to derive a sense of accomplishment and validation for their actions. Psychologically, their return was seen as an act of voyeurism in its purest form, with arsonists and murderers statistically more predisposed to undertake the perverse practice.

Was the man who attacked her here?

One by one she peered at the fuzzy faces, waiting for her gut to flinch, to announce, *That's him!*

She squinted at women, children, men . . . finally homing in on a man standing alone at the back of the pack. He had short sandy hair and wore what looked like mirrored aviator sunglasses.

Are you him? she wondered. She peered closer, the tip of her nose almost touching the screen.

Her landline rang, startling her. She reached over and picked up the handset. "Hello?"

"Maggie. It's Sasha."

"Sasha?" Maggie leaned back from the screen.

"I know it's getting late. I hope I'm not disturbing you."

Maggie sat up. "No, it's fine. Is everything okay? I wasn't expecting . . ." She fumbled for the right thing to say, then opted for the obvious. "It's good you called. How are you?"

"Coping," Sasha answered. There was a noticeable rattle in her voice, as though something was stuck in the back of her throat and needed spitting out. "Right now the best way I've found is to take things one minute at a time."

Maggie kept her eyes on the video. "I was going to call . . ."

"Maggie, it's all right. I know you've been busy. Laremy came over this evening. We cried together and prayed for Clay. It might sound crazy, but it was therapeutic. He told me about the other man you saw getting out of Clay's car that night, and what it means. It's a relief, knowing Clay isn't responsible for any of it."

Maggie was tongue-tied. She didn't know the exact details of Sasha's conversation with Lieutenant Dunbar, but she knew that whatever he had said to her, it had been selective.

Was the damage control his way of protecting her?

"I wanted to tell you myself," Maggie said. "But with one thing after another, I didn't find the time." She didn't mention that Smits had also forbidden her to make contact.

"That's why I'm calling," Sasha said. "I heard what happened. In Titusville. This afternoon. I felt I should reach out."

"You spoke with Andy?"

"He's a good listener. We've spent hours talking since . . ." Her words trailed off, and Maggie heard her swallow, twice, failing each time to unblock her throat. "I couldn't ask for a better friend right now."

"It's good you've got Andy's shoulder," Maggie said. "It's what Clay would've wanted." Maggie closed her eyes, silently admonishing herself for overstepping. The truth was, she had no idea what Clay would have wanted. "How are the boys?" she asked, hoping to divert Sasha's attention away from her blunder.

It worked; she sensed Sasha brighten.

"Bless them," Sasha said. "They're being brave. It's mostly for my sake, I know. I'm so proud of the way they're conducting themselves right now."

Maggie felt herself smile. "Listen to me. I'm calling them boys. But they're young men now, aren't they? They're a credit to you, Sasha, and to Clay. I'm glad you're all together."

On the other end of the connection, Sasha had gone quiet. Maggie could hear her breath rattling in the microphone. Not for the first time, Maggie wondered how she might feel if she were in Sasha's shoes.

Out of the corner of her eye, she caught sight of herself on the laptop screen, closing the Sentra's door a fraction of a second before it flung wide open again, knocking her off her feet. A ring of crumbled glass blowing out from the shattered windows. The recording shaking as the concussion wave hit the onlookers, scattering them.

Maggie reached out and hit the pause button.

She heard a tremor rise in Sasha's breathing.

"Sasha, is there something you want to share with me?"

"Maggie, there is," she said quietly. "But I'm not sure where to start."

"The beginning's always good."

"Well, I feel bad," Sasha said. "And I need to get it off my chest. I need to be honest with you, Maggie. I wasn't completely transparent the other day, and it's been weighing heavily on my conscience ever since. Clay received a phone call that night."

"New Year's Eve?"

"Yes."

"What time?" Maggie was thinking about the number she'd found in the call log on Clay's phone, and Donna Krick reporting back from Digital Forensics that she had been unable to trace it.

"Minutes before he left home."

Maggie almost said, *Didn't you think that information was important?* but she bit her tongue instead, knowing her being judgmental was the last thing Sasha needed. "Why are you only telling me this now?"

"I suppose it slipped my mind. My head was in a spin."

"Do you know who the call was from?"

"I don't." Sasha's reply came with a delay, the pause significant enough to tell Maggie that either Sasha knew otherwise, or she suspected she might know the caller's identity. "But I think it was the real reason he left that night when he did," she said. "Going for milk was just the excuse. Laremy told me about the woman you saw in the security recording. The one talking with Clay right before he . . ." Again, she couldn't bring herself to say it. "Anyway, when Laremy told me about her, it made sense that she was the one who phoned Clay."

Maggie drew an unsteady breath. "Sasha, this is difficult for me to say and definitely difficult for you to hear. But I need to be honest with you as well. I found a text conversation on Clay's phone. A list of clandestine meetings. Dates, times, and hotels. When I've seen this kind of thing in the past—"

305

"He promised me he wasn't."

Maggie bit the bait. "Having an affair?"

"Yes." This time Sasha's response came too quickly, almost defensively. "For months, every time I asked, he said I was imagining things. But a wife knows when her husband is being dishonest. And if she doesn't, then she's in denial."

"Is that why the two of you were arguing more than usual lately?"

"Yes. But how . . . ?"

"A concerned neighbor."

"Oh. I didn't realize our fights were impacting the neighborhood."

On screen, Maggie was lying on her back on the blacktop, a raggedy ring of broken glass surrounding the Sentra, the air shimmering with heat and vapor. She could see Corrigan on his back, a few yards behind the car, his face a bloody mess.

A cold breath moved across Maggie's skin.

"I just had this *feeling*," Sasha was saying, her voice suddenly racked with hurt. "I just knew he was seeing somebody else. I could *sense* it. But he wouldn't admit to it, no matter how many times I brought it up. He was the innocent party, and I was the one losing my mind."

Maggie cleared her throat. "Sasha, I'm sorry."

"I loved him, Maggie. But he made a fool out of me."

"No, Sasha. He made a fool of himself, hence the term *fooling around*. You're not to blame for what he did. That's all on him."

Sasha went quiet again, seemingly while she thought about Maggie's words.

Maggie's gaze traveled beyond Corrigan to the police cordon, where Shaw was in the process of falling to the ground, clutching at her thigh. Ramos crouching behind her, his back to the explosion, covering his head with his arms.

"The boys must never know," Sasha said, her voice hushed. It was both a request and an instruction.

What could Maggie say? She was all too familiar with the effect her own mother's affairs had had on the family. The pain of betrayal seemed to go on forever. As her father had once said, "Even the shortest fling has a far-flung reach."

"It will ruin them," Sasha continued. "I can't let that happen."

"Sasha, my lips are sealed."

"Thank you, Maggie."

"Anytime. For the record, while we're being honest, I know about the call Clay received right before he left for the store. I figured it could be from the woman he was arguing with."

"They were arguing?"

Dunbar hadn't told Sasha the full facts, Maggie realized. Just that Clay had been filmed talking with another woman.

"Actually," Maggie said, "by the looks of it, she was giving him a dressing down. It wasn't an easy conversation to have, or to watch."

"I see." Sasha said it in a way that meant that she didn't. "Can you describe her, Maggie?"

"Not properly. She kept her face hidden from the camera the whole time she was at the store. She was about your build. Dark skinned. Red nail polish. A black ring on her right hand."

"A *black* ring?"

"Yes. It looked like engraved wood."

"Was it on her right thumb?"

"It was." Maggie sat up. "Sasha, do you know who she is?"

"I think I do, Maggie. It sounds like De-Andra."

It took a second for Maggie to make the connection, by which time Sasha said, "I have to go," and hung up before Maggie could object.

Maggie stared at the handset.

The only person with that name that she knew was De-Andra Dunbar, the wife of Lieutenant Laremy Dunbar, Sasha's brother.

◆ ◆ ◆

Maggie was still staring at the handset when it rang in her hand.

The caller ID said *Unknown Number*.

Automatically, she checked the time, realizing it was a little late for cold callers, and she answered with a wary hello.

"Miss Novak?" It was a man's voice. He sounded nasally, stuffy, like he had a head cold.

"Who's asking?"

"I'm calling about your father."

Maggie sat up straight, planting her feet on the floor. "Who is this?"

"A neighbor. Your father gave me your number a while ago, in case of an emergency. I'm sorry to trouble you. I didn't know who else to call."

Maggie stood up, her skin suddenly prickling at the thought of something happening to her father. "Is my dad okay?"

"He's fine. I just can't get him out of my front yard, is all."

"What?"

"I don't know what's going on with him. I'm no doctor, but he seems confused, and I can't get him to go home. I realize it's late, but could you come over?"

"Sure." Maggie went through to the hall and scooped her keys from the table. "Listen, I'm sorry for your inconvenience. What's your address?"

"Just down the street from your father's. The corner house with the Winnebago in the driveway?"

Maggie recalled seeing the recreational vehicle parked a few doors down from her father's house in Red Bug Lake, each of its tires flat, its bodywork discolored with green algae. Her father had called it a landmark in the neighborhood. But it was more like a blot on the landscape.

Maggie opened the front door. "Give me twenty minutes?"

"Thanks, Miss Novak. See you soon."

Outside, the rain had passed, but the lush Florida landscape was still wet, a coolness hanging in the damp air.

What was going on with her father?

Maggie popped the locks on her Mustang and dropped into the driver's seat. Rock music blared from the speakers as she started the engine. Something from Aerosmith. She switched on the headlights, then reversed out of the driveway a little too fast, tires screeching as she backed out into the cul-de-sac.

Her father had been acting strangely for a while now. Not all the time. Intermittently. In conversation he seemed lucid, coherent, rational. It was his behavior that was occasionally odd, unpredictable.

Does he have a brain tumor?

The thought gave her chills.

She stepped on the gas as she drove uphill through the Hammocks.

As far as she knew, no one in the Novak family had ever been diagnosed with anything like that. According to the family medical history, the Novaks lived to a ripe old age, only stopping when something stopped them. Her father was the brainiest person she knew, his analytical mind having provided a good living for his family over the years. How cruel would it be if it turned out that the one thing that had been his saving would end up being his undoing?

Again, she didn't want to think about it.

She slowed for the intersection with White Road, then made the right, accelerating beyond the speed limit as the pavement opened up in front of her.

He'd always seemed strong and healthy. One of those people whose immune systems repelled viruses like bullets bouncing off Superman's chest. In many ways, he'd seemed indestructible to her. Permanent. But the reality was he was getting old, and with age came infirmity. These things were bound to happen. It wouldn't do any harm to have him checked over. Anything could be happening with him.

She'd never seen him more stressed than since he'd retired.

She made the right onto Clarke Road, driving past the dark hulk of West Oaks Mall lurking behind the trees. She could see breaks in the cloud cover overhead. Jet-black night sky peeking through, salted with stars.

Maybe it was nothing at all. Maybe it was a blip, or just his age, and this kind of random behavior was to be expected from now on. Maybe she had to accept that nothing lasted forever.

As though to drive the point home, R.E.M.'s "It's the End of the World as We Know It" came on the radio, and she reached over, turning it off.

"Hey," a voice sounded from behind her. "I was enjoying that."

Heat bloomed in Maggie's chest, and she almost let go of the wheel. She snatched a glance over her shoulder, her mind suddenly racing into overdrive. Every nerve electrified. Every sense on high alert.

There was a man sitting in the back in shadow. He had on a hoodie with the hood up, and a white hockey mask covered his face.

Fire swept through her lungs.

"Keep your eyes on the road and your hands on the wheel," he said, his voice muffled by the mask.

Instinctively, Maggie lifted her foot off the gas, intending to stomp on the brake and throw the intruder into the back of the passenger seat. From there she could bring an elbow down on the nape of his neck, incapacitate him long enough to get the upper hand. But she hesitated, rethinking her next move as his gloved fist came into view holding a gun, the muzzle pointed at her face.

"Don't even think about trying anything courageous," he said, as though reading her thoughts. "Don't make me shoot you in the face. Just drive. You're safer driving. We've got some talking to do."

Chapter Thirty-Nine

UNDER CONSTRUCTION

The flames ran wild in Maggie's chest, her thoughts crashing as she glanced in the rearview mirror at the inhuman face staring back.

She wanted to say, *Who are you? What do you want?* but both questions were asinine, and not very original in any case. She knew exactly who he was, and she knew exactly what he wanted.

He was *the killer*—the man she'd seen in the video leaving Clay's car minutes after Clay's suicide. The same man who had abducted Stucker and then tried to kill her on the boat. And she had no doubt in her mind that he was here to finish what he'd started.

Asking *anything* seemed pointless.

She flicked her gaze to the glove box, her thoughts turning to matters of self-defense; then she remembered with dismay that she'd left her Glock in the house.

The realization came as a sickening blow.

In her haste to rush to her father's side, she'd left everything except the landline handset behind. She hadn't even brought her purse. The handset was on the passenger seat next to her, within reach, but useless this far from home.

The muzzle nudged her cheekbone.

"I said keep both hands on the wheel." His voice was nasally, stuffy, like he had a head cold.

Out of the corner of her eye, she saw him reach through the gap between the seats and take the handset.

"It was you, wasn't it?" she said. "On the phone a minute ago, pretending to be my dad's neighbor. You used my fear for his welfare to lure me outside."

"You've got a fancy new intruder alarm and a bunch of nosy neighbors. I had to bait you out of the house somehow."

"If you've harmed my dad in any way . . ."

"Relax," he said. "This is between you and me."

Maggie released a tense breath, cursing herself for failing to notice the man in the back seat when getting in the car.

In not too dissimilar circumstances, her abduction from home in November had seen her driving through the night at gunpoint, too. Only that time, she'd known that backup was on its way. This time around she was on her own, and no one was coming to her rescue.

Her surviving the night was all down to her.

Maggie contemplated her options. She could flash the headlights at oncoming vehicles, or swerve the Mustang off the road into the trees, make a run for it in the dark. A large wooded area stretched along this side of Clarke Road. Long tracts of shadow between the streetlights. Plenty of places to ditch the car and disappear. If she kept her bearings, she could make her way back home through the woods on foot, raise the alarm.

What she couldn't do was wrestle with an armed killer and expect to come out of it on top.

The muzzle pressed at the back of her jaw.

"Just so we're clear," he said from behind her. "I won't hesitate to shoot you and every one of your family members if you try to escape."

Maggie glanced in the rearview mirror again. His masked face was in shadow, the hood obscuring the shape of his head. "Why are you doing this? Is it really all just payback for what happened to Lay-Z Creek?"

She studied his reflection, trying to gauge his reaction despite the mask.

"Take a left at the lights," he said.

Maggie flicked her gaze back to the road ahead. The intersection with West Colonial Drive was coming up, traffic lights piercing the dark. There were no other vehicles on the street, and the signals were on green. Maintaining the car's speed, she swung the Mustang into the left-turn lane, tires squealing as the car followed the long left turn onto SR 50.

"Slow down," he told her. "Keep to the posted speed limit. Don't do anything to attract attention."

"Where are we going?"

He sniffed, coughed. "You'll know when we get there."

Colonial Drive bisected Central Florida. It ran east-west from one side of the state to the other. Maggie knew that on their present course, they would reach downtown Orlando in ten minutes, and eventually Titusville, of all places, fifty minutes after that. A hundred offshoots between there and here, with quiet back roads crisscrossing the county.

She thought about all the secluded spots, the untamed woodland, the overgrown swamps, all the isolated backwater places in which the killer could dispose of her body. Although more than twenty million people called Florida their home, the state was mostly wilderness, composed of inhospitable wetlands and shallow reedy lakes. Add to that the tropical climate and any number of carnivorous animals, and the likelihood of a dumped body being found off the beaten path wasn't great.

Probably, he didn't want her to be found.

Maggie's hands were clammy on the wheel, her thoughts coming thick and fast.

"How is this going to play out?" she asked. "Are you going to make it look like suicide? Or, are you just going to shoot me and dump my body?"

"Shooting you would make us even," he answered glibly.

It wasn't the answer she was hoping for. Her one small consolation was knowing that he wouldn't shoot her while she was driving. The repercussions would be unpredictable and certainly put his own life in jeopardy. Driving gave her time to think, to engage with him and keep him talking.

Could she talk sense into him?

"I'm curious," she said. "How did you coerce Detective Young into killing himself?" She glanced in the mirror. "That is what you did, isn't it? That was your doing, right? You talked him into blowing his brains out." She waited for a response, but none came. She told herself to keep talking. "Either way, it was a smart move. The elaborate plan of yours. Making us think he'd committed suicide as well as wanting his partner dead. The whole setup stopped us looking for a killer. So how did you do it? How did you force my colleague's hand? It must've taken some doing. Detective Young was the definition of hardheaded." She stared at his masked reflection. "You can tell me. It won't make any difference to what's going to happen."

"Just drive," he said.

"I thought you wanted to talk?"

"Not about that." He sniffed again, coughed.

She heard him clear his throat, then saw him lift the bottom of the mask slightly and spit phlegm into the foot space behind her seat.

DNA evidence. Spat in her car. The killer, she knew, had no intention of the car being found either.

Maggie waited a few seconds before saying, "You know, in a weird kind of way, I understand where you're coming from

315

with all this. Wanting revenge the way you do. If I were in your shoes, and it was someone dear to me who died in custody, I'd be angry, too, especially if it was preventable. I'd want justice. In fact, I'd campaign for it. But I'd also have to accept the facts, no matter how much they conflicted with my own personal take on things." She watched his reflection again, looking for anything to confirm she was on the right track. "The coroner ruled Creek's death accidental."

"No," he said quietly. "People lie."

"And so what're you saying—vigilante justice is the answer? I agree in righting wrongs, but I can't agree with vigilantism. There are other ways of going about it."

"I tried."

"You didn't try hard enough. I read your letter. That was you, wasn't it? The letter with the biblical quote." Maggie was speculating again, fishing, trusting her intuition and trying to tap into his humanity. "It was moving. Your family sound nice. Good people. It's no surprise they were devastated. Do they know you're here doing this? Is this what they want, too—an eye for an eye?"

"You have no idea."

"I know Detective Young had a wife and two sons. Like yours, they're a loving family. His boys were doing great in college. But now they'll have to live the rest of their lives without their father. You did that to them. Help me understand why. Because from where I am, it doesn't make any sense. After seeing what death did to your own family, you still went ahead and wrecked another. That's the bit I don't understand. Do you have children?"

She sensed him lean forward in the seat, and she risked a quick peep over her shoulder, only to find his masked face a few inches from hers, his breath rasping against the plastic.

"I know what you're doing," he said. "It won't work. Save your breath. You're going to need it."

Then he sank back into the shadows.

Maggie's stomach was in knots.

One after the other, she wiped her sweaty palms off on her pants.

In silence, they passed darkened strip malls, brightly lit restaurants, clusters of gas stations. The highway had been resurfaced in recent years, and the blacktop glistened like wet leather after the rain.

As instructed, Maggie kept to the speed limit, traffic lights courteously turning green as they approached them. A handful of vehicles traveling in their direction. The occasional headlights dazzling from the other side of the road. The bad weather had kept people indoors, and West Colonial Drive was all but deserted.

Maggie wondered if any state troopers were parked on the roadside, and how she could get their attention if they were.

Could she risk her life on it?

What about her family's?

She had to face the facts. Right now she was in an impossible situation. She was buckled up and trapped in the driver's seat, committed to steering a two-ton vehicle at a constant forty-five miles per hour while her abductor sat pretty behind her, covering her with a handgun.

In no way could she defend herself.

She couldn't even twist around and try to disarm him. In fact, with her hands as good as tied to the wheel, she couldn't do anything except drive. But once they reached their destination, things would change. The car would stop. She would be able to move more freely. And if they got out of the car, that's when her hand-to-hand training would come into its own.

Of course, it was all guesswork. For all she knew, he had plans to shoot her in the back of the head the moment she switched off the engine. Maybe she wouldn't even know anything about it. One second staring out the windshield, the next . . .

Maggie drew a deep breath and told herself to focus on the positives.

She was still alive. And where there was life, there was hope.

If he'd wanted simply to kill her, he would have shot her in the driveway, or sneaked in the house in the dead of the night and shot her in her sleep. The fact that he hadn't taken the simplest option told her that he had a preferred kill spot in mind. Somewhere he could carry out the murder on his terms, for whatever reason. And there, at that remote location, would be her best shot at freedom.

The intersection with John Young Parkway came and went. Maggie spotted the Sheriff's Office coming up on the right, a sudden sense of pride and hope bristling within her.

The killer saw it, too; the muzzle pressed more firmly against her cheekbone.

"Don't," he warned.

Through the roadside trees, Maggie caught glimpses of the floodlit parking lot. Rows of white sheriff's cruisers and one or two deputies walking to their vehicles.

She kept her foot on the gas, and within seconds, the Sheriff's Office was left behind, and with it any chance she might have had of bringing attention to her abduction.

"Take the interstate," he said, nudging her with the gun.

"Which way?"

"East."

That would take them out of Orlando, she knew, through Altamonte Springs and Lake Mary, eventually intersecting with I-95 at Daytona Beach.

Where was he taking her?

She had to keep him talking, build mutual trust.

Fostering a civil communication was a crucial part of crisis negotiation. It could mean the difference between life and death, and at the very least, it could buy her time.

"What's with the hockey mask?" she said, looking at him in the mirror.

"Privacy."

"But it's just you and me. Why don't you let me see your face? It's not as though I'll be able to describe you to a sketch artist. You're going to kill me anyway, right? You hold the ace card here. You've got nothing to lose at this point."

He didn't answer—Maggie suspected he was thinking it over, debating the pros and cons of revealing himself to her—then he nudged her face again with the gun.

"Don't miss the on-ramp."

Maggie eased off the gas as the multilayered interchange with I-4 appeared out of the dark.

Striped construction barrels lined the roadway leading to it, orange lights glowing on their tops. Tall cranes standing over the interchange, silhouetted against the clouds.

As part of the Ultimate Improvement Project, this section of the interstate had been undergoing new construction for some time now, expanding the number of lanes as well as erecting a whole new road bridge spanning Lake Ivanhoe. The plan was to improve traffic flow across the county, but for months the construction had caused nothing but headaches and major delays.

Maggie drove underneath the elevated roadway. She took the next left, following the narrower lane as it ascended to the interstate. Concrete barriers and more orange construction drums on either side.

"Slow down," he said. "There's a site entrance coming up on the right. Take it."

Where the on-ramp climbed to meet the interstate, Maggie could see a noticeable gap in the construction barrels. It was an opening leading into the construction site and the new bridge currently being built alongside the existing one.

Maggie touched the brake, then swung the car through the gap in the concrete barrier. Grit rattled around the fenders as the Mustang bucked on the uneven surface. Once again, she thought about leaping out of the car and making a run for it, then had second thoughts as the muzzle stroked her cheekbone.

"Keep going," he said. "Not long now."

The temporary road sloped gradually upward, running parallel to the existing interstate. Maggie drove between mounds of sand and composite, passing the hulks of heavy construction machinery, sitting dark and silent for the night.

There was no construction crew here at this hour, and most of the construction site was unlit. Even so, Maggie could make out the half-built curve of the new bridge as it reached midway across Lake Ivanhoe before terminating in a sudden cutoff over the black water.

She wondered if there were any night security officers and if they were alert to her trespassing.

"Where are we going?" she asked.

"See the concrete mixer?"

She looked.

Up ahead, where the bridge began to strike out above the lake, a mixer truck was parked against the temporary concrete barrier, its lights off and its drum revolving.

He was going to entomb her in fresh cement, she realized. Shoot her out here on the deserted bridge, then cover her in the wet mix. Bury her in the body of the bridge, right here in the heart of the city.

Fear clutched at her heart, so tightly that it hurt.

There was nowhere left to run.

She should have acted before now. Made her move before her options had been narrowed down to *this*.

With panic burning through her, she stood on the brake, pressing down with all her strength.

Chapter Forty

THE END OF THE ROAD

The Mustang's hood dipped, and the car came to an abrupt standstill, throwing Maggie against the seat belt. She heard the killer smack into the back of the passenger seat. Then she felt the gun jab into her ribs.

"What are you doing?"

Maggie didn't answer. She sat there, unmoving, staring at the cement dust swirling in the headlights, her mind suddenly clearer than it had been in ages.

She knew that fear could be a lifesaver, holding someone back from taking hazardous chances with their own safety. But she also knew that fear could be a killer, sending someone into a blind panic and under the wheels of a bus.

In both cases, fear was in complete control.

"Keep moving."

She knew what she had to do.

In a weird kind of way, her entire life had come down to this moment.

Did she want it to end *now*?

She stomped her foot on the gas.

The sudden burst of acceleration took the killer by surprise, throwing him back against the back seat.

Maggie pushed her foot down hard.

Energized, the Mustang leaped across the pavement.

In the mirror, Maggie saw the killer trying to right himself, level the gun on her. Adrenaline squeezed her heart again, and she yanked at the steering wheel, half turns, first one way and then the other, repeatedly, each time throwing him sideways, this way and then that, preventing him from recovering long enough to bring the gun to bear.

The Mustang eating up the road.

In the corner of her vision, she saw his fingers clutch the passenger seat headrest, and she let go of the wheel with one hand, hammering his fingers with her fist until he let go.

Then she yanked the wheel hard again, left then right, tires squealing, suspension protesting. She heard him crash into the side window, hard enough to crack his skull.

The Mustang charged onto the unfinished bridge.

Up ahead, dozens of A-framed **ROAD CLOSED** barricades marked the end of the roadway, blocking off the deadly drop. Orange lights warning people to *stay back*. Beyond, the pavement ended abruptly, twenty feet above the black water, as though the concrete had been sheared off, leaving a dark chasm and a sudden terrifying drop.

Fear burned through every inch of her.

But she wasn't *afraid*.

Fear was not her enemy.

Lightning flashed, and a deafening bang sounded in the car. Cymbals ringing in her ears. She noticed a small smoking hole in the dashboard, realizing that the killer had discharged his weapon.

The next bullet could take her head off.

Hot fear kicked in again, and she used it as a strength, standing on the brake again.

The sudden deceleration threw her forward and the killer into the back of her seat. She saw the gun fly out of his hand and clang onto the dash, scooting up against the windshield.

Skidding on the unfinished surface, the Mustang plowed into the first **ROAD CLOSED** barricade. Plastic crossbeams flying up the hood and smashing into the windshield. Thunder clapping and a spider's web of fractures radiating across the glass.

Bang! And another barricade clattered across the hood, flipping over the roof.

The car wasn't going to stop in time.

Maggie's lungs were on fire.

The next A-frame went under the wheels, whacking against the underside of the car and jerking the steering wheel out of her grasp.

She glimpsed the end of the roadway coming up fast, and she grabbed the wheel again, rotating it hard to the right as far as it would go.

Still skidding, the Mustang spun 180 degrees. Maggie clung on for dear life as the rear wheels dropped over the edge and the car collapsed onto the concrete with a bone-shaking thud. Momentum carrying it a few feet farther. Metal grinding against concrete. Then it ground to a juddering halt, seesawing precariously on the precipice.

And silence rushed in.

Maggie realized she was holding her breath, and she let it out. She looked around her, assessing the situation, her heart thudding wildly in her chest.

The car was teetering at a forty-five-degree angle, tilted backward over the end of the roadway, the headlights pointing at the sky, the trunk aimed at the water. In the mirror she could see the killer sprawled in the back seat, his hood fallen down, but his mask still in place. She saw him push himself up, as though groggy, then look past her. She tracked his gaze to the gun on the dash.

He lunged for the back of the passenger seat, his movement causing the car's tilt to steepen even more. The gun began to slide off the dash, gravity pulling it down toward him.

Maggie threw out a hand, trying to catch it as it fell. But it dropped past her fingers and out of reach, falling right into the killer's hand.

Without hesitation, he pulled the trigger.

Chapter Forty-One

LIFE IN THE BALANCE

Maggie blinked with shock as the bullet buried itself into the headrest, an inch from her eye. Then adrenaline burst through her system, flooding her with superheated fuel. She swung around, fumbling with the door handle, intent on leaping to safety before he could fix her in his sights again.

But fate had other plans.

The gun's discharge had pressed the killer into the back seat, and the sudden shift in weight was destabilizing the Mustang's already perilous position on the edge. With a howl, the car started to tip all the way back. Metal screaking as it slipped against the concrete overhang.

Maggie flattened herself against the driver's seat, pressing her head against the headrest, knowing and dreading what was about to come. She saw the hood come up, headlights probing the clouds as the car tilted toward the vertical.

Hardly breathing, she coiled her fingers around the steering wheel and held on with all her might.

There was a moment of inactivity, a suspension of all sound and movement, as though the car had found a new equilibrium and was *stuck*.

Then it fell, silently, like the blade of a guillotine.

And Maggie braced herself as she dropped with it into the abyss.

Chapter Forty-Two

TOMBSTONE

A voice screamed in her head, *Maggie! Maggie, wake up!* and she came to with a jolt, her eyelids springing open, as though somebody had slapped her across the face. It took a fraction of a second for her bruised consciousness to fully coalesce with reality, and for her brain to figure out that she was still sitting in the driver's seat, facing upward like an astronaut waiting for liftoff.

Through the cracked windshield, she could see the car's headlights illuminating the ribbed underbelly of the bridge.

The car was in the shallow lake, standing upright on its back end.

She let out a shaky breath and *assessed*.

No other sounds apart from the ringing in her ears and the gentle ticking of the engine.

Her vision seemed a bit blurry, the readouts on the instrument panel appearing brighter than normal, vivid, almost luminescent in the dark, like the light was flowing in waves from the dashboard.

She had no idea how long she'd been out.

Seconds, minutes?

Lucky.

The word came as a whispered word in her head.

Without question, she was lucky to be alive. At the very least, lucky that nothing seemed to be broken, or *missing*. She'd attended plenty of the aftermaths of car wrecks on the highway, inspecting crushed vehicles that had tumbled from overpasses, seen the victims trapped inside, bent and bloody, or thrown through windshields onto unforgiving concrete. If it hadn't been for her headrest, the twenty-foot fall would surely have snapped her neck.

Behind you.

With a start, she remembered that she wasn't alone in the car, and she twisted in the seat so that she could see the killer.

Behind and *below* her, he was lying flat on his back across the rear window, unmoving.

Maggie switched on the interior lights.

Water swirled underneath him, the rear plastic window buckled and pushed into the car by what appeared to be a block of concrete. The Mustang, she realized, had landed on top of a mound of rubble in the bottom of the lake, becoming wedged upright on the construction debris. Standing tall like a black monolith. As a result, several lengths of rebar had penetrated the car, pointing up at her like lethal stakes in a mantrap.

And the killer was impaled.

One of the iron lengths had punctured his leg and was now protruding up through his thigh. Two feet of hard metal, shiny with blood. More blood soaking his pants and infusing the water around him.

The lake.

It came as another sobering realization. The Mustang, presently standing vertical on its crumpled trunk, was half-sunken. Dark water sloshing against the door windows, level with the side mirrors, and more of it streaming in through the ruptured rear window underneath the killer, slowly filling the inside of the car.

A smell of algae and metal and . . . *gasoline*?

Maggie unclipped her seat belt and rolled over onto her knees in the driver's seat, her hair falling past her face as she looked *down* at the killer.

Incredibly, his hockey mask was still in place.

No sign of the gun.

The car shook and sank a couple of inches deeper into the debris pile. Water gushing in around the broken rear window, filling up around the killer.

At this rate, she estimated she had minutes at most before the water level inside the car matched the outside.

If she didn't do *something*, they could both drown.

Yet, she hesitated, a selfish impulse for her own safety elbowing its way to the front of her thoughts.

Right *now* was the best time to escape both the car and the killer. She could heave open the driver's door, or drop the window while there was still power to the circuitry, swim clear.

But that would be as good as condemning the killer to death by drowning. Once she opened the door or the window, she knew, lake water would come pouring in, filling the car in seconds, killing the killer.

Could she live with *that* outcome?

The car shuddered again, the sound of metal under immense pressure reverberating through the bodywork, and it tilted slightly to one side.

Maggie wondered how much time she had before gravity won out and the weight of the engine pulled the front of the Mustang down into the lake.

Move. Now.

She did. She dropped a leg through the gap between the front seats and balanced her foot on the edge of the back seat. Then, holding on to the headrests for support, she brought her other foot down beside the first.

The killer seemed to be out cold, losing blood from the wound in his leg, his body buoyant as lake water swelled under him.

It was going to be difficult extricating him in the cramped space, and virtually impossible once the car was fully submerged. The inrushing water was already a foot deep and filling fast.

Maggie dropped to her haunches, her gaze locked on his mask, suddenly curious.

Take a look.

Maggie's pulse quickened as she hooked shaking fingertips under the rim and gently pried the mask clear from his face.

The killer's eyes were clamped shut, puffy and blackened, and most of his nose was missing, as though it had been bitten off. Rags of bloody skin in an open wound. A dark furrow running vertically up his forehead and into his hairline, crusted with dried blood.

The shoot-out on the boat.

Maggie had shot him in the face, she realized. That's why he had fallen from the flying bridge, probably stunned and blinded. That's why he sounded like he had a head cold. The bullet had obliterated most of his nose, plowing a vertical gouge in his brow.

His face was like something from a horror movie.

And a cold gasp clutched her throat.

Despite all the blood and the bruising and the horrifying missing nose, she *recognized* the killer.

Chapter Forty-Three

CURIOSITY KILLS

No longer mere whispers, Maggie's thoughts came rushing in from the wings, tripping themselves up as they clamored to take center stage and be *heard*.

The old saying went that *seeing was believing*. But Maggie couldn't believe her eyes. Not one bit. She was positive that the poor light and *shock* were conspiring to play tricks with her vision. Maybe she'd bumped her head during the fall, and she was *seeing things* that weren't there? It had to be the answer. What other way could she interpret what her eyes were seeing? How else could she reconcile the fact that the person behind the mask, the killer, was none other than . . .

"Deputy Ramos?"

Maggie's voice sounded distant, frail, coming from a faraway place.

She blinked, hoping to replace Ramos's image with that of an unknown assailant, someone she could *despise*. But his remained the same familiar face she had come to know so well over the last few months.

How can this be?

Ramos was one of the good guys. Somebody she considered an acquaintance. Someone she trusted, *would* trust with her life. He had a loving family. Strong ties in his community. A rising star in Patrol Division. Someone with a bright future ahead of him. He was kind and considerate, dedicated. A good husband. A good father. A cold-blooded killer.

Maggie stared at Ramos's face as a carousel of conflicting thoughts went round and round in her mind, flashing with emotion.

Surely, *surely*, Ramos *couldn't* be the killer.

There had to be another explanation.

And yet . . . here he was. Undeniably *him*. Floating on his back in her car, unconscious, bloody water lapping his face.

How did this happen?

What terrible twist of fate had compelled him to *murder*?

Maggie was still staring when Ramos's eyes flicked open.

Her first reaction was to say something to reassure him, that despite everything, she wanted to help, not harm. But he didn't let her get her words out. He seemed to size up his predicament in a split second, and chose a deadly response to it.

Before she could utter a single syllable, his hands came up and seized her by the throat, stifling her breath and with it her voice. His attack caught Maggie by surprise. In the same moment, his arms straightened like pistons, his elbows locking, and he lifted her up and away from him.

Maggie grabbed at his wrists with both hands, trying to peel back his fingers from strangling the life out of her.

The car quivered like a dying beast, metal shrieking as the whole vehicle began to tilt and collapse wheels first into the water. The motion dislodged the trunk from being half-buried in the rubble, and Ramos howled as the rebar retracted halfway out of his thigh. But his screams were short lived. As the car dropped into the lake, a torrent of rusty water rushed in through the broken rear window, flooding over his face. Maggie expected his grip to loosen as he choked on the inrush. But it remained firm, his nails digging deep into her flesh.

She swung her fist at his face, but it was ineffective, splashing through the water, missing by inches. She pushed with her legs, trying to pry his hands loose, but she didn't have the angle. Her feet slipped off the rim of the back seat, and suddenly her whole body weight pressed down into his clutch, effectively closing her windpipe.

Ramos was staring at her through the blood-tinted water, his eyes magnified. Tiny bubbles leaking from his lips.

Was he *smiling*?

Was he *enjoying* this?

The water level reached her chin.

She tried to wrench herself free, thrashing and aiming to land a lucky blow, all to no avail.

Then things went from bad to worse.

Ramos pulled her under the surface. Water flooding into her ears, seeping into her mouth. Her lungs screaming at her to *breathe*. In the same instant, the interior lights flickered and went out, plunging them into darkness.

This was it, she realized. Ramos was going to kill her, here in her wrecked Mustang. Hold her under the water and squeeze out every last ounce of her breath until her heart stood still and her oxygen-deprived brain shut down.

She had no way of knowing how long he could hold his breath, but she did know that what little air she had left in her own lungs was rapidly evaporating.

She had to break free.

Now.

Maggie planted her elbow in Ramos's stomach, as hard as she could, ramming it under his ribs and screwing down. She heard a muffled howl rumble through the water, sensed his grip loosen ever so slightly. She leaned all her weight into him, crushing his diaphragm.

His hands sprang clear of her throat.

Maggie didn't hesitate.

With both hands, she pushed away from him, scrabbling up to the sloping roof, desperate to find a pocket of air and cool the flames rampaging through her lungs.

She broke the surface and gulped, her throat raw and rasping.

Less than a few inches of air.

She felt Ramos grabbing at her legs.

She filled her lungs and ducked back under, pulling away from him, over into the front of the car. The Mustang was completely underwater now, settling in the lake, the dash dark and no headlights piercing the gloom. She groped for the driver's door handle and tried the door. It wouldn't budge. Her fingers found the window switch, and she toggled it without any effect. The wiring must have short-circuited. The Mustang was dead in the water.

She went up and grabbed another painful breath.

The air pocket less than an inch.

If she wanted to survive, she had to get out of here *now*.

She went under, into the dark water again, this time bracing her back against the passenger seat headrest and bringing up her legs. Then she kicked both heels at the cracked windshield. Kicking again and again through the water, shock waves coursing up her spine. Fire in her lungs. Acid in her windpipe. Kicking until the window seal tore loose, and the laminated glass flopped onto the submerged hood.

Then, with her heart banging wildly, she dragged herself out through the opening, pulling herself hand over hand through the murk to the surface, where she burst out into the cool night air, her senses spinning, her lungs gasping.

She spat out water, looking frantically around her.

She was in the middle of the lake, the nearest shoreline at least fifty yards away. Above her, the unfinished bridge blocked the night sky, overhanging its concrete support pillars like a giant diving board.

Through the whistling in her ears, she could hear crickets chirping and the distant rumble of traffic passing by on the old interstate bridge.

She'd been seconds from death, and yet the world hadn't even noticed. It had continued on, indifferent.

Maggie trod water and gathered her wits.

Ramos hadn't surfaced.

Barely a few yards below her, he was still trapped inside the car, bleeding out and probably already drowned.

She pictured his mourning widow standing at his graveside, sobbing, black mascara running down her cheeks while Ramos's cute little boy held her hand, looking glum as his daddy's casket was lowered into the ground.

Ramos had let his family down.

Ramos had let the Sheriff's Office down.

Most of all, he'd let himself down.

It wasn't enough to *know* that he had chosen to kill her colleagues and her. Maggie wanted to know *why*.

A beam of light struck her from above, as though the sky had opened up and a heavenly glow had picked her out.

Maggie squinted at it.

"You okay down there?" a man's voice shouted.

"Call nine-one-one," she gasped.

The light lifted, moving away.

335

"Wait," Maggie shouted, and the beam came back to dazzle her. "Don't go. Keep the light shining down here for a minute."

Then, breathing deeply, she filled her lungs to capacity and dived back under the water, following the diffused light to the wrecked Mustang on the bottom of the lake. She swam right through the gaping hole where the windshield had been, pulling herself over the headrests and into the back.

Ramos was a limp and lifeless body suspended in the dark water, only barely attached to the rebar. Maggie hooked her hands under his armpits and pulled him clear. Then she swam around and under him, pushing him up and out of the smashed window ahead of her.

With lava in her veins, she grabbed his hoodie and kicked toward the light.

Chapter Forty-Four

CLOSURE, BUT AT WHAT COST?

Days later, Maggie leaned on the hood of the motor pool sedan and took a moment to *think*. This was the point, she thought, that if she were Nick Stavanger, she'd light a cigarette and embrace the pseudocalmness it brought as the nicotine teased dopamine from her brain.

But Maggie wasn't Nick, and she didn't smoke, and her skin crawled at the thought of what was to come.

In the glare of the midday sun, the Department of Corrections facility in Wedgefield looked like a military outpost in the middle of a jungle. Guard towers and barracks surrounded by tracts of twisted trees and mesh fencing topped with razor wire. One or two buzzards wheeling against the cloudless sky.

Maggie touched her fingertips to the blue-green bruising on her throat. The soreness had gone, but not the memory of being choked.

Several intense days had passed since her death-defying plunge off the half-built bridge at Lake Ivanhoe. Several days in which she'd found time to process events more fully and come to some sort of terms with the fact that one of their own had undertaken the ultimate betrayal of trust.

News outlets across the state had run with the *cop-turned-killer* story, with headlines pointing fingers at what they called "the growing culture of vigilantism in American society," with endless hours of media speculation and TV pundits united in their opinion that killer cops were endemic of a badly corrupted system.

How can police officers protect the public when they're busy trying to kill each other?

As always in cases like this, the reporting had been taken to the extreme, and Maggie had avoided being dragged into any kind of public debate, keeping a low profile despite pleas from the press to *talk*. The local TV news had broadcast *live* the recovery of Maggie's waterlogged Mustang from the lake, retracing her steps that had started with her abduction and ended with the capture of a cop killer. Every facet of the Sheriff's Office was reeling from the publicity storm, and damage control was the order of the day.

But there was no escaping what Ramos had done, or what would no doubt be its long-term negative repercussions on OCSO's public image.

A trusted deputy had targeted detectives, and people wanted answers, especially the state attorney.

To that effect, Maggie had several face-to-face meetings lined up over the next few days, and she knew that she would have no easy answers for the difficult questions ahead.

But at least she had Ramos's confession.

Two hours ago, Ramos's lawyer had hand delivered a signed admission of guilt to the state attorney. A ten-page sworn affidavit in which Ramos had laid out his motivations as well as confessing to all charges, including first-degree murder, two counts of attempted murder, assault on a police officer, bomb manufacture, reckless endangerment, and coercion.

Maggie had read Ramos's statement before coming down here, becoming increasingly uncomfortable in her own skin as she'd learned exactly how and why he had undertaken his evil deeds: his renting the storage units in Clay's name; putting his experience with IEDs to good use when building the pipe bomb; leaving the unit's key on Clay's key ring that night in Clay's car; stalking her colleagues for weeks beforehand, discovering Stucker's illegal import business; sending the suitably ambiguous text messages to Stucker's phone as bait, intending them to prick Stucker's guilty conscience; following Clay to several hotels in the city, learning of his extramarital affair and the identity of the person he was sleeping with; cornering Clay and coercing him to end his life.

The nature of Clay's affair had come as the biggest shock of all, and Maggie still wasn't sure how she felt about the whole thing.

It turned out that Clay hadn't been seeing another woman behind Sasha's back after all.

He'd been sleeping with a man.

And Ramos had taken pictures on his cell phone to prove it—high-definition photos of Clay with his male lover at various city locations. Multiple instances over as many weeks. Ramos showing Clay the proof that night in Clay's car and using it as influence to coerce him into taking his own life.

Trapped and desperate, Clay had done what he must have felt he needed to do, which was to kill himself on the understanding that his family would never know his darkest secret.

Ramos's statement had left Maggie with chills. And she was still having a hard time reconciling Ramos's extremes. How did a good-hearted family man turn into a cold-blooded killer? None of *this* was the Ramos she knew, or *thought* she knew. It was like he'd had a complete shift in personality. How did something like that just *happen*?

She drew a deep breath and began to walk toward the single-story brick building and the doorway marked VISITOR ENTRANCE.

Ramos had been silent for days now, refusing to speak with anyone except his family and his lawyer. But then he had requested to speak with Maggie, this morning, alone and in person, and Smits had told her to attend the meeting.

Even so, she didn't have to do this, she knew. Smits would be grouchy, but he'd understand. She could turn around, get back in the car, and go about her business. She had plenty of casework to occupy her mind. Dead bodies piling up. Silent victims screaming for justice. When it came to Ramos and his warped sense of justice, it wasn't as though she was without answers.

In his statement, Ramos hadn't held anything back. In fact, he'd gone into great detail about the stresses in his personal life—his *motivators*, as he called them—explaining how his son's illness had put an unbearable strain on his marriage the last twelve months; about hiding his true feelings in public; about his emotionally unstable wife going to pieces when Lay-Z Creek was killed.

Maggie and the team had been surprised to learn that Ramos's wife was his connection to Creek. Apparently, she and Creek had spent a good deal of their childhood together, housed in the same foster home, thinking of themselves as brother and sister. For her, Creek's death had been the final straw in a tumultuous year, and it had sent her into a stupor and Ramos's world into meltdown.

Maggie had most of the answers, but not all. She had agreed to come down here, not because Ramos had requested it, but because it could be her one and only opportunity to hear it from his own lips: *Why had he tried to kill her?*

It was cool inside the visitor center. Maggie surrendered herself to the screening process and left her personal effects in a tray at the sign-in desk. A burly FDC officer handed her a stick-on visitor badge with her name printed on it, and then he led her along a corridor to the visitor suite. The corridor smelled of dirty mop water, and one of the overhead fluorescent bulbs blinked and clunked like something out of a scary movie.

"You know the drill," he said as they came to a reinforced door near the end of the passageway. "Should you require assistance, I'll be right here." He waited for her to acknowledge his words.

"Understood," she said, wondering if he made the same statement to the male visitors.

The officer rattled a key in the lock and stepped aside. "All yours," he said.

Maggie reached for the door handle, then paused, taking a moment to compose herself.

Through the mesh-strengthened glass panel, she could see a simple square room, painted powder blue. Bright daylight streaming in through a double row of glass bricks where the ceiling met the rear wall. In the middle of the floor, a metal table was bolted to the polished cement, its surface dulled from years of visitors and thousands of overlapping handprints.

At the table, Ramos sat in a wheelchair, his bruised eyes closed and his handcuffed hands clasped together against his chest, prayer-like. The bullet track in his forehead was an angry red line, pointing at a surgical dressing taped over the remnants of his nose. Over the top of his white undershirt, he wore a blue tunic with the words FLORIDA DEPARTMENT OF CORRECTIONS stenciled in white.

As though sensing her watching, he cracked open his eyes, and a glimmer of a smile bent his lips as he saw her looking in through the glass.

Maggie hadn't seen Ramos since he'd left the hospital two days ago, and a conflicting mix of revulsion and compassion washed over her.

In one sense, he was lucky to be alive.

The deadly duo of traumatic blood loss and oxygen starvation had left him at death's door, putting him in a coma for days, during which time he'd undergone emergency surgery to plug the bore-hole in his thigh, as well as cosmetic surgery to repair the gaping hole where his nose used to be. At one point it had been touch-and-go, she'd heard, learning later that Ramos had flatlined for almost a minute before doctors had managed to resuscitate him. The day after, a slightly altered version of the disgraced deputy had resurfaced into the world, and after extensive tests, his doctors had deemed him fit enough to be transferred to the medical wing of the Central Florida Reception Center here in Wedgefield.

In another sense, Ramos was unlucky that he'd survived.

It had been a miracle—Maggie extricating him from the wrecked Mustang, dragging him to the shore, and administering mouth to mouth. But the combination of hypovolemic shock and brain hypoxia had caused cerebral damage, seizures. Complications that would dictate all aspects of his lifestyle from now on. The wheelchair was just the start.

Maggie opened the door.

"Detective Novak," Ramos said before she could say anything. "I was beginning to think you'd stood me up."

His voice was clipped, she noted, nasally and slurred, as though he were intoxicated and struggling to form sentences. But Maggie knew he wasn't under the influence of anything except strong pain-killers. According to Ramos's hospital notes, his speech defect was symptomatic of his major brain trauma, and likely to be perma-nent, even after extensive therapy.

Briefly, he offered her a lopsided smile, as though he was hoping that it would make her see him as he had been and not as he was.

But Maggie wasn't interested in making friends with monsters.

Without speaking, she sat down in the chair facing him.

"The doctors aren't giving up on me," he said, even though she hadn't asked about his health. "They say they can rebuild my nose, and with physical therapy I might even walk again. They tell me this is as bad as it gets. What do you think?"

"I think you're in better shape than the last time I saw you."

He offered her another weak smile, his head wobbling slightly.

Inside Maggie, sympathy and antipathy vied for dominance.

Not only was she struck by Ramos's affected speech, but also by his physical change. His olive skin had an ashy cast to it, and his eyes seemed larger, darker, his face rounder—as though, not satisfied with scrambling his mind, the seizures had somehow had a say in his outward appearance, too.

"I read your confession," she said. "It was unexpected. Why the sudden change of heart?"

"Protection for my family." He said it matter-of-factly, as though it was a guaranteed outcome. "I didn't want them put through a public trial. They don't deserve blowback for my actions. My confession protects them."

Without doubt, Ramos's official statement had been the right thing to do, but Maggie wasn't sure it would shield his family from being hounded by the press, or others, not the way he wanted it to, not when the complete facts got out and the world learned exactly what he'd done and why.

Life, as his family knew it, was already over for them.

Ramos was staring at her, his head on a tilt. "Even after I tried to kill you, you saved my life."

"I would've done the same for anyone."

"It might be for nothing. I'm a cop. I've seen what happens in prison to people like me. My days in this world are numbered. Once they relocate me to gen pop, it's only a matter of time." His wan smile came back again, but it was laced with irony. "I'll be lucky to last a week."

It sounded extreme—that Ramos would be killed the moment he mixed with the other inmates—but unfortunately, his fear was

343

valid. It happened. Not all the time. But often enough to raise genuine concerns.

"I can speak with the state attorney," Maggie said. "Request isolation in recognition of your confession."

Ramos looked disturbed at the thought. "And spend the rest of my days by myself? No, thank you. Isolation is my idea of hell. I'd sooner take my chances. We're not meant to go through this life on our own. I'd go loco, cooped up in solitary all the time. Can you imagine?"

Maggie could. The idea of permanent loneliness had crossed her mind several times recently, more so since her close shave with death two months ago during the Halloween Homicide case. So far, her adulthood had been spent mostly on her own, with her doing her own thing, answerable to no one, with just a few casual relationships of any length to speak of. For a long time, independence had been Maggie's preference, but she wasn't getting any younger, and the notion of growing old without a significant other to share her life with had lost any appeal it once had had.

She leaned on the table. "Ramos, why did you want to see me?"

"For the same reason you wanted to see me." He motioned to the dark patches on her neck, made by his own hands. "The bruising's almost gone. That's good."

Maggie felt revulsion stir inside her. Even though she wanted to tell Ramos exactly what she thought of him, she knew she had to keep her composure. On the drive over, she'd warned herself not to let Ramos in, not to engage with him emotionally. The last thing she wanted was to give him the wrong impression, indicate even casually that she was in any way okay with any aspect of what he'd done. She'd trusted him, *liked* him. She wasn't anywhere close to being in a place to *forgive* him; his betrayal still *hurt*. She needed to keep this visit relevant and as short as possible, for her own sanity.

"Let's be clear about this," she said. "I'm not here for a social visit. I don't need to hear how you felt justified in going after my colleagues, or how you got it into your head that their deaths would somehow make things okay between you and your wife. You can explain all that to the prison psychiatrist. I only need one thing from you, Ramos. And that's to know why you tried to kill me."

Ramos leaned toward her, to the limit of his chain, his posture intimidating. Maggie could feel the heat coming off him, smell the blood on his surgical dressing, and the staleness of his breath.

"Do I need to spell it out?" he said quietly. "It's simple. You killed my partner."

"Me?" Maggie was taken aback by his reasoning, or lack of it. "But *you* planted that bomb, Ramos. Take some responsibility here. Shaw's death is on you, not me. You killed her."

"No." He strained against the chain, snarling. "That's not what you said."

Maggie felt spittle on her face, but she didn't flinch.

Ramos glared. "That morning, outside the emergency department, you told me her death was your fault. You were to blame, you said. *You.* Admit it. She'd be alive today if you hadn't opened that door."

An image of Deputy Shaw lying in a pool of her own blood in the Walmart parking lot filled Maggie's thoughts. Ramos on his knees, desperately trying to tie the tourniquet around his partner's thigh. Bright crimson blood squirting all over him.

Noisily, Ramos yanked the chain, straining to reach her, inches from her face. *"You killed her!"*

He swung his head, viciously, trying to connect with hers.

Maggie's reflexes kicked in, and she pushed backward, standing up with enough force to send the chair toppling over. In the same instant, the door swung open, and the FDC officer came bursting through. Maggie pushed her way past him, rushing out into the corridor, her senses spinning and her whole body ringing like a bell.

"Retribution is coming after you," Ramos called. "You hear me, Detective Novak? One way or another, you're going to pay for what you did."

Maggie made it halfway along the corridor before she hunched over and threw up.

Chapter Forty-Five

NEVER SAY NEVER

L ocated five minutes from Maggie's home, the popular family restaurant in Ocoee was rowdy for this time of day, a sad bunch of happy hour addicts crowding the bar—Maggie and Steve included.

Dressed in black, the two of them were perched on high-backed barstools, Maggie trying to come down to earth softly after the emotional upheaval of the last couple of hours. Her visit with Ramos, followed by Deputy Shaw's funeral at Greenwood Cemetery, had taken a toll on her nerves, and all that she wanted to do for the rest of the day was *normalize*.

Getting tipsy at this hour wasn't her usual way to unwind, but it was an appealing alternative to moping around at home and feeling sorry for herself. Besides, such a concept was *alien*.

A sister had fallen, and Maggie had needed a pick-me-up.

Now, her lips burned with bourbon.

She held the spicy liquid in her mouth until the fire started to numb all sensation, finally swallowing it down, the flames scorching her throat and acting as a temporary distraction.

"Take it easy," Steve said without glancing up from the beverages card. "You won't enjoy your food."

"Watch me. Funerals always make me hungry. I could eat the entire menu right now." Maggie pulled a long swig of cool beer to quench the heat in her throat.

As embarrassing as it was, her stomach had been rumbling throughout Shaw's interment, and a stopover at Maggie's favorite chain restaurant on their way back to her place had been essential. After watching Shaw's mother weep into the American flag draped over her daughter's coffin, Maggie had needed to touch base with familiarity, and the hungry howl of her belly had called all the shots. More to the point, it was four in the afternoon, and she and Steve had nowhere else they needed to be.

But neither the bourbon nor the thought of quieting her hunger pangs made Maggie feel any less on edge. Her confrontation this morning with Ramos had affected her more than she'd expected it to, his words still echoing around her head and creeping her out. Wrapping her brain around his change in personality was nothing less than challenging, and Shaw's funeral had only exacerbated her unease—so much so that she'd come away from the wake feeling slightly out of sync with reality and in desperate need of *grounding*.

She had seen the damage of Ramos's actions firsthand. She knew she would never truly understand what he'd done and attempted to do. That was for people like Steve to dissect and debate over. Her job was to put it to bed, congratulate herself on maintaining a healthy conversion rate, and move on to the next case. But theory rarely matched reality. Ramos's words—*You killed her*—were haunting, and Maggie suspected they would haunt her for a long time to come.

Steve cleared his throat. "They've put together some interesting margaritas here," he said, pointing to the beverages card and doing his best to deflect.

Maggie made a face. "Not a huge fan."

"Me neither." He pushed the card aside and turned to face her. "Okay. Now that we can breathe easy again, can we talk?"

"We never stopped."

On their way to the funeral, Maggie had spoken with Steve about the case details in depth for the first time. Since returning from his conference last weekend, Steve had picked up on the basics of the investigation, including her calamitous encounters in Titusville and at Lake Ivanhoe, but the raw specifics of her abduction at gunpoint, once revealed in full, had visibly shaken him, and she knew explanations were in order.

He'd held her hand through most of the funeral service, ostensibly to reassure her that she wasn't alone in *this*, but Maggie suspected that the hand-holding had been more for his benefit than hers. She had to remember that what seemed everyday ordinary to her as a law enforcement officer was often shocking and disturbing to regular citizens.

"You were going to tell me about Clay's affair," Steve said, leaning his elbow on the bar and his chin on the heel of his hand.

"I was?"

"As we arrived at the cemetery. Just before we got out of the car. Your exact words to me were, 'Remind me to tell you about Clay's affair—you won't believe it when you hear it.' Then you left me hanging, and I've been on tenterhooks ever since."

"It was a nice service, though; wasn't it?"

"Maggie . . ."

She took a breath. "Okay. All right." She held up the empty shot glass. "But I'm going to need another one of these." She gestured at the bartender—*Same again*—and he acknowledged her request with a nod.

Steve was looking slightly unsettled.

"You might want to slow down there a little," he said.

Maggie narrowed her eyes at him. "Steve Kinsey, are you telling me how to behave right now?" She said it only half seriously, but it took Steve a second to answer.

"Me?" he said. "I'd never dream of such a thing. More than my life's worth. What I am saying is, major afternoon drinking is not like you, Maggie. Or, me, come to think of it. Even though it feels pretty good right now."

"You're just worried you'll have no hope of keeping up if this turns into a bender."

"I'm worried, period." He raised his beer to her, then drank some and wiped his lips. "So," he said, "getting back on subject. You were saying about this affair of Clay's?"

"Worse than you can ever imagine."

"Try me. I have a pretty good imagination. I was top of my class in conceptual studies."

"That's not quite the same thing, and you know it."

The bartender placed another two bourbon shots on the bar. Maggie smiled her thanks.

"I was wrong," she said.

"You were?"

"Clay didn't have a mistress."

"He didn't?"

"Nope." She picked up the shot.

"Maggie Novak, are you teasing me? I thought he was having an affair."

"He was."

"Okay. So how does that work?"

"Think about it." Maggie brought the bourbon to her lips. "There's only one other possible explanation."

Steve looked puzzled. She could imagine his cognitive wheels moving up a gear as his mind tried to make sense of her statement. Then, all of a sudden, enlightenment dawned in his eyes, and she saw his jaw drop, the same way hers had when she'd learned the nature of Clay's lover from Ramos's confession.

"There you go," Maggie said and downed the shot.

Steve picked up his own bourbon and slung it to the back of his mouth, visibly shuddering as its fieriness swept through him. "All this time," he said. "Clay was seeing another man?"

"He was."

"Oh boy. I didn't see that one coming."

"Me neither. I don't think any of us did."

"What about Andy?"

"As shocked as the rest of us. I think Sasha had her suspicions, and that's why they were having marital issues, but I don't think she knew for sure he was seeing a man."

A server balancing dishes like a circus performer checked off each item on their order as she laid plates on the bar in front of them. While Steve had played it safe, opting for the smokehouse burger and fries, Maggie had ordered a full slab of ribs and everything that went with it.

Steve asked the sixty-four-thousand-dollar question: "Do you know who he is?"

Maggie waited until the server had moved on before telling him. "Laremy Dunbar," she said quietly.

"Your lieutenant?"

"One and the same."

Steve gaped a little.

"He's also Clay's brother-in-law," she added. "That was part of Ramos's leverage. If news of the affair came out, it would've ruined two marriages and the whole family dynamic. Clay lived his whole life as a man's man. His sons worshipped him like he was a superhero. It would've hit them the hardest."

"And Clay couldn't live with the prospect."

"Apparently not."

Steve's surprised expression slipped into skeptical. "Even so, Maggie, committing suicide is a pretty drastic solution. Don't you think? Even when you're backed in a corner like that, surely there's another option other than *death*. Worst-case scenario, his boys might've hated him initially, but would've probably come around to the idea eventually."

"Not always. I've seen families break up over less and never speak to each other ever again."

She knew Steve would know she was speaking from a personal perspective, and that he shouldn't even attempt to delve any deeper.

"Still," he said, "better to have a gay dad than no dad at all." He picked up a french fry and popped it in his mouth.

For someone who dealt with shades, Maggie thought, Steve could be very black and white at times.

"And besides," he said, then paused to devour a mouthful of fries, "Clay was a big guy. Why didn't he simply overpower Ramos?"

"Because he told Clay he had a contingency plan. Something he'd set up with an attorney. If anything happened to him, letters were to be mailed out, telling everyone the truth about Clay and Dunbar. Either way, Clay couldn't win."

Steve shook his head. "Wow. I can't imagine being in that position."

"Me neither." Maggie had traipsed through several imaginary scenarios in her head over the last few days, placing herself in the crosshairs and wondering what she would have done differently than Clay.

Steve cut his burger in half. "So this woman Clay was seen arguing with in Walmart . . ."

"Confirmed as De-Andra Dunbar. Clay's sister-in-law. We questioned her. Turns out one of her friends had seen Dunbar and Clay at a hotel together when Dunbar was supposed to be at the office. De-Andra challenged him about it, but she said he laughed it off, saying the meet up was work related."

"But she didn't believe him."

"No. She called Clay that night, to hear his version of events. He told her he couldn't talk because he was on his way out to the store. Plus, he made the mistake of telling her to keep her nose out of it. And De-Andra saw red. That's why she was down there, at Walmart, gunning for Clay."

Steve took a bite of his burger. "Happy families, huh?"

"Well, the heartbreaking thing is, Sasha and De-Andra both learned the truth anyway, which means Clay killed himself for nothing." Maggie stared at the rack of ribs on her plate, not too sure that it was hunger causing the pangs in her belly anymore. "It's all just a complete and utter mess."

"Here," he said. "This might cheer you up." She saw him dip his hand into his jacket pocket and bring out a small black box. "I was going to wait until we were alone later. But you look like you need an infusion of happiness right now."

He opened the box.

Maggie stared at the diamond ring inside, all her mixed emotions regarding New Year's Eve and Steve's proposal suddenly rushing back and competing for headspace. For a moment she was overwhelmed, unable to separate one emotion from another.

"I collected it from the jeweler's this morning," Steve said as he plucked the ring from its cushioned slot. "They did a great job resizing it. Hopefully it's a better fit this time."

Maggie felt herself frown. "I said *yes*?"

Steve looked at her like she'd spoken in Chinese. "You don't remember?"

"I was drunk. My memory is hazy at best."

353

"I guess that explains why you've been acting a bit quiet with me lately. I chalked it up to Clay's death. When really it was all down to you forgetting your answer. Oh boy." He sounded hurt.

Maggie bit her lip. "Steve, I'm sorry."

Then he laughed. "Relax," he said. "I'm pulling your leg. We were both pretty wasted that night. I'm surprised you can remember *anything*."

Maggie shot him a playful scowl and punched him on the arm.

He motioned at her to give him her hand.

She hesitated, all at once feeling each one of her conflicting emotions trying to elbow the rest aside.

Is this what you want? she asked herself.

The question had been playing on her mind all week, evoking fear and uncertainty, but also something else. Something that she hadn't been able to dismiss.

After all her introspection, her analyzing, her dismantling of her defenses, she'd come to realize something she'd known for a while now: her feelings for Steve were *real*.

It didn't matter if Nick thought him "vanilla." It didn't matter if Loomis secretly believed him not to be "the one." It didn't matter that Steve wasn't anything like *her*.

What mattered was that Steve made her *happy*.

Was there any better reason to be together?

"So," Steve said as he took her hand in his, "since you're slightly less inebriated now than you were the first time we did this, allow me to put you through it all again." He held the ring to her fingertip. "Maggie Novak, will you marry me?"

She was aware of people starting to look. Heat rising up her neck and into her cheeks. "Just to be clear. I said *yes* the first time around, right?"

"You did."

"And I'm a woman of my word."

"You are."

"Then I guess you already have your answer." She slid her finger through the ring, then leaned over and kissed him on the mouth, hard, tasting beer and salt.

No turning back now.

Someone shouted, "Congratulations to the happy couple!" And everyone at the bar started clapping.

"The next round's on my fiancé," Maggie said as she disengaged, and the clapping turned into cheers.

"You kill me, Maggie Novak," Steve said through his smile.

Maggie grinned. "Never. But let's take things easy. Okay? There's no rush. If we're doing this, I want it to be right."

"I agree. But just to throw it out there, I'm thinking Vegas."

Maggie snickered. "I'm not." She pictured the photo she'd seen of Andy Stucker and Klementina getting married in Sin City, and how cheesy it had looked. "For now, let's just play it by ear and see where we end up." She raised her beer. "Deal?"

Steve clinked his glass against hers. "Deal."

Maggie's new cell phone chimed. She glanced at the screen. It was a message from Dispatch, calling available homicide detectives to attend the discovery of a dead body at Lake Ruby in Vineland.

Ordinarily, Maggie would have called back without reservation, advising the operator that she was en route to the scene. But she'd spotted a look in Steve's eyes, a look that urged her to think twice.

She slid her phone back on the bar.

"Bold move," Steve said.

"Well, it's time I made some changes. I can't keep burning the candle at both ends and thinking I can single-handedly solve every murder case that comes along."

"Even though you can and you do?"

Maggie smiled. "But at the expense of everything else, right? The thing is, Steve, I'm not getting any younger. If I want my life to be a marathon and not a short sprint to the finish, I need to start pacing myself. And that includes making more time for the people who matter the most."

"I'll drink to that." He signaled the bartender, asking him to fetch a bottle of champagne, but Maggie caught his arm.

"Not for me," she said. "I'm good."

"You're sure?"

"Put it this way. I'd like to remember saying *yes* this time."

Steve canceled the order and squeezed her hand reassuringly. "We'll make this work," he said. "I promise."

But the very fact that he'd felt the need to say so struck a chord of concern in Maggie.

They ate, keeping the conversation light and optimistic, and as far away from any mention of work or funerals as they could.

But every now and then, when Steve's gaze was on his food, Maggie's eyes were drawn to her phone, part of her wondering about the nature of the homicide at Lake Ruby and what she might be missing out on.

Author's note

Thank you for reading my second Maggie Novak thriller. Your support is sincerely appreciated. I hope you enjoyed it. If you did, please tell everyone!

To be the first to hear about my next Maggie Novak release, and to enter exclusive competitions to win my signed books, please join my growing reader list at www.keithhoughton.com, where you are more than welcome to drop by and say hello.

Also, if you look hard enough, you can find me on Facebook, Twitter, and Instagram at https://www.facebook.com/keithhoughtonbooks and https://twitter.com/KeithHoughton and https://www.instagram.com/keithhoughton_author.

See you there!

Acknowledgments

First, as always, I want to thank my dear wife, Lynn, for loving me despite my faults. It isn't easy living with a writer. At times, my characters distract, and my thoughts inhabit worlds from which she is excluded. It takes patience and tolerance to put up with me and my daydreaming, and I am truly blessed to have her support, guidance, and friendship—without which none of this would be possible.

Lynn, you are my rock, my muse, my soul mate. You define me. Thank you for being you!

I want to thank my family for their love and laughter. Our gorgeous twin daughters: Gemma and Rebecca. Our suave son-in-law: Sam. Our beautiful granddaughters: Willow, Perry, Ava, and Bella. And our lovely parents: Lynn's mum, Lillian, and my mum and dad, June and Bill. And also my brother-in-law, Mark, who has lived with kidney failure for years now and never complained once. Together, you guys are my world.

I want to thank Amazon Publishing and the brilliant Thomas & Mercer team for continuing to believe in me and my writing and for their tireless support of my T&M books throughout the year. In particular, I want to thank Laura Deacon, editorial director, for trusting in my vision for Maggie Novak and for allowing me to turn my dream into reality yet again. Special thanks also go to Hatty Stiles for putting my books in front of readers and to Eoin Purcell for keeping the show on the road.

I want to thank Charlotte Herscher, my developmental editor, for showing me that I am not as clever as I think I am. She forces me to face the difficult questions and then to come up with believable answers. My stories are better because of her.

I want to thank Lori, my copyeditor, and Susan, my proofreader, for making me look like a pro.

Last, but not least, I want to thank you and the rest of my reader fans for reading my books. Without you, I'd have to get a real job.

Thanks!

About the Author

Keith Houghton spent too much of his childhood reading science fiction books, mostly by flashlight under the bedcovers, dreaming of becoming a full-time novelist. When he was thirteen, his English teacher—fed up with reading his space stories—told him he would never make it as a science fiction writer. Undeterred, Houghton went on to pen several sci-fi novels and three comedy stage plays while raising a family and holding down a more conventional job. But it wasn't until he started writing mystery thrillers that Houghton's dream finally became reality. Though his head is still full of space stories, he keeps his feet planted firmly on the ground, enjoying life and spending quality time with his grandchildren.

Houghton is the bestselling author of the three Gabe Quinn thrillers—*Killing Hope*, *Crossing Lines*, and *Taking Liberty*—as well as the stand-alone psychological thrillers *No Coming Back*, *Before You Leap*, and *Crash*. Please visit www.keithhoughton.com to learn more.